Juno Rushdan is a veteran US Air Force intelligence officer and award-winning author. Her books are action-packed and fast-paced. Critics from *Kirkus Reviews* and *Library Journal* have called her work 'heart-pounding James Bond-ian adventure' that 'will captivate lovers of romantic thrillers.' For a free book, visit her website: junorushdan.com

K.D. Richards is a native of the Washington, DC, area, who now lives outside Toronto with her husband and two sons. You can find her at kdrichardsbooks.com

WYOMING UNDERCOVER ESCAPE

JUNO RUSHDAN

THE PERFECT MURDER

K.D. RICHARDS

MILLS & BOON

First Published in Great Britain 2024
by Mills & Boon, an imprint of HarperCollins*Publishers* Ltd
1 London Bridge Street, London, SE1 9GF

www.harpercollins.co.uk

HarperCollins*Publishers*
Macken House, 39/40 Mayor Street Upper,
Dublin 1, D01 C9W8, Ireland

Wyoming Undercover Escape © 2024 Juno Rushdan
The Perfect Murder © 2024 Kia Dennis

ISBN: 978-0-263-32253-8

1124

This book contains FSC™ certified paper and other controlled sources to ensure responsible forest management.

For more information visit: www.harpercollins.co.uk/green

Printed and Bound in the UK using 100% Renewable Electricity at CPI Group (UK) Ltd, Croydon, CR0 4YY

WYOMING UNDERCOVER ESCAPE

JUNO RUSHDAN

For all who served in the Marine Corps. Once a marine, always a marine. Thank you for your service.

Chapter One

Rip Lockwood crossed the field of his elderly landlady's property, heading to his Airstream parked a few hundred feet away, to grab a screwdriver to repair her dishwasher. Wishing he'd worn his jacket in the chilly November night air, he noticed his front door ajar. Only cracked a couple of inches, but he hadn't left it open.

He drew his gun from its holster on his ankle and trained it on the door. Glancing around, he searched for anyone lurking outside as a lookout or any sign of a parked getaway vehicle. Nothing that didn't belong and no one around, from what he could tell.

A slam from inside the trailer, followed by dishes clattering.

Creeping closer, he caught the creaking tread of heavy footfalls across his floor. More than one person. He listened carefully. Two were skulking inside.

"Hurry up," one said from deeper within, trying to keep his voice low.

Rip eased onto the wood deck under the awning and up to the door. Pleased with himself for oiling the hinges last week, he swung the door open wide and rushed inside the Airstream.

Two men—one with a tall, burly frame and the other with

an average build—wearing black hoodies and ski masks spun in his direction. The tall one grabbed the microwave from the counter and hurled it at Rip.

He blocked the blow of the sturdy appliance, but a third guy emerged from the bedroom behind him and charged. No way to sidestep the inbound assault in the tight confines, Rip took aim. But the heavyset guy tackled him around the waist. Rip's weapon discharged at the same time, three bullets hitting the ceiling. He and the guy fell out of the trailer, tumbling off the deck while wrestling, and hitting solid, cold ground.

Unfortunately, the stocky guy landed on top of Rip. Another squeeze of the trigger and a shot fired off low to the side, the slug spitting bark from a tree. The thickset man landed a blow across Rip's face before knocking the gun from his hand and sending it sailing across the grass.

Rip threw a hammer fist up into the man's chest, the meaty part of the swinging blow hitting the solar plexus. Gasping for air, the wind knocked from his lungs, the heavy guy fell backward.

The tall one rushed forward with the microwave hoisted overhead, ready to bring it down on Rip's skull. Rip rolled out of the way an instant before the appliance smashed onto the ground. Still on his back, Rip used the position to his advantage and kicked at the other man's knees. Felt a kneecap give way with the snap of broken ligaments. The man hollered in pain.

As Rip tried to climb to his feet, a punch caught him in the ribs. A second fist struck him in the kidney. The thickset guy hit hard, like a boxer. Rip could guess who it was, but rather than focus on identifying him, he needed to immobilize him first. He spun, vision blurring, swinging his elbow up and around, using the added momentum to drive the blow hard into the side of the guy's head. If he'd punched him with that much force, Rip would have broken his hand, whereas his elbow barely registered it.

The heavy guy staggered, clearly disorientated, but he was strong and could take a solid punch. Rip charged straight at him, a wounded bull, lifting the heavy man off his feet and slamming him backward against the ground.

Steel glinted in the moonlight. His gun.

They both went for the weapon.

Then Rip reconsidered. Instead, he launched a fist into his assailant's face, throttling him with jabs until his attacker was dazed.

Where was the third guy?

Adrenaline hot in his veins, Rip reached for his gun. In his peripheral vision he spotted a shadow moving. His fingertips grazed cold steel. The third assailant tried punting his head off with a front kick. Abandoning the gun, Rip jerked away from the incoming boot, but not fast enough. The tip caught him in the jaw.

The tang of blood filled his mouth. He scrambled up onto his hands and knees, reaching for the sheathed Marine Corps KA-BAR on his hip. Or rather, the one that should've been on his belt.

Swearing, he realized he'd left the knife in his trailer.

Mr. Average, who'd gotten in him the jaw, stood with gloved hands clenched and a knapsack on his back. The tall man, now limping, pulled a 9mm gun from his waistband that had been concealed by his sweatshirt.

Rip groped around for something, anything he could use as a weapon, and his fingers closed around a large rock.

"No!" the average one said to the tall guy, his tone sharp with alarm, his palm raised. "Remember, you can't shoot him."

The voice familiar, Rip thought he might be able to pinpoint it.

The man holding the gun hesitated. "No, I just can't kill him."

Rip threw the rock, hitting the guy holding the gun square in the forehead. The man swore, stumbling backward and holding his head with one hand while maintaining a shaky grip on the pistol with the other. Rip spun on to his knees, ready to lunge.

A shotgun cocked, not too far in the distance, pumping a shell into the chamber. The sound was loud and unmistakable. "You're trespassing!" Mrs. Ida Hindley called out. She was his landlady and friend and the closest thing to family that Rip had left. "You better leave because I shoot to kill."

That warning was meant for Rip. He dropped to the ground before Ida opened fire. She could only see a few feet clearly in front of her and that was in bright light. Eighty big steps away, at night, she was just as likely to shoot him as his attackers.

The shotgun cracked, sounding like a mini explosion, the shell getting dangerously close to the big guy.

The three assailants took off toward the woods, one hobbling impressively fast.

Ida pumped off one deafening shot after another, changing her aim each time, determined to hit something. Even if it only ended up being trees and his trailer.

The men disappeared into the darkness.

Motorcycle engines grumbled to life, the sound faint, the sight of the bikes concealed by the woods. They must've been parked on the auxiliary road near the property. Seconds later, the bikes sped off, and Ida was finally out of ammo.

Rip lumbered to his feet and started making his way to

Ida. She had lowered the shotgun to her side, but better to be safe than sorry. "It's only me," he said, in case she had extra shells in the pockets of her robe. "They're gone."

Getting closer, he spotted her late husband's snub-nosed revolver in her other hand.

"Are you all right?" she asked.

"I'll live." He slipped the shotgun from her trembling hand, touched his jaw and winced. "You're going to kill someone one day."

"Only a trespasser who deserves it." Giving him a sly grin, she took the arm he offered, and they headed to her house. "I dare anyone to doubt that I would, son." Even with her frail body racked with rheumatoid arthritis, white hair in rollers, wearing winter boots and a flannel bathrobe over pajamas, she was a formidable woman who shouldn't be tested.

"Well, I'm not fool enough to doubt you, Auntie Ida." They might not be related by blood but were still kin.

Shoving the revolver in her pocket, she wheezed, and he slowed their pace.

Tragedy had claimed the lives of their closest relatives. When he was a young teen, Ida had taken him in along with his younger brother. Despite her love and lectures and desperation to keep them away from the motorcycle club their father had been a part of, they had joined the Iron Warriors MC anyway.

If only they had listened.

If only they hadn't chased after some illusory birthright.

If only Rip hadn't failed to protect his brother, he might still be alive.

If only…

"Now, what was all the ruckus about?" she asked.

"MC business," he said.

"Iron Warriors business or Hellhounds?"

The Iron Warriors were his, at least those who still wore the MC cut displaying their patches and insignia, and he had their unwavering loyalty. The Hellhounds, the newly formed OMG, outlaw motorcycle gang, were his cross to bear.

Somehow Todd Burk had dragged the club so deep into illicit and illegal activity, right under his nose, that Rip had to put a stop to it, drawing a line in the sand. In the end, Rip had made a mess of things and caused his club to split.

Those who agreed that they should not deal drugs stood with him as Iron Warriors. The vast majority who didn't, who loved the money, who craved power and refused to give any of it up, had broken away with Burk as their leader and become the Hellhounds.

The group's existence was yet another failure Rip had to atone for and deal with.

He helped Ida up the steps of her back porch and inside the house. "It's best if that's all you know." Gently, he set her down in a chair.

"There's been a lot of ugly, unfortunate *MC business* around here and in town lately." Ida was back up on her feet, plodding to the refrigerator. She grabbed milk and went to the stove.

"Precisely why I don't want you to pull another stunt like that," he said, setting the shotgun on the kitchen counter. "Understand? I don't want you to get hurt."

She waved a dismissive hand at him. "I've had eighty-nine good years on this earth. They weren't always easy, but I've gotten to see the world, make my mark on it, known the love of family and cherished friends." She put a delicate hand on his arm and squeezed. "What I will not do is hide in here while someone I care about is in danger out there."

She pointed through the window at the land in the direction of his trailer.

"I don't want you to risk your life for mine." No one should die to save him.

Giving a dry chuckle, she poured milk in a pan and turned on the fire. "Remind me, how old are you?" She counted on her fingers. "Thirty-five?"

"You flatter me. Thirty-eight."

She opened a cabinet and grabbed hot chocolate. "My life has been full and rich, though not with money." Another dry laugh. "When my time comes, I'll be ready. And I want you to be at peace with it. But you've got more than half your life ahead of you, son."

Things had only escalated with Burk, going from bad to worse. Rip had been extorted, shot at, and had his tires slashed. No matter how hard he tried to avoid bloodshed that would only lead to a war, he wasn't so sure he'd outlive Ida. And after tonight's incident, with her getting involved, he'd reached a crossroads.

If he allowed this mayhem to continue, Ida would be burying him before the new year.

"I wouldn't be so sure about that." He dug out the cold compress from the freezer and put it on his face. "I haven't done much good with the first half of my life." Maybe there wasn't much point in the second half. "What do I have to show for it?"

"You left this small town and the club to join the military because I begged you to."

And he'd also left his brother behind, who refused to leave.

Rip had seen the dark side of the MC culture and when Auntie Ida pleaded, no, *dared* him to see what else there might be in the world for him, he didn't back down from the challenge.

Ida got out mini marshmallows and caramel syrup and set them on the counter, but not the chocolate syrup when she knew he liked a drizzle of both on his cocoa.

He was lucky to have her in his life, someone willing to shoot his attackers and make him hot chocolate. Dropping into a chair, he propped an elbow on his leg, resting his head in his hand, and put the compress to his face.

"You saved lives in the Marines," Ida continued. "Looking around here, you can't see it. But dig out your Navy Cross and look at that. It's proof you made an impact. Not only on those you saved, but for their mothers and fathers and siblings and spouses and children. You also came back home to make an even bigger difference." He opened his mouth to protest, and she raised her palm, silencing him. "You haven't achieved what you set out to do. Not yet." She handed him a cup of hot cocoa. "Not yet," she repeated. "But there's still time. And where there's a will, there's a way. Even if we don't like the way forward or it happens to be unexpected, there comes a point where we have to make a choice. Do we keep at it, using the same methods that haven't worked. Or find a new way to fight."

There was time. As a Marine Raider, he was trained to deal with disaster and eliminate too many types of enemies to name. Stopping terrorists was his specialty. He was going to use his skill set and whatever time he had left to take down Todd Burk.

War wasn't a possibility that he could prevent. It was already on his doorstep, and he was in the thick of it. But the one thing he knew how to do was fight a war.

He needed to be ruthless to win. Even if doing so killed him.

Ida picked up two mugs and left the kitchen.

"Why did you make three cups of cocoa?" How did he not notice until now?

She shuffled down the hallway and he followed behind her.

Red-and-blue flashing lights pulled up in front of the house.

"You called the sheriff's department?" he asked. Irritation sparked through him. "I can't talk to the law about MC business."

No one snitched. Not even about this. That was the code. They lived by it. Died by it. Honored it. Even a legit biker and upstanding citizen like him did not get the authorities involved.

"But I got the pretty deputy to come," she said.

Gritting his teeth, Rip sighed. There were a couple of female deputies in the sheriff's department, but instantly he knew she was talking about the gorgeous one he had a complicated relationship with. "You asked for the one who hates me?"

And Ashley Russo had every reason to despise him, the club and everything the MC stood for. No matter how hard he'd tried to break down her wall of disdain—and he'd tried very, very hard—it was never enough to get her to change the way she looked at him.

There was a rap at the door. Light from the headlights and flashing strobes outlined a slender athletic shape wearing a cowboy hat through the glass pane of the door.

"I thought you two had some kind of thing going on. That you were at least friends," Ida said.

"Friends trust each other. That's not the case here. We've formed a tenuous…." He was at a loss for what to call it. Association? Acquaintance? Civility? No word was quite right. "I guess we do have some kind of a *thing*." But it was held together by gossamer threads. One wrong move on his part and it would snap.

"That does explain all the questions she asked me a few weeks ago about whether you were living on the property against my will and if you were paying a reasonable rent or if I wanted you to leave. But I cleared it up. Set her straight about you. She gave me her card, with her personal cell phone number on the back, and told me to call her anytime, especially if there was trouble. So I did, tonight."

"What? Why didn't you tell me? When was she here?" *How was any of that friendly?*

Another knock. This time louder.

Ida looked at him with a wry grin. "There's a thin line between love and hate. Now open the door and act like the man I raised you to be."

"She blames me for the death of her brother," he admitted, his voice low.

He remembered like it was yesterday, the conversation Ashley had overheard at her brother's funeral, the way she came up to him, a fearless seventeen-year-old girl, slapped his face, pounded on his chest and screamed her anger and grief.

Ida's smile fell. "Is she justified?"

Rip didn't pull the trigger but shared the blame for Angelo's death and for his own brother's. "In a way, yes."

"Then it's high time you took responsibility for it and started righting your wrongs."

Scratching his head, he wished Ida had warned him she had called the authorities. More specifically, one deputy in particular.

Ida switched on the porch light and the one in the foyer and gave him a *get-on-with-it* look.

Dropping the cold compress onto a side table, Rip stalked

up to the door and opened it. His gaze met the deputy's, her whiskey-brown eyes narrowing a fraction. He gave her the once-over, surprised she wasn't in uniform. Her dark hair hung loose, falling past her shoulders rather than pulled into a ponytail or the tight braid she sported whenever he'd seen her working. Form-fitting jeans accentuated her long legs and rounded hips. A tucked-in flannel shirt and leather jacket didn't do much to flatter her figure. But her classic hourglass shape on her five-foot-seven frame made it impossible to ignore the fact she was no longer a girl.

He flicked a glance over her shoulder. She had driven her personal truck, using portable red-and-blue emergency lights that could easily be mounted to the dash or windshield with suction cups, rather than a patrol SUV. "Are you off duty?"

The deputy unhooked her badge from her belt and held it up, making it clear she was working even if she might be off duty.

"I'll ask the questions." She gestured past him into the house.

The star in her hand reminded him what he *didn't* like about her. Rip stepped aside, opening the door wide.

She came in, bringing with her the cold and the crisp, clean scent of frost.

Ida handed the deputy a mug. "I made it just the way you like it. With mini marshmallows and caramel syrup."

"Thank you," she said. "But you shouldn't have gone to the trouble."

Rip glanced down at his mug. He had neither the zhuzh of marshmallows nor syrup.

Sipping his plain cocoa, he shut the door and followed them down the hall. His gaze slipped below the deputy's waistline and belt with flashlight, pepper spray, handcuffs and holstered gun, and locked onto the gentle sway of her hips. He liked her curves, and she had plenty of them. Appreciated the strength of her body from a combat standpoint. But he had to fight against the primal physical interest, the spark of heat that flashed inside him whenever she was near.

Inside the kitchen, he hurried to the table and helped Ida ease down into a chair. In the evenings her arthritis got worse, making her stiff.

The deputy glanced around the room, her gaze lingering on the shotgun on the counter, and took out a notepad and pen. "I'm responding to a report of shots fired. The best way for me to do my job efficiently is if you're honest when answering my questions," she said, all business, staring right at him as she spoke. "You might not be a Marine anymore, but tonight I need you to abide by the same uncompromising integrity of the corps instead of your MC code of silence."

"Once a Marine, always a Marine," he said, not turning away from her face, which he liked even more than her figure.

Satin-smooth complexion. The golden brown hue of her skin showed her multiracial heritage. Italian on her father's side. Creole on her mother's. Not that it was one thing about her, like her high cheekbones, but rather the complete package, the sum of her parts, that he found captivating. He could look at her for hours and often struggled not to stare.

"A distinguished Marine," Ida chimed in, her voice full of pride. "Ripton lives by a set of core values that have formed the bedrock of his character."

"Really? Is that so?" The deputy didn't filter the sharp skepticism from her tone. "What kind of core values?"

He understood the law enforcement game she was playing. When a cop thought they might have trouble getting answers from a person, they warmed them up, getting them talking about something the reluctant party was comfortable with first.

Unfortunately for her, he'd been playing this game far longer and was better at it.

"I do my best never to lie unless there's good cause. But I never cheat. Never steal. Don't break the law." Honor, strength to do what was right, commitment—an unrelenting determination to achieve victory in every endeavor—made him who he was.

He'd tried to tell her this before but she either didn't listen or didn't believe him.

"I only hope that's true." She stepped closer, dangerously close, inches separating them, studying his face as if searching for the truth, and heat flared again, coaxing him to thaw. Enticing him to strive for something far deeper than friendship with her.

But he backed away from the deputy, going around to the other side of the table. Regardless of how attractive he found her or how drawn to her he was, or that he needed to, and intended to, make amends for her brother, he had to be the same with her right now as he would be with any other badge investigating. Stone-cold.

An iceberg that wouldn't crack.

Chapter Two

Staring up at Ripton Lockwood, with her being at least six inches shorter than him, Ashley fully expected him to answer every question with a half-truth or simply evade giving a real answer at all. He might still consider himself a Marine, but instead of wearing a military uniform, he usually wore a biker cut.

Though he didn't have on the leather vest covered in patches now.

He was not only a member of a notorious motorcycle club but also the president of the Iron Warriors.

The MC had been a blight in the towns of Laramie and Bison Ridge for as long as she could remember. Corrupting the youth, recruiting them into their ranks with sparkly promises, neglecting to disclose that not everything that glitters was gold.

A few things gave her a glimmer of hope that Rip might be honest about tonight's events and, if so, possibly help her with her one-woman crusade. Ida Hindley's high praise of him. The DEA's recent deep-dive background report on him that only showed two red flags: his motorcycle club affiliation and no verifiable source of legitimate income. There was also the fact most of his rotten-apple bikers had broken away, forming a new, dangerous faction—the

Hellhounds—under Todd Burk. The man who had brutally killed her brother.

Now the Hellhounds seemed hell-bent on putting Rip six feet under.

Maybe the enemy of her enemy could be a real ally?

The way he answered her questions would tell her. "Mrs. Hindley told me you were fixing her dishwater, left to get a tool from your trailer, and then she heard gunshots."

Rip stared down at her with that uneasy stillness to him. He possessed a coiled readiness, a wariness that made her nerves hum, giving him a more lethal vibe than any other MC gang member. Nothing on the job ever made her nervous.

But he did.

He wasn't quite like the other bikers. Guarded, sure, but he didn't taunt authority as though invincible, certainly didn't back down from it, and he didn't run in a pack.

For all the years she'd seen him around, she'd usually encountered him alone. More baffling was his living situation with Mrs. Hindley. Apparently, Rip had taken care of her debts, saving the land she was about to lose due to outstanding unpaid property taxes, and still paid her rent.

The question was where did he get the money?

He didn't have a nine-to-five job, and whenever she asked about employment, he'd given cagey responses.

The elderly woman had been eager to explain why Rip had done so much for her, but Ashley had been called away to respond to a 10-80, chase in progress.

She was bound and determined to figure out what Rip's deal was.

"That's right," Mrs. Hindley said, holding her cocoa between her hands. "And then I called you."

Instead of 911, which puzzled Ashley, but she wasn't going to squander this rare opportunity.

"Walk me through what happened," she said.

Rip pushed up the sleeves of his shirt, revealing corded forearms and tattoos, then pulled out a chair for her to sit. His gaze never left her, always watchful. Especially of her.

She decided to change course. "Why don't you show me where the altercation happened while you walk me through it?"

"Out at my Airstream." He turned to Ida. "Will you be all right until I get back?"

Sipping her cocoa, Ida waved a hand at him. "I don't need a babysitter. You're the one who needs looking after."

Grabbing his black sheepskin bomber jacket from a hook, Rip smiled and gave a low, husky chuckle far sexier than Ashley wanted it to be. He opened the back door and, standing against the jamb on the threshold, held it for her.

She hesitated.

Not that she feared him. Oddly, not once had he ever made her afraid. She simply didn't care for his politeness, how careful he was never to stand too close—*she was the one always stepping within arm's reach, maybe to test him*—the way he seemed aware of his height and strength and how intimidating it could be.

The dark jeans and gray Henley he wore did little to hide his sculpted chest and muscled arms. Another stark reminder of his physical capabilities.

If only he acted less chivalrous and more despicable, it would be easier to cling to her lingering doubts about him.

"You'll be safe in the dark alone with me, Deputy. Don't worry, I won't bite. Unless you want me to." His slow grin made her skin tingle.

It was devilish and inviting, and she had to fight very hard not to grin back at his effortless charm.

She'd been alone with him plenty of times and always felt safe, but they'd never been together in the dark. This flirty banter of his was just a game, so she decided to play by putting her hand on the hilt of her gun. "I'm not worried because I'm armed."

Ashley brushed past him, their bodies grazing, and she couldn't ignore the hard, rugged wall of muscle beneath his clothes. The smell of him. Soap and leather and pine. Up close, his eyes were a startling blue-gray that commanded attention. His features were sharp and chiseled, his square jaw unshaven. The sheer size of him never had her strategizing how best to take him down if necessary, because she didn't consider him a personal threat.

In fact, whenever she drew near him, her stomach fluttered as it did now.

Instantly, she became aware of her mistake. Physical contact. She wished she'd had him lead the way and gone out behind him.

Rip might be ridiculously—*disarmingly*—good-looking, but she refused to be attracted to a selfish man who ran from responsibility when he could have prevented her brother's death.

He shut the back door and slipped on his jacket.

Ashley walked beside him. "How long have you lived here?"

"Depends on the perspective."

An answer that told her nothing. He was good at giving those. "I need to know for my investigation and the report. You agreed to cooperate."

"Did I?" He raised an eyebrow. "Don't think so."

She thought back to the brief conversation in the kitchen. He was right. "You said you wouldn't lie."

"I said I do my best not to." He flipped up the collar of his jacket against the wind. "And I haven't lied to you. *Ever.*"

Another flutter whipped through her on his last word, but she deliberately tamped it down. "Why did you call me if you're only going to stonewall?"

"Ida called you. Not me."

She stopped walking. Once he did too, she hiked her chin up at him. "Would you prefer a different deputy to handle this?"

Shoving his hands in his pockets, with a hint of a smile on his face, he stared at her. That incisive, intense gaze and the sharp intelligence behind it made her squirm a little on the inside.

"I'd prefer none at all," he said, running his fingers across his head. Gone was his slightly too long sable hair that fell past his collar in favor of a buzz cut that made him look harder, edgier. Sexier.

"I already called it in to the station. So, it's me or someone else."

"You're in civilian clothes and driving your personal vehicle. Why are you here off duty?"

Technically, she wasn't off duty. For the past couple of months, she'd worked around the clock on a special assignment. "Ida called. I told her that if she ever needed me, I would come."

"Because you're worried about me?"

Odd way to phrase it. "Because I'm worried about her with you."

His jaw twitched as he seemed to chew on that. "I prefer you. Over the others. Since I've got no choice." He turned and continued to his trailer.

At the Airstream, she pulled latex gloves from her pocket, slipped them on and looked around outside, noting the damaged microwave oven on the ground.

Rip picked up a gun and held it up by the hilt. "It's mine. Discharged four times. Once out here, hitting a tree. The other three inside the trailer into the ceiling."

She opened an evidence bag, and he dropped the subcompact gun—SIG P365, she guessed—inside. "I thought you'd be a good shot, as a Marine."

"I am. When I intend to shoot, I don't miss. All the shots were accidental. The discharge happened during a scuffle."

She glanced at his hips. No holster. "Where were you carrying?" she asked, shaking the bag.

Pulling up his pant leg, he revealed an ankle holster.

"Got a concealed carry permit?"

He took his wallet from his inner jacket pocket and fished it out.

She looked it over. The permit was in order. She handed it back to him. "Shouldn't have your gun too long. This is only a formality. Procedure. I'll call you when you can get it back." His number was one of the few she had programmed in her phone, though she rarely had reason to use it. "Why do you live way out here, so far from town, on Mrs. Hindley's land?" she asked, trying again now that he was talking.

Since age nineteen, Ashley had lived in Bison Ridge, away from town, in the house her grandmother had bequeathed her. It was peaceful, surrounded by nature. Not unlike here.

"It's an arrangement that works for both of us."

Still being cagey.

"I noticed your motorcycle parked at Mrs. Hindley's house instead of in your driveway out here." The suspects would have heard his engine approaching and probably would've hightailed it out of there before he got close enough for an altercation if they only wanted to rob him or trash his place. "Why?"

"Ida needed a refill on her blood pressure medication. She wanted me to wait until the morning to get it, but I insisted since the pharmacy in town was still open. I parked at the house when I got back. We chatted for a while. Then she wanted me to look at the dishwasher because it had started leaking."

"Walk me through what happened," she said, and Rip explained everything from finding his door open to Mrs. Hindley firing her shotgun. "Can you describe what they looked like?"

"They wore ski masks, black hoodies and gloves. One was average height and build. The other was an inch taller than me but with slightly less bulk. The third one was thick around the middle. Stocky."

"Any distinguishing marks? Visible tattoos?"

"No. But the tall one is limping after the altercation."

"Did you recognize their voices?"

He hesitated and then shook his head. "Can't put a definitive name to any of them."

His choice of words had been careful. Too careful. "But you have some idea who they might be?"

"I don't care to speculate. Sorry, Deputy."

But if he did, no doubt he'd name three Hellhounds.

Sighing, she stepped inside the trailer and looked around. It was in a shambles. Broken dishes on the floor. Cushions ripped open and stuffing pulled out. The mess would take a solid day to clean up and furniture would have to be replaced.

Three guys to trash one trailer was a lot. Overkill really,

unless they'd wanted the backup in case they encountered Rip. Three against one and he'd done substantial damage. Impressive.

"Did they take anything?" she asked.

He stood near the door under the bullet holes. "I haven't had a chance to look, but I don't have anything of value. I don't keep cash in here."

She walked over to him. "What about drugs?"

"I don't do drugs. Never used. Never dealt it. Also, don't condone the trafficking of it."

She searched his face and, strangely, believed him. If he was into drugs, she supposed he'd give her one of his *non-answer answers* to avoid lying.

Passing him on her way back outside, she caught the masculine smell of him again. Her body tightened against it. Outside, she was grateful for the fresh air.

"You know this is a crime." She gestured at the trailer.

"What, assault with a microwave?" he asked, the corner of his mouth hitching up.

She bit back a smile. "I wasn't referring to that." She pointed higher, to the colorful pepper-shaped lights strung up along the awning on the outside of the Airstream. This was her first time at his home, and she realized how little she knew about him. "Putting up Christmas decorations before Thanksgiving."

The holiday feast at her parents' house would be next week. This was the hardest time of year for her, for the entire family, since her brother had been killed right after Halloween.

"You're one of those, huh? A believer that the holidays shall not overlap. Ida is the same. She calls the lights sacrilege. But I like having them up for longer than a month. The festive feel of it, though I've got nothing to celebrate."

She eyed him for a moment. "We can sweep for finger-prints, but since they wore gloves, I doubt we'll get any other than yours and those of visitors."

"No visitors. Not even Ida comes in here."

"No lady friends?"

He leaned against the side of the trailer, that laser focus of his full bore on her. "Are you asking as part of your investigation?"

Honestly, she wasn't sure why she'd asked. "Curious."

"No lady friends, Deputy."

"You mean that you bring here. I guess that's what your clubhouse is for." The MC had a clubhouse, if it should be called such, that Rip had built. Once again, raising the question of how it was paid for if not by illicit means? A massive single-story building that took up almost half a block. She'd heard the rumor that every member had his own bedroom at the club. After they partied hard, everyone had a private space to sleep or continue having fun with a woman. Not only that, but they also reportedly had a bar, game room, armory, conference room, gym, and a stage with stripper poles. *Classy.*

"If that's what you want to think, go ahead, but you'd be wrong about me."

"Why so cryptic?" She wasn't inquiring about MC secrets, only if there was a woman in his life, or occasionally in his bed. Not that she cared either way.

"Why so curious?" he countered.

"Can't help it." Particularly when it came to him. "It's what I do—ask questions, investigate, solve problems."

"I meant no lady friends. Period. Before you ask, no, I'm not gay. Only single. And when the clubhouse belonged to the Iron Warriors, I never used the room designated for me to sleep with women."

Something important in his comment registered.

"What do you mean *when* the clubhouse belonged to the Iron Warriors?" The answer dawned on her, but it didn't make any sense. "The clubhouse belongs to the Hellhounds now?"

A shadow crossed his eyes. "I gave it to them."

"What?" That wasn't akin to giving a bully your lunch or the money in your wallet, but more extreme, like giving them your entire house or life savings. "Why?"

Rip wasn't the type to roll over and give in. Was he?

Her gut clenched at what this could mean. The Iron Warriors were losing the battle against the Hellhounds. Rip was losing.

Where would that leave the town? If Rip and his guys were a blight, then Burk and his posse were a plague.

"The answer to that question is none of your concern," he said, his tone matter-of-fact, his stance unyielding. "Has no relevance on your investigation."

"It's connected. Todd forming a new gang. You giving him your clubhouse. The clubhouse you built for them. The other day, Ida told me someone slashed your tires. And now this. I'm sure there's now one Hellhound with a limp. Be honest with me."

"You want the truth?"

"Yes."

"Move on," he said, and she caught the warning as well as the worry in his voice. "Ida only called you tonight because she thought I might be in trouble or hurt. I'm fine."

She squared her shoulders, irritated at his straightforward manner of telling her zilch. Glancing back at the trailer, she tried to regroup. "Deputy Livingston will be out to sweep for prints. Maybe one of them got sloppy and we'll get lucky."

"Not necessary. I'd prefer not to have any further intrusion in my home if we can avoid it."

Frustration welled inside her. "Can I give you some advice?"

"Certainly. Doesn't mean I'll take it."

"In this turf battle between the Iron Warriors and Hellhounds, don't become a person of interest." She needed him free to help her, not investigated or locked up behind bars.

"Well, I *am* an interesting person."

She sighed, her breath crystallizing in the air. "Anything else you can tell me about what happened here tonight?"

"Nothing. And believe me, I wish I could."

"Thanks for the paperwork I'll have to do tonight since I have to file a report that will lead to nothing." She put away her notepad. "If you find anything missing, let me know."

Little point to her coming out here, let alone looking at his trailer, though it was nice to finally see where he lived. Maybe she could make this trip worth her while. She had to ask him sooner or later for help and couldn't wait for him to make another random visit to her house.

"Sorry about the paperwork and that I couldn't be more helpful," he said, almost sounding sincere. "I wish I hadn't taken up so much of your time while you're off duty, Deputy."

His politeness and formality were galling.

"You and I have history," she said. He owed her for her brother's death, and she was going to make him clear that debt. But over the years, he'd watched out for her and ceaselessly endeavored to build something beyond their complicated bond of obligation. In the back of her mind, she couldn't be sure he wasn't trying to use her. A powerful thing if a motorcycle club president had a cop in his pocket.

"That we do," he agreed.

"You show up at my house maybe twice a month to check in on me." Sometimes it was closer to every eight to ten days. Rip seemed to always be doing that. Looking out for her. Making sure she was okay. At first, they only talked outside on her porch. Then he started bringing food—tacos, empanadas, savory croissants from the café, delectable, irresistible items that got him inside the house, and once even a bottle of whiskey. She'd told him she preferred tequila. For her recent—twenty-fifth—birthday, instead of giving her the usual bath oils, luxury candles or silk kimono robes that she loved but would never buy for herself, he'd given her a bottle of Clase Azul twenty-fifth anniversary tequila. Someone at the office told her it cost three thousand dollars. Good thing she hadn't mentioned who'd given it to her, or they would've thought it was a bribe. That was what she'd suspected after learning the price. "It's weird, the way you only call me Deputy. Even when we bump into each other in town and I'm in plainclothes. Or when you're at my house."

He always parked around back, like his presence at her home was a dirty secret, and maybe for her it was, but she never let him past her kitchen.

She'd been grateful for the distance the use of her title provided, preventing them from ever getting too close, but now she needed that distance erased.

Rip folded his arms. "That's what you are."

"It's my job title. Not *who* I am." In a small town, it was hard to be someone else once you clocked out of your job, but she didn't always have to be Deputy Russo. "Use my first name. When you do, I'll know you haven't forgotten. About my brother. About the misery you could've prevented."

Something flashed across his face. Guilt? Pain? Whatever it was, it was real, honest.

"I haven't forgotten," he said. "I'll never forget. Burk will pay for Angelo. For everything. I swear it."

The words hit her, not as a blow, but more as a sudden, swift bear hug. Strong and reassuring.

He was a hardened Marine who had sworn to defend his country—once he'd even sworn to protect her, too, on the day her brother was buried. Back then, she couldn't hear it, wouldn't believe it. Now she suspected Rip didn't take oaths lightly.

Still, she didn't trust him completely either, which put her in a difficult position, because she was going to have to put her life in his hands.

"Why do you live here? Mrs. Hindley is itching to tell me." Ashley needed Rip to share, to open up further. DEA Agent Welliver had hammered home the importance of it when trying to cultivate an asset. Oddly, it made her wonder if that was what Rip had been up to all this time, with the visits to her house, asking her personal questions—trying to recruit her, but to what end? "I want to hear it from you. Will you give me that?"

He sighed. "My parents died when I was thirteen. Ida took us in, me and my brother, Thatcher. *Hatch*, that's what everyone called him. She cared for us when no one else would. She had lost her husband and her daughter and needed someone to love. Would've been less heartache for her if she'd rescued a couple of stray dogs instead and let us go to foster care." The regret in his voice was thick.

His candor touched something deep inside of her she hadn't expected.

"I'm out here to look after her," he continued. "To give her what company I can. Fix whatever breaks. Get her groceries. Make sure she takes her medication. She needs me now, though she'd spin a different tale, so I'm here."

Rip was an enigma. He'd told her things about himself, details that painted him as a good guy. A great one in fact. All of which she doubted and questioned until talking to Ida. Ashley had seen many things that made her wonder why he was ever in the MC, much less a club president. Sponsoring blood drives, holding fundraisers for the elementary school to cover the cost of pre-kindergarten, the way he was helping Ida when he didn't have to. How he watched out for Ashley. Not once had she had any problems with the Iron Warriors since he took over the club. Rip was both laudable and lamentable.

She struggled to reconcile the dichotomy.

"What happened to your brother?" She knew that Hatch had tried to rob a strip club one night while drunk, with some other bikers. He'd been caught and, while in prison, someone had killed him. Stabbed him with a shiv. According to the report, one of the guards suspected it had been related to a drug deal.

If Burk had been involved, Rip might let something slip.

His lips firmed. "I failed him. The same way I failed yours."

Ashley approached him, cautiously, as one would a wild animal being cornered. Not that she expected him to attack her. But her situation meant risking her life all the same. She couldn't afford to make a mistake. Not with him.

She drew as close as possible without touching him and could see the stormy blue-gray of his eyes in the illumination from the string lights above his head.

He stiffened, pressing his back to the side of the trailer as though he wanted to get away from her. But he didn't walk off, only shoved his hands in his pockets.

"I need your help," she said, her voice a hair above a whisper, even though they were alone.

His brows pinched together. "With what?" His tone matched hers.

"Taking down Burk, once and for all."

Straightening to his full height, he leaned in a little. "I warned you to stay away from him. Told you I'd handle it."

"Yeah, seven years ago. How has that been going for nearly a decade?" she asked, and he lowered his gaze. "You don't get to do that. I want you to look at me."

He lifted his head, his eyes meeting hers, but everything about him frosted over, putting distance between them, even though they were only inches apart. Might as well have been miles.

"I'm going after him," she continued. "But I need you." She had to be careful about how much to tell him until he agreed to help her.

"*Need*, huh. Tempting words coming from you," he said with sudden, cool remoteness that still managed to warm her. "But I'm not sure what you're saying. Are you asking to get dirty with me?"

Ashley hated the power he had over her, to make her belly flutter or her thighs tingle with the slightest innuendo. She cursed him in her head. "I have sensitive information I'm going to act on. I could use your help."

"I can't work with a cop. Cooperation is one thing. Collaboration is quite another. The code—"

"Forget about the MC code. For once. Please."

He stared at her for a long moment, as if looking straight through her, down to her soul.

When he didn't respond, she asked, "Did you mean it when you said you'd protect me?"

He gave a curt nod. "Of course."

"Then help me," she implored with every fiber of her being. It might be the only way she could take down Burk's operation and get out alive. "Do you have any idea what this takes?" To her chagrin, she heard her voice threaten to break and he dropped his head back against the trailer. "For me to come to you and ask? Please, I need you on this."

"I can't." His jaw tightened. "Just leave this to me. I'll handle it," Rip said, anger or annoyance edging his voice.

"When? In the next seven years? Seven days? Do you even have a week? Because you can't handle anything if you're dead. Tonight was only a taste of what's to come. Burk is turning up the heat on you. The word around town is it won't stop until you're finished. As in cold in the ground." She studied him, hoping to see a crack in the ice wall he'd thrown up between them. Nothing. "Forget it. I knew asking you was a waste of time. I'll do it on my own."

She spun on her heel, but before she could take two steps, he caught her wrist and whirled her back around, stealing her breath.

It was the first time he'd ever laid a finger on her. At her brother's funeral, she'd wailed as she thrashed him, beating him with her fists, and he'd done nothing to stop her or defend himself. He'd simply taken it until her parents had hauled her off him.

But now he had her wrist locked in an iron grip and dragged her so close she could feel the heat of his body. His eyes flashed hot enough to singe, a muscle in his jaw ticking. His face was so near hers his chocolaty breath brushed across her lips. She couldn't tell if he wanted to kill her or kiss her, and for a heartbeat she wondered what his mouth would feel like on hers.

"I don't know what you're planning," he said in a harsh whisper as his thumb stroked along the inside of her wrist. "But whatever it is, I'm telling you it's a bad idea. Stand down and walk away from it, Ashley. Do you hear me?"

Her pulse pounded from his touch. From his fury. From the bittersweet sound of her name on his lips. From the jolt of unwelcome desire.

From his blunt order that shook her to the core.

How dare he try to tell her what to do?

She was no longer a teenage girl. She had been with the sheriff's department since she was of legal age to join. For nearly seven years, she'd worn the badge and done as he asked, staying away from Todd Burk, his MC brother, while he *handled* it. Not anymore. She was done waiting. "Shame on you. For asking me to back down. For not helping me, when I have never asked you for anything. I've finally got a chance to stop Burk and I'm taking it. I'll handle it while you keep running from your responsibility."

Ashley yanked her arm free from his tight grasp and marched off toward her truck.

DEA Agent Welliver had given her the tip she'd been waiting for. The final piece had been Rip, but…

Shaking her head, she whisked away her disappointment. She didn't need him. It would be riskier without him, a lot riskier, but she could do it alone.

Come hell or high water, she wasn't going to be like Rip. She wasn't going to fail.

Her mission wouldn't end until she stopped Burk's drug-running operation and the man was behind bars or dead.

Chapter Three

Pushing through the front door of the first-ever Iron Warriors clubhouse, Rip hated the emotions running riot through him. Anger. Shame. Defeat.

No. Only a temporary setback.

Rip had lost a battle, but not the war.

Taking off his sunglasses, he sat in a rickety chair and looked around. In the early afternoon light, the ultra-rural cabin situated in the middle of nowhere looked even more dilapidated. Almost a twenty-minute drive outside of Laramie or Bison Ridge, it was a sufficient spot for privacy, to gather with his men and strategize without any of their plans getting leaked.

For far too long, Rip had been trying to take care of the problem named Todd Burk, without any of his other brothers in the MC being collateral damage.

The task had proved impossible.

Todd had layers and layers of separation from most of the illegal activity, insulation by the very men Rip had been trying to protect.

The sheriff's department had done half the work of cleaning up the club, without Rip's involvement, by shutting down Burk's prostitution ring with help from the FBI. Todd had a few civilian sleazeballs running the day-to-day of handling the women and clients. Two low-level Iron Warriors had been collecting the money, funneling it back to Todd. They were arrested but refused to incriminate Burk.

Nasty business that had opened Rip's eyes to what had been transpiring unbeknownst to him. A couple of months later, he learned about the drug trafficking when his own brother was killed. Hatch had been behind bars for armed robbery, serving nine years. A dangerous, foolish act that never would've happened if Rip had been around instead of serving in the military. Hatch kept getting into trouble in prison and his sentence extended with every infraction. Then his brother had gotten caught in the middle of a turf war between rival gangs selling narcotics behind bars. That was how Rip discovered Todd had been sneaking drugs into the prison somehow and turned Hatch into a dealer.

Rip had dug around with the type of professional scrutiny he'd used in the Marines.

Todd's operation was extensive. Not only was he dealing locally, but also to every university and college within a four-hour drive of town, poisoning communities and killing kids.

What Rip hadn't been able to ascertain was Todd's supplier, the schedule and location of major shipments, how the cash flowed and was being laundered. He also couldn't prove that Todd was behind any of it. Rip could only decree that the club would not mess with drugs. No transporting or dealing them.

But Todd had been prepared and called the decision to a vote.

One Rip lost.

Those same guys he'd been trying to protect had stabbed him in the back, figuratively, siding with Todd and trading in their Iron Warrior cuts to be Hellhounds.

Now Rip would get as ruthless as required to complete the job, even if it meant half of the new OMG ended up behind bars. A necessary sacrifice as long as he kept Ashley out of the fray.

He looked over at the few men seated that he had left, a whopping four, whom he'd called together this afternoon.

"Meeting here feels like a slap in the face," said Quill, his vice president. A senior Warrior twenty years older than Rip, Quill had seen the club go through many phases and lots of change, but even he was having difficulty with this one. "Being in this run-down shack while the *Hellhounds*—" he spit on the floor "—are in the house that you built."

To clean up the club and steer it toward the straight and narrow path, Rip had to give them a way to earn money. Legitimately. He fell back on what he knew. Combat and defense. He'd formed the Ironside Protection Service. Whether someone needed a single bodyguard or full squad detail, conspicuous or covert, Ironside answered the call. Once they developed a solid reputation, work had begun to pour in, the gigs had gotten better, more lucrative. They had raked in plenty, to pay for the tricked-out clubhouse, to keep them flush in cash and, he had thought, mistakenly, to appease their greed.

The whole time he was busy focused on building a law-abiding legacy, Todd was just as busy expanding the criminal enterprise. The worst part was that Todd had the brains and clever sense to keep it quiet and his methods concealed from Rip and those loyal to him.

JD grimaced. As the group's sergeant-at-arms, he was third in rank. "How could you give it to those ungrateful, traitorous fools?" JD asked.

For so many years, Rip had been careful, not keeping anyone too close because he couldn't afford any additional vulnerabilities. But last month Todd had taken his one weakness and exploited it anyway.

"Give me the clubhouse or I'll spill blood," Todd had said. "And not just the Iron Warriors'. I won't waste a bullet on Ida. But you won't be around forever to protect the pretty little deputy, and once you're out of the picture, she'll pay the price." A wicked grin pulled at his mouth. "It won't be quick, and it won't be painless. Maybe a couple of guys will show her a 'good time' first." He licked his lips.

Disgust swam through his veins as he recalled it. After Rip *showed* Todd what he thought of that proposal, with his fists, going so far as to break his nose, he'd given Burk the keys and signed the deed over to him.

"A building isn't worth bloodshed," Rip said.

Quill rolled his eyes, leaned back in a creaky chair and put a boot up on a table, kicking up dust. "Let those boys build their own place. Danger comes with the territory for us. If we get to hold on to what's ours, we can take whatever they dish out and give it right back."

They could.

Ashley couldn't.

She was smart and strong and a sharp deputy, but the badge wouldn't keep her safe. The depravity Todd was capable of, combined with his utter lack of respect for women—the guy even beat and cheated on his own old lady—meant he'd order some lowlifes under his thumb to hurt Ashley, bad, and then kill her. Not only to get to Rip but just for fun. "I don't want a war spilling over into town. Innocent people will suffer the consequences," he said.

"Are you talking about Ashley Russo?" JD asked, and all the other curious gazes in the room swung to Rip.

It was common knowledge that he'd watched over her and ensured no Iron Warrior messed with her, but he'd kept it secret from Ashley how he managed to do that. Todd's vile threat only made Rip more determined to shield her. From everything, including herself.

"I am," he admitted. "But also, Ida. And your families. Once bullets start flying, bystanders could be hit."

Quill nodded. "You make a good point. The sheriff's department will only make things difficult for us, and cops are likely to die if Todd becomes so unhinged as to go after *your* deputy."

My deputy?

A part of him enjoyed the sound of that far too much. Ever since he'd seen her swimming in the lake with some friends, almost nineteen years old, climbing out of the water in a modest one piece, laughing, sparkling, radiating light, he'd considered how it would be if she was his.

The more pragmatic side of him was aware she didn't even like him and deserved much better than he could offer. So, he kept his distance and put Quill in charge of watching her, ensuring her safety with the full power of Ironside services at his disposal.

But the way she'd asked for his help, the imploring look on her face, the plea in her voice had been a sucker punch straight to his heart. That was the last conversation he'd wanted to have with Ashley. Upsetting her. Angering her. Disappointing her.

Denying the one request she'd ever made of him.

He'd almost caved. *Almost.* But helping her would not only go against the code but also meant allowing her to get in the middle of this war, which was exactly where he didn't want her. He needed to figure out her reckless plan and stop her before it was too late.

Her defiance last night, when he was only trying to keep her out of the line of fire, still had him bristling.

"This is going to come to a head, sooner rather than later," JD said. "There's only room for one club in this town."

An unfortunate truth. It was the reason Todd had called a vote to split the club instead of replacing Rip as president. This left those not loyal to Todd isolated and vulnerable to attack.

Todd was eventually going to try to kill him unless Rip got to him first.

"Rather than a full-frontal confrontation, there's a better way to handle this," Rip said. "Ironside is mine. They can't bring in cash through it without me. The authorities already shut down their prostitution ring." He'd had no idea women were being trafficked and pimped out in portable tiny homes that routinely changed locations. But Todd had at least three or four degrees of separation preventing law enforcement from charging him. "The only thing left is drugs."

"I heard he's expanding that," JD said. "He's got big plans."

Rip nodded, having caught wind of the same rumors. "And we need to know what they are."

"It'll turn out like every other attempt to get Todd." Quill heaved a loud, long sigh laced with weariness. "Teflon won't go to jail."

Since the cops could never make a charge stick to Todd, the club had given him the apt nickname "Teflon."

Rip also doubted the man would ever see the inside of a prison cell and wasn't counting on Todd's arrest as part of his plan. "He's most likely getting his drugs from a cartel. We need to figure out the inner workings of his operation and bring the hammer down. Find a way to seize a shipment. A big one that he can't recover from financially. One that puts him in the crosshairs of the cartel."

"So they take him out for us," JD said.

Rip nodded. A lot of moving parts to piece together to make it happen. But possible.

"That might work," Quill said.

Based on the expressions of the others, they weren't opposed to the idea, but they weren't sold on it either.

"How are we supposed to do that?" asked Saul, one of the skeptics.

"We start with a weak link. A little guy in the food chain," Rip said. "One of his dealers. Someone who will talk to us, but also someone we can rattle to keep quiet about sharing information. Any ideas who we can squeeze?"

JD snapped his fingers. "Yates. He acts tough, but it's smoke-and-mirrors. I'm telling you that dude will rat to save himself when it comes down to it. I think he might even do it just because he doesn't like Todd and the way he gets treated."

Burk didn't respect many of his brothers. That was why it had come as such a shock to Rip that so many had sided with him. Was it out of coercion? Fear? Bribery?

It certainly wasn't out of loyalty or love.

"But what if Yates doesn't know enough?" Quill asked. "Todd is a slippery snake. I'm sure none of the dealers will know everything we need to make this happen."

A safe bet that Rip wouldn't wager against. Getting information from one of the dealers was only a maneuver that would lead to another. Rip had already made a preemptive move before he'd given Todd the clubhouse. He'd left behind a parting gift. A voice-activated audio transmitter with a SIM card hidden in the room or rather the *chapel*, where they held *church*, their official club meetings. When its built-in sensor detected a sound over sixty decibels, it automatically dialed a preset number, Rip's primary burner phone. Then he could listen in. Thus far, he hadn't learned anything noteworthy, but at the same time, it also meant Todd wasn't aware of the bug.

"Yates isn't going to be the endgame guy," Rip said. "One step at a time. First, we find out what he knows, then we take it from there." His men nodded. "Something else I need you to do. Talk to the boys who we thought were loyal, who we never assumed might side with a drug dealer. Find out why they're wearing different patches now." At the moment, Todd outmanned them. Anything Rip could do to whittle down the numbers and spare some good people jail time, he would. "And be discreet."

Chapter Four

Ashley zoomed the telephoto lens in on the front of the Hellhound clubhouse. Ten bikes were out front. Over the past several hours that she'd been seated in an unmarked patrol SUV across the street, she'd snapped pictures of six members. None of them had a limp. But instinct told her to be patient.

Apparently, the ones inside, whom she hadn't seen, weren't early risers. Nearly noon and they hadn't shown their faces yet. She didn't know if any women were inside. Besides the Harleys, no other vehicles were parked out front. Not that there couldn't be some concealed in the adjacent four-bay garage.

They'd accepted a food delivery about an hour ago.

Why were they all holed up in there on a Saturday instead of at home with girlfriends, wives, their families? Half of them had kids.

Mustering together, getting their stories straight.

She looked around. There wasn't much traffic out here on Rock Grinder Lane. No homes or businesses in the desolate area on the far outskirts of town, aside from a couple of warehouses farther down the dirt road, a trucking company and a defunct cement plant. Other than a few 18-wheelers and vans that had passed earlier, there was plenty of privacy for the OMG.

The front door of the clubhouse swung open. Todd Burk sauntered outside smoking a cigarette, followed by three members of his crew. One was average height and medium build. Another was a heavy guy with a barrel-shaped torso. The last guy, bringing up the rear, was tall and had a distinct limp. Every time he put weight on his bad leg, he winced.

"Gotcha," she muttered to herself, snapping pictures of them talking.

Not that she had fingerprints, a detailed description of them to go on, or any evidence to link them to the attack last night on Rip. But those were the perpetrators.

Ashley only had to prove it. She took a couple more photos.

Todd patted the tall one on the back, saying something to him and the others. The three guys nodded as Todd turned, glancing around. His gaze landed on her.

She zoomed in for a close-up of his face.

He smiled, though there was nothing pleasant about it. His grin was pure evil. He gestured for the others to go back inside, then he jogged across the lot through the opening in the gate, and over toward her.

Stay away from Burk. Rip's voice rang in her head.

But she had kept her distance. Nothing she could do about the man crossing the street. She certainly wasn't going to speed off like she feared him. Even though she'd been afraid of the man since she was seventeen.

Ashley set the camera in the passenger's seat, started the SUV and lowered her window. Heart thrumming, she unfastened the strap on the holster at her hip with the flick of her thumb and rested her hand on the butt of her duty weapon.

Todd took one last drag from his cigarette and flicked it to the ground.

"That's littering," she said as he approached.

"Good afternoon to you, too, Deputy Russo. Feel free to write me a citation. I'd be happy to pay. I must admit I'm surprised to see you here."

Anger always overrode her fear when she saw him, but this was the first time they'd come face-to-face and spoken. "Someone broke into Rip Lockwood's trailer last night and attacked him. I'm here investigating. You wouldn't happen to know anything about that, would you?"

"No, ma'am. A break-in and assault. How unfortunate. The thought of a former brother under siege." He gave a mock shiver. "Terrifying. It's good the sheriff's department is investigating. But it looks like you're just taking pictures. Which is fine. I welcome it. Nothing to hide. In fact, I was counting on someone from your department swinging by today." Another vicious grin tugged at his mouth. "Just surprised that it's you." He let that dangle between them for a moment. "Want to come on over, ask us some questions inside *my* clubhouse?"

No way that was happening. "Why are you surprised it's me out here?"

"Well, your boyfriend paid a steep price to keep the devil away from you, but in spite of that, here you are, taking pictures, in front of the devil's house. Tempting him." He licked his lips. "Not wise. I bet Rip doesn't know you're here. He would not be happy." Todd shook his head as though reprimanding a child.

"What price did Rip pay?"

He raised his eyebrows. "You don't know?" A dark chuckle rolled from him. "Then I can't say. I don't want to be the one to spoil the surprise. But the gesture was grand. Undeniably romantic. You should ask your boyfriend."

Hearing Rip referred to as her *boyfriend* irked and intrigued her. Why on earth would Todd or anyone else for that matter think such a thing?

"There's nothing personal between me and Rip," she said flatly, not wanting him to see he'd struck a nerve.

A look of surprise and she dared guess possibly even delight swept over his expression. "You're not his old lady?"

"Old lady?" That was a serious term of endearment reserved for a woman a biker was committed to. But there was nothing romantic or sexual between her and Rip. No *ship* of any kind. No relationship. No friendship. Nothing.

"Yeah. I get you wanting to keep it secret. You've both got to keep up appearances with you wearing a badge. But you can tell me. You two a thing?"

Something prickled through her, some kind of omen, at him pressing the question, at him asking at all. If people thought that, if the sheriff did, could it hurt her job, damage her reputation? "Not that it's any of your business, but no."

Wicked satisfaction spread wider over his face.

She realized with a sinking sensation in the pit of her stomach that she'd somehow made a mistake. But she'd only been honest.

Todd drew closer, resting his forearm on the frame of the open window.

She tightened her grip on her gun.

"You may not be intimate with your protector, but make no mistake, it's personal. Rip really should remedy that technicality." Todd sucked his teeth. "One never knows how much time they've got. Life can be short. With the slew of mishaps that he's endured recently, he probably hears a phantom clock counting down in his head. *Tick. Tock. Tick. Tock.*" He chuckled again, making her skin crawl. "Are you sure you don't want to come in?" He hiked a thumb over his shoulder at the clubhouse. "We make a mean cup of coffee. Could probably scrounge up a Danish or a doughnut for you, too."

"Yeah, I'm sure. The boys will all say they don't know anything, the same as you. Their alibi will be that they were here at the club."

"Sounds about right." He winked at her, and it was all she could do not to wrap her hands around his throat and squeeze. "Suit yourself, Deputy. You drive safely back to the station, you hear?" He tapped on her door, jogged back across the street and slowed to a hurried stride, disappearing into the clubhouse.

Doing a U-turn, she rolled up the window and cranked the heat. She headed toward town, churning over everything Todd had said. A lot to unpack.

No doubt in her mind, Rip was in grave danger.

As much as she wanted her concern for him to be strictly related to the operation she was planning and the part she had hoped he'd play, it was hard to deny that it was also deeply...personal.

Hating that Todd Burk had been the one to make her face that uncomfortable truth, to feel it, she groaned.

She glanced in the rearview mirror. Through the dust on the dirt road that her tires kicked up, she spotted a black van behind her.

Todd had expected the sheriff's department. Probably to question his crew about last night. Whenever they were interviewed, they always told the same lies, as if reading from a script that Todd wrote. But the way he'd been looking forward to the arrival of law enforcement was concerning.

It niggled at her even more how strangely pleased it made Todd to learn she wasn't Rip's woman.

Ashley watched the black van speed up a bit. She told herself that it couldn't be anyone after her. Not in broad daylight while she was in a patrol vehicle. But still she sensed something was off. Just nerves after speaking with Todd, her brother's murderer, inches away from her face, taunting her. Given that she'd yearned so long for justice, and she finally had a chance to hurt the man that had killed Angelo, who could blame her?

Pressing down on the gas, Ashley drove a little faster, anxious to get off the barren strip of road and to reach the well-populated town center.

The van stayed back behind her some distance. She couldn't make out the driver, front passenger or license plate in the cloud of dust. What had made her think the person behind the wheel had been chasing her?

Todd hadn't threatened her, and after all, she'd only been taking pictures.

Still, she couldn't shake the unease curling through her midsection. She got on the radio. "This is Russo, who else is on patrol?" With her splitting her time and focus between the sheriff's department and the DEA, she couldn't remember.

"It's your favorite deputy," Mitch Cody replied.

He was a good guy and they got along well. "Where are you right now?"

"Black Elk Trail. Why? What's up?"

Not far from her. Only a few minutes away. "It's nothing. I'm on Rock Grinder, passing Cloverleaf now," she said, referring to the cluster of dirt roads named after boot spurs. "I was over at the Hellhounds clubhouse. Had a chat with Burk."

"I'm sure it was pleasant." His voice was laced with sarcasm.

"He invited me in for coffee and doughnuts."

"Ooh la la. Aren't you special."

As a matter of fact, she got the impression that she was, somehow, because of Rip, but not in a good way. "Anyhow, there's a black van behind me. I can't make out the plate. I don't think it's following me. Probably from the trucking company." But she wasn't sure and that was what troubled her. "It's silly, but something in my gut told me to check in."

The van sped up, closing the distance between them.

"Never ignore your gut." His tone sobered. "I'll head your way."

Ahead, the road made a sharp turn to the right and then back to the left. Only a little farther and Rock Grinder would connect with the wider, better-paved main street into town, which Mitch would turn onto any second.

Ashley came around the corner as the sun peeked through the clouds, shining over the landscape. She caught the glint of something up on the horizon ahead of her. Checking the van's distance behind her in the rearview mirror, she spotted a man lean out of the passenger's window, wearing a gaiter scarf pulled up over his nose, a second before she heard a loud distinctive crack—*a gunshot*—followed by another.

Both back tires on her patrol SUV blew.

Tightening her grip on the steering wheel, she fought to maintain control of the vehicle, but it was impossible. The rear end fishtailed, the tires skidding across the loose earth at the edge of the road. The SUV keeled hard to the right and rolled, sliding on its top before crashing into a tree in the ditch below the road, the passenger's-side window shattering on impact. The airbag deployed, making her cough from the dust particles released in the air.

Stunned, Ashley hung upside down, the seat belt cutting into her. The airbag was now hanging deflated in her face. For an instant, she couldn't move, couldn't breathe.

The sound of the other vehicle's engine roaring toward her fired her into action.

She hit the seat belt button, tumbling onto the headliner of the ceiling covered with pieces of the window. Glass shards cut into one palm. Aware the van had stopped, she drew her weapon and got back on the radio. "Shots fired. I repeat, shots fired. My tires were hit. My vehicle crashed in the dry ravine just before Nine-Point Star Trail. I'm in need of assistance. Suspects are still on the road."

Ashley fumbled for the door handle.

Jammed. The door wouldn't open.

If she crawled through the broken passenger's-side window that faced the road, it would leave her exposed to possible gunfire.

She aimed at the driver's window and pulled the trigger. Glass shattered.

The engine of the van revved and tires peeled off, screeching. She kicked away the remaining fragments of glass around the frame, scrambled out and got her bearings with her Glock at the ready.

Ashley ran up the incline, out of the ditch, and took aim. She fired two shots, one hitting the back door before the van turned onto the main road.

Sirens blared. Seconds later Mitch raced by in pursuit of Todd's thugs.

Drawing in a deep breath, she winced. Her ribs throbbed

and her skull ached. She touched the wetness on her forehead and looked at her fingers. Blood.

Todd Burk had come after her.

Whatever protection Rip had provided over the years was gone and they were out of time.

Now, she needed to go after Burk. Tonight. There was no telling what might happen tomorrow.

PARKING AT THE crime scene at Fuller's Pharmacy, Ashley glanced around for the sheriff. She spotted Deputy Livingston suited up in protective clothing—white overalls with a hood, goggles, face mask, gloves and plastic overshoes—to prevent DNA cross contamination. Holding his kit, he headed inside. As she cut the engine, Sheriff Daniel Clark walked out of the pharmacy, tugging off his latex gloves.

Ashley climbed out of her truck. She was no longer woozy from the accident and the emergency room had cleared her for duty. No concussion and nothing broken. She ducked under the yellow police tape cordoning off the area in front of the drugstore.

"I heard about what happened," Sheriff Clark said. "Are you okay?" He gestured to the small bandage on her forehead.

"Only a scratch. It's fine."

"It's not fine," he said, his expression stern.

Of course, it wasn't. Deputy Mitch Cody had apprehended the driver and shooter. A couple of prospects, two young guys hoping to become full members of the Hellhounds.

"Did the perps talk?" he asked.

"They claim they didn't like the sheriff's department taking pictures and acted without any of the other Hellhounds' knowledge."

The sheriff pursed his lips. "And Burk? What did he have to say for himself?"

"According to Mitch, it was the same story. Burk even had the audacity to act horrified that potential members of his club would shoot at a cop."

"Do you think they went after you because of your association with Ripton Lockwood? Hurt him by hurting you?"

More likely to offend Rip than hurt him by going after someone under his protection. It seemed like a leap, but then again Todd had a lot to say about Rip and the questions he'd asked her gave the impression he believed she was Rip's old lady. "Anything is possible."

"Regardless of the reason, I should've had you hand off this investigation to Cody first thing this morning. The MC has an issue with cops and an even bigger one with female cops."

Rip wasn't like that. He didn't have a problem with women in positions of power or authority, but when she'd joined the sheriff's department, he'd told her in no uncertain terms that he didn't care for her putting on the badge. Not because he disliked cops, but he didn't want her in harm's way, let alone pursuing the bad guys.

"Mitch has got it from here," she said.

"The Hellhounds and Todd Burk can't think they're going to get away with this. An attack on you is an attack on all of us. On the law itself. I'll pay them a visit later. Bring Cody and the fire department."

"Why the fire department?"

"Because I've got a sneaking suspicion that I'm going to smell smoke when I get there. Might have to bust through a few walls to make sure it's not electrical."

The sheriff was a good man and only wanted to look out for his people, but things were going to escalate. Todd's reign of terror was just getting started. The sooner he was dealt with the better for everyone. "What do you have inside?" she asked, wanting to change the subject.

"Homicide. Someone shot the pharmacist once in the head, twice in the chest and slit his throat."

"Unusual. Not what we typically see in a robbery." Perpetrators were normally in a rush to grab what they could and get away from the scene. "One in the head. Maybe in the chest. But not three bullets and a fatal knife wound."

"I think someone was sending a message," the sheriff said.

What kind of message and sent by whom? "Was it the father or the daughter?" Fuller's was the largest drugstore in town. Multigenerational, family owned and operated. Kind, decent people.

"Father. I need to track down the daughter to see what she knows. She was scheduled to work today. Looks like she logged in earlier on one of the computers, but there's been no sign of her."

Over his shoulder, Ashley watched the news station van along with the purple Jeep that belonged to journalist Erica Egan parking near the scene. "Media is here."

"I'm surprised it took them so long." The sheriff glanced behind him. "I better go speak with them. Did you need something? Shouldn't you be resting?"

No rest for the weary. Or the wicked. "The hospital cleared me. I just wanted you to know I'm going dark for the next couple of days."

"The DEA is sending you undercover?"

Debating again about whether to be forthright with the sheriff, she decided against it. "Something like that. The situation is urgent. A window is open. Now or never." She had jumped at the chance to be assigned as a liaison to the DEA's Rocky Mountain task force. Finally, she thought she'd be able to cut off Todd Burk's drug operation at the source. How naive she had been to assume the DEA cared about her small town or any of the others that Burk was poisoning. They had their own targets and objectives, and though she'd done plenty of good work with them, none of it had brought her any closer to her goal of stopping Burk. So she was going undercover. Technically, she was still attached to the task force and working within the constructs of their mandate, but the DEA wasn't directly sending her. "I'm tracking down the drug supplier to the—" she caught herself from saying *the Iron Warriors*, the change was still surreal "—Hellhounds. I'll be out of pocket and unreachable until I'm done."

"Can you say where you're going?"

The less he knew the better for them both. In case things went awry, she didn't want any of this to blow back on him. Only her butt would be in a sling. "North."

"Tell Agent Welliver to keep you safe. I want my deputy back in one piece, preferably unharmed."

This went against her instincts, her training, her deep-seated desire to do things by the book, but drugs had now spread to the high school. Kids were getting addicted and dying younger and younger. Lives were at stake. Including Rip's and hers. This was bigger than the rules. It might be the only way to clean up the town and get rid of Todd Burk.

Just this once, she had to go rogue.

She gave the sheriff a measured smile. "I'll let you know as soon as I get back."

"You do that." He turned toward the media approaching the crime scene.

Her cell phone rang. Heading to her truck, she pulled it from her pocket and looked at the caller ID. The man must have a sixth sense. "Russo," she answered.

"Checking to see if you're squared away," Agent Welliver said. "Were you able to get Lockwood as an asset?"

"Not quite." She got into her truck out of the cold and started the engine.

"My recommendation is to keep working on him. I did a deep dive into Lockwood. No red flags other than his association with the motorcycle club. Honorable discharge from the military. Glowing performance reviews. His last commander said that Ripton was a man of focus, commitment and sheer will. He'll be your best way in and with his Special Forces background as a Marine Raider, you couldn't have a better person at your side."

She swallowed her bitter disappointment. It could take weeks to convince him to help her, and with Burk getting more hostile with each passing day, they were out of time. "If you could assign one of your agents to assist me for a couple of days—"

"We've been through this. The DEA is after big fish. Major dealers. Heavyweight gangs. Cartels. Not low-level dealers. The best I can do is pass along any intelligence to you that might be of interest."

According to one of Welliver's informants, a small motorcycle club in southern Wyoming, which had been narrowed down to her town, got their drugs from a pill mill—a place where bad doctors and clinics handed out prescription drugs like candy—and made their contact through someone known as LA, who was with another MC. The Sons of Chaos up in Bitterroot Gulch.

The town was outside of her jurisdiction as a deputy, but as a liaison of the task force, she had legal authority throughout the province of the Rocky Mountain Division of the DEA to investigate.

"Maybe the sheriff can get another deputy to help you," Welliver suggested.

They were short-staffed as it was, and Sheriff Clark was under the impression she was getting all the support she needed from the DEA. Her approach was thorny and not without great personal and professional risk, but necessary.

"That won't be possible," she said.

"Probably for the best anyway. You'll need a real biker with you to get anything out of the Sons. You need Lockwood."

Shaking her head, she slapped the steering wheel. "I've tried."

"Have I taught you nothing?" Welliver gave a dry chuckle. "Try harder."

The lessons she'd learned from him had been hard and ugly and most she wanted to forget. He operated in the gray, as she was doing now, all for the greater good. If she succeeded in this and needed DEA cover in explaining her actions, he'd provide it. If her op fell apart, then—

"You've mentioned that he feels protective of you. Something to do with the death of your brother. Exploit it. Better yet, sleep with him."

The suggestion was a complete blindside, leaving her stomach fluttering. First Burk, now Welliver. "What, sir?"

"If you do, I think you'll have him wrapped around your little finger."

"No, it wouldn't work." Not on Rip. He wouldn't take the bait. Even if she thought that he might, she'd never consider doing it.

"Might sound indecent but agents use a honey trap on occasion because it does work. If he's been protecting you from the Warriors all this time, then there's an emotional element that runs deeper than guilt or obligation. Trust me.

If you get physical with him, the guy will do whatever you ask. I can practically guarantee he'll help."

"I can't."

Not that Rip was lacking in physical appeal. It was the exact opposite. Last night when he'd touched her, there had been something beneath the anger, a different kind of heat. No matter how hard she tried to convince herself the sparks had merely been a product of the argument mixed with adrenaline, she still wondered what his lips would feel like on hers.

Every time he'd visit, the rumble of his bike drawing closer, a thrill of anticipation went through her. After a while, she'd stopped feeling guilty about the way her pulse quickened when he came into sight. He had a way of pushing her buttons. Every single one of them. Gave her that strange, fluttery feeling with a look. Made her thighs tingle with simple innuendo. She'd always suspected he'd be an amazing lover. Once, after a couple of shots of tequila from the bottle he'd brought over, she'd been tempted to invite him to her bedroom for dirty, hot, pity sex, no strings attached, but then he'd addressed her as deputy, and the thought of Angelo and Burk—a man Rip viewed as his MC brother—had sobered her.

Why did Rip have to be a biker?

Then again, a dyed-in-the-wool biker was precisely what she needed right now.

Regardless of how much she wanted justice, she wouldn't trade her body, manipulate Rip using feminine wiles. Not that it would work anyway. Rip's charm could come across as flirtatious, but he wasn't attracted to her. Constantly reminding her she was nothing more to him than a deputy and an obligation.

"That's not a line I'm comfortable crossing," she added. "I won't operate that way. I'll find his pressure point and push."

But she already had, and it hadn't worked.

"Then Russo, you need to find an active *trigger* point. The difference being the latter is very painful. And make it hurt when you push. I'm talking excruciating. If your op turns up anything worth my while, let me know. Remember, you can't do this alone. To try would be suicide. Good luck." Welliver disconnected.

Ashley racked her brain over how to persuade Rip to do this without seducing him. Because that was not an option. He was against the dealing of drugs and had big reasons to take down Burk. Now more than ever. But working with a cop went against his MC code.

She had to give him a compelling justification to overlook that detail. Something he couldn't ignore. Something bigger than that code. Maybe she'd been too careful last night about not revealing her plan. He'd only help her if he understood the magnitude of the risk she was taking, the high degree of danger involved.

Being cagey like him got her nowhere.

The one thing she couldn't share quite yet was that Todd had sent his prospects after her. Telling Rip would only distract him from the bigger picture. Knocking Todd's lights out would be temporary and would only provoke the devil to act more violently. The only real solution was putting an end to Burk's drug business and locking him up behind bars.

To do that, she would have to trust Rip. She needed to put the rest of her cards on the table with him and let the chips fall where they may.

She took out her phone and sent Rip a text message.

Your gun is cleared. I'll give it back. Meet me at Angelo's grave. Thirty minutes.

Chapter Five

Rip had a bad feeling about meeting the deputy, much less at her brother's grave. Yet, there he was, riding his Harley, headed for Millstone Cemetery.

Deep in his gut he knew she was still determined to carry out whatever plan she had, no matter how dangerous.

He was equally determined to keep her from painting a bull's-eye on her back.

Pulling up to the cemetery, he spotted Ashley's parked truck and something inside his chest clenched.

Chance had put him on a collision course with her seven years ago. Rip had heard about his brother's arrest, taken leave from the Marines and gone home to find out what happened. While there, Quill had told him about Angelo Russo. A first-year college student who had been in the wrong place at the wrong time and witnessed Todd trying to take advantage of a teenage girl. Todd had killed Angelo. Threatened the girl and her family into staying quiet. And had gotten rid of the gun tying him to the crime.

All speculation and deduction. Todd had only ever alluded to being responsible, at least to Rip.

Quill had insisted Rip go with him to the funeral to pay their respects to the family. At the time, he didn't understand why the older biker wanted him to go, but once there, he realized it had been an emotional ambush.

"Your father always wanted you to be an Iron Warrior," Quill said.

"And I joined." He'd wanted to wear a cut and ride a Harley since he was five, but the club didn't fulfill him the way he had imagined it would. Fantasy had been better than reality.

"Only to leave. When you were meant to lead."

The Marines had given him an unexpected sense of purpose and belonging and family the MC never had. Just like Ida told him it would. "I'm on the career track." He'd gotten great assignments, tough, but career-builders that put him in the fast lane for promotion. "I was thinking about being a lifer."

A four-year enlistment had turned into ten. Why not make it a full twenty or more?

"A lifer?" The dismay in Quill's voice was cutting. "You made a vow to us first."

"I'm still an Iron Warrior. Wear my colors whenever I ride, no matter where I am in the world. When I'm here, I attend church," he said, referring to their meetings.

"Not good enough. Your leaving created a vacuum that Todd Burk has filled. The boy is a bad seed. Has sway like I've never seen before. If you had been here, in charge of the club instead of Larson, the way you were supposed to be, the way your father meant you to be, none of this would've happened. Your brother wouldn't be in jail along with those others. It was Todd who put them up to the robbery. And Angelo Russo wouldn't be dead," Quill said, the words stabbing Rip like a hot knife to the gut. "The only reason Burk felt so confident and cocky to kill that kid is

because he's got a gang on his side. You never would've allowed that snake to wear the patch and get a choke hold on the MC by getting more filth like him to join. Todd is running amok, getting worse every year, and will drag the club in a direction it was never intended to go by any of the founding members like me and your father. This is on you, Rip. You were selfish and ran away from your responsibility. There are many who'd still support you to take up the mantle. How many more brothers need to get locked up? How many more kids need to die before you take your place as president?"

"Is it true? You could've prevented this?" a tiny female voice said as a teenage girl dressed in black, with dark brown hair in two long braids, stepped out from behind a tree. Her face was still damp, her cheeks flushed, her eyes swollen and red from crying during the service. Ashley Russo. *"It's your fault my brother's dead?"*

The men make the club. *He'd heard that a thousand times. The president guided the MC, but his real power resided in whom he did and didn't allow into the club. One devil could be like a cancer, spreading, eating away at what was healthy, slowly killing what was once good.*

The Iron Warriors always had a dark side, but didn't abide rape and didn't gun down teens. Quill and a few of the others had been grooming Rip to lead. Someone young, strong, principled, with fresh ideas, who would protect the moral constructs of the bylaws. But he'd never wanted the job, which they'd said made him perfect for it. And so, he'd run from the responsibility to lead.

Rip was an eerily excellent judge of character, the closest thing he had to a superpower, and never would've let someone like Todd Burk join if he had been president. The Iron Warriors were supposed to defend the town. Not decimate it.

As he stared at the girl, seeing the devastation in her eyes, the sorrow on her face, her pain called to him, and with his heart aching for her, he gave the only answer that he could. "Yes."

Her anguish flipped to anger. She stormed up to him and slapped him hard, her small palm making his cheek sting. "Then you should've been here!" She curled her hands into fists and beat his chest. "You should've stopped him!" Her screams were bloodcurdling, the sound resonating in his soul as she shouted and sobbed.

Quill moved to grab her, but Rip held out an arm, stopping him.

This innocent young woman was grieving and in anguish. She couldn't do this to Burk, but she could do it to Rip. And he let her.

Until her parents raced over, horrified. It took them both to haul the slip of a girl off him.

"I'm going to kill him!" she cried. "I'm going to kill Todd Burk!"

"Stay away from Burk," Rip said, his voice low and firm. "I'll take care of him."

"She didn't mean it," Mr. Russo said, his voice shaky with fear.

"I meant it!" the young woman spit out. "I'll kill!"

"Please don't let that animal hurt her." Mrs. Russo's face was awash in agony and alarm. "He's already taken our son. Don't let him take our daughter, too."

"I'll protect her." Rip took a tentative step toward them but stopped when the mother cringed and the father held up a hand in warning. "No Iron Warrior will hurt her. I swear it."

The girl's parents wrapped their arms around her and hurried away.

"How are you going to keep that promise?" Quill asked. Rip turned to him. "I haven't signed my reenlistment contract yet." Something kept telling him to wait. To hold off as long as possible. Most Marines had to sign twelve months before their service date ended. Raiders could wait up to six months, a special exception that no one talked about, because of the stressors of the job. "Rustle up support for me in a vote as president. I've got a ton of leave saved up. I'll be back as soon as I can. Until then, I want the girl to be watched and protected. Make sure she stays away from Todd and vice versa. Anyone who messes with her, even looks at her wrong, they'll have to deal with me."

RIP CAUGHT SIGHT of Ashley. She was kneeling at her brother's grave, brushing leaves off the headstone. As he approached her, he braced himself for yet another ambush.

He eased up alongside her. "I know why you asked me to come here. Effective, I'll give you that." Being back at Angelo's grave was a poignant kick to the gut. "But my answer will still be the same. I need you to trust that I have a plan to take care of Burk." He'd told her he would handle it and for too long he hadn't. But this time would be different.

Standing up, she gave him his gun.

His gaze flew to the bandage on her forehead. "What happened to you?" he asked, erasing the distance between them. "Are you all right?" He reached for her face, and she jerked away.

"Car accident. This is nothing," she said, gesturing to her head.

It took every drop of self-restraint not to reach for her again and double-check she was okay. She stood there, staring him down with those expressive eyes, and he suspected she'd only shoo him away once more if he tried.

To give himself something to do with his hands, he tucked the gun into his ankle holster. "How did you get into an accident?" She was proficient at everything. Always so serious and scrupulous. An excellent defensive driver.

"That's not what I want to discuss," she said. "You think you know why I asked you to come here, but you're wrong."

Silence fell between them. Not in a hurry to fill it, he waited for her spiel, steeling himself not to let whatever she had to say weaken his resolve.

Her face was stiff, her body tense, her obvious dislike of him palpable, which for some reason made him want to draw closer when he needed to stay as far away from her as possible.

"Once I leave the cemetery," she said, "I'm heading up to Bitterroot Gulch. Someone in the Sons of Chaos hooked Todd Burk up to his supplier. I'm going to find who and I'm going to cut off his drug operation at the source."

As she spoke it was like an invisible hand had reached into his chest and grabbed hold of his heart and squeezed. "You make it sound so simple."

"There's a difference between simple and easy. Regardless, it has to be done."

"The Sons are no joke." He knew those guys and was well acquainted with their president, Ben Stryker. Rip had a couple of things in common with the man. They were both prior military and tough as nails, but that was where the similarities ended. That gang wasn't to be trifled with. "You're playing with fire and you're going to get burned. If they find out you're a cop, they won't hesitate to do unspeakable things to you and then kill you."

She hiked her chin up at him, her expression so stubborn and her face so beautiful it hurt to look at her. "I guess I better not let them find out."

Scrappy as ever.

"You can't just walk in there and pretend with that group. Have you even been trained for undercover work?" He seriously doubted it. She might be able to dress the part, but that was all. If by some miracle they didn't see beneath the facade she tried to put on, then they'd be entirely focused on her as a woman. Waves of dark brown hair and fiercely vibrant whiskey-colored eyes in a striking face that was a real gut check. Not to mention her body. Guaranteed to destroy a man. Heat prickled the back of his neck thinking about the way they'd look at her. They'd treat her like a biker groupie, though they had cruder terms, whose sole purpose was to slake the appetite of the guys. None of the above options was acceptable. "The Sons are a pack of animals. Those guys are a brutal, cutthroat bunch."

"That's why I need you. But since you refuse to help me, I'll have to do it alone."

Alone? "Sheriff Clark can't send you in there with no backup," he said, searching her face, and then saw the unthinkable.

She averted her gaze, a slight tilt of her head, as though hiding something, but also folded her arms, a defensive posture. He not only watched out for her, but he'd also studied her, knew her tells.

"He's not sending you, is he?"

"I'm on a task force with the DEA," she said, still not looking at him.

A chill slithered down his spine. "They most certainly wouldn't send you in alone."

"They go undercover alone all the time."

"It's what they're trained for. Not you."

"I can pull it off." But uncertainty flashed in her eyes.

"You're a lousy liar, Ash. You wouldn't even be able to

bluff your way through a hand of poker with them. You can't seriously be thinking about trying to infiltrate the Sons of Chaos to get information. What are you playing at?"

"This isn't a game. And I'm done thinking about it. I'm doing it. Today."

"You're jumping into this too fast." She'd only first approached him about this yesterday.

"It has to be tonight," she said. "I can't afford to wait any longer."

"Why not?"

Averting her gaze again, she touched the bandage on her forehead. Then she caught herself and dropped her hand.

"How did you get into an accident?" he demanded.

"Work," she said, flatly, the one-word response not telling him a thing. "There's a window of opportunity with the Sons of Chaos. A Saturday night is my best chance. I'm going to do this."

Why was she rushing? "Hold off one week, and I'll give it serious consideration," he said, testing her. Considering and doing were not necessarily the same. A lot could happen in seven days to change her mind.

Her eyebrows drew together in contemplation that lasted a blink. "I can't wait that long. It has to be now."

"How about I call Sheriff Clark and see what he has to say about your plan?" he asked, not really thinking it through. He wouldn't jeopardize her job, but he also couldn't let her flirt with disaster.

Ashley whipped out her cell phone, pried off the back cover, and popped the battery out. "Go ahead." She shrugged. "The sheriff knows I've gone dark. And by the time you get him to believe you, president of the Iron Warriors, over me, his trusted deputy, which will take a while, it'll be too late."

Frustration burned at the back of his throat. What was she doing? "This is madness. I could call the Sons, tell them you're coming." Not that he had a number to simply dial, but if he dug, he might be able to get one.

"As you pointed out, they'll kill a cop. That's not the kind of call you'd make."

True. He'd never endanger her that way. "No matter how this shakes out, your job will be on the line if you try to go through with this."

Another shrug from her. "The only reason I ever put on the badge in the first place was to get Todd Burk. If I accomplish the goal, all will be forgiven. If I fail, the prospect of getting fired won't matter because my parents will have to bury me here——" she pointed to the empty plot beside her brother's "——next to Angelo."

She was willing to risk her badge and her life. "You would do that to your mother and father? They shouldn't have to bury another child."

Her eyes hardened. She was gearing up to be even more defiant, and in that moment, she reminded him of the innocent, reckless, daring-to-be-fearless girl who had slapped and punched him in this very cemetery. A different kind of man, a different kind of biker, would've made her pay for it. Might have even hit her back. But that wasn't him. All he had wanted back then was to take away her pain and keep her safe. The same as he did now.

"You would be the one doing it to them," she countered.

Too headstrong for her own good.

"You're asking me to break a vow," he said. "I'd give my life for you but that I won't do. Not even for you." If only she knew how much he'd already done and was willing to do on her behalf.

"I'm not asking you to break one. I'm asking you to keep

two. You swore," she said, jabbing his chest with her finger, "justice for Angelo and to protect me. I'm asking you to keep both vows now. Or have you been stringing me along, simply placating me all this time?" Her words sucked the air right out of his lungs. "You can stay here and continue to do nothing besides offer platitudes and make empty promises. Or you can come with me. Help me. Not because I'm a deputy. Because I'm a sister seeking justice for her brother. A woman desperate to make her town safe again. Protect me, like you swore you'd do."

"I've been protecting you since you were seventeen." It hadn't been easy, especially once she became a law enforcement officer. The sacrifices he'd made, the scrutiny he'd been under. And now, no longer having the full might and force of his club behind him, with his chapter divided, could he still keep her safe while Todd remained unchecked? "Let me go instead of you. Stay here, out of unnecessary danger."

Her lips firmed. "Danger is everywhere. Closing in every day."

"For me, yeah. But you can stay away from it rather than throwing yourself headlong into it."

"For you *and* me," she said, and he wondered what she meant. "For the whole town. There's no hiding from it." She took a deep, shaky breath and let it out. "You think it's perfectly fine for you to go out and risk your life while there are different rules when it comes to me? I don't think so. This is my fight. I'm not sitting on the sidelines. Todd Burk has to pay for everything he's done. And I aim to be the person collecting."

The need for justice had driven her to become a cop, and he suspected it haunted her like a ghost, overshadowing every decision she made.

"Not just for my brother," she added, "but for everyone

Burk has hurt or poisoned or killed. Get me through this with the Sons of Chaos and help me track down the supplier and, regardless of the outcome, any debt to me will be paid."

She was doing her best to box him in.

And he hated it.

She was a complication that he didn't need or want.

"Don't do this, Ash."

She eased forward, coming so close the tips of their boots touched, their bodies brushing. To a passerby, they probably looked like lovers, and that thought sent an ache through him.

Ashley tipped her head back, looking up at him. "Is there anything between us, besides your sense of responsibility?" She moistened her pink lips, and his gaze fell to her mouth and snagged there a moment. "Anything more?"

For him, plenty more.

Plenty that ran far deeper than he wanted her to know because she was off-limits. Every time his efforts at friendship with her had been met with skepticism or cool curiosity, a part of him was grateful he had failed to get closer. Because deep down when he paid her visits at her house, he no longer wanted to be confined to the kitchen and was ready to be invited into her bedroom. She stirred up his protective instincts as well as his desire. A powerful combination he was finding hard to resist.

But to tell her as much would give her ammunition to use against him and only a fool would do such a thing. "Anything more, like what?"

Stepping back, she lowered her head. "Never mind." She swallowed hard, her throat muscles jumping with the movement, and shoved her hair behind an ear. "I'm going with or without you. I'll follow this lead and put an end to Burk's drug trade, hitting him where it hurts, even if it's the last thing I ever do. The choice is yours, Rip. Whatever you decide, remember that you'll have to live with it." She marched off without giving him a chance to utter a response.

An icy breeze sliced through his jacket. He didn't mind the cold. In fact, he embraced the frosty wind. It helped cool off his temper so he could think straight. He had a lot to process.

Everything about this predicament grated. Ash going undercover. Rushing in. Unprepared. Unauthorized. With the Sons of Chaos. All alone.

His rule-abiding deputy was suddenly playing fast and loose with every rule in the book. And so help him, she was going to get herself killed.

Chapter Six

A tricky thing—not showing a hint of fear around those who could smell it, like sharks catching the scent of blood in the water. Even more challenging when it was the one emotion Ashley felt, second only to her resolve.

Being afraid did have the upside of keeping her mind sharp.

She sat sipping cola at the bar in Happy Jack's Roadhouse, doing her best to appear relaxed. In the mirror behind the shelves lined with alcohol, she looked over the twenty or so heavily muscled, tattooed bikers wearing leather vests with varying amounts of patches adorning them. Some wore hoodies or long-sleeved shirts under their cuts while a couple wore nothing at all despite the frigid temperature outside.

The Sons of Chaos owned the roadhouse—a seedy dive on the main floor with their private clubhouse upstairs—as well as the rinky-dink motel next door where she'd parked her truck in case she needed to make an inconspicuous getaway. The outlaw biker group used both businesses to launder money.

Two nights a week were open to the public. Thursdays were only for ladies looking to have the thrill of being with a biker. On Saturdays anyone, except for cops, was welcomed, making it the one night of the week she'd risk strolling in as long as she didn't have her badge. But she had gambled that she would also have Rip at her side and lost.

A flashing neon sign in front proclaiming Crime Happens Here had given her pause, but she'd still sauntered past the lined-up assortment of customized Harley Davidsons and hot rods into the roadhouse.

Inside, the place was crawling with bikers, their women, prospects. She'd spotted their president, a man they called Stryker, along with the vice president, but they were constantly surrounded by others. A couple dozen ordinary Joes and Janes were in the mix, playing pool, throwing darts, grabbing a bite to eat, dancing. Most of the women really should have been wearing more clothing than they had on. Attire ranged from sexy casual to downright skimpy. One even dared to prance around in cutoff shorts and cowboy boots. No way she was riding the back of a bike dressed like that in November.

To Ashley's surprise, more than a handful of women sported denim cuts that, on the back, read *Property Of* along with a man's name at the bottom.

The Iron Warriors had never considered any of the women they associated with or loved as property. And they had a policy of accepting any male prospect they deemed worthy regardless of skin color. A stark distinction from the Sons as she looked around, but they didn't seem to mind diversity among their groupies.

Feeling silly in her getup, Ashley kneaded the muscles in the back of her neck. Skinny jeans so tight she could barely breathe. Thigh-high boots. Backless, cropped, halter top. She was aiming to blend in and had overshot beyond her comfort level, going a tad too revealing. The problem was she had never had the wild, party phase. Her life since her brother's murder had all been about being prim and proper and then being a deputy. No parties. Hardly dating since guys seemed to lose interest after one dinner. She didn't really do makeup. And never did *this*—go to a bar and flirt with men to get information.

She wished she'd kept on her leather jacket after a big, brawny, hairy brute claimed the stool beside her and wouldn't stop trying to chat her up.

"Hotties don't pay for drinks." He leaned closer, his breath smelling of liquor and garlic. "Her next one is on us," he said to the bartender, who nodded.

"Thanks." She caught herself cringing ever so slightly in the mirror and forced herself to straighten and smile. "But I'm good."

He rested his massive hands flat on the bar top. Tattoos were inked on his blunt knuckles. From her vantage point, it took her several seconds to decipher what the upside-down letters spelled.

Lost. Soul.

Instead of *O*'s there were skulls.

She imagined how much damage those hands could do. Fists through walls and windows. Pounding flesh and cracking bone. The answer was a *lot* of damage. Not feasible taking him one-on-one, in the event things went awry. In spite of his relentless interest, this Neanderthal wasn't the right one to probe for information.

"Not much of a talker, are you?" he asked.

"Only when I have something to say."

He grinned, making the corded muscle of his inked neck flex. "I like the quiet ones." He put a meaty hand on her thigh. "Less talk. More action," he said, making her stomach twist.

The biker stroked her leg. His touch was worse than cobwebs across her face in a dark basement. She resisted the overwhelming urge to jerk away.

Picking up her drink, she spun 180 degrees on the stool, removing his hand discreetly. She looked around, trying to give him the message to move on. Her gaze kept darting to the door. Part of her clung to the unlikely possibility that Rip would walk into the roadhouse any second. She'd been in Bitterroot Gulch for over an hour. It took time to surveil the place, change into this ridiculous outfit and muster the courage to go inside.

Rip would've been there by now if he was coming.

She'd wanted to trust that his vow to protect her had been real. Not some hollow line. That when faced with the choice between keeping the MC's code and keeping his vow to her, he'd pick her in the end. To meet his responsibility to get rid of Burk head-on, so she no longer had a reason to hold any grudge against him.

A motorcycle growled up outside. A sliver of hope percolated in her chest. Seconds later, the door swung open.

Another biker waltzed in with his arm slung over the shoulder of a redhead.

Her heart dropped. It wasn't Rip.

I'd give my life for you.

That was what he'd told her, but Rip was a liar.

He always seemed to be there when she needed him. Flat tire on a dark road. He'd happened to ride by and changed it. As she was dropping off groceries at the soup kitchen, hands full, he'd appeared out of nowhere before a downpour started. Held an umbrella over her head and helped her carry the bags inside. The night she'd had too much to drink in a bar that never should've served her since she was underage, he'd snatched the car keys from her hand and taken her home. She'd come to expect Rip to be there, especially at a time like now.

If she was being honest with herself, it went much deeper. She wanted to know he truly cared about her for some silly reason. Maybe because he'd spent so many years striking up casual chats that felt intensely intimate and got her to admit personal things, swinging by her house at night to make sure she was doing okay, giving her piercing looks that reached into her soul and heated her belly, trying to convince her he did care until she almost believed him.

She didn't want to simply be an obligation. She wanted to be a choice. For him to choose her. Not that any of it made sense.

Worse, she was such a fool for thinking the twisted bond they had ever meant anything.

"I'm Jimmy." The big scary biker turned around on his stool and rubbed the side of his leg against hers. "What's your name, sweetness?"

Why couldn't he take a hint? She crossed her legs, eradicating the contact. "Would you believe me if I said Sugar?"

"No, but I'm happy to call you whatever you want."

If this situation had the potential to turn into a brushfire, then this guy was gasoline.

Her plan had been to chat up one of the ladies affiliated with the club, get a feel for which Son to approach. But her stalker had been all over her the second she walked in.

Maybe if she didn't make any more eye contact with him, he would buzz off.

"Yo, Jimmy." A Son wearing a red bandanna tied around his head strutted up along the other side of her. "Can't you see she's not interested? Time to give someone else a crack at her."

Jimmy swore as he made a vulgar hand gesture.

The other guy laughed, not intimidated. "Leave her alone, man. I heard your old lady is on the way over. If she sees you talking to her, she'll cut this chick. And I kind of like her face the way it is."

"Me, too," Ashley said, shifting in her seat toward Red Bandanna. "Would love to keep it unblemished."

Swearing again, Jimmy got up and skulked off.

"Thanks for saving me from his old lady's switchblade," she said.

"She's not really coming. When he finds out, he'll be back. So you've got until then to sit on my lap and show me some gratitude," he said, and a sour taste coated her tongue. He called over to the bartender. "Give me a Coke like the lady."

Red Bandanna had been watching and listening. She wasn't sure if she should be flattered or concerned.

"No shots or a beer for you?" she asked, putting on a pleasant smile.

"Been clean for two years."

She swallowed a groan at having first drawn a scary creep and now the only sober guy in the place. Would he even have the information she needed?

"Congratulations." She set her glass down on the bar. "Excuse me, I need to use the bathroom."

What she really needed was to regroup.

She hopped off the stool, grabbing her purse and leaving her jacket. The restrooms were situated partway down a short, narrow hall. At the end of the dimly lit corridor, she spotted the neon red Exit sign. For a moment, she considered using it. Just pushing through the door and getting out of that place. But she'd come here to achieve an objective. Running from the Sons of Chaos and Bitterroot Gulch would only lead her home, where Todd was waiting. She had to stay and finish what she had set out to do.

Besides, on taking a closer look at the door, she saw a sign that read Emergencies Only, Alarm Will Ring.

Ashley shoved into the bathroom. Going to the sink, she opened her purse. Inside it, she flicked off the safety on her personal firearm. A Beretta, and beside it was another gift from Rip. A stun gun. She had the unsettling sense she might have to use one or both before the night was over.

Staring at her reflection in the mirror, she washed her hands. The rough bangs she'd cut herself to hide the gash on her forehead didn't look too bad. She pulled red lipstick from her purse and reapplied. That and some mascara was the extent of her makeup, and fortunately it had been enough to attract two bikers.

Only the wrong two.

She had to make the most of Red Bandanna. He might not know about the drug supplier, but he could find out for her. She just had to be more persuasive with him than she had been with Rip.

Ashley finished drying her hands and tossed the paper towels in the trash bin. She opened the door, leaving the bathroom, and ran into a wall of muscle and the stench of alcohol. "Jimmy."

Before he muttered anything, she rushed past him into the hall, making a beeline for the main area. The last thing she needed was for him to force her back into the restroom, where he'd have her cornered and she'd have to use her gun. The equivalent of pouring gasoline on the brushfire. All the Sons of Chaos would come running.

Her new objective was to get out of that hallway un-scathed.

"Hey." In a few strides, Jimmy was in front of her with

a hand planted on the wall, blocking her from taking another step. "My old lady isn't coming. We're free to have some fun."

She suspected they had very different definitions of *fun*. "I don't want any trouble. Just another drink at the bar."

Ducking under his arm, she scrambled to escape out of the narrow, dim corridor but didn't get far.

He wrapped his arms, thick as tree trunks, around her waist, hauled her to him and swung her around, pushing her back against the wall. "Let's go take a ride on my bike. What do you say?"

Her heart thundered in her ears and her body turned to lead. "Not interested."

"First time I ever met a *mama* who wasn't."

She always found the word odd used in such context, but uglier terms existed. "Maybe that's because I'm not a groupie."

He grabbed her bare arms, pinning her to the wall, and leaned closer. "Then why are you here, Sugar?"

The hairs on Ashley's neck pricked as fear washed over her. She'd have to roll the dice with Jimmy instead of Red Bandanna. "Drugs."

"Selling?" He cocked his head to the side. "Or buying?"

She raised her chin. "Buying."

"Why didn't you say so? I can hook you up." He pulled out a little baggie with a variety of pills, keeping a strong grip on her arm. "Name your pleasure."

"I'm looking for more than you can supply. A lot more. I heard LA is the one to talk to. Can you introduce me to him?"

"Him, huh?" Jimmy's eyebrows knitted together as he narrowed his eyes. "How about you pop a pill first to prove you're not a cop?"

She didn't let any fear show even though the emotion nearly suffocated her.

"How about you take your hand off her and back away!" a deep, familiar voice said, making her pulse spike.

A voice that haunted her dreams. Rough and husky. Dangerous as a blade.

Rip.

Ferocious energy pumped off him as he stormed down the hall toward them. His eyes blazed with fury.

He came.

Her heart did a somersault in her chest, relief surging in her veins. She'd never been happier to set eyes on him.

"Saw her first," Jimmy said. "You'll have to wait until I'm finished."

Four bikers hurried down the hall behind Rip. More Sons of Chaos.

Can't be good.

"I say you're done. Right now. You've got two choices." Rip stepped up to him until they were toe to toe. He was dressed all in black, only his patches adding pops of color. "Remove your hand or I break it."

Jimmy's gaze raked over Rip's cut under his sheepskin jacket. "I don't care if you're a Prez or not. This is the Sons' house."

"And this is my old lady," Rip ground out with a fierce intensity that sent a shiver through her.

Jimmy hesitated, eyes flaring wide, like the words had stunned him as much as they had her.

She understood enough about biker culture to know that it meant she was off-limits to everyone else, regardless of club association.

Jimmy dropped his hand as if it had been burned and

then raised both palms. "She didn't say anything about having an old man."

Rip advanced on him, vibrating with rage, fists at his sides. Jimmy staggered backward.

One of the Sons clasped Rip on the shoulder. "Ease up, Rip, he didn't know," Stryker said. "Misplaced anger. Your old lady should've told us."

"Yeah, you're right." Rip whirled and shot her a look that could cut through steel. Those intense blue-gray eyes of his stayed locked onto her as he closed the distance between them in two quick, threatening strides, causing her stomach to go into freefall.

Her pulse beat wildly as she stood rooted to the spot, strangely transfixed.

He pointed a finger in her face, something he'd never done before. "Next time you make it clear you're mine." The rough and rumbly words made her skin tingle. "Better yet, listen to me and when I tell you *not* to do something…" He let his voice trail off, his gaze boring into her, and the longer the silence stretched on, the more her nerves tightened until she trembled. "Don't do it," he said, in a deep, throaty growl.

She opened her mouth to give him some argument, but her mind blanked. "Sorry, baby." The words slipped out in a whisper.

He brought his hands up, cupping her cheeks, tilted her face toward his, and claimed her lips with his own.

Rip was kissing her. And it was hot and unyielding and possessive. Not controlled and characteristic of his rigid discipline. Or anything like she imagined, and she had thought about it whenever she drew too close to him.

But this was different. He was kissing her like he was starving. Consuming her. Needed her more than his next breath.

His tongue plunged deeper, sliding against hers. All Ashley could do was surrender to the spark of heat that flashed into a blaze inside her. She threw her arms around his neck, coming up on the balls of her feet to better meet him, giving in to the passion and promise in the kiss that had her forgetting about their audience.

His hands moved to her hips, and he lifted her up from the floor into his arms. She wrapped her legs around him, confused how all the fury that had been blasting off him a second ago had erupted into this.

Him pressed against her, his fingers fisting in her hair, his strong arm looped around her, his hot mouth on hers, and desire she'd never known surged through her.

Then he ended the kiss as abruptly as he had started it. They were left gasping for air, chests heaving. She opened her eyes, meeting the most intense, heated stare in her life, and her breath caught.

"Why was she here without you?" Stryker asked.

A muscle flexed along Rip's jaw. "Give us a minute." He didn't take his gaze from her. "I need a word with my woman in private."

The sexual current running between her and Rip had her body humming with electricity.

"Yeah, all right." Stryker waved the Sons out of the hall, and they left.

Rip set her feet down on the floor and pressed his hands to the wall on either side of her face and brought his mouth to her ear. "Sorry about the little show we had to put on. We needed them to believe it."

The declaration quickly sobered her. Of course, he was just acting.

The man was good. A little too good. But they both did what they had to. No big deal. Meant nothing.

So, why did her heart sink?

"You all right?" he whispered, his breath warm on her skin. "Did that guy hurt you?"

"No. I'm fine. But I didn't think you'd come."

"I'll always come if you need me, Ash." His voice was a sexy, rough rasp. He made her name sound sensual. As if it were a caress.

Rip stroked her cheek, a gentle brush of his knuckles across her skin, a reverence that erased her doubts about what he valued more—his commitment to the code or to her.

He meant his vow to protect her. Ida and Welliver had told her Rip had saved lives in the Marines, earning one of the highest military decorations. The hero. Rip had that complex in his soul. She only wished she'd realized sooner.

"I can't bear the thought of you getting hurt in this," he said. "So, my options were either kidnap you to keep you from going. Or help you so you didn't get yourself killed."

"You understand my job is dangerous." She kept her voice low.

"This is different. You're in my world." He sighed. "Listen, I know how much you hate me, but for us to get through this, we've got to pretend to be a hot and heavy couple." He pulled back and looked down into her face. "Can you do that?"

Rip thought she hated him?

Ashley met his gaze. "I'm pretty good at bluffing," she said with bravado she didn't feel. "I'll give them an Oscar-worthy performance."

"I'm going to have to touch you. If you recoil, can't sell it—"

"Answer one question. Did it feel real, the way I kissed you back?"

Chapter Seven

As real as the air he breathed.

She'd kissed him back with a wild hunger that set his blood on fire.

"Yeah, it did," Rip said, realizing it was all illusion. He could only imagine what a struggle that must have been for her while he'd been in pure heaven. Not taking into account the Sons of Chaos that had been standing around watching.

He'd been interested in women and thought he had a crush on Ashley. But holding her and kissing her, he'd come to the revelation that he *wanted* her.

Wanted her in a way that he shouldn't, in a way that he could never have.

His desire was supposed to stay buried, a burning ball of yearning and guilt and anger, deep in his core. Never allowed to surface, to be dealt with, but it stared him in the face now.

The low-cut, practically backless powder blue top she wore hugged her ample cleavage. The midriff exposed an enticing flat stomach but had given him the pleasure of feeling her silky soft skin. High-heeled boots accentuated the length and curves of her legs. He'd always had the impression of her being tall, though it was merely the way she carried herself. Not that she was short, but in the skimpy top and heels, with no gun on her hip, she seemed much less formidable than usual.

Vulnerable. That was the word.

She looked vulnerable. And the most beautiful thing he'd ever seen.

It had been an uncomfortable realization when he saw that Son towering over her, with his hands on her. Made his blood boil. Granted, Rip had been relieved that she wasn't tied up somewhere, bound and gagged, but still.

Every instinct that flared had been primal. Visceral. The need to protect her a fist in his throat.

But he had to find a balance between his concern for her, his genuine affection, his frightening hunger for her and the need to keep his emotions in check.

Rip didn't normally have an issue maintaining a handle on his temper. But he had come close to punching that Son in the face and knocking out his teeth. He couldn't afford to make a mistake like that. Not when it could cost either of their lives.

"But I caught you by surprise," he added. "Now you're going to be anticipating it. I don't want to creep you out."

"Jimmy creeps me out. Not you."

Now he knew the jerk's name. "That's small comfort."

"To set the record straight, I don't hate you, Rip. Tried to, but never succeeded. I've just been angry. Partly at you. Mostly at Burk. At the Iron Warriors. At the lack of justice. I hated myself more for not being able to put Burk behind bars myself than I ever hated you."

He caressed her face. "I can understand that, and I know pretending to be with me isn't helping. I wish there was another way, but there isn't now."

"Kissing you wasn't so bad." She bit her bottom lip and

he wanted to claim her mouth again. "You're really rather good at it."

Pride swelled in his chest. It had been a while since he had locked lips with anyone, but he'd never kissed a woman the way he'd just kissed her. Full of relief and hunger and an urgent need that overwhelmed him.

Ash put her palms on his arms and ran them up to his shoulders, bringing her body closer until her breasts pressed against his chest. "I won't have a problem acting like you're mine or selling it to them." Rising on her toes, she feathered a kiss on his lips, and he didn't want to notice how right or good she felt in his arms, nestled against his body. "Think they're buying it?" She gestured with a tilt of her head.

He glimpsed down the hall. Sure enough, they had a captive audience.

"So far, so good. Did you give them your name?" he asked, not sure what alias she might've used.

"Sugar."

He glared at her, and she shrugged. "What if they had demanded a name? Taken your wallet to check your ID?"

"Someone in the DEA got me an ID. Ashley Roberts."

Sighing, he gave a nod of approval that she'd planned for that. He knew she'd worked on a DEA task force, which required her to bounce between Cheyenne and Fort Collins, but had been unaware about the need for a fake ID.

"We need to get out there," he said. "Once again, sorry for how we'll have to play it. For the way I'll have to touch you. And for the things I might have to say." The Sons treated their women like property and would only respect him if he did the same. He'd have to swallow his disgust and get into the role.

"It has to be done." She cleared her throat. "This is important. When we get out there, should I apologize?"

"To them? Hell, no. But saying it to me in front of them was the right thing. Good call." He took her hand, and they started down the hall. "Follow my lead."

"Whatever you say, *baby*."

The endearment warmed his chest, despite being a part of the act.

Holding Ash's hand, Rip strode over to Stryker, who waited, seated at a table with his vice president and two other Sons. There was only one empty chair.

"She can wait over there with the other women." Stryker gestured across the room to the pool table where the scantily clad biker chicks had gathered.

Rip dropped into the chair and tugged Ash down onto his lap. "She stays where I can touch her." Just because the Sons wouldn't touch his *old lady* didn't mean the scowling women across the room wouldn't. Ashley could hold her own, but if they could avoid a brawl of any sort that would be best. "No worries. She knows when to be seen and not heard."

Leaning against him, she draped her legs across his lap and slid an arm over his shoulder.

Stryker cracked his knuckles. "If she were mine, I would've punished her in the hall instead of kissing her."

One of the dark things about the MC culture he always had difficulty with was how women were regarded as second-class citizens. The club was a means to an end for Rip, to safeguard Ash and deal with Burk, but with the Iron Warriors he didn't tolerate abuse in his presence. The one time Todd had tried to lay a hand on his girlfriend in the clubhouse, he'd put a stop to it and threatened to break his hand next time. *Property Of* cuts had never been acceptable in his club and he'd added to the bylaws that they never would. Some MCs encouraged cheating. He believed in loyalty. Not only among the men but also for the women who supported them.

"Well, she's not yours." Rip put a hand on her thigh and curled an arm around her waist, tucking her closer. "And I don't like to damage what's mine." If he ever had the honor of being anything more to Ash than her protector, he'd cherish her every single day. "Can I talk to you without your boys?"

"Afraid not." Stryker shook his head. "Jimmy told us she's here looking for drugs. Didn't know you had a junkie on your hands. But it makes this club business."

Interesting. Rip hadn't anticipated that, and he'd considered a great many things before waltzing inside Happy Jack's.

It must have caught Ashley by surprise, too, based on the way she shifted in his lap, rubbing her soft curves against him, distracting him with her heat and sultry feminine scent.

A real relationship with her was out of the question, so he did his best to suppress his body's reaction. And failed.

He hoped she couldn't feel the way she aroused him, but there was no hiding it from her. What was wrong with him? How could the possibility of imminent bodily harm coupled with the friction from Ash against him cause such an intense physical reaction?

Must be the punch of adrenaline and the flare of hormones.

Rip reeled his thoughts in line despite the intimate way she stroked the back of his head with her fingers and pressed her lips to the side of his neck. "How is it club business?"

"Todd always griped about how you wouldn't let him deal." Stryker tipped his beer bottle up to this mouth. "You could go to him for what you need if it was just to get her high, but instead you allowed the matter to tear the Iron Warriors in two. Jimmy said she wants a supplier."

"*I* want a supplier," Rip clarified through clenched teeth. "Todd's. She was being overly eager, trying to find out for me." He rubbed his hand up and down her leg, stroking her thigh. "How does that make it a concern for the Sons?"

"We're getting to that." Stryker took another swig of beer. "Why the sudden interest in drugs? It's not your thing."

"But competition is. Todd wants to come for me and what's mine, so I'm coming for what's his."

With a sigh, Stryker set the bottle down. "Therein lies the problem. To connect you with his supplier is asking the Sons to take a side in your little civil war. Requires a vote, man."

His vice president leaned forward, resting his forearms on the table. "We could call a meeting upstairs, bring the matter to the table, but it'd be a waste of time. You won't have the numbers."

The Hellhounds had more support than the Iron Warriors. So much more in fact they were confident Rip didn't stand a chance of winning a vote.

He wanted to put a fist through the wall. "I need this," Rip said, considering a last-ditch play. Focusing on business and lining the pockets of the Sons might be enough to sway things. "I'll kick back five percent of my profits as thanks for making the connect."

"It still won't pass a vote," the VP said.

Since there never would be any profits, he could go up a bit, but if he ventured too high it would raise a red flag. "Okay, let's say ten percent."

Stryker stood, scraping his chair back across the wood floor. "We can't help you."

Ashley glanced at Rip, her eyes going wide in concern. But this discussion was finished.

Rip set her feet on the floor, shuffling her up as he stood. He took her hand in his and squeezed, silently telling her to act cool about the setback.

Stryker walked around the table. "Sorry, man." He put a palm on Rip's shoulder and steered him toward the door. "If you'd come sooner, right after your club fell to pieces, I could've done more."

Sooner? How could a month have made a difference? Stryker was trying to tell him something, but what?

On the way out, Ashley grabbed her leather jacket from the back of a stool. If Rip hadn't been in the middle of Happy Jack's filled with Sons of Chaos, he would've helped her put it on. But chivalry was dead in that place.

Opening the front door, the Sons' president glanced over his shoulder and Rip did likewise. No one else was close by. As Rip passed him, crossing the threshold, Stryker said in a voice so low it was barely audible, "HT for ten."

Doubting Ashley had even heard the man, Rip gave one curt nod. Holding her hand, he went down the steps, practically pulling her along.

"We have to go back," she said in a harsh whisper.

The woman was going to be the death of him.

"Nope. Not happening." He hurried down past the bank of bikes to his. The Harley was in Ida's garage. Instead, he'd taken his Triumph Rocket. The motorcycle was sleek and powerful with ridiculous torque that hit the road like a berserker.

"We gave up too easily. We have to go back and try again."

Sometimes you need to know when to quit. "I know how badly you want this."

"Need this. It's the only way."

"We have to hold tight for ten like Stryker asked."

"When did he ask and what for?"

"Do you trust me?"

Ash didn't hesitate, she simply nodded.

He lifted her, seating her on his bike. "We need a reason to sit out here for a few minutes. Since neither of us smoke, we've got to keep up the ruse a little longer." Cupping her cheeks, he leaned in and kissed her.

The rush hit him again like water from a fire hose quenching the thirst of a man who'd been walking in the desert. Just as potent and intoxicating as before. Maybe even more so because when she wrapped her legs around his waist, holding him tighter, her fingers diving in his hair, rocking her pelvis against him, he groaned in her mouth.

Sure, they needed a plausible justification to hang around in the cold, but he would use any excuse for another make-out session, to hold her and treat her like she was really his. A taboo fantasy came to life. He'd always considered her off-limits, even after she grew into a woman and he'd seen her swimming that day, water glistening on her skin, shining bright as the sun, making everything inside him clench tight with need.

The world around him faded away, except for her and the possibilities he shouldn't be thinking about popping into his head. Of what he wanted with her if only he was someone else. Not some biker in an MC, fighting for his life. Not someone she was angry with and blamed for the delay in justice for her brother. Not someone a cop would be ashamed to be with. Not someone thirteen years older with his best years behind him.

If only.

He used those precious minutes. To imagine. To indulge in the feel of her lips and the warmth of her body pressed to his and the taste of her. To memorize the new carnal knowledge that would torture him later.

At the sound of approaching footsteps, a set of two, he pulled himself back, but stayed planted between her thighs. She blinked up at him, trembling, mouth slightly agape, dark eyes wide, uncertain.

Rip glanced over his shoulder. Stryker and his old lady were coming.

He looked back at Ash and ached to kiss her once more. Realizing this was probably his last chance, he took it. He dipped his head, catching her bottom lip between his teeth in a playful nibble, and kissed her again. Quick and hard. Then he eased away, helping her off the bike, and tugged her beside him. With his heart throbbing painfully from every twisted emotion those kisses had roused, he forced himself to focus on the business at hand.

"I'd tell you to grab a room at the motel, but it's wiser if you didn't stay the night," Stryker said. "You need to get your old lady a *Property Of* vest. Would've saved everyone some grief. Here's some patches."

The other woman offered Ash an envelope.

A fresh wave of anger rolled over Rip as he shook his head. "Not my style."

"Yeah, man, I'm aware," Stryker said. "You're too nice when you've got to be merciless. It's the reason you're losing the war at home. Trust me, you want it."

There was something more to the envelope. Rip nodded and Ash took it.

"Go grab us a room." Stryker smacked his woman's butt, and she hurried off toward the hotel, tottering on her high heels.

"What happened last month?" Rip asked, cutting to it.

"As soon as Todd formed the Hellhounds, he reached out to us. Asked to get patched over."

The news was a hard blow Rip didn't need. His heart couldn't countenance the prospect. "He wants to turn the Hellhounds into a Sons of Chaos charter of Laramie and Bison Ridge?" That would give Todd powerful allies aligned with his interests, committed to supporting him in a war.

Stryker nodded. "He wants to roll you out, man. Only one club is going to survive in your neck of the woods. Todd has made a lot of friends here. After Thanksgiving, we're holding a vote with all the other charters on whether or not to let him join. I think it'll pass. That's why we can't officially assist you in your request."

Yeah, but he was sharing this information for a reason and not from the kindness of his dark heart. "And unofficially?"

"Unofficially, you're looking for LA. My sister, Lou-Ann," Stryker said, and Rip recalled one or two brief interactions with her. "She works for a dealer who operates a drug camp that runs a bunch of addicts. She used to pick up the junkies at a predesignated site, every two weeks, then drive them around for the day to various pharmacies filling scrips written by dirty docs. Big cities from Casper to Colorado Springs. Afterward, LA and the addicts would get flown to the camp, or the ranch as they like to call it, where they drop off all the pills, spend the night, and do it all over again the next day."

"Are you sure this is a major supplier? How much could they possibly get in a day?"

"LA told me that she brought in anywhere from 4,000 to 6,000 pills. A day. All controlled substances. Mostly opioids."

"That's major, but Todd is dealing more than that."

"Anything the dealer can't get with a scrip they get through a cartel."

Finally, a break. The lead they needed. "Can you give me her number?"

"I would, but she got promoted. Now she's at the ranch, managing distro. Out there, no cell phones and no guns for the workers, only for security."

Ashley put her hand on Rip's back, no doubt annoyed she had to stay silent, itching to voice the questions running through her mind.

Rip slid his arm around her waist. "Where's the ranch? Who runs it?"

"Don't know." Stryker shrugged. "Despite calling it a ranch, they're mobile and change locations every so often, but LA never discussed whereabouts or the owner. LA doesn't have loose lips. It's how she survives in that business."

"Then how do I find her?"

"Inside the envelope is the address of a pickup point. My guys would sometimes provide protection for her on the road, for the first day's run, making sure no one jacked her payload. She started by loading up a van with junkies at the pickup. Her runs always began on the weekend. Usually lasted two to three days. At night, they go to the drug camp. Give the workers food and their payment in pills. They like to do a big run before holidays, and Thanksgiving is in a few days. LA took off yesterday. Which means they're gearing up for processing. They either picked up some addicts earlier today or will tomorrow. You might get lucky if the pickup point is still active. Your best bet is to hang around there. Go as early as possible. Act like junkies looking to work for pills. If you make it to the ranch, tell my sister that Benji sent you." Rip raised an eyebrow, and Stryker added,

"It's what she used to call me when we were kids. That'll let her know I really sent you. Maybe she can grease the wheels and help you cut a deal."

"You're sure that's Todd main supplier?" Rip asked.

"His only supplier. Everything he gets comes from those guys."

"I appreciate this, but what do you want for it?" Everything had a price.

"The ten percent you offered," Stryker said. "Only it comes straight to me. Not the Sons."

Greed wasn't enough for him to risk cutting out his club and going against their wishes. Presidents of an MC guided the club, they weren't dictators who ruled. Getting caught would result in severe consequences. "Why are you helping me?"

"I'm not helping you so much as I'm trying to hurt Todd. Earlier this year, at Sturgis, he got rough with some of LA's friends. One girl went missing. LA made the mistake of confronting him about it instead of coming to me first. He put his hands on her. Probably killed that friend of hers, too, who went MIA. If you mess with my little sister, you mess with me. Also, that dude can't be trusted. The way he stabbed you in the back and tore your club asunder." Stryker gave a low whistle. "I don't need that dirty fool wreaking havoc for me or the constant headache of worrying about when I'll get a knife in my back. If you can manage to crush him before the Sons vote on whether or not to patch his crew over, don't worry about the ten percent. We'll call it square."

"Thanks."

"Don't thank me yet. There are some Sons inside who don't much care for the way you operate. Letting her—" Stryker gestured with his chin to Ashley "—get away with that stunt she pulled, not making it known she was with you. That's something we would punish."

"Let me guess." Rip sighed, filled with frustration and exhaustion. "They also happen to be buddies of Todd."

"You got it. Look man, I have no beef with you. But some in the club already consider Todd to be an unofficial brother ahead of the vote. You're coming for his business. A righteous move in my opinion. But everyone knows the Iron Warriors are at their weakest. If you were full strength, it would be different, giving many a reason to pause. I suggest getting out of Bitterroot Gulch. Now. And expect some unfriendly company along the way."

Rip shook his hand.

"I'll do what I can to give you a head start," Stryker said. "Try talking them down. They think I'm out here schooling you about your lady. The fact that you 'accepted'—" he used air quotes, "—the *Property Of* patches might cool some heads."

Rip gave Ash a full-face helmet to put on while he grabbed the extra one that he had secured on top of an overnight bag with a pair of bungee cords to the back of his motorcycle. "Any time you can buy us would be good." Seconds, minutes, he'd take it.

Nodding, Stryker turned back toward the entrance of the roadhouse just as three bikers strode outside.

Rip shoved on his helmet and activated the two-way Bluetooth communication system. Grabbing his small overnight bag, he slipped the strap over his head, slinging it across his torso.

Ashley did likewise with her purse. "What about my truck?" she asked.

"Where is it?"

"Parked at the motel."

One red-faced hothead stormed around Stryker, but the president grabbed him by the arm as he continued to speak.

Rip got on his bike and cranked the engine, bringing it to life with a fierce growl. "Is your service weapon or badge inside your truck?"

"No. Left both at home." She climbed on behind him, resting her slim denim-clad thighs snug against the outside of his legs and fastened her arms tight around his waist.

"Then forget it. I'll send a tow truck to pick it up. I know a guy. We need to get out of here." He preferred together anyway, one ride. "Are you armed?"

"Always."

That was *his* deputy.

A pang of regret cut through him. What he wanted more than anything was for Ash to be his. But that was something that could never be.

He squashed the inconvenient desire and every distracting thought.

Because the one thing that mattered most was keeping her safe.

Chapter Eight

A cold knot settled at the base of Ashley's spine as they sped away from Happy Jack's Roadhouse.

She glanced over her shoulder and thought she saw people following them, but she couldn't tell if her tired brain mixed with the surge of adrenaline was playing tricks on her.

Rip raced down the long sleepy street as they headed for the highway and the relative safety of the open road.

"We'll get an hour or two away," he said in the helmet mic, over the comms system. "Get our bearings at a hotel and strategize how to handle the info Stryker gave us."

"Sounds good." The moment of calm gave her a chance to try and piece together what had just happened. "What does it mean if the Hellhounds become Sons of Chaos?" she asked. "Big picture."

"It would mean I'm out of time. It would mean added protection for Todd. That stopping him would be even harder. I can't believe how far out he's planned this."

"At least now we have a chance to hurt Todd by cutting off his supplier. Maybe even to goad him into doing something that the sheriff's department could nail him on."

"Yeah, but it's messy. Now I'm exposed no matter how this plays out."

"With Todd?"

"With everyone. Todd will know soon enough that I'm going to come for him and how. They're going to mention you. If Todd tells the Sons that you're a cop, I don't know what the future will look like for me," he said.

The thought of this hurting Rip, upending his world, had the knot inside her coiling tighter. She wanted to save her hometown by stopping Todd Burk, not ruin Rip Lockwood's life in the process.

"Why didn't you listen to me and let me handle it?" he asked.

"Why didn't you just come with me to begin with?" she asked, throwing it back at him. "If we could've spoken to Stryker privately, this would've played out differently. His entire club wouldn't know."

"I needed to think. You only wanted to rush."

"Think about what?"

"How to help you without breaking a bylaw, the code," he said, and of course, he hadn't chosen her over the MC but had found a loophole. "Then I had to figure out exactly where you went. Once I connected the dots with it being a Saturday, only one place made sense."

"And what was the brilliant solution that kept you from breaking the code?"

"I called a vote to change it. With only five of us, the bind we're in with the Hellhounds, and considering my relationship with you, it passed, no problem. But it took time to make it happen."

"And what if it hadn't passed the vote?" Would he have abandoned her?

I'll always come for you if you need me, Ash.

Was that true?

She heard the growl of motorcycle engines roaring up

behind them and turned to see flashes of yellow and black, three bikes coming up on their rear.

Gunfire erupted. One bullet pinged his bike.

"Should I shoot back?" She wasn't sure how the logistics of that would work. Firing behind her while holding on to him with only one arm.

"I'd prefer to outrun them," he said. "I'm going to need you to hold on tight. Wish you were wearing chaps."

Was he worried they might wipe out?

She stiffened against him, snapping her thighs securely around his as she tightened her arms on his waist. He cranked open the throttle and the bike exploded down the asphalt like a bullet.

The freezing wind whipped over them. The dashed lines in the middle of the road whizzed by so fast they almost appeared unbroken.

Her muscles twitched, aching to be released, needing to do something other than rely on Rip and his expertise in handling a motorcycle.

The length of black pavement separating them and the Sons in pursuit, who were shooting at them, continued to stretch.

"Fast bike," she said. "We're going to make it."

"Don't jinx us."

Too late.

A siren whined. Red-and-blue flashing lights appeared from the darkness and zoomed up behind them.

"They might be able to assist."

Rip didn't slow as they continued to fly down the road. "The Sons have got the police in their pockets around here. We're just as likely to catch a bullet from them as we are from a biker. Or worse, the cop stalls until they catch up to us."

The patrol cruiser wasn't far behind.

A train whistle blew.

Up ahead, the white crossing gate was already lowered in front of his lane ahead of the train tracks. Yellow warning lights blinked. A train was coming, headlights ablaze.

He was going to try to outrun it and make the crossing.

She was all for taking chances, but one wrong maneuver, one miscalculation in the slightest, and ten thousand tons of steel would turn them into roadkill. "Rip, don't."

"We have to." His voice was steady, firm. "Don't let go."

What choice did she have? But could they clear the crossing in time?

The whistle blew again, reverberating in her bones. The long, high-speed freight train hurtled down the tracks, drawing closer to the crossing.

Twisting the throttle, he accelerated, and the bike surged even faster, the engine straining. Her stomach launched up into her throat as she clutched on to him for dear life, pressing the side of her head to his back.

The darkness, the rush of wind, pushed in on her, squeezing the air from her lungs. She dug her fingers into the thick leather of his jacket, hoping, trusting, praying.

He whipped across the dotted yellow line over into the lane for oncoming traffic and they rocketed around the crossing gate, barely zipping over the tracks—the glare from the freighter's headlights blinding—before the train roared by within inches of the rear tire.

The gust of the compression wave rocked them on the bike, the tail end swinging out. Rip slowed and rebalanced them and kept going.

Releasing the breath she'd been holding, she looked behind them. In between the train cars, she saw the police cruiser jerk to a halt, dust whipping into the air. The lights of three motorcycles pulled up alongside the vehicle.

A close call.

Deep down, she suspected there would be more to come.

IN THE MOTEL room off the interstate, Rip and Ashley had gone over the information Stryker had passed to them and strategized a flimsy plan to get to the drug camp. Start at the main initial point where the addicts waited to be picked up to make their rounds at pharmacies. With any luck, the location was still being used and tomorrow would be a pickup day.

"All the information I had to go on to get this far was intelligence from Agent Welliver with the DEA," Ashley said, seated next to him on the king-size bed. "He was in charge of the task force I'm technically still attached to. We should call him. See if he's willing to assist now that we know it's not just pills on the ranch."

"Worth a try."

The heat in the room had finally kicked in. He stripped off his jacket and MC cut. His cell phone rang. He dug it out of his pocket. "It's Quill," he said to Ash. "I'll put him on speaker. Just keep quiet. No more secrets or withholding information between us, okay?"

She nodded. "Agreed."

"Yeah," Rip answered.

"I spoke with the boys who we didn't expect to cross over to the dark side," Quill said.

"What reason did they give?" It could've been anything. Calling in political favors, backstabbing, bribery.

"It varied. Larger cut of the profits from Burk's new drug venture for two of them. But three guys weren't pleased with how you handled the situation."

Rip scratched at the stubble on his jaw. "What do you mean?"

"You tried to issue a decree of no drugs without taking

a vote. They're upset that you didn't trust the system. Trust in them to have your back. Being a potentate who crushes the will of his people is being someone who destroys the backbone of an organization which you pledged to lead. A Prez must convince his members. Not coerce. Not decree."

Regret pooled in him. He'd been afraid to take a vote. And in acting out of fear, he'd created the very situation he hoped to avoid.

Ash put a hand on his leg. The concern in her eyes was a small comfort.

"They're right. I should've trusted them." Rip clenched his teeth and swallowed past the bitter lump in his throat. "Did anyone get info from Yates on what Todd's big new venture is?"

Quill sighed. "About that. Shane Yates is dead."

"How? When?"

"Sometime tonight. He replied to a text around seven thirty, agreeing to meet at the old clubhouse at nine, ready to spill details about Burk's operation. Never showed. JD swung by his place to check on him. The sheriff's department was there. Along with a detective from the Laramie PD. The Delaney chick. Crime scene tape was up. Wheeled a body bag out."

The sheriff's department and LPD? Seemed like overkill. "What's happening?" Rip asked, not really expecting an answer.

"No earthly idea, but the winds of change don't seem to be blowing in our favor. If I learn anything else, I'll call."

"I might be out of pocket and hard to reach the next day or two. If I am, don't worry about it. You'll eventually hear from me."

"Okay. Stay safe."

Disconnecting, Rip turned to Ash. "Can you find out

what happened to Yates? He was one of Todd's dealers. We thought he'd be the weakest link to tap for information. He agrees to talk to us and then turns up dead. I don't like it."

"Sure. I'll pretend as though I'm checking in." She picked up the landline and called the sheriff's office. "Hey, Mitch. This is Ashley," she said over the speakerphone. "I'm out on assignment. Just checking in to say that I'm alive and well. What's going on in town? Anything new?"

"Everything is going to hell in a handbasket. Me and the sheriff went over to the Hellhounds hangout. Along with the fire department. Sheriff Clark tore through some walls with an axe. Burk seemed to get the point."

Rip slid Ash a curious glance and gestured for more information.

She shook her head and mouthed, *Nothing*.

Sounded the exact opposite of nothing to him. The sheriff was a levelheaded, cautious man. Rip thought he was well suited for the job and had even voted for him. Clark would never provoke anyone, least of all the Hellhounds, by busting holes in the wall of the clubhouse without good cause.

"Anything else?" she asked. "Any leads on the murder of the pharmacist?"

"No, but we've got another body. Two in one day. One of the Hellhounds. Shane Yates. Killed the same way as the pharmacist. One bullet in the head. Two in the chest. Throat cut. But it looks like the perp was in a hurry on the way out and dropped the knife used. Something to go on. LPD is bringing in Burk for questioning. Apparently, Yates was an informant for Detective Hannah Delaney. She's hot under the collar. I expect she'll hold Burk for as long as she can just to mess with him even if she can't dig up enough evidence for charges."

The police could hold him up to seventy-two hours before

the prosecutor decided whether to charge him. The timing was a much-needed boon. The longer Burk was behind bars limited to making only one phone call the better.

The Sons of Chaos who had Todd's side in this war wouldn't be updating him on the events at Happy Jack's anytime soon. Rip only hoped it would be long enough for him and Ash to accomplish what they'd set out to do.

Once Todd learned about tonight's exploit, that he and Ashley were working together to bring him down, there was no getting around the fact that Rip would be left in a dangerous situation. Exposed. He'd have to make a tough choice.

One that was going to change his life forever.

Chapter Nine

Ashley paced near the landline on the bedside table. "You told me that if I found anything of interest to contact you," she said to Welliver, with Rip listening nearby. "Drugs from a cartel should catch your attention."

It was almost midnight, and the DEA agent was still in the office working. He had enviable stamina. A true workaholic. She knew getting assistance from him might take convincing, but she hadn't expected a flat-out *no*.

"Which cartel?" Agent Welliver asked.

"I don't know."

"How much product?"

"I don't know."

"Where's this supposed drug camp or ranch located?"

She raked a hand through her hair. "I. Don't. Know."

"I appreciate your eagerness and commitment in getting this far. Really, I do." Welliver sighed. "Once you have more for me to work with, we can speak again. But tell me one thing, did you go into Happy Jack's alone?"

She flicked a glance at Rip. He sat on the bed, hands clasped, resting his forearms on his thighs.

"No," she said. "I had help."

"How did you convince him to do it? Did you sleep with Lockwood?"

Her stomach twisted into a pretzel.

Rip's gaze flashed up to her. His brows pinched together.

She reached for the receiver to take the call off speaker. Rip lunged, snatching her wrist, stopping her. He shook his head. *Leave it on.* He mouthed the words at her, indicating he intended to listen.

"No, sir," she said, her cheeks heating. "I told you I wouldn't do that."

"Really?" The surprise in Welliver's voice was like nails on a chalkboard. "I don't know what kind of hold you've got on this guy, but whatever it is, it's worth gold."

She squeezed her eyes shut, bracing against the embarrassment. The sheer humiliation.

"Get yourself and Lockwood into this drug camp. Find out what you can."

Jerking her wrist free from Rip, she grabbed a water and turned away from him, not able to look him in the eye. "I'll ask him. No guarantee he's willing to go that far." Not after learning she treated him like an asset. *Thanks, Welliver.* "Worst case, I go in alone." She twisted off the top and drank from the bottle.

"If you're telling me that he waltzed into the Sons of Chaos den with you and got you that information, then I'm telling you this guy will go off a cliff for you."

She choked on the water going down her throat. Chancing a glance at Rip, she hated what she saw. He was glaring at her, jaw tight, lethal energy starting to simmer beneath the surface.

Ashley was going to be sick.

"I'm impressed," Welliver said. "Once this all shakes out, he might face serious blowback."

Now he points this out. How this would leave Rip *exposed.* She should've considered any potential consequences to Rip sooner instead of operating with blinders on, solely fixating on nailing Todd Burk.

"If there is fallout for him, what can we do for him?" she asked. "What are his options?"

"Not if but when. And short of disappearing? Not much."

Her jaw went slack. "What?" She looked up at Rip.

He turned his back to her and crossed the room.

"Yeah," Welliver said, casually, "that happens in situations such as these."

Her heart pounded in her chest, a sharp pulsating roar that filled her ears. "If this could burn him, destroy his life, why didn't you warn me of the repercussions? Give me a heads-up?"

"Look, kid, you've got a tough exterior, but inside you're soft. You've got a heart. I didn't think you'd have the stomach to go through with it if you knew. But don't beat yourself up over this. Lockwood was a Marine Raider for ten years. Trust me, that dude considered every conceivable risk before helping you," Welliver said, only making her gut twist harder. "Focus on finishing this. Complete the op. Find the drug camp. If you can confirm ties to a cartel or anything big enough for me to take more interest, then I can help you. Best I can do. Hey, Jasper is in the next office. We've got something in the works tonight, but he wanted to speak to you if you've got a minute. Says you haven't been returning his calls."

Just when she thought this conversation couldn't get any worse, it did. "No, um, I, um," she caught herself stuttering, "I'm too busy to talk to him."

"Yeah, I bet. You've got your hands full with Lockwood."

Rip plopped down onto the bed and dropped his head into his hands.

Her chest tightened. "I've got to go."

"You know how to reach me," Welliver said.

Ashley hung up. Slowly, she turned to Rip and stared at his back. "I didn't know," she said.

"Know what? That you'd blow my life apart with this?"

She went over to him and sat beside him. "If you realized that this could happen, why did you come?"

He jumped to his feet. "You dropped a bomb on me that you were going to the Sons and ran off! You left me no choice!" he ground out, and her head spun, her heart aching. "What am I to you? Just some asset?"

Hesitation tensed her shoulders. She opened her mouth but was at a loss for the right words. "I don't know what you are to me."

For a long time, she'd thought of him as the one to blame for Angelo's death, right along with Todd. Later, his actions had separated the two men. Rip had been kind and sort of flirty in his aloof way, always offering to be there for anything she needed. Their conversations redefined him into a would-be protector. But she never knew what was real and what he simply wanted her to believe.

She'd convinced him to help her with this, like an asset. Because she needed him.

But he was never something to be used and discarded.

Rip leaned against the wall, muscled arms crossed over his chest, jaw set hard.

He'd risked everything for her, going to lengths no one else had ever done. Kissed her and touched her and made her feel things she didn't think possible.

The primal attraction heating her blood now as she looked at him left her breathless. But she didn't know what box to put it in, what label to give him.

"Who's Jasper?" he asked.

The question knocked her farther off-kilter. "What?"

"Jasper."

"He's, um, a DEA agent I worked with on the task force." Answering shouldn't fluster her the way that it did, as though she had something to hide, but she didn't want to talk about the other guy. Think about the things she'd done with him that she wished she could do with Rip.

"That's what he is. Who is he to you?"

She lowered her head. "No one."

It shamed and confused her that more heat existed when she was in the same room with Rip, a guy she'd convinced herself for years she had to despise, than with any of her past dates, including Jasper Pearse.

"I've never lied to you," he said. "Have enough respect for me to be honest."

This shouldn't be so difficult to spit out but it felt like admitting to an affair when there was nothing between her and Rip. "Jasper and I slept together while working on the task force in Fort Collins."

No other man had ever followed up after a date, showing any eagerness to get to know her better. Other than Jasper. Her interest in him had been lackluster at best, but it was an opportunity to finally explore something romantic. Something sexual. It had been her first and only time being intimate with a man, but she'd felt more desire, more raw, hot need for Rip when he had his hands on her than she'd ever had for Jasper. No one but Rip had kissed her so thoroughly, so passionately that he had possibly ruined her for every other man out there.

Something about her attraction to Rip unnerved her. An attraction he couldn't possibly reciprocate.

"Are you two still together?" Rip asked.

She was startled by the odd undertone she could have sworn she heard in his voice.

Was he jealous?

What if all this time it was desire lurking beneath their arguments, the flirty banter, the endless tension and prying conversations that always got too personal?

That sudden thought seared into her brain like a brand, glowing red-hot and strangely urgent.

"No, we're not together. It was a brief, casual fling."

"How brief?"

"Why are you grilling me about an encounter with an agent, who I have no feelings for by the way, like some over-protective big brother?"

The color drained from his face as he grew still. Too still. Too quiet.

"We need to focus on Todd Burk," she said, redirecting the conversation. "We have to finish this. As soon as possible."

Staring at her, he said nothing. An emptiness fell over his eyes, the cool distance between them growing, spreading.

"There's something I haven't told you. About the car accident I had." She realized she was fidgeting with her hands and stopped. "Burk was behind it."

"What are you talking about?" His voice sounded hollow. Whatever numb mode he'd flipped into, he was still there, unsettling her. "He wouldn't hurt you, not until I'm out of the way."

Rip sounded so certain, but… "You're wrong."

"What am I missing, Ash?" His gaze sharpened, and he watched her far too closely. "What else haven't you told me?"

The harsh question came across like an accusation. One she deserved.

She'd deliberately hidden the circumstances surrounding her accident. Now there was no avoiding it. She had to tell him.

Ashley took a breath, steeling herself for how he might react. "I was taking pictures in front of the clubhouse. I think I found which three bikers attacked you. Anyway, Burk spotted me. He came over for a chat. Taunted me about some high price you paid. For me. To protect me. By the way, what was he referring to?"

"The reason I gave him the clubhouse," he said flatly, and she ached for how much he'd sacrificed. "Get on with what you were saying." His tone was ice-cold.

"Todd called the gesture romantic. I told him in no uncertain terms that there was nothing between us. Then he asked me point-blank if I was your old lady, which sounded preposterous."

Rip narrowed his eyes. "And you said?"

She stared at him like the answer was obvious. "The truth. That I wasn't. I left and then two prospects followed me, shot at me and ran me off the road."

Clenching his fists in front of his face, he shoved off the wall with panther-like grace. "I told you to stay away from him."

"And I did. Sort of. He approached me, not the other way around."

He stormed over to her, exuding masculine power, and she was strangely more comfortable with his anger than his silence. "The one safeguard, the biggest thing keeping you safe, you just stripped away. Like that." He snapped his fingers.

Seated on the bed, she tipped her head up at him. "How is that possible? What did I do?"

"After your brother's funeral, I had to go back to the Marines for a little while until my paperwork was processed. Do you remember an incident behind Delgado's?"

She thought back, combing through her memories, and came up short.

"You worked at the bar and grill part-time in high school," he said. "Went to throw out the trash. Spotted some Iron Warriors on their bikes. Decided to go over and make a scene. Threatened Todd."

Her shoulders sagged as she recalled. "Yes." It wasn't her proudest moment. She'd been in so much pain, the grief suffocating her, and then she'd seen Todd Burk and couldn't stop herself from venting her anguish.

"When you walked away and went back inside," Rip said, "Todd let it slip what he was going to do to you. Quill interceded, told Todd the only thing, the one thing that would stop him. The story he spun was that after the funeral, before I left, I was comforting you and fell for you. I staked my claim to you while I was home on leave...and that you were my old lady as far as the club was concerned."

She rocked back as though what he'd said had been a physical blow. "I don't understand." The words *my old lady* got caught in her mind and spun there. "Wouldn't I've had to know that I was your girlfriend, to pretend with you, like we did tonight, to pull that off?"

Letting out a heavy breath, he lowered his head. "Quill told everyone that it needed to stay quiet since you were only seventeen. When I came back to town, that explained why no one ever saw us together in public, except for us talking. As soon as you were of legal age, you joined the sheriff's department. Gave a different reason for us not to go public. They all think that you and I are together and that we want to keep it under wraps. Besides Quill."

Stunned, she sat there. "All this time, you've been lying about being with me?"

"I never asked Quill to lie or actually repeated it, but I perpetuated the story with my silence," he said, as though that made a difference. "Because it worked. Old ladies are off-limits. Period. The one rule Todd would respect until he eliminates me, but you've taken that away."

She reeled from the admission. "Wait. Help me wrap my head around this. For seven years, if I'm supposed to be your old lady, then you haven't had a real girlfriend or gotten serious about anyone?"

He shook his head. "No."

Narrowing her eyes at him, she found that hard to believe. "For seven years, *seven*, you haven't slept with anyone?"

"On occasion." He shrugged. "I'd go to Cheyenne. No one regular. Kept it discreet."

Oh my God. That was why he didn't have any female visitors at his trailer or sleep with women at the clubhouse. To add credence to the lie that they were together. In love. Committed.

"You can't collaborate with a cop, but you can sleep with one?"

"Yeah," he said with a reluctant nod. "There are clubs that have patches for a thing like that."

Gross. "Do you?"

"Of course not. I'd never brag or exploit you."

She believed him. He'd have too much honor to wear that kind of patch. But this story boggled her mind.

"What about me?" she asked, perplexed, trying to piece it all together. "I mean, how would you have explained it if I'd had a boyfriend." In high school, she'd been focused on getting good grades, graduating, taking it one day at a time without her brother, not dating. But once she'd started working as a deputy, she'd tried to build a full life. She wanted marriage, a family, thinking it might fill the hole inside.

"I figured I'd cross that bridge when I eventually came to it. But you haven't had a boyfriend, have you? Quill would've told me. Or you would've. Other than this *Jasper.*"

And she thought she would have shared it like she had countless other things, such as her awkward date with Dave, personal things about her family, things she'd never whispered to another soul.

But she hadn't. And Jasper had happened out of town. All the way down in Fort Collins. Where Rip and other Iron Warriors hadn't been watching.

The ugly truth of everything gelled and smacked her in the face. She leaped off the bed and strode over to him. "Are you the reason I haven't been able to date? That I haven't had a boyfriend? That after one dinner, every single guy, except for Jasper Pearse, seemingly lost interest in me?"

"How would I be the reason?"

"It's the only thing that makes sense. Has Quill been scaring them off? Have you?"

"What?" The denial on his face slowly shifted, realization dawning in his eyes. He shook his head like he didn't want to believe it and then took out his phone. Punched in a number. Put the call on speaker.

After the seventh ring, Quill answered, "What's up, Rip?" He sounded like he'd been roused from sleep. "Thought I wouldn't hear from you for a while."

"I'm going to ask you straight and you better answer straight. Have you been sabotaging Ashley's dates? Keeping men away from her?"

"Huh?" Quill asked with a yawn.

"Give it to me straight," Rip demanded.

"Well, yeah. Me and JD let it be known subtly. We

planted a rumor around town that you two were together. Word spread faster than pink eye among toddlers. That did half the work."

Ashley thought back to a couple of years ago when Mitch had joked that the reason he couldn't ask her out was because she had a biker for a boyfriend. She hadn't taken it seriously, thinking it was his way of letting her down easily. It wasn't the first time someone had made that kind of teasing remark, but she'd chalked it up to how Rip would stop and talk to her whenever and wherever in town while he didn't give anyone else from the sheriff's department or most civilians for that matter the time of day.

"When any guys went sniffing around her," Quill continued, "JD and I rode up on them. Told them to lose her number. If they pushed back, well, then JD got off his bike. Looked them in the eye and told them to stay away from her. Every time they caved."

She should have chosen stronger men.

But that would explain why Dave, a nice guy who shared her fondness for Mexican food, had literally run from her when she bumped into him at the post office and asked if he wanted to grab some tacos and margaritas a second time. Because he'd been scared off. By Rip's henchmen.

"You brought JD into this?" Rip asked.

"Had to. I'm not as intimidating as I used to be. He understands and can be trusted."

Rip's free hand clenched into a fist at his side. "I never told either of you to do something like that!"

"You asked me to watch out for her after you caught *feelings* and didn't want to be the one keeping tabs. It had to be done. Let's say she started dating, got into something serious, then the story that you two were together would've unraveled faster than a yo-yo and painted a target on her back.

If Todd ever found out the truth, she wouldn't be safe. And you know it. I won't apologize for doing my job."

"Unbelievable," Rip snapped. "You should have told me."

"Don't ask, don't tell, right? You didn't ask about my methods, so I didn't feel obliged to tell. Figured it was best that way for both of us. Straight enough for you, brother?"

Rip stabbed the disconnect icon on his phone and huffed a breath. "I'm sorry, Ash. This is my fault. I set out to protect you and roped Quill into helping me. This wasn't how it was supposed to be done. I never should've let this happen, let them interfere in your life."

Shock didn't simply surge through her. That was too simple. A mix of everything did. Surprise. Fury. Betrayal. Confusion. It rose up, twisted together and turned into rage with one target. Him. "But you did." She could spit nails. "Todd sent his goons after me because I told him the truth. Because you didn't bother to let me in on the big lie. Instead of keeping this a secret from me, you could've talked to me about it and explained. Given me a choice, a say in the matter."

"Talk to you about it? It's not as though you've made it easy to look out for you. You never listen to me. Or do what I tell you. Taking pictures at the clubhouse. Chatting with Todd. Running off to the Sons of Chaos. And where am I? Here, with you, ready to jump off a cliff, apparently, while my life is about to be blown apart, because I'm too foolish to help myself."

"I didn't ask you to vow anything to me any more than you asked Ida to take you and your brother in." Maybe he would've been better off if he had never made any promises and stayed away from her. "Don't get me wrong, everything you said is valid. The bind you're in with the clubs because of what the Sons know is on me and I'm sorry for it. But do you have any idea how your actions, Quill's, have made me feel? How it's damaged me?"

Rip's brow furrowed. "Damaged you? I don't understand."

"I could never figure out why no one was interested in me. At first, I thought the hot guys were simply out of my league. I came to terms with reality, accepted that I wasn't beautiful, lowered my standards. Told myself that the only thing that mattered was if a guy treated me well. Not what he looked like. Not if he excited me. Or made me feel anything at all inside besides boredom. Because the problem had to be me. I needed to try harder. I went so far as to force myself to go out with someone I didn't even like, only to have him reject me, too." The gnawing emptiness inside her opened up, spreading through her. "For years, I've gone through that. Do you know what it does to a person?"

A sense of defeat eventually crowded out the desperation. Hope and the chance for love slowly withered.

Being with Jasper hadn't been better. Their time together had left her emptier than being alone, so why bother.

Holding her gaze, Rip stood frozen, but she didn't want to see the pain echoed in his expression as though he were the one wounded.

Chapter Ten

"Ash…" He shook his head. "You're beautiful." So beautiful it hurts. "You deserved the attention of every guy out there even though you were better than all of them. I didn't think about how that story might grow and get out of hand. The way it might affect you." Maybe a part of him hadn't wanted to think about it, to question why a woman as stunning and smart and spirited as Ash was single. Deep down, he'd been too relieved not to have to cross that bridge. Not yet anyway. How blind he'd been. "I never meant to hurt you. I didn't realize."

"Why would you? How would you know the consequences of that lie or the repercussions of maintaining it? How lonely I've been." Her voice broke right along with his heart. "How badly I've wanted to be touched. To be wanted." Tears welled in her eyes. "To have what everybody else does. Affection from someone who has my back in this world."

Rip had no idea of the depth of her pain, and she would never know how truly sorry he was that she'd suffered.

But he had her back, no matter the circumstance. If only he was capable of being a vigilante, he would have taken out Burk long ago. Instead, he'd tried to do things the right way, to see her brother's murderer serving time behind bars. But in waiting, in being patient, he'd unintentionally robbed her of something she'd needed. For her to think she lacked in any way tore him up.

Easing closer, he curled his hands around her shoulders. Her cinnamon-anise scent filled the space between them and worked its way into his senses, overriding his anger at the mess of things. He pulled her to him and lowered his mouth to hers.

Letting out a shocked gasp, Ash shoved him away. "Stop it. You don't have to do that. Keep putting on an act. Pretend to be attracted to me. Give me a pity kiss to make yourself feel better about destroying any chance I had at a love life for the past seven years."

An act?

Sure, he'd hidden how deep his feelings for her ran because she never seemed interested. Any attempts he made to flirt were met with a cool, almost confused reception, like they were speaking two different languages. Every positive thing about him he'd tried to share she'd dismissed, choosing instead to look for the negative. Perhaps she'd simply never believed any of the good things, including his attraction to her.

If so, he'd done them both a disservice. No more being subtle. Time to be blunt.

"I wasn't pretending." Rip sighed. "My feelings for you have never been fake. I know you've never liked me. I didn't mean to overstep just now, but it was killing me, listening to you think you weren't desirable. You have no idea how men look at you. Even in your uniform I see it." He scrubbed a hand over his face, tamping down the jealousy that flashed through him as he recalled it. "I've wanted you for a long time. Thought about what it would be like, us, together. As a real couple. You're all I think about. All I hope for."

Rocking back on her heels, Ashley swallowed like something was stuck in her throat. "The kiss wasn't just an act for you?"

"The kiss was necessary. We had to get through it at Happy Jack's with the Sons believing we were a couple, but I didn't have to get *that* into it. Multiple times. I used it as an excuse to do what I've longed to for a while because I'm attracted to you. Want you in the worst way." There, he'd said it. Put his cards on the table.

A ragged breath punched from her lips as if squeezed from her lungs. Silence descended. Her gaze wandered as she rested against the dresser. Loose strands of hair hid her face, but he didn't need to see her expression.

He was probably the last man she'd want and if by some chance that spark had been mutual, he had to consider his entire world was about to change. But he didn't want her to think he'd bail or that she owed him anything. "Our history, our current set of circumstances, complicates things. I want you to know that I'm going to help you see this op through to the end. No strings attached."

"Thank you." Ashley let out a low breath. "It's not that I've never liked you," she said, her voice soft. "I thought I couldn't trust the things you've told me, couldn't believe in the goodness I've seen in you." She looked up at him. "Until tonight. Everything you've done...wiped away the doubt that's been keeping me from accepting how I feel about you."

He eased toward her, hoping she felt as deeply for him as he did for her.

"You're a good guy, Rip. I wish I could've seen it sooner. Believed everything you showed me. I'm sorry I dragged you into this. I wish there could've been another way. I didn't mean to ruin your life where you might have to go into hiding."

"Sometimes stuff has to happen, I guess. Without the way things played out at Happy Jack's neither of us would've been as honest as we have. Found out the truth." He'd never regret getting the chance to hold her, kiss her, and imagine.

She studied his face. "What if the vote to change the by-laws of the Iron Warriors to work with a cop hadn't gone in your favor?"

"The odds were pretty good, but I'd be here anyway. I would've waited until after we finished doing whatever is necessary to end this thing with Burk before I stripped off my patches and walked away from the club." He was prepared to give it all up.

"Really? For me?"

"This thing between us started out as an obligation I took upon myself. I'm not sure what it's become. All I know is that I'd do anything for you. The affection I have for you is real, and I want you in a way I've never wanted another woman."

Ashley pressed her palms to his chest. "I want you, too. Kind of scares me how much." She curled one warm hand around his arm and slid the other over the back of his neck. Her fingers stroked his hair, enticing him to soften.

But he couldn't ignore the uncertainty in her eyes. He no longer doubted that she wanted to sleep with him, but how did she feel about him?

"What am I to you?" he asked.

She was quiet, that beautiful gaze of hers stark. Perhaps she was surprised that he persisted in raising the question but also once more considering an answer. Then she looked away.

Again, she didn't know.

Not that he blamed her. First, she was angry at him and now she wasn't. Had questioned his character and now trusted in him without hesitation. Denied her attraction to him and now wanted to explore it.

But bikers and cops didn't mix.

Not to mention they were in different places in their lives. There would be fallout from his actions tonight. Once he rid his town of Todd Burk, one way or another, he'd have to leave before the Sons of Chaos came after him for payback.

"This isn't a game for me," he said.

"For me either." Lifting onto the balls of her feet, she leaned in, her mouth reaching toward his.

Rip locked down every muscle in his body and pulled his head back. "I won't be satisfied with one night." He stepped to the side, crossing the room. "With a brief, casual fling like you had with Jasper." The thought of that guy, any guy, touching her burned a hole in him. "I'd want more." A lot more. More than he had a right to have. Not simply rough, hot pleasure in a dark hotel room. The elusive more of a connection that was physical and emotional and serious.

"You don't understand. Jasper was convenient and he was interested," she said, as though that made things better.

"I'm convenient and clearly interested." A convenient asset, who could no longer hide his attraction to her.

Pressing a palm to her forehead, she lowered her gaze. "I slept with him because I didn't want to be a virgin anymore, okay?" Her voice was low, embarrassed. "But I didn't feel anything for him. That's why it was a meaningless fling." She looked up at him. "But this, us, it feels different."

Jasper was her first lover. Jealousy tangled with guilt and coiled within Rip. She'd simply given her virginity to the first yahoo who made it to a second date. Had a meaningless experience because she'd been denied the ability to have anything else.

He wanted to punch Quill and then himself for boxing her into that position.

"It wouldn't be fair to ask you for what I want." Even if she could give it. "The way I allowed Quill to handle things prevented you from dating and playing the field." Though Rip hadn't realized such horrible interference was happening, ultimately, the responsibility fell on his shoulders. "I won't take that away from you anymore. I'm thirty-eight. Doesn't feel old to me, but I'm already graying, and I've sown my wild oats. I know what I want. Who I want." Even if he didn't deserve her. "I can't undo my mistakes, but I can give you time. Without me or the club hovering, sabotaging your efforts to find what you've been looking for. Once we get Todd, put an end to him and I fix what I broke in the club, my obligation will be done. I'll move on from Laramie. And you can be free."

She blinked, her eyes filling with hurt, surprise slackening her features.

He didn't have time to choose his words carefully because if she kissed him again, he'd break apart and cave.

Rip snatched his jacket and helmet. "I'm going to run to that big twenty-four convenience store at the rest area we passed on the interstate. Get you some things for tomorrow. Sweatshirt. Sneakers. I've got an extra toothbrush in my overnight bag and you can sleep in one of my T-shirts. Don't wait up for me."

He left the room, shutting the door behind him.

Getting on his bike, he wrestled with his feelings. He wanted to make love to her more than anything, but she was special and deserved a man who would be serious about her. Who would be able to stick around and give her everything. To be everything for her.

Once some lines were crossed, there was no going back.

No doubt in his mind what she meant to him. He'd sacrifice everything, including his own desires, to make sure she got the chance to have the life she deserved.

ASHLEY CONSIDERED GOING after him but had no idea what to say.

What am I to you?

Because she didn't have an answer, he was prepared to push her away for good.

Something banded around her lungs, tight and squeezing. A depth and breadth of emotions she'd need time to sort through.

The secrets, the feelings they'd each unloaded were big and powerful and overwhelming.

She unzipped his bag, got toiletries and a T-shirt. A long shower gave her a chance to process, think, unwind. The water poured down on her, too hot, pricking her skin, but Ashley didn't care. When she toweled off, anxiety hadn't subsided, and putting on Rip's T-shirt didn't make it better. She climbed into the bed under the covers.

Sleep was impossible. She lay in bed, adrift and uncertain. Her life was caught in a whirlwind. This was the eye of the storm. The quiet, the calm, before more pieces of their lives got ripped away, changed forever.

Unease ticked through her over how Rip had left things. He'd been in her life, protecting her for seven years, letting his feelings for her grow, slow and steady and sure. But for her a cork had popped on the mix of emotions she'd kept bottled inside. Gushing and fizzing, overflowing into a mess.

Now he wanted her to simply contain it because circumstances made it inconvenient.

That part was unfair.

She stared at the red digital numbers on the clock. It wasn't until after two in the morning when she heard the purr of Rip's bike pull up outside.

He tiptoed into the room, not making a sound with the shopping bags, closing the door with a soft click.

"You don't have to be quiet. I'm not asleep." She sat up, bringing her knees to her chest under the covers and wrapping her arms around her legs.

He set the bags down on the floor. "You need to get some rest."

"We both do. But I need to talk to you first."

"You don't have to say anything."

"I do." She sighed, wanting to take her fizzy feelings and pour them into a neat glass he'd understand. "There are three phone numbers that I have memorized and know by heart. The landline to my parents' house, the sheriff's office and your cell phone."

"What does that have to do with anything?"

That was everything. He was one of the most important people in her life and she was only now realizing it.

"I don't know what you are to me because I never gave myself a chance to unpack it. During all the time we've spent together, throughout every conversation, every quick meal at my house, I've doubted you. While you were getting to know me, sharing who you really were, I refused to believe anything you told me was honest. Real. Until Ida and Welliver convinced me I should be looking at you differently." She released a heavy breath. "Whenever you're within arm's reach, I've been drawn to you, always tempted to get closer, daring to do so, curious to see what might happen, despite the fact you seemed determined to keep your distance. I tried to deny how attracted I am to you, constantly fighting against it. Told myself that it was just oxytocin, dopamine, norepinephrine. A chemical reaction in my brain that I couldn't trust."

Crossing his arms, he leaned against the wall. "The whole universe is a chemical reaction. But it's still real."

"You're right, and tonight changed everything."

"How so?"

"For one thing, you proved to me you're committed to stopping Burk. But there's more." She went to get up.

But he raised a palm, warding her off. "Stay there. Under the covers. Please."

"Then you come closer. Sit by me."

Rip hesitated a moment and then eased across the room and sat on the edge of the bed near her feet.

"Jasper gave me attention. Pursued me. I liked it and thought that meant I wanted him. But I was wrong. On my dates with him, I found my mind veering to you. Wasn't sure why. Sex with him—"

"I don't want to know." He hung his head and clasped his hands.

"It'd been fine. Nothing thrilling. Or sweet. Or special. But tonight, with you, was all that and so much more when you touched me and kissed me." Fireworks went off inside her body. "It was like my heart was beating so hard it was going to come straight out my chest. You made me ache, Rip, with real desire." She'd never experienced a hollow sensation between her thighs akin to pain. Never felt like she might die if she didn't get a man's hands all over her body. Not until him. "I don't want to fight what I feel for you anymore."

She crawled out from under the covers and climbed onto his lap, settling her knees on either side of his thighs. Staring into his eyes, she slid her palms up his chest and then to his shoulders.

Rip stiffened while everything inside her eased. "Ash, please don't. You need to be free of me. Free of Todd. Free to see what your life could be without the pressure of this weighing on you."

Sometimes high pressure and intense heat were necessary to forge something new.

"I don't know what you are to me, but I need to figure it out." Despite the undercurrent of confusion, the suddenness of the tide washing away false beliefs, she couldn't ignore the truth that being close to him, like this, felt right. Absolutely right. Him. Here. The two of them. "What I do know is that you make me want to take off my clothes and throw caution to the wind and forget about every rule, Rip." She pulled the T-shirt over her head and let it hit the floor, exposing her body to him.

A harsh, shuddering breath rushed from his mouth as his gaze fell over her. "You need time. A chance to find someone, anyone else. Not me taking advantage of you. I promised myself that I wouldn't do this. That I wouldn't make love to you. Told myself that I wouldn't even take off my pants when I got back to the room."

Smiling, she cupped his handsome face and caressed his cheeks. He was an honorable man. Strong, fierce Rip, with his rugged good looks, cropped hair, stormy blue-gray eyes and that golden skin. Such a good guy, but right now, she wanted him to be bad in the best way. "Touch me. Hold me. Talk to me about all the things you've been trying to share but I've been too stubborn to hear. And if it makes you feel any better, I'm not asking you to break a promise to yourself. You can keep your pants on. But at least let me take your shirt off."

She pushed his leather jacket back from his shoulders. Tugged his arms from the sleeves. Stripped off his Henley.

All hard-packed, well-honed muscle, without an ounce of fat. She slid her arms around his neck, pressing her body to his, skin to skin, melting into his warmth. His pulse raced beneath her touch as he stiffened.

"You and I are an impossibility." His somber tone tugged at her heart. "Where do you think this could go from here?"

"I don't know, but don't draw a hard line. Not when the sand around us keeps shifting. This thing between us runs deeper than anything I've ever known. Give me a chance to understand it. To fully feel it."

His piercing gaze was unwavering on hers. The awareness between them, the raw attraction, finally acknowledged, vibrated like sparks in the air, crackling with a new kind of electricity.

She brushed her lips over his and she trembled, or he did. Maybe both of them.

His jaw tightened, and still, he didn't put a finger on her.

Her heart couldn't take another rejection. Not from him. Not when she'd never wanted anyone more.

"Please, Rip," she said, filling her voice with every drop of desire running through her.

He looped an arm around her waist, cradled her cheek in one of his hands and stared at her like he was deliberating.

So, she slid her mouth against his and kissed him, insistent, determined, rocking her hips over the bulge in his jeans. Need twisted deep inside her. She yearned to explore his body until every contour was etched in her bones. No matter what happened tomorrow, or next week, she'd at least have that and this feeling.

Alive.

Electric.

Connected.

She clung to him. Pushing against him as if she could

push herself all the way *into* him. Her pulse was a hammer, hard and resilient, thundering out a message—*don't let go, don't let go, don't let go.*

And finally, he kissed her back, his tongue sweeping over hers, delving deeper, drinking her in, erasing any questions or concerns, leaving only the powerful feelings she had for him. And in his arms, it was all that mattered. It was everything.

Chapter Eleven

The truth had a way of surfacing, regardless if it was convenient. The honesty Rip and Ash had disclosed changed things between them, for better or worse.

But redrawing physical boundaries complicated everything.

Rip sat behind the steering wheel of Ash's vehicle. The tow truck had dropped it off before sunrise and the driver had collected his bike, agreeing to take it on to Laramie for a steep fee. Then they drove to the address in Casper listed on the paper Stryker had given them. To a transport hub where they'd been waiting three hours.

Looking through binoculars, he stared out the windshield, staying vigilant, forcing himself not to look at Ash asleep in the passenger's seat, trying not to replay last night in his head. She'd taken off the T-shirt and had nothing underneath. All those soft, supple curves more beautiful than he'd imagined. Her killer body perfect to him. Sexy Ash.

Gutsy Ash.

Off-limits Ash.

Or at least she had been in some ways, but in one very important way to him she still was.

She had no idea how badly he wanted her. He'd tried to do the right thing, the noble thing, and he'd given her what he could. Kisses. Comfort. Tenderness. Pleasure again and again, with his fingers and his mouth, touching and tasting, and he'd reveled in her sweet cries of satisfaction. Then she'd asked for more, for him to be inside her. Need roared up like a wild beast, clawing through him, and he ached to have her. If he'd had protection in his wallet or had bought some at the store, he might've been a weaker man, but instead he kept his pants on as promised.

Ashley had been robbed of so much, he just wanted to give, not take.

Making love to her when he only had to leave later would've torn something from him. Something deep he didn't think he'd ever get back.

A part of his soul.

After the Marines and the club, he didn't have all that many pieces left.

Across the street, a small group of desperados had formed at the far end of the hub at the last bus shelter. Only seven. Every one of them had the anxious, fidgety vibe of an addict. Two looked as though they hadn't changed their clothes or showered in a few days and held a trash bag, partially full of items. The others had knapsacks, and one woman carried a huge tote capable of holding almost anything. They all appeared to be in rough shape.

With no one else around, they also stood out.

"Hey." Rip caressed her face with the back of his hand, brushing his knuckles across her cheek. "Time to get up." He hated to disturb her and wished he could've risked her sleeping longer.

Ashley stirred. Yawning, she stretched.

He took a small vial of peppermint oil he purchased from the store out of his pocket and applied a drop near the corner of each eye.

"What's that for?" she asked.

"The oil is an irritant. It'll give me those telltale red eyes that junkies tend to have." He slipped on a cheap pair of sunglasses. "Takes a few minutes to work."

"We got movement?"

"I think we're in luck." He handed her the binoculars.

She stared in the direction he indicated. "Either that or they're waiting for a ride to a Narcotics Anonymous meeting." She turned to him. "How do I look?"

They'd messed up the new clothes he'd bought, a sweatshirt and sneakers for her, and a flannel shirt for him by rubbing a jagged rock across the material, to tatter the fabric and scruff the shoes, giving their attire a worn-in appearance. If he'd had time, he would've gotten things from a thrift store to save them the trouble.

But her hair was pulled up in a smooth ponytail and her face too fresh and pretty to fit in.

"You need to be a bit rougher around the edges."

She removed the elastic band, fluffed her hair and redid the ponytail, making it sloppy with loose, chaotic strands framing her face. Pulling mascara from her purse, she flipped down the visor and lifted the cover of the vanity mirror. She applied mascara, but not to her lashes, and strategically smudged it underneath her eyes on the lids. She now looked like a party girl who'd had a hard night but was still beautiful.

"Much better."

They'd debated earlier and agreed it was best to play a couple. No way he'd be able to suppress his protective instincts if she was put in a compromising position.

"How much longer do you think until they get picked up?" she asked.

He shrugged. "No way to know for certain. Most of the

pharmacies around here open at nine, but Stryker said to be here early." He glanced at his watch. Seventy thirty. He popped open her glove box and shoved his primary burner phone linked to the voice-activated listening device at the clubhouse as well as his personal cell inside. "We should get out there. Try to blend in."

They exited her truck.

He braced against the frigid breeze with only an inexpensive fleece-lined windbreaker and the flannel shirt over his Henley to keep him warm. In a similar position, Ash shivered beside him as they crossed the street and turned the corner, heading toward the group.

They each had a backpack with protein bars, water, toothbrush, cheap burner phones that would be handed over in the event they were picked up and a rolled-up sleeping bag strapped to the bottom. Since he had no idea exactly what they were walking into, he erred on the side of caution.

With so many moving pieces, they didn't know where they would ultimately end up. So, he'd arranged for the same tow truck driver, Ganow, to collect her vehicle again and run it down to Laramie if necessary. Considering the exorbitant amount he was being paid, the guy didn't complain. Worst-case scenario, the drug dealers didn't show to pick up the group of addicts, there would be no need for the tow truck, but the guy still got paid. Win-win if you were Ganow.

As they neared the shelter, a scruffy guy with blotchy skin and an overgrown beard wearing a blue ballcap stared at them. The others noticed them but didn't take too much interest.

Once they were close enough, Rip gave a head nod to Mr. Bearded Blue Ballcap, BBB.

The guy didn't do likewise, only narrowing his eyes in

response. BBB was going to be a problem. The only question was how big of a problem.

Joining the seven individuals, they stood inside the shelter, shielded from the wind.

Rip put his back to a corner in the shelter, where he could see any approaching vehicles. Ash leaned her side against him, resting her head on his chest, and he curled a loose arm around her.

Six more strolled in while they waited.

An hour or so later, an unmarked white passenger van pulled up. The driver hopped out. A guy in his late twenties. Mirrored sunglasses. A well-worn leather jacket. Turtleneck. Torn jeans. Steel-toe boots. He finished smoking a cigarette and put it out under his bootheel.

He opened the passenger door and waved the group over. Everyone filed out of the shelter and up to the van.

The man opened a drawstring bag and set it on the floor of the van. "You know the drill. Cell phones inside."

A guy stopped in front of the driver and extended his arms. The driver patted him down, probably checking for weapons and wires, and searched his knapsack. Then the guy dropped his phone in the bag and climbed into the van.

So on it went until it was their turn.

Rip stepped forward, with Ash behind him. He caught the flash of a gun in the shoulder holster beneath the man's jacket.

"Hold on, you weren't here last time."

"We couldn't make it," Rip said, gesturing to Ash.

The driver eyed him and then looked Ashley up and down, taking her in too closely. Rip chalked it up to male interest and not suspicion. Not that either was good. The latter meant trouble now. The former meant trouble later. No telling what those guys at the ranch expected from female junkies, who were normally willing to do anything to get their next fix.

Everything inside told him to persuade Ash to stay behind, but he was certain she wouldn't agree.

"I don't know either of you," the driver said.

With a sigh, Rip shook his head. "Well, LA does. I'm used to riding with her. This is my girl's first time. But LA will vouch for us."

The driver cocked his head to the side. "Oh yeah? You sure about that?"

Rip took off his sunglasses, squinting at the light. His eyes should be nice and red by now. "Positive."

The driver scrutinized him for a moment as if trying to decide what to do. "You willing to bet *both* your lives on it? Because if LA says she doesn't know you, I guarantee you'll each get a bullet in the head."

Hesitation would only convey doubt. Rip opened his bag and extended his arms for the pat-down as his answer.

The driver nodded. "Okay. I'm up for a game of Russian roulette. Let's see whether you live or die."

Rip was used to taking high-stakes chances as a Marine Raider, accomplishing the mission as his sole focus. What he wasn't willing to do was gamble with Ash's life. She was a competent and capable cop, but asking her to stay behind—when she'd refuse because she mistakenly thought being a cop meant she was cut out for this—would only raise a red flag.

They were in this now. He just had to make sure he kept her safe.

After a less than thorough pat-down, where the guy had missed the gun in Rip's ankle holster, he waited for his bag to be searched. In the few seconds it took, Rip noticed the tight weave of the fabric on the drawstring bag for the cell phones. Inside, it was lined with a shiny silver material. A Faraday bag—blocked GPS signals to prevent location tracking and stopped remote spying. Whoever this crew was they were serious players, but if they had weaknesses at the pickup point, there would be more later that he could exploit.

Rip dropped his burner phone in the bag, waited for Ash to be searched and to dump her burner as well. Then they climbed in.

The driver started the vehicle.

They rode for about ten minutes before pulling up in front of a shady-looking pain clinic on Elk Street. There were no other buildings on the block beside the shoddy one-story. The sign on the door read Closed.

"Come on." The driver cut the engine and ushered them out. At the exterior metal screen door, he rang the bell three times and waved at the camera positioned above it.

They were buzzed in, the lock disengaging. The driver held the door open. They funneled in, forming a line. One by one they were directed into an office that only had space for a small desk and chair. A man wearing a white lab coat, presumably the doctor, sat collecting IDs. Not bothering to raise his head and look at anyone or even speak, he entered information into a computer and then handed back the identification card along with twelve signed prescriptions per person.

The driver took a thick envelope from the inner pocket of his jacket, dropped it on the desk, and they left. In the van, he collected the prescriptions.

Next stop was a small pharmacy three minutes away. They parked right as the place opened for business. The driver handed each person a scrip, enough cash to pay for it, and herded them inside.

STANDING IN LINE at a higher-end drugstore in Fort Collins, Ashley shuffled forward. The pace had been grueling. A merry-go-round of stopping at pharmacies, everyone filing out with their belongings rather than leaving them in the van, turning in the prescriptions, little to no wait getting them filled—courtesy of working for drug dealers, they were paid in cash, and then off to the next location.

No big chain store pharmacies. Only smaller, independent ones, lots of mom-and-pop places. They spent around fifteen minutes inside, thirty at most, with the driver, whose name she'd learned was Drexel, always waiting outside out of view of the cameras. Most likely didn't want to be captured on the surveillance video.

Whatever agreement had been reached with the owners of the pharmacies had been done in advance.

Getting back in line behind her after using the restroom, Rip curled his left arm around the front of her, tugging her backpack against his chest, his fingers stroking her throat.

A wicked heat curled through her belly, pooling deep inside her, and the memory of last night flooded her mind. The way he'd held her. Caressed her. Tasted her. Gave her such intense pleasure. The only problem was it had all been one-sided. He told her how much he'd enjoyed it, making her writhe with want, hearing the sounds of her satisfaction, but it wasn't the same as them coming together as one.

He pressed his mouth to her ear. "You good?" Concern was heavy in his tone.

"Yeah," she said low. Her nerves had settled now that she understood this part of the process and knew what to expect. The next part, where they were off to the camp, would kick up fresh jitters.

Nothing she couldn't handle.

She was well trained. Not DEA agent or Special Forces

trained but ready, prepared for anything. She could get through this. Still, she was aware that Rip's protective instincts tended to kick into overdrive where she was concerned.

In front of her, the weird guy with the beard and ballcap stepped up to the pharmacist and handed over his prescription and ID.

"Not too late to back out," Rip whispered.

"As if." He needed to realize that her life wasn't more valuable than his. They could do this together, as a team.

"I figured as much. Just checking."

Her turn came. She followed the same procedure as the last eight times and then stepped to the side. Rip was the second to last to go up to the counter.

Those who had already turned in their prescriptions were already in the pickup line, paying with the cash Drexel had given them outside the store, and grabbing their white bag of pills.

"I'm going to go ahead of you," Rip said. "Use whatever time we've got to see if I can get Drexel to lower his guard a bit around me. If I can make inroads here, it'll be easier at the farm."

"Sure. I can buy you a minute or two by going to the bathroom. But I don't think it's going to be easy with Drexel."

He slid his arms around her shoulders, tugging her closer. "Speaking of not easy, things might get rough at the farm."

"I get it. I can do this." Security probably liked to have a good time with the women, trading sexual favors for pills, but she had Rip as an excuse. If she got cornered, a knee to the crotch would solve that problem. As for the countless other what-ifs, she'd take them one at a time.

He gave her a probing glance for a moment. "I know. You wouldn't have gotten this far if you couldn't." His tone was warm, and from the look in his eyes, she could tell he meant more than this, here and now, but also the academy and every tough thing she'd been through as a deputy. "I believe in you." He gave her a quick kiss on the lips. "Do you trust me?"

She would trust him with her secrets, with her life. With her heart. "Of course."

"No matter what I might have to do, no matter what twists or turns come...*trust me*."

"Always." But his words sent a jolt of nervousness rushing through her.

"Next!" the pharmacist called out, not bothering to use their names, seemingly anxious to give them their pills and get them—the dregs of society—out of their place of business.

Rip went up to the pickup counter, grabbed his white bag and headed for the exit.

Ashley turned to the woman with the humongous tote. "Go on ahead of me. I've got to use the bathroom." She started toward the restroom and glanced over her shoulder.

Rip was speaking to the security guard at the front door before he headed outside. He dropped his bag with the oxycodone into the larger bag that Drexel held open as he waited for them on the sidewalk.

Hurrying inside the bathroom, she took the opportunity to use the facilities and wash her hands. No telling how long until the next pharmacy or where. She left the restroom.

Only a couple of regular customers were in the store.

A tense-looking pharmacist waited for her. Ashley gave her the cash and took her bag with the oxy from the woman and headed down the aisle.

She was just about to reach the door and caught Rip's eye. His attention flickered between her and Drexel. The two were engrossed in a lively conversation, with the driver appearing more at ease with Rip.

Perhaps it had worked.

"Excuse me, miss." The security guard stepped forward, blocking the door. "I need to search your backpack."

Her heart fluttered. "What? Why?"

"I have reason to believe you stole something."

"There must be some mistake."

"Please take off your backpack and unzip the front compartment."

Stunned, she slipped off the straps and turned the backpack around to face the security guard. "I didn't take anything."

"I hear that all the time from you people."

She didn't take the comment as racist since the guard was Black and attributed it to her being in a group of addicts.

Across the street, a police cruiser pulled into the gas station and parked. Two officers got out and went into the convenience store.

The security guard unzipped the front compartment of her bag and peered inside.

"Satisfied?" she asked.

Frowning, he pulled out two bottles of perfume. "This is three hundred bucks."

Ashley stiffened, her legs turning watery, not understanding how it got in her bag. "I didn't put that in there." Her mind spun trying to make sense of it.

"Sure, you didn't." The guard grabbed her wrist. "I've got to call the cops."

"What?" She tried to jerk her arm away without getting physical. The two officers stepped out of the gas station, holding cups of coffee, and lingered as they spoke. "No. We can talk about this."

"You can talk all you want to the police," the guard said.

Drexel shouted something at Rip and pointed for him to go over to the drugstore.

Rip yanked the front door open.

But it was Drexel who asked from farther back, "What's the problem?"

"She stole something. I've got to call the cops. It's a class two misdemeanor."

Ashley glanced at Rip to see how to play this.

His expression was inscrutable, his blue-gray eyes going stormy, and her chest constricted.

Rip looked over his shoulder at Drexel. "My girl's a hard-core junkie, sorry," he said to him. "She does stuff like this sometimes. She isn't worth this kind of trouble."

A cold chill splashed down her spine, numbing her heart. Ashley shook her head, not believing this was happening.

"We've got to go." Drexel turned, facing the gas station, where the officers still hadn't gotten back into their vehicle. "I don't need any headaches on this run. We cut her loose. Get her pills and we're out of here." The driver made a bee-line for the van.

She was ready…prepared for anything. Except for Rip betraying her.

Her stomach felt as though it had dropped into the spin cycle of a washing machine, churning and flipping.

Why hadn't he pulled this stunt at the first pharmacy? Why now? Why wait all day until they got here?

All the way to Fort Collins.

They were in Fort Collins, where she had people that she knew, who could straighten things out and give her a ride. He'd been planning this the whole time.

Rip marched inside the store and snatched the white pharmacy bag from her fingers. She narrowed her eyes at him and gritted her teeth, too blindsided to speak, anger drumming in her veins.

"This isn't betrayal," he bit out, as if reading her mind. "It's protection. I won't play Russian roulette with your life. Call a friend and go home."

Then he turned his back and left her behind.

Chapter Twelve

The wounded look on Ash's face once she realized what he'd done had taken a slice out of his heart. Still haunted him. Those sultry brown eyes—that warmed him like a shot of whiskey when her heated gaze fell on him—had flared with shock and then narrowed to cold slits. But pain had washed over her expression.

Another pang wrenched through his chest. He didn't want her to think this reflected what he thought of her capabilities or was some sexist judgment on his part.

It was purely selfish.

If something happened to her, when he could've prevented it, he'd never forgive himself. Headed to the farm, he needed all his attention on only one thing. The mission. With no distractions.

Worrying about her rather than the task at hand would've split his focus and gotten them both killed.

Once they'd finished at the last pharmacy in Colorado Springs, they'd driven to a municipal airport east of the city and loaded onto a Cessna—based on the size he guessed a Caravan outfitted mainly for hauling cargo—where a grungy pilot had been waiting. They sat on benches rather than seats, and the aircraft took off.

The plane passed Devils Tower—a distinct, iconic butte

that loomed 867 feet above the trees—and began a descent to land. They were back in Wyoming. The far northeastern part of the state.

Rip stared at the roll-up door for loading cargo. It was the same kind used for skydiving.

The Cessna touched down on grassland with a bumpy landing and rolled to a stop.

Drexel got up and yanked on the wide door, getting it halfway before using both hands to finish rolling it up. "Come on. Everyone out." He hopped onto the ground and led the way to a parked van nearby.

Another man, who wore a skullcap beanie and glasses, was behind the wheel.

As they got off the plane, BBB elbowed Rip, shoving past him. He'd let it slide this one time. Causing a scene wasn't his goal, but he let that guy push him around and it would only end up being a bigger deal later.

Everyone climbed into the van and settled in for the ride. Ten minutes later they drove into a camp. Tents, makeshift shelters, a couple of decrepit school buses, and a fifth wheel camper and a large trailer both connected to trucks formed a horseshoe. This was the drug camp.

The van came to a stop, and they exited. Everyone began forming a line in front of a third guy, and he followed suit.

"Lumley, I'm going to see the boss," Drexel said to the current driver, holding up the bag from the day's haul.

Lumley nodded. Drexel headed for the fifth wheel camper.

The third guy was lean, rangy and not too tall, with scruff on his face. He stood handing out payment in pills. The line inched along steadily, everyone waiting their turn.

Rip scanned the area, searching for Lou-Ann. He wasn't

sure if she'd remember him. Plenty of bikers had crossed her path over the years.

Near a picnic table, he spotted her stirring a large pot of something situated over the fire. Her blond hair was in a choppy, angular bob. She'd put on some weight. No longer rail-thin, she had a little meat on her bones. He was tempted to head straight for her, but all the addicts were only interested in pills. So, he stayed in line to blend in.

BBB came up from behind him, elbowing him to the side, trying to cut the line in front of him. Rip was fed up with this guy and hooked BBB's leg with his foot, tripping him. BBB couldn't regain his balance. Momentum carried him forward and he face-planted into the dirt.

Not knowing when to back down, BBB jumped to his feet. "Who do you think you are?" he said, lunging for him.

Rip had his fist ready to punch the junkie in the face and ring his bell nicely.

But the one in charge of the line got between them. "No fighting. Or you're out of here." He turned to BBB and dumped one pill into his palm from a large container.

"Hey, where's the rest? I'm supposed to get three, Perry!"

"You fight, you get less. Next time keep the peace." Perry looked at Rip. "Same for you." He doled out one pill for him. "Go get something to eat." He gestured to the picnic table.

The others were in line in front of LA, getting bowls of soup and then grabbing things from the two cardboard boxes on the table. Rolls were in one and snacks in the other. People were walking away with protein bars and chips.

Rip increased his pace without trying to look overly eager. He couldn't have a real conversation with her while everyone else was hanging around nearby, but he at least wanted to give her a heads-up.

The door to the fifth wheel camper swung open.

Drexel hurried outside and ran to the firepit, where LA continued to serve soup. "Lumley," he called over the other one.

Another man appeared in the doorway of the camper. Curly hair. With his height and wide shoulders and the light creating a shadow behind him, he was a menacing figure. He lowered a respirator mask from his face and leaned against the jamb, watching.

That was no ordinary camper. They were doing something with drugs in there.

Rip approached the fire. His gaze met LA's and he held it, steady, confident.

Drexel pulled his gun and the addicts scattered like roaches, disappearing into the darkness.

Rip kept walking until the muzzle of the gun touched his chest.

"LA, do you know this dude?" Drexel asked. "He claims he was with you on some of your runs?"

Squinting, she stared at him and cocked her head to the side like she wasn't sure.

"We first met at Sturgis," Rip said quickly. "Benji—"

"Shut up!" Drexel moved the gun from his chest to his head. "She shouldn't need any reminders if she knows you."

Lumley drew a gun from his waistband at his back but kept it down at his side.

"Yeah, I know him." LA nodded. "Rip Lockwood. He's cool. My brother made the connect for him to do a couple of my runs."

With his name put out there, his exposure only grew. He couldn't catch a break. At this rate, he'd have to go deep underground for the rest of his life. Provided he survived the ranch.

Drexel lowered his weapon, put the safety on and returned it to his holster. "Your lucky day. You get to keep breathing. No hard feelings."

"None taken," Rip said.

Drexel and Lumley walked away.

The others kept a safe distance, giving Rip the opportunity he needed, but he didn't know how much time he'd have.

"What are you doing here?" LA asked in a whisper. "You're no druggie."

"So, you remember me."

She arched an eyebrow and looked him over from head to toe. "You're a hard man to forget, Rip. Explain. Why are you here?"

He grabbed a disposable bowl and went to the pot.

"I'd skip the soup if I were you." She glanced around. "They lace it with rat poison. They don't want the same druggies sticking around forever, giving the DEA a chance to turn one of them into a snitch. The steady regulars only last three to four months. Always plenty of addicts out there to take their place."

His stomach clenched. He set the bowl down. "Todd Burk is making a big play at home. Believe me, I want to see him hurt more than you do. I need to sever this pipeline of his, making him hemorrhage until he bleeds out." Rip grabbed a couple of protein bars from one of the boxes.

LA smirked, appearing downright devilish in the firelight. "Music to my ears. That SOB has it coming."

"I heard about your friend at Sturgis and what he did. I'm sorry. But she's just one in a long line of his victims." He thought about Angelo Russo. Todd's comeuppance was long overdue.

"Not sure how you're going to accomplish that goal."

"Maybe I'm a buyer, offer to pay for Todd's product at a

higher price because of the war going on at home." Even if the DEA wasn't interested in the bust, some law official in the county would be. Setting up a sting was high risk, but also high reward.

"Won't work." LA shook her head. "Not unless you've got more than seven hundred fifty thousand dollars on you right now."

"What?" he said in a harsh whisper.

"Buyers pay up front in advance of receiving their product. Todd has already forked over seven fifty."

Where did he get that kind of cash? His operation must be much bigger than anyone thought.

"I've already put a bug in the boss's ear." LA zipped her fleece jacket and pulled on the hood. "Todd claims this is his last shipment from us. I've heard he intends to set up his own drug camp close to home. That he's already intimidating doctors and pharmacists. His plan will hurt our business. The boss isn't too happy about it. So, he's taking steps to make him pay. Pay big." She pivoted and nodded to the camper. "They've cut his entire shipment of product with fentanyl."

It wasn't uncommon for dealers to grind down pills, add fentanyl and use a pill press to reshape the drugs, making them resemble real prescription drugs such as oxy, Xanax, Adderall and much more. The process was time-consuming and tedious. The worst part was that dealers weren't chemists. It only took two salt-sized grains of fentanyl to be lethal. Dealers did it to increase profits, stretch their supply and expand the number of addicts by juicing the potency of the other drugs.

"The boss is being generous with the fentanyl in this shipment." She warmed her hands by the fire. "It'll probably kill a quarter of Todd's customers. The rest won't get the same high as his regular product and will go looking elsewhere. Namely us. Those who die will bring him a ton of heat from the authorities. This is going to be a lose-lose for Todd."

Not to mention the unsuspecting people, many of them college students, who'd be getting far more than they bargained for. So many kids were going to die to make Todd suffer.

Rip kept the horror from surfacing on his face. "You must be talking about a lot of fentanyl."

"We sell quite a bit. Get it from the cartel."

"Mendez?"

LA shook her head. "Sandoval."

"There has to be another way for me to get my hands on that shipment." He had brainstormed about other ways to accomplish the goal in the wee hours this morning and all day in the van. "When is it supposed to go out?"

She shrugged. "Not sure. Maybe Tuesday or Wednesday."

"Tell me about your boss?"

"Farley." LA glanced at the fifth wheel camper, and his gaze followed her line of sight. No one was outside besides Perry, who was smoking a cigarette near the travel trailer. "He's Canadian. Ex-military. The guys who fly the planes used to work with him."

That was his way in. "Can you introduce me? Tell him I'm interested in working as security for him. Making deliveries, runs, anything that pays well."

"Tricky," she said, raising her eyebrows. "The boss doesn't take a shine to everyone. Especially not strangers. I had to prove myself doing runs for a year before he moved me over to distro."

"How does the distribution work?"

"Varies. Local drops made from wherever the ranch is located at the time, we do by van. Farther out, we use one of the planes. Drop the load with a beacon. Buyer tracks it via GPS."

"I need to meet him."

"I don't know." Glancing around, she stuffed her hands in her pockets. "Get yourself situated in one of the buses. Claim a cot. I'll see what I can do."

"Hey, all I need is an intro. No need to vouch for me any further. I'll do the rest."

Chapter Thirteen

Ashley sat in the passenger's seat of the sedan. They'd passed the sign that read Welcome to Laramie, Home of Southeastern Wyoming University.

The college was the biggest draw to the town. She'd gotten her bachelor's degree in criminal justice while working as a deputy, considering it one more tool in her arsenal in the fight against Burk. When all along, her greatest tool was also her greatest weakness.

Rip Lockwood.

Her chest was tight, achy. Her heart swollen and bruised over Rip's deception. He wanted to sugarcoat his betrayal as protection, but it stung, nonetheless. Because it meant he didn't trust her enough to be honest.

She couldn't be mad at him. Not while he was out there risking his life to take down Todd Burk. If only he'd let her help, be his partner in this. She was the one who'd brought him in on the plan after all. Besides, this burden was both theirs to bear.

They passed the smaller, unassuming sign marking the border of Bison Ridge.

Ten minutes later, Jasper pulled up to her house and parked beside her truck.

Ashley donned her emotional armor and girded her feelings. "Thanks again. For the ride back to Wyoming. For coming down to the police station to clear everything up when Welliver wasn't available."

"It's really no problem." He flashed a kind smile. "If this is what it takes to get to see you again, then I don't mind. I wish you'd called sooner. But I still can't believe this Lockwood fellow. What was he thinking ditching you like that?"

One thing for her to question Rip, but Jasper wasn't allowed. "He was doing what he thought was right. To keep me safe."

"Doesn't he realize he isn't authorized to act on his own?"

Technically, neither was Ashley, but she didn't know how much Welliver had shared. "He's a Marine. Special Forces."

"Used to be a Marine. That was what, seven or eight years ago?"

Irritation flared inside her. "Once a Marine, always a Marine. Whatever the situation, he'll be able to handle it and when the time comes, he'll contact the proper authorities."

"Are you sure he's not going to go vigilante and ruin any chance of you building a case?"

If Rip were going to turn into a vigilante and take matters into his own hands, regardless of the law, Todd would already be dead and buried in an unmarked grave where no one would ever find his rotting corpse. "I'm sure. Thanks again." She clutched the handle and opened the door.

"Mind if I come in to use the bathroom?"

She tensed, but how could she refuse. He'd spent too much time at the police station straightening things out and then an hour on the road to bring her home. "Of course."

Hurrying up to the front door, she racked her brain on how to get rid of Jasper without being rude. This wasn't her forte. In fact, she'd never been the one doing the rejecting before.

She unlocked the door and let him inside. "The bathroom is right through there," she said, pointing down the hall.

Setting the backpack on the floor, she couldn't wait to wash her face, shower, and try to get some sleep. Though she doubted she'd be able to rest, not knowing what was happening to Rip.

The toilet flushed and the faucet ran in the two-piece bathroom. She had her spiel ready. It would be short and sweet and would hopefully work without ruffling any feathers.

A moment later, Jasper came toward her with a sweet smile.

Yawning like she was exhausted, she stretched. "Wow, it's so late."

"After that long drive, I'm parched. Can I have something to drink?"

Who would say no to water? Besides a rude ingrate. "Certainly." She led the way.

In her kitchen, she grabbed a glass from the cupboard and went to the sink, wishing she had bottled water that he could take to go.

"Now, this is the kind of drink I'm talking about," Jasper said, excitement in his voice.

She glanced over her shoulder as she filled the glass with water.

Jasper was holding her extravagant, decorative three-thousand-dollar bottle of tequila. "Clase Azul. Ashley, I had no idea you had such fine taste. The sheriff's department must be paying better than I thought."

"It was a gift. Birthday present from someone special." From someone who thought she was special.

"I've got to try a shot of this. It might be my only chance.

Do you mind?" Jasper beamed, his green eyes bright, his face warm, his blond hair perfectly coiffed.

He reminded her of the frat boys at SWU she'd hoped would ask her out and call her back for a second date, eons ago. It would've only resulted in what she'd found with Jasper.

Nothing of consequence.

She was done with boys who didn't excite her, who didn't know how to pleasure a woman in bed, whose loyalty ran surface-deep, who wouldn't put her above everything else.

Who were so consumed with taking that they didn't understand the true meaning of sacrifice.

"I do mind, actually." It wasn't about sharing. If the tequila hadn't been a gift from Rip, she would've gladly given the entire bottle to Jasper, regardless of the cost, simply to get rid of him. "If you drink, you'll use it as an excuse not to drive. I'd feel bad about asking you to leave and get behind the wheel with alcohol in your system. Then things would get awkward between us because I don't want you to stay."

His perfect smile fell. "But why? I don't understand. Did I do something wrong? I thought we were starting a good thing. Didn't you have fun last time?"

Sex was supposed to be fun and passionate and meaningful. With Jasper, she'd only checked the no-longer-a-virgin box. That was all.

What she'd shared with Rip had been in a different universe. Undoubtedly one-sided in her favor, he'd done things to her that she'd only read about, stopping short of letting him go to home base or letting her give him any of the sweet pleasure he'd spoon-fed her body, but she'd been as affectionate as he'd allow.

Connection—that was what she had with Rip.

Ashley dug out one of the plastic cups she used for her

protein shakes and transferred the water. "You're a nice guy, Jasper, truly you are. It's just… I'm seeing someone else."

Surprise flashed across his face. "So soon? Already? I didn't realize we were even over."

"We never really started." Two dinners, one night of humdrum sex, and no further communication. "Did we?"

"Welliver told me not to get my hopes up, but I was certain I had a shot at something more with you."

"Why would you think that when I haven't returned any of your calls?"

"I guess ghosting a person should send a clear message, but I kept coming up with explanations for it because it's never happened to me before."

Welcome to my world. "I'm sorry if I hurt your feelings. I should've had the decency to explain. I know better than most how it feels. You didn't deserve to be treated that way."

"No, it's okay," he said, giving her a crestfallen look. "Who's the lucky guy? Please don't tell me it's that old, washed-up Marine turned biker?"

"He's far from old or washed-up." *More like mature, high-skilled, could-probably-kill-you-with-a-pencil Marine.* "And yes, it is." No hesitation. No doubt. No shame. "I'm with Rip Lockwood."

What exactly that would mean in the days to come, she wasn't quite sure, but for now her heart wasn't interested in anyone else.

LYING ON TOP of his sleeping bag that he'd placed on a cot in the bus, Rip stared at the ceiling. His mind churned; his body was restless.

He hoped LA could work out the introduction that he needed. With close to a million dollars on the line, not to mention countless lives, if he could sabotage that shipment laced with fentanyl, it would be a deadly blow to Todd. A move like that would be knocking down the perfectly positioned domino and the rest would fall, an unstoppable chain reaction until Todd Burk was dead or in jail.

The floor of the bus creaked. Feet shuffling slowly toward him.

Rip spotted BBB trying to creep up on him. Sighing inwardly, he lowered his eyelids to appear asleep while watching this dude, who thought he was being stealthy.

BBB had something sharp in his hand, a knife or homemade shank. Whatever it was, it could kill him. Hunched low, BBB slunk closer, easing past his feet, up beyond his legs, and raised the weapon in his hand, poised to thrust it in his chest.

Rip swung his legs around, knocking the man to the side, and jumped up as he grabbed BBB. He wrenched BBB's wrist hard, enough to sprain but stopping short of breaking it, snatched the shiv from him and pressed the sharp tip of the weapon to his jugular.

"I'm the last guy in the world that you want to mess with," Rip ground out. "Come near me again and I'm going to flip your off switch. Got it?"

Eyes wide with terror, BBB nodded. "Y-y-yeah. Got it." He scurried away and scrambled off the bus.

LA passed the scaredy-cat on her way in.

Rip hid the improvised weapon in his pants.

"You're up," she said. "Farley will meet you, but you have one chance to make an impression. Don't blow it."

He took off his windbreaker and the flannel shirt he wore over the Henley. "I won't."

As he left the bus following LA, the cold air nipped him. A temporary discomfort he ignored. He spotted Perry carrying a batch of drugs from the camper to a shipping container that was eight feet by eight feet. He held parcels of pills in various colors, roughly the size of bricks, maybe sixty or seventy of them, bundled together in plastic wrap. It looked like a small bale of pharmaceuticals. Perry set it on the ground and unlocked the storage container.

The man with wild, curly hair waited in front of the travel trailer. To his left beside him, Lumley and Drexel were chatting and smoking cigarettes. In the golden lights under the awning of the trailer, Rip saw that Farley's hair was red, his eyes a watery blue, his face weathered with a long, jagged scar running across his left cheek.

Farley stood, peeling an apple with a switchblade, but Rip didn't miss the tactical knife holstered on his hip. It was a Karambit. The small knife had a razor-sharp double-edged blade that curved inwardly, nearly semicircular, ending in a vicious point. In action, with the large round steel finger holes on the handle, a Karambit reminded Rip of a tiger's claw. A nasty piece of business if the one wielding it knew how to use it properly.

The only other person Rip had encountered carrying one had been Special Operations like him.

"So, tell me, why should I give a junkie, who'll do anything for his next fix, two minutes of my time?" Farley asked.

Two was better than one. "For starters, I'm not a junkie."

Farley cast a furtive glance at LA, who started fidgeting.

Drexel pulled his weapon again and pointed it at Rip. The kid was too eager to draw. The skullcap-wearing Lumley wasn't sure what to do and grabbed his handgun as an afterthought.

Farley raised a palm, giving them the sign to hold, but Lumley was the only one to lower his weapon. "Let the man explain what he's doing here if not working for pills."

"My girl is a junkie," Rip said. "I'm here because I need serious work with serious pay."

"Oh, really." Farley slid a slice of apple into his mouth. "How do you feel about serious risk?"

"Wouldn't be here if I couldn't handle it?"

"Are you a cop?"

Tipping his head to the side, Rip pulled up his shirtsleeves, revealing the tats that told his story from motorcycle club to Marine Corps. "Do I look like a cop?"

Farley narrowed his eyes. "I don't like smart mouths."

With his 9mm still raised, Drexel took a step toward Rip.

"He's the Prez of the Iron Warriors," Lou-Ann said. "He ain't no cop."

Gritting his teeth, Rip wished she'd let him handle it from here.

"If you're the president of the Iron Warriors, why aren't you working with Todd Burk?" Farley asked. "Doesn't he have to kick back a part of his cut to the club?"

"We didn't see eye to eye on the percentage points. Long story short, Todd formed a new MC. The Hellhounds. Now, we're at war. I'm looking to stick it to him any way I can. Requires the right sort of friends and resources."

Farley stroked his jaw as he scrutinized Rip, especially his tattoos. "It's rare, but not unheard of for things to go wrong during deliveries. I happen to know that Burk is indebted to the cartel. If he's not able to make a profit from his impending shipment, it would create trouble for him. The lethal kind. But I don't like blowback on my business."

"You mean, you don't like to get your hands dirty," Rip said.

The corner of Farley's mouth hitched up in a grin. "That's what middlemen are for. Let's say I hired you to handle Burk's next shipment. Free of charge to me, as a test. If his product happens to go missing, you take all the heat and deal with Todd Burk, so I never have to again. Dead men can't cause waves."

"What happens to the product?" Rip asked, though he already intended to turn it over to the DEA.

"Who's to say?" Farley shrugged. "If it got lost, finders keepers. But I'd want a taste of the profits."

"Ten percent."

"Forty. It's not as if you paid for it, and I remain your dealer in perpetuity."

Rip gave it a minute, pretending to weigh his options.

Clearly, Farley was a gambler. He was betting and betting big that Rip would eliminate Todd Burk for him, sell the tainted drugs, kicking back a whopping forty percent of the profits while taking the heat from the authorities once people started dying from the spiked drugs.

"You've got a deal." Rip offered his hand to shake on it.

Farley's half grin spread into a smile. "Not so fast. How do I know you're capable of *dealing* with Burk?"

Rip moved fast. He snapped his hand up, grabbing the body of Drexel's gun, and shoved the muzzle sideways to stay out of the line of any accidental discharge. Then he twisted the gun a half turn counterclockwise, nearly breaking Drexel's wrist. The gun fell to the ground. As Drexel howled in pain and clutched his wrist, Rip kicked the gun to the side into the darkness.

Keeping a lightning pace, he turned on Lumley. Skullcap was fumbling to draw his pistol. Once he pulled it free from his waistband, Rip snatched it. Stepping back, rather than aim it at anyone, he disassembled it. Removed the magazine. Ejected the bullet in the chamber. Pressed the two buttons on the side and slipped off the slide. Popped the spring free. Pushed out the barrel.

Eighteen seconds.

He held out the pieces for Lumley to take.

"A bit of a showoff, but I like you." Farley chuckled. "Were you MARSOC?" he asked, gesturing to Rip's tattoo of the Marine Special Operator insignia.

"Yeah. From the Karambit, I'd take it you were Canadian JTF," he said, using the acronym for the Joint Task Force.

"You'd guess correct." Farley's gaze dropped to his ankle. "You're also packing."

Rip tugged up the leg of his jeans, exposing the gun in his ankle holster. "What can I say? You've got shoddy security."

Drexel glared at him.

"Well, good help is expensive." Farley held out his palm and waited.

Reluctantly, Rip pulled out his gun and handed it over to him.

"SIG P365." Farley pulled back the slide, checking to see if a bullet was in the chamber. There was. "Nice weapon." He aimed it right between Rip's eyes. "I only do this kind of dirty business of backstabbing and double-dealing with people I can trust. Can I trust you, Rip Lockwood?"

No honor among thieves. Farley couldn't trust Rip any more than Rip could trust this drug dealer who had neglected to mention the entire shipment was laced with fentanyl.

"No. If I said yes, you'd know I was lying. What you can trust is that I'll take care of Todd Burk. He won't be your problem anymore."

Farley narrowed his eyes again. Then he cracked a smile. "As I said, I like you." He emptied Rip's magazine of bullets and handed it back empty. "Take a picture of Burk for me when you tell him his shipment got lost. I want to see the look on that weasel's face."

"I'll see what I can do."

This time they shook on it.

Chapter Fourteen

Dressed in civilian clothes, with her badge and her service weapon clipped on her belt, Ashley walked into the sheriff's department to let Clark know she was still breathing and to get an update on everything.

She kept her Stetson on, not intending to stay too long. Nodding hello to the deputy stationed at the front desk, she walked to the half door at the end of the counter and waited to be buzzed in.

The door clicked open. As she walked in, she glanced at the sheriff's office. He was inside talking to a striking, petite blonde.

Detective Hannah Delaney.

Her picture had been splashed all over the *Laramie Gazette* in recent months. She'd been put through the wringer. No law enforcement officer had gone through more hell than her, and Ashley did not envy the woman. However, Hannah had managed to catch the University Killer after nearly being his last victim, and gotten engaged to her partner on the case.

All is well that ends well. Ashley's grandmother used to say that.

Mitch flew out of his chair from behind his desk in the bullpen and hurried over to her.

"Where's the fire, Cody?" she asked, brightly.

Staring at her, he searched her face. "You haven't heard," he said in a whisper.

"Heard what?"

He took her by the arm, hauled her to the break room the size of a closet, stopped in front of the coffee maker and shut the door.

Drama was the last thing she needed this morning. "This is very cloak-and-dagger. What's up?" Then she caught the worry in Mitch's eyes.

"LPD released Todd Burk."

An icy wave of fear flooded every cell in her body. Fear for Rip. "No, no, they can't let him go." What if the Sons of Chaos reached out to him about everything that had happened in Happy Jack's? Not if. But when. Had they already called him? If so, would he think of contacting his supplier? Would he be able to? "I thought they were going to hold him for at least seventy-two hours."

"Detective Delaney had no choice but to cut him loose."

"But why? I don't understand."

With a sigh, Mitch put his hands on his hips. "The knife used to kill Shane Yates was the same murder weapon used to slit the throat of the pharmacist."

"Okay? What does that have to do with why they let him go?"

"We got prints off the knife. They didn't belong to Todd Burk."

"When have a set of prints at a crime scene ever matched his? It's probably some Hellhound who we need to interrogate because the odds are extremely high that Todd ordered the murder."

"You're not listening to me." Mitch clutched her shoulders as if to steady her, and dread crawled up her spine.

"We got a match on the prints. They belong to your biker boyfriend. Rip Lockwood."

Shock rocketed through her. What the hell?

She jerked free of his grip. "It's not Rip. He didn't kill anyone." Her mind whirled a second before focusing. "His place was burglarized Friday night. The knife must've been stolen."

Mitch looked anxiously uncomfortable. "You didn't list anything as missing."

"I meant to," she said quickly, without thinking. "It took him time to go through his things. He mentioned the knife was missing. But I didn't have a chance to report it because I had to go dark on something for the DEA." She grew lightheaded from the lie and the room started spinning. She hoped she didn't sound as suspicious as she thought she did.

Mitch frowned and crossed his arms. "What kind of knife was it?"

Swearing inside her head, she spun on her heel away from him. She pictured Rip. Sometimes he wore his Glock in a shoulder holster. Sometimes on his hip. She didn't know about the ankle holster. But he usually had a fixed blade. "KA-BAR." She opened the door.

Mitch slammed it closed. "Did he report it missing?"

"Let me open the door."

"If you march into the sheriff's office looking and sounding like you do right now, if you go in there and lie or try to protect Lockwood, you will lose your badge. Maybe not today, but when this all shakes out and the truth comes to light—"

"The facts, the evidence will prove without a shadow of doubt that Rip is innocent."

"Is he worth what you're about to do?"

"Yes." She tried to open the door again.

He leaned on it with his full weight, shutting it. "I'm your friend. Just walk back out the front door instead. Get in your car. Drive off. Calm down. Think it through. If what you're saying is true, then he doesn't need you to put up a defense for him in front of your boss. Let his lawyer do it for him."

"Move."

"Think it through, Russo."

"He didn't do this! If Rip was a cold-blooded killer, he would've taken care of Burk years ago."

"Right now, you need to be a deputy. Not his girlfriend."

Stepping away from the door, she took a deep breath. "You're right."

"I am?" Mitch cleared his throat. "I mean, of course I am. I just can't believe you're actually listening to me."

She needed to think clearly. Above all, she needed to be honest. Lying wouldn't help him.

"Did he really mention the knife was missing?"

She shook her head. "He hasn't had a chance to clean up his place, much less go through everything. But he wasn't wearing it when I was called over about gunshots reported. And I didn't see the knife on him the next day either. The three Hellhounds who broke in must have taken it from his trailer."

"Okay." Mitch nodded. "Just tell him to get a lawyer and turn himself in."

"I would...if I could."

"What is that supposed to mean?"

Her chest tightened with worry for Rip. "I need to update the sheriff on what I've been doing."

"And it concerns Lockwood?"

"It does." She'd dragged him into her one-woman operation to cut off Todd's drug supply and now he was alone, exposed. Vulnerable.

Because of her.

Lowering his head, Mitch sighed even louder this time. "Russo, what kind of hole have you dug for yourself?" Her friend looked at her with disappointment in his eyes.

"A big one." She held his gaze. "Please, get out of the way."

Mitch stepped aside.

She shuffled past him in the small space, opened the door and marched to the sheriff's office. Glancing across the hall, she looked at the empty chief deputy's office. She wished Holden Powell had been on duty today. Her brother, Angelo, had been Holden's best friend in high school. He'd have her back in this and would understand the lengths she had to go to in order to get Todd Burk. Knocking, she met her boss's gaze.

Sheriff Clark waved her in. "Deputy Russo. I'm happy to see you alive and well. This is Detective Hannah Delaney."

Ashley shook Delaney's hand while the detective remained seated. "Pleasure to meet you, ma'am. I admire your work and sympathize with everything you've been through this past year."

"Sometimes the job throws you into the meat grinder. If you're lucky, you come out in one piece, but never quite the same."

"I'm sure you've got some dark stories to tell."

The detective flashed a grim smile. "You have no idea."

"Detective Delaney, if that was all," Sheriff Clark said, standing, "I need to get an update from my deputy about a case she's working on."

"It would be best if she stayed." Ashley glanced between them as the sheriff's eyebrows pinched in curiosity. "What I have to tell you might have some bearing on her case."

"The Shane Yates murder?" Delaney asked.

"Yes."

"Well, go ahead." The sheriff gestured for her to speak.

For a split second, she debated how honest to be, but deep down she knew she had to tell him everything. "On Saturday, I left on a mission that was DEA-related."

"Yes." Clark nodded. "I'm aware."

Get on with it. Spit it out. "I misled you to believe that the DEA was sending me in with one of their agents. But they didn't feel the case warranted taking up their resources. They only want to go after big fish. Agent Welliver provided me with actionable intelligence, helped me strategize and then encouraged me to recruit Rip Lockwood as an asset and to have him assist me as my partner undercover, which is what I did."

Clark reared back, a stony expression washing over his features. His gaze flicked over her shoulder, behind her, to the hall. "Deputy Cody, unless you have a good reason to lurk outside my office, I suggest you return to your desk and get to work."

Ashley didn't bother to turn around; she could hear the shuffle of Mitch's footsteps hurrying off.

"Continue," Clark said, folding his arms across his chest.

Ashley clasped her wrist behind her back, standing formally at ease. "We went to Bitterroot Gulch on Saturday. Got information from the Sons of Chaos regarding Todd Burk's drug operation and then stayed the night in Misty Creek. I know that Shane Yates was killed that night between seven thirty and ten."

"How do you know that if you were out of town?" Detective Delaney asked.

"Because Bobby Quill from the Iron Warriors called Rip. I listened to the call on speakerphone. They all wanted to get information from Yates about the Hellhounds' drug operation. Yates responded to a text at seven thirty agreeing to meet them at their old clubhouse at nine. When he didn't show up, JD drove by his house. He saw the crime scene, you—" she nodded to the detective "—and a body bag. I also know that Rip's prints were found on the murder weapon."

The sheriff and Delaney exchanged a furtive glance.

"Explain," he said.

"I can't tell you how I know that, but I know for a fact that Rip didn't kill Shane Yates because he was with me that night. I can't speak to his whereabouts for the Fuller murder, but if the same weapon was used then it was the same person who committed both murders."

Clark glanced across at the bullpen through the window and shook his head, his gaze no doubt locked on Mitch. "What time did you leave town together on Saturday to go up to Bitterroot Gulch?" He opened his pad and grabbed a pen.

"We left separately, sir. But it's a three-and-a-half-hour drive to Bitterroot from here. He met me at Happy Jack's Roadhouse a few minutes after nine. We didn't stay long together inside. Maybe twenty minutes. We hung around the parking lot for another ten, waiting for Stryker, the president of the Sons. He gave us critical information that Rip is acting on now. Then we left and we were followed and shot at by three Sons."

"Can you prove Lockwood was with you in Bitterroot around nine last night?" Delaney asked.

"There were cameras outside of the roadhouse, which would have captured our arrival and departure." As well as their make-out session in the parking lot. "Also, I noticed a traffic camera at the main intersection less than a quarter mile on the only road that leads to Happy Jack's. We passed it separately on the way in and together on the way out. The motel we got a room at in Misty Creek also had surveillance cameras in the office. He was captured on it. I'm certain of it."

"Deputy Russo, did you and Lockwood share a room?" the detective asked.

Ashley stiffened. "The surveillance footage should be sufficient evidence to clear Lockwood of Shane Yates's murder. I don't see what bearing our accommodations would have on the case."

"You don't see, or you don't want to see?" Detective Delaney asked.

Ashley looked at the sheriff.

"Under normal circumstances," he said with a heavy breath, "I do my best to turn a blind eye to your association with Rip Lockwood because quite frankly I'd rather not acknowledge it. But since the nature of your relationship has significant bearing not only on a murder case but also a DEA-related operation, loosely related might I add and in a dangerous manner that I am not comfortable with, we need you to answer the question."

"We shared a room," Ashley admitted.

Detective Delaney crossed her legs. "Are the two of you involved?"

"It's complicated."

"I'll make it simple," the detective said. "Yes or no?"

"Yes. But as I've stated, there's proof that he was in Bitterroot at nine p.m. and could not be the person who murdered Yates. It is my belief that three Hellhounds broke into Rip's trailer on Friday to find something with his prints that they could use as a murder weapon. He injured one of them. A big, tall guy with a limp. Deputy Cody has the pictures I took of the three who I think are responsible for the break-in. Todd Burk is setting up Rip. I thought he wanted to kill him, but apparently framing him for murder is just as good to get him out of the way."

"To what end?" the sheriff asked.

"To have it all, with no opposition. Rip Lockwood is the one person that Todd Burk fears." Rightfully so because Rip had him in the crosshairs now. "The DEA-related operation was leading us to Burk's supplier at the ranch, a drug camp somewhere. But with Burk no longer being held in custody, Rip's life is in grave danger."

Detective Delaney straightened. "Wait a minute. Did you say a drug camp?"

"Yes."

"Before Yates was killed, he called me. Scared. Left a message that he had information about what Burk was planning next. Something about a *camp*, but it didn't make any sense at the time and I never got a chance to clarify."

"The drug camp that Stryker described was where they collected all the pills they received after a run. I rode undercover with Rip on part of one yesterday. They took us to a pain clinic. A doctor was paid to write various prescriptions for a bunch of addicts. For oxycodone, Percocet, Adderall. But mainly oxy. There was a man, Drexel, he was the driver and security, took us around to different pharmacies from Casper to Colorado Springs, though I only made it to Fort Collins, where we filled the prescriptions. Some kind of deal had been worked out in advance with the pharmacists. All smaller drugstores. Family-owned. Like Fuller's. Most just hurriedly went through the motions of filling the scrips to get us out of there, but a few looked as though they had been intimidated and coerced into compliance. What if Burk is trying to set up a similar operation here? And what if Mr. Fuller didn't want to cooperate and Burk found out that Yates was an informant, so he had them killed?"

Delaney was probably a fantastic poker player. Her expression didn't give away anything she was thinking.

"Ashley, it's not like you to color outside the lines," the sheriff said. "I want to know how long you've been misleading me about your work with the DEA, how deep it goes, and the specifics of everything you've done off-book. Anything you tell me will be fact-checked with Agent Welliver." Clark gave her a stern look of warning, but Ashley guessed that Welliver wouldn't return his calls until after he learned the results of the mission that Rip was still on. "Then I have to begin a formal investigation into your association, *relationship*, with Ripton Lockwood to see if it may have tainted any prior cases. Close the door and take a seat."

WEARING HER STETSON, Ashley walked out of the sheriff's office without her badge or service weapon. Suspended pending the results of the department's investigation.

White noise that had started in her ears as the sheriff began asking probing, invasive questions continued along with her out-of-body experience. It seemed she was floating to her truck rather than walking.

Sheriff Clark had doubted every word she said, she saw it in his eyes, but at least Detective Delaney had wasted no time starting the process to track down the surveillance footage in Bitterroot and Misty Creek. The Laramie Police Department would probably have it by lunch, certainly no later than the end of day, and Rip would be cleared of Shane Yates's murder and hopefully that of the pharmacist as well.

The only other good thing to come out of the interrogation was the three of them agreed Todd Burk was mostly likely behind this.

She climbed into her truck and simply sat there with no idea what to do next.

The loss of her badge didn't bother her. She only became a deputy for one reason and one reason only. To see Todd Burk behind bars. As long as justice was served, the results of the investigation didn't matter.

But she had no way to contact Rip and warn him that Todd was no longer being held in custody.

A buzzing sounded in her truck. She checked her cell phone to see if she had it on silent. But it wasn't coming from her cell.

The sound was coming from the glove box. She opened the compartment and tracked the buzzing to Rip's burner phone.

Ashley grabbed it. Instead of a phone number on the screen there was a six-digit code. She opened the flip phone and put it to her ear.

On the other end a bunch of men were cheering, whooping and hollering.

"All right, all right! Settle down. I told you I would be back lickety-split!" Todd Burk's voice.

Her pulse spiked. She stared at the phone, piecing together what she was hearing, how she was hearing it. Rip must have planted a listening device in the clubhouse.

She put the burner on speaker, took out her own phone and started recording.

"The cops can't hold me," Todd said. "No matter how hard they try."

"Teflon! Teflon! Teflon!" the Hellhounds cheered.

"Okay, let's get to business, boys," Todd said.

"Shane Yates is dead," a less than enthusiastic Hellhound said. "Murdered. You've got to call a vote for a member to meet Mr. Mayhem."

A vote to murder a brother in the club.

"Yates was a rat. He's been snitching." Todd went on to say foul things about Detective Delaney, calling her disgusting names. "He's not dead because of me. This is on her."

"We sided with you because you promised you'd be different." The same dissenter. "Rip didn't call a vote on you selling drugs, so we walked. On principle. But you're the same."

"I'm nothing like Lockwood!"

"You don't want to lead. You want to rule. That's not what we signed up for." Chairs scraped wood. She couldn't make out how many. Maybe three. Possibly four. "No member meets Mr. Mayhem without a vote. Snitch or not. We're out."

A door slammed.

"It's all right, boys. Let those weak punks walk. We don't need them anymore anyway. They served their purpose, sided with us in the vote that allowed us to form our own club. Now we can finish this with Rip. No vote necessary."

"He left town on Saturday," a different guy said. "Before Yates met Mr. Mayhem. He might have an alibi. Rip is one lucky dude. Maybe he can be persuaded to stay out of our way. He used to be our brother."

"Past tense," Todd said. "He's not a Hellhound. If he's not stopped, he'll bring down the empire we're building."

An empire of drugs and dirty money and death. Todd and his Hellhounds weren't building anything. Only destroying.

"Are you sure this is the best way to handle things?" a new voice questioned. "Letting Rip take the fall for the pharmacist and Shane? I mean, what if it doesn't work? Like Lyle said, he wasn't even in town when you had a brother killed. This might not stick to him and then he'll come for all of us. I don't know about you, but I don't want to be on his 'to-do things' list. Rip can be a scary, deadly dude when provoked. First you go after his deputy and now you frame him for murder. I'd call that provocation."

"Not me, *we*, brother. We're in this together," Todd said.

"I didn't vote for any of this!" a new dissenter called out. "I was in favor of expanding and starting our own drug camp. Not starting a war with Rip Lockwood."

"Quiet! Yeah, I wanted the cops to deal with Rip," Todd said. "So, I could see that self-righteous do-gooder rotting behind bars while I took everything that was his. Including his pretty deputy. But fortune shines on us, brothers. I heard from the Sons of Chaos. Guess who was in Happy Jack's with a cop the other night trying to get info on our drug supplier?"

"Rip wouldn't go in there with a cop, regardless of whether she's his old lady," someone called out.

"But he did! He called her his old lady, and they described her to me. Hot little number with light brown skin and long brown hair. Apparently, they were all over each other. We haven't seen Rip with a woman besides her. Definitely Deputy Russo. She must've lied to me the other day when I asked her about the two of them. Makes no difference now. I reached out to our supplier this morning. Just so happens Rip is with him. I told Farley that Rip is working with a cop. We don't have to worry about Lockwood anymore because his luck runs out today and I'm going to be there to watch. I've got the coordinates. Less than hour's drive north of town. All we have to do is go there and wait. He'll be delivered along with our drugs. Dead on arrival."

Chapter Fifteen

"Change of plans," LA said. "They upped the timeline for some reason. They're delivering Burk's shipment today. Be ready."

Change wasn't always good.

Rip finished eating the protein bar he'd purchased himself before arriving and washed it down with water. No need to take unnecessary chances consuming anything from the camp when all the food might be poisoned.

Putting on his windbreaker, he jammed the homemade shank into his pocket. He grabbed his backpack and got off the bus.

Perry went to the shipping container, unlocked it and opened the doors wide.

In the light of day, Rip had a full view of the contents. The quantity of drugs inside was staggering. A mother lode the DEA would salivate to get their hands on and be eager to take credit for the seizure of. This would make up for any wrongdoing on Ash's part or at least be taken into consideration if she were censured for breaking the rules.

Perry took a bundle of drugs out of the shipping container and locked it. The shipment had lashing straps crisscrossed and cinched tight around it. Hooked at the top was a small red device—the beacon.

"Load up!" Drexel called out.

The addicts crowded around the picnic table stopped eating and smoking. They gathered their belongings and began piling into the van.

Farley stepped out of the travel trailer, wearing sunglasses. His wild red hair was a hot mess in the wind. Taking a minute, he stretched his neck, arms, back, rolled his shoulders. Rip had done likewise before the sun was up. Farley slipped on a utility field jacket over his holstered gun and Karambit blade and started toward a second vehicle. "Rip!" He waved him over.

"Hey, what's up?" Rip asked, unease trickling through his veins.

"We're taking a separate plane to make the delivery," Farley said as Perry loaded the shipment into the van.

Rip stared at Farley. "You're coming?"

"I want to see to it that things go smoothly." Farley clasped his shoulder. "I need the warm fuzzy that you get to Laramie with the drugs. From there, it's up to you to deal with Burk."

Rip nodded, but his senses went on high alert. Farley preferred the middlemen to handle this sort of thing, so what was the real reason he was tagging along?

He suspected the answer meant trouble, but he played it cool. Got in the back of the van without protest or hesitation. Farley sat beside him.

Lumley drove with Perry riding in the passenger's seat.

A plane waited, engine running, on a landing strip that stretched off into vast, barren terrain punctuated by small piles of rocks. In the distance, trees, a range of mountains and Devils Tower were visible.

They parked and climbed out.

Lumley opened the back van door so Perry could grab

the shipment of drugs, but when he closed the door, he was holding a tire iron.

A blade or blunt instrument made the best weapon on an aircraft if you wanted to land in one piece. They boarded the plane without uttering a word. The aircraft was slightly smaller than the Cessna. A twin otter that had the same type of roll-up door.

Farley took a seat in the cockpit next to the pilot. With Lumley to his left, holding the tire iron, Perry to his right, Rip, on guard, buckled in.

The plane took off.

The two henchmen were antsy, gazes bouncing from the windows to the pilot, to Rip, to Farley.

None of this boded well for Rip. The lackeys didn't concern him. Farley was the unknown variable with his Special Operations background that made him wary.

They'd been in the air maybe forty-five minutes, definitely less than an hour, when Farley got up from his seat and shoved out of the cockpit. "We're here."

A shot of adrenaline that always came before a fight sparked through Rip's synapses. Muscles coiled. Ready for the inevitable moment to arrive.

Perry undid his lap belt. He went to the roll-up door, yanked it open, letting in a surge of cold air, activated the beacon on the shipment and tossed it out of the plane.

Hovering near the cockpit, Farley removed his sunglasses and slipped them into his top jacket pocket. "I got a call from Todd Burk this morning. He was released from police custody and couldn't wait to tell me that your supposed junkie of a girlfriend is a deputy with the sheriff's department. He also had a lot of colorful things to say about you. Like the only thing you'd do with a shipment of drugs is turn it over to the authorities."

"This is a war," Rip said, "and Todd's a liar. You can't trust anything he says."

"That may be true. In fact, it is true. Todd's a stinking liar for sure." Farley grinned, the facial expression tugging the skin around the gnarly scar on his cheek, making him look even more menacing. "But I'm going to take that weasel's word over yours on this because I know that he's a no-good criminal. Can't say the same about you." He pounded a fist on the wall of the cockpit. "Circle back around," he said to the pilot. Then he looked at Rip. "Time to jump."

"No parachute?" Rip asked with a wry smile.

Farley chuckled. "Why couldn't you be on my side of the law? I wasn't lying when I said I liked you."

"Get up." Lumley nudged Rip's arm. "And get moving. Burk is down there waiting to see you hit the ground. We promised him a show."

"Well, we don't want to disappoint him," Rip said, but it wasn't going to be him hitting the ground like a pancake if he had anything to say about it.

Lumley shoved him this time. "Let's go."

Near the open door, Perry stood hunched from the low ceiling, waiting for him.

Rip shook his head. "No way."

Staying back near the cockpit, Farley simply watched.

Lumley moved the tire iron to his left hand and grabbed the hilt of the 9mm stuffed in the front of his waistband with his right. "Unbuckle your belt. Now!"

Rip was seated at such a close range. The odds were high that Lumley could get off a shot and hit him somewhere that would do plenty of damage without puncturing a hole in the aircraft.

So, Rip did the only thing he could. He unbuckled his lap belt and got up.

Then Perry made the mistake of moving forward to grab him.

Training kicked in. Rip was a machine, programmed by the Marines for one purpose: to put down the enemy.

He fired a left-handed jab to the man's solar plexus, a tight network of nerves below the sternum, knocking the wind from him as he doubled over. Not giving Perry a chance to regain his breath, Rip grabbed him and whirled 180 degrees in anticipation of Lumley's next move.

Sure enough, in a panic the jerk had already pulled his gun. Lumley squeezed off two rounds. One bullet struck Perry in the back and the second in the head.

"Don't fire, you fool," Farley shouted. "You'll get us all killed."

Dropping the dead guy, Rip backed up closer to the door and prepared to take down the next one.

With a deer-in-the-headlights look, Lumley lunged at him. The guy swung wildly with the tire iron, but Rip pivoted out of the way, and Lumley hit nothing but air.

Rip launched a punch to his windpipe. When Lumley dropped the tire iron and gun and clutched his throat with both hands, his mouth open, struggling to breathe, not even a wheeze getting out, Rip knew he'd crushed his windpipe. He thrust Lumley toward the open door and kicked him out.

Something hard came down across Rip's skull, and piercing pain tore through the side of his head. The world blurred. He dropped, his head slamming against the steel bench, and hit the floor.

Farley. Farley had hit him with the tire iron. The former JTF operator had moved quick as lightning because he was also trained to kill.

Rip tried to regain his bearings, tried to swim through the dizzying haze of pain.

Move. You have to move.

Every second counted. He needed to end this fight quickly or the other guy would.

Farley yanked his leg, hauling him to the opening.

Frigid air rushed over Rip, energizing him. Adrenaline fired hot in his system, clearing his mind, but his head throbbed like someone was beating on his skull with a chisel.

Grabbing him by the windbreaker, Farley managed to shove Rip's head and shoulders out the door.

But with his right hand, Rip snatched onto a strap dangling near the rear wall, used for tying down cargo, and held strong.

Rather than trying to wrestle him out of the plane as one of his lackeys might've attempted, Farley drew his Karambit knife, hoisted the blade up and drove it down.

Rip reacted without hesitation, without emotion, without thought, and blocked with his left hand.

The blade plunged into his palm. Ignoring the excruciating pain, disregarding the fear of falling out the aircraft and plummeting to the ground, Rip let go of the strap keeping him onboard and grabbed the shiv from his pocket. Then he thrust the pointed end of the improvised blade up under Farley's chin.

The redheaded man stilled, a shocked expression on his pale face. Rip pulled the weapon free and stabbed again. This time in the jugular. It was done. Blood ran down Farley's throat, dripping onto Rip. He shoved Farley off him, knocking him deeper into the plane, and the former JTF operator keeled over.

Scrambling away from the door, Rip yanked the knife from his hand, letting it clatter to the floor. Not taking any chances, he checked Farley. The man was dead, his eyes open and vacant.

Rip peered out the door. Below on the ground, he spotted a black van and a couple of motorcycles—Hellhounds—in a wide-open space. The Snowy Mountain Range wasn't far to the southwest. They were somewhere north of Laramie, with no town around for miles.

Just then he caught sight of patrol cruisers from two different counties racing up, red-and-blue lights flashing. They surrounded the Hellhounds from the west and south, cutting off any escape.

Rip caught his breath, grabbed a gun and shuffled to the cockpit. Keeping the safety on, he aimed the weapon at the pilot.

"Don't kill me," the middle-aged man said, his eyes growing wide.

"I'm not going to kill you. But you are going to land. Right down there."

The pilot looked around at the ground. "I don't think there's enough room to taxi before I can stop."

"You had less space where you picked us up. Do it."

"Uh-uh." The pilot took another glance. "Pretty rocky down there. We could crash."

"I said I wouldn't kill you, but it's about to get a whole lot rockier for you if I shoot you," he said, aiming at the man's knee. Not that Rip needed to go that far. The pilot was scared of the cops. Rip needed to override that fear with the prospect of something worse. "Take us down and land."

After a moment longer of hesitation, the pilot nodded. "All right."

Rip's head pounded and ached. "You got a med kit?"

The pilot gestured to the wall behind the seat.

Rip popped open the kit, dug out some gauze and medical tape.

As the pilot circled twice, gauging where to make his approach, Rip quickly bandaged his hand, though it wouldn't do much to stop the bleeding. Once the pilot finally decided, he brought the twin otter down, taxied and braked to a stop.

"You're getting out first." Rip waved him along with the gun, and the pilot moved to the back of the plane.

The blood from the wound in his palm had already soaked through the gauze. Getting up, Rip winced from another gut-wrenching stab that went through his head, his vision blurring again. Pure adrenaline still pumping through him was muting the pain and keeping him moving. But it wouldn't last. He dreaded to think what state he'd be in once it wore off.

The pilot hopped out onto the ground and raised his palms.

Rip dropped the gun before he eased off the plane and held up his hands.

Several Hellhounds were in handcuffs. Freddy, Arlo and Clive—the same ones he suspected had attacked him at his trailer. They were loaded into the backs of cruisers.

And Todd Burk. He was down on the ground, face-first, arms behind him, a knee in his back, as he was being cuffed. As they hauled him up, his gaze found Rip's.

Seething, Todd glared at him, and Rip smiled even though it cost him a jolt of pain.

Deputies from the neighboring county approached him and the pilot, guns at the ready, issuing instructions.

Doing as told, Rip and the pilot got down on their knees and put their hands behind their heads.

A door from one of the Laramie cruisers flew open. Ash jumped out and ran, headed straight for him. She shoved past Sheriff Clark, who tried to hold her back, and kept sprinting for him.

Rip's heart lit up brighter than a stadium on Super Bowl Sunday.

Sheriff Clark hurried behind her. "It's all right!" He shouted to the other deputies. "Let her through. Rip Lockwood is with us."

For a split second, Rip wondered why she'd been inside the vehicle in the first place and why the other deputies didn't already know she was with the sheriff's department.

But every thought evaporated once she was in front of him, helping him up from the ground, her face slack with shock, her eyes wide with worry.

"Oh my God!" Ash's gaze fell over him. "You're covered in blood."

"Most of it is not mine." Grateful to be alive, he wanted to hold her, kiss her, but he was a bloody mess and there wasn't much time. His vision blurred again. Pain ballooned in his head like his skull wanted to explode.

Sheriff Clark came up beside them. "Good grief. What happened to you?" He glanced inside the plane and gasped. "Or rather, I guess you're what happened to them."

Ash touched the side of his head, and he winced. "You're bleeding. We need to get you to the hospital."

A deputy slapped handcuffs on the pilot.

"You're going to need him," Rip said, gesturing to the middle-aged man, "to fly you back near Devils Tower, where he picked us up. From there, it's a ten-minute ride..." He pushed through the fog encroaching on his brain to think. "Due east. You'll find the drug camp. Agent Welliver will want to know. There's fentanyl from the Sandoval cartel and enough drugs to make it more than worth his time." He kept spewing every little thing he could remember. "Farley was in charge, but he's dead in the plane. Lou-Ann, LA, she knows about the dealings with the cartel and Burk. If someone cuts her a deal, she'll talk." He thought about her serving rat poison to the addicts they used as workers. "But the deal shouldn't be too good."

"Okay." Sheriff Clark nodded. "We'll take care of it."

"Come on." Ash curled an arm around his waist, slinging his left arm over her shoulder, like he needed her help walking.

And maybe he did, because a blinding bolt of pain lanced his head.

He took four steps forward, the world spun, and everything faded to black as his legs buckled.

Chapter Sixteen

Numb. Ashley was numb as she continued to wait for Rip to open his eyes and talk to her. In his hospital room, she lay in the bed alongside Rip, her head on his shoulder, her hand on his chest, listening, feeling him breathe on his own. The blinds were drawn, dampening the afternoon light without making the room too dim.

The hardest part had been the thirty-six hours he was in the ICU on a ventilator. The nerve-racking sounds of the machine, the overwhelming smell of disinfectant, constant reminders of how close he'd come to death. She didn't know if she could bear any of this, how to face the prospect of him not making a full recovery. So, she'd pushed such thoughts from her mind. As she'd sat in the chair, holding his hand and watching over him, one thing repeated over and over in her head.

I can't lose you.

I can't lose you.

Once he was moved to a regular room, relief had set in, but she still couldn't bear to leave his side for more than a few minutes. Not until he woke up. He was only here in the hospital because she'd dragged him into all this.

Ashley was considering going to the cafeteria for a cup of coffee when Rip stirred and finally opened his eyes.

Leaning up on her forearm, she peered down at him.

His gaze wandered before landing on her. "Hey, you." He sounded foggy.

She caressed his cheek, so happy to see him awake tears pricked her eyes. "Hey, you."

"My throat…"

"You were intubated," she said, and his eyes narrowed in confusion. "Want some water?"

He nodded. Groaned. Struggled to sit up.

"Take it easy." She helped him adjust and then grabbed the cup that she had ready for him. Once he was propped up and seemed more comfortable, she put the straw to his lips.

Rip sipped generously, draining the cup of water. "How long was I out?"

"Two days."

"Two?" He was quiet for a long moment. "Have you been here the whole time?"

"I have. I didn't want to leave you." She got an extra pillow from a table near the chair, put it behind his head and climbed back into the bed. "They put you into a medically induced coma to alleviate the swelling in your head and allow your brain to rest. You opened your eyes after they took you off the ventilator, but you fell back asleep. The doctor said it was from the medication, but that you're a remarkable healer." She rubbed his arm. "You're going to be fine."

He raised his left hand that was bandaged and clenched his fingers until he winced.

"Nineteen stitches," she said. "You're very lucky according to the surgeon who operated on your hand. Well, that's what everyone around here is saying. All the doctors and nurses." She caressed his cheek. "Which makes me lucky."

He lowered his eyes. "Are you still angry that I left you behind?"

"No." Her worry and fear for his life overrode any anger. "I understand why you left me in Fort Collins." If he was in better shape, she would've told him who had given her a ride home, but in his current condition she didn't want to risk upsetting him.

"What happened with the camp?" he asked.

"A major drug seizure for the sheriff's department and DEA. LA was arrested. She was willing to spill her guts about everything for a lighter sentence. All thanks to you."

Reaching for her, he brushed strands of hair from her face. "Thanks to us. That bust never would've happened if not for you. Your stubborn persistence. You're the one who got the lead from the DEA and made sure I didn't waste time getting up to Happy Jack's. If I had waited a day or two, planning, trying to handle it on my own, we would've missed the window of opportunity and Todd would've gotten his last shipment. Did Agent Welliver cover for you with Sheriff Clark?"

"He did. Spoke very highly of me and commended my efforts in recruiting you." But she had already been honest with her boss and nothing Welliver had to say was going to undo her suspension or could help with the internal investigation.

"Is everything okay with your job?" he asked, as if reading her mind.

The man had nearly died, and he was worried about her. "It's complicated. We can talk about it later. I'm just happy you're going to be okay and that Todd Burk is finally going to prison for a long time."

"They did catch him red-handed picking up a shipment of drugs."

"And we have a recording of him admitting to framing you for murder."

"Murder? What did I miss?"

"A lot. Is your KA-BAR knife missing?"

He thought for a moment and then nodded. "Yeah. I left it in my trailer. Those guys broke in and I couldn't find it afterward."

"They stole it. Used it in the murders of Dr. Fuller, the pharmacist, and Shane Yates. But I was your alibi for Yates. There's surveillance video of you in Bitterroot, proving you couldn't have been here in town at the time of his murder."

"How did you get the recording?"

"The burner phone you put in my glove box rang."

"The bug I planted in the chapel, the meeting room, must have been voice-activated. I forgot to tell you about it."

"When I answered the phone, I heard Burk bragging about everything. Including how his supplier, Farley, was going to kill you that day. I recorded it on my phone, but I was out of my mind with worry for you." With fear like she'd never known. She held his face in her hands and kissed him lightly.

But he moved his mouth from hers, and unease wormed through her. "The Sons of Chaos will be coming for me sooner or later. Word will get out about LA to the Sandoval cartel and then I'll be on their radar, too. I'm leaving town, Ash. Today."

She swallowed around the sudden lump in her throat. "You're not going anywhere today. They're running some more tests on you later this afternoon and the doctor needs to determine if you need rehab."

"I can do rehab anywhere. *If* I need it."

"The doctor isn't going to discharge you today."

"This isn't prison. They can't keep me against my will. I'll leave when I'm ready regardless of paperwork."

Putting her hand on his chest, she held his gaze and softened her voice. "You had a severe head injury. Let them finish running their tests today, to make sure that you're fine. It takes hours to get results." Everything in the hospital took forever. One long waiting game. "Tomorrow, if you're still determined to get out of here, you can do it then. Please. For me. For my peace of mind."

He sighed. "I'll wait until tomorrow," he said, and she smiled. "Only if you agree not to stay."

Her smile fell. "What?" Drawing closer, she rested on her elbow, lowered her face close to his and cupped his cheek. "Don't do this. Don't push me away. Not after everything we've been through together."

"You've been in this hospital for two days. Get some air. Go rest. Do something else besides fret over me. I'm fine."

"You're *going to be* fine. Provided you take the time to heal and listen to the doctor. You're not invincible."

"Never thought I'd see the day where you were begging to keep me in bed."

His flirty banter was back, which meant he was truly on the road to recovery.

"You could have plenty more of those days." She brushed her lips over his and held his gaze. "You just have to want them. Want me."

Someone near the door cleared their throat, drawing their attention.

Quill and JD entered the room.

"Sorry to interrupt," Quill said. "We can come back later."

"No." Rip waved them in. "Ash was just leaving."

"To get a cup of coffee," she quickly added and glared at him. "I'll be back." Then she leaned in, bringing her mouth to his ear. "Whether you like it or not. If you think you're going to slip out of the hospital and sneak out of town, think again." Putting her hand on his chest, she snuggled up close and kissed him on the lips in front of his MC brothers. The long, slow kiss left no doubt about her feelings for him, and maybe because they had an audience or he was too tired to fight her, whatever the reason, he kissed her back, soothing her heart.

She climbed out of the bed, grabbed her purse and, ignoring the confused stares of the Iron Warriors, left the room. In the hall out of sight, she stood still a moment and listened.

"You're welcome, brother," Quill said with an attitude.

"What are you talking about?" Rip asked. "Welcome for what?"

"For her. Looks like she's your old lady after all. And that would not have happened if we hadn't been scaring off every dude that came near her."

"I'm still not happy about your interference, but I don't know what she is," Rip said. "What I do know is that I have to leave town as soon as possible and she's not coming with me."

We'll see about that, Ripton Lockwood.

RIP WAS A man of his word. The measures he'd taken over the years had derailed Ash's love life. Now that Todd Burk was in jail on charges that were going to stick, she could be free. To live her life as she wanted. To date. To have fun. To find love. To settle down in town, where she had a career and her family and roots.

Not running away and going into hiding with him.

"Have you heard anything from the Sons?" Rip asked.

JD nodded. "Oh, yeah. Stryker found out his sister is in jail because of you. The Sons want your head on a pike."

"Your old lady's, too." Quill raised his eyebrows.

"They asked the Hellhounds to take care of you two,"

JD said, "but they're a mess after Todd and the others got busted. At least that's what Will tells me."

Will was one of the surprise voters that had been against Rip because he hadn't trusted in the process and in the members to make the right decision.

Rip believed that deep down, Will was still loyal to the Iron Warriors and under new leadership, he'd return.

"Get the word out that Ash is with the sheriff's department. It'll be a deterrent. Once the Sons know I'm gone and I've left her behind, they'll think I don't care about her. But before I leave, I'll talk to Sheriff Clark about getting her protection and give him enough information to take to the FBI about the Sons and their prostitution ring. That'll put many of them in jail and leave the rest in real chaos." LA didn't know about Ash, which meant she'd stay under the radar of the cartel.

JD crossed his arms. "You can't go starting a war with the Sons by giving the FBI information without a vote, Rip."

"You heard Will. They want me dead. I'm already at war with them. That's why you need to strip me of my patches and excommunicate me. To protect the Warriors from any blowback."

Quill blanched. "No. No way. We won't do it. There has to be another alternative."

"There isn't." Rip had given it serious consideration. Strategized all the options. "Quill, I want you to support JD for president."

JD shook his head. "I don't want the mantle."

Smiling, Rip understood what the others had tried to teach him years ago. "That's one of the reasons why you're perfect for the job. You'll do great."

Ashley walked back into the room, holding a cup of coffee. She stopped at the foot of his bed and met Rip's gaze, and his chest tightened. She was so beautiful. So full of light. Special.

He didn't want to leave her, but he also didn't want to endanger her.

The best thing to do was to set her free.

"I appreciate everything you guys have done for me," Rip said to them. "Everything I've asked. For trusting me. For having my back. For watching out for Ash." He took a breath, finding it difficult to continue. He wasn't the sentimental type but was getting a bit choked up. "Even though I won't be an Iron Warrior anymore, you'll always be my brothers."

Ash stiffened, her eyes going wide in surprise.

"One drink before you leave town?" Quill asked.

Rip gave a noncommittal gesture. "I can't make any promises."

"I don't want this to be the last time I see you. In a hospital bed. Not wearing any underwear." Quill grinned.

Rip chuckled. "I'll see what I can do."

"You were a great Prez, Rip. I learned a lot from you," JD said.

"Make me proud. Lead them in the right direction."

Quill and JD took turns tapping a fist on Rip's shoulder. On their way out, they did the same to Ash.

There was a knock on the door. Chief Deputy Holden Powell came in and tipped his cowboy hat in greeting. He was the one man Rip thought might've ended up with Ashley. He had been her brother's best friend. Holden and Ashley had chosen to be deputies at the sheriff's office, and worked long hours together. But according to Ash, Holden always treated her like a little sister and now was happily married to a nurse.

"Holden," Ash said, "what are you doing here?"

"I wish it was better news," the chief deputy said gravely.

JD eased toward the door. "We'll get going."

"You two might want to hold on." Powell stepped deeper inside the room. "Since it's Thanksgiving tomorrow, the district attorney wanted Burk and the other three Hellhounds to be moved to county lockup today. Earlier, as they were being transported, they managed to break out."

Rip swore under his breath. *Teflon.*

"In the process, they killed Deputy Livingston and injured Deputy Cody," Powell continued.

"Oh no!" Ash moved closer to Powell. "Is Mitch going to be okay?"

"He's out of surgery. Lost a lot of blood. Needed a transfusion. But he's going to make it."

Ash's face hardened. "You should've told me sooner."

"I'm sorry. I know you two are good friends, but you were waiting for Rip to wake up. I didn't want to add more to your plate of worries until I had to. The US Marshals have started a countywide manhunt for Burk and the others. In the meantime, we're working with the Laramie Police Department to have an officer assigned to each of you around the clock," he said to Ash and Rip.

Todd and the others would be looking for a place to hide. Someone vulnerable, someone alone whom they could exploit. "Ida. She'll need protection while I'm in here."

Holden tipped the brim of his hat up. "The LPD can only spare enough personnel to watch each of you."

"Ida is fine." Ash came around to the side of the bed and put a hand on his arm. "She's been with my parents the last few days."

"She went willingly?"

Smiling, Ash nodded. "Not a single complaint."

Didn't sound like his Aunt Ida.

"My mom had been checking on her several times a day to make sure she was all right and was taking her medication. Eventually, she just invited her to stay over. Ida seemed more than happy to have the company," she said, and that was a great relief to Rip. Ash turned to Powell. "You can have one officer watch our family. The other one can cover both of us. We'll stay together."

She was good at boxing him in and getting what she wanted. He'd give her that.

But *our family* struck him in an unexpected way. It almost gave him hope he and Ash could be together, their families joined as one.

Powell looked at Quill and JD. "We're hoping the Iron Warriors could keep an ear out and let us know if you hear anything."

JD nodded. "Of course. The sooner you catch them, the better for all of us."

"Everyone needs to stay vigilant," Chief Deputy Powell said. "Todd Burk and his cohorts are armed and desperate. With the marshals searching for them, we think it won't take long for them to be apprehended."

Ash's gaze found Rip's. The look in her eyes made his heart constrict. Too many emotions surfacing, battling for dominance. He didn't like it clouding his judgment, thawing him when he needed to be ice-cold—the only way to make tough decisions.

"I'm still getting out of the hospital tomorrow," he said to her. "But I won't leave town. Not until Burk has been captured."

Chapter Seventeen

In her parents' kitchen, Ashley finished putting away the last of the food. "I really appreciate you going to so much trouble to make Thanksgiving special."

"It was nice to have more people at the table this year," Mom said. "Instead of it being the three of us. And I'm pleased you finally brought a man to dinner. I didn't expect it to be that one, a biker, but you seem happy around him. Light up whenever you two are in the same room. Your father and I have noticed how he looks at you, too."

"How is that?" She still wasn't sure what was going through Rip's head.

He acted determined to push her away, but she was known for her stubborn persistence.

Mom gave a knowing smile and a soft chuckle. "The man is in love with you."

Air caught in her throat. *In love.* Their relationship had been a complicated, slow burn and then a sudden rolling boil. He'd give his life for her, and she wanted to spend her life with him. Love…was the perfect word.

"Are you sure?"

"I'm certain of it. The real question is how do you feel?"

She went to her mother and took her warm hands in hers. "I didn't realize how deeply I felt for him until I saw him covered in blood and watched him collapse. Sitting with him in the hospital, I would've given anything for him to open his eyes. Anything."

"I never knew what to make of Rip, but after everything he went through to get Todd Burk arrested, he's got our approval. We just want you to be happy."

"I will be. Once Burk is back behind bars." And Rip accepted they were meant for each other. "Tomorrow, I need to sit down with you and Dad and share my plans for the future."

"Not tonight?"

Ashley needed to get Rip on board with the plan first. "Tomorrow." She hugged her mom. "I love you."

"I love you, too, sweetheart."

She went into the living room.

Rip and her dad were coming down the hallway from the bedroom.

"We just tucked Ida in for the night," Dad said.

"She really loves it here. Thank you for taking care of her while I was gone." Rip shook her dad's hand. "There's something I'd like to ask, though it might be a huge imposition."

Ashley sensed what it would be. "Rip, I think you should wait until tomorrow. We'll come back. Okay?" One clear discussion about leaving would be best. "It's late and I'd like to get going."

Eyeing her, Rip hesitated.

She looked away from him and hugged her dad. "See you tomorrow. Love you."

"Love you more, jelly bean."

Hating when her dad called her that, she groaned.

Rip followed her through the living room.

She opened the front door and stepped out onto the porch.

"An officer will stay parked out front until the US Marshals find Burk and his crew."

"Don't worry about us. You two go enjoy the rest of your evening." Dad lingered in the doorway, watching them get into her truck, and waved as they drove off.

"Drop me at my trailer. The other officer will stay with you."

"Rip—"

"Ash, we're not going to argue about this. I said I won't leave town. I'm not going to run off."

"Fine, no arguing." She turned on the radio and drove. Ten minutes into the ride, rather than take the road that led to the Hindley property, she took a left, heading for Bison Ridge.

"This isn't the way to my place."

"No, it isn't, because we're going to mine."

"Ashley."

"Is that going to be a thing?"

"Is what?"

"You using my whole name when you're cross with me?"

"I want to go to my trailer."

"The one you haven't cleaned up? Sure thing. But first, I want to show you something."

"Okay. I'll play this game. What?"

"Something you've never seen before."

He growled, the low rumble in his chest sounding sexy instead of scary. "Tell me what it is."

She pulled up in front of her house and threw the truck in Park. "That would spoil the surprise. But trust me, it's important. Afterward, I can take you straight home, if you still want to go," she said, and he narrowed his eyes at her. "I'd take that deal if I were you. It's the best one you're going to get." She pocketed her car keys.

"Fine." He got out, slamming the truck door, and stomped up to the porch.

The police officer parked behind her vehicle.

She went to the driver's side of the patrol car and he rolled down the window. "We're going to be here for the rest of the night. Can I get you some coffee or something?"

He held up a thermos and a plate of dessert covered in plastic wrap. "Your mother was kind enough to take care of me and the other officer who is watching your family's house. Have a good night."

"Thank you." It was a shame those officers had to be out in the cold, keeping guard on Thanksgiving, but hopefully the marshals would end this ordeal with Todd Burk once and for all.

Ashley hurried up the porch steps, past a brooding Rip, and opened the door. She stepped inside, but he stayed on the porch.

"What's wrong?" she asked. "I promise it's a good surprise. It won't upset you and we won't argue."

"It's just that you've lived in this house for five and a half years, I've been here countless times, but this is the first time I've come in through the front door."

She reached for him, taking him by the arm, and pulled him across the threshold. "Why did you always come around back?" She closed the door, locked it and put on the chain.

"You didn't seem thrilled about my visits. In case your family or a friend stopped by, I figured it would be best if they didn't see my bike."

She took his hand. "I felt like you were just as bad as my parents, checking up on me, giving me a hard time for living out here by myself."

"A young, pretty woman living alone with no neighbor in shouting distance tended to worry me. A lot."

She led him down the hall. "It made me feel like you underestimated me. My ability to handle myself if something were to happen."

"I never underestimated you, Ash. I just prefer to overestimate other people's capacity for evil."

"Guess I didn't think of it that way." She stopped in front of her bedroom. Holding his gaze, she backed up into the room, tugging him along with her.

He halted in the doorway. "What are you doing?"

"At first, I was annoyed when you'd stop by, but after a while, I looked forward to your visits. Every time I heard the rumble of your bike coming, pulling around back, I'd get these electric tingles and a part of me couldn't wait to see you."

"You hid it well."

"I'm sorry. I just wanted to be sure this thing between us was real, and not you trying to manipulate me, or use me because I was a cop. That you really wanted to see Burk in jail. It was taking you so long to handle him."

"Revenge would've been easy, but you wanted justice. He was slipperier than I anticipated."

She set her purse on the dresser and held out her hand for him.

Rip sighed like the weight of the world rested on his shoulders. "Why are you doing this? I have to leave. Soon. Your family, your job, your life, are here."

"You're asking the wrong question. Ask me the right one. The one from the motel."

His gaze bore into hers. "What am I to you?"

She took a deep breath, but she wasn't confused or unsure. This time she was certain of her answer. "You're my anchor. The one I confide in." She shared so many things with him first, some she'd never even told her parents. Wanting to be a deputy. Enrolling in college. The problem she had with a sexist professor. Her worst nightmare—that the authorities would never get Burk. How she wanted to get married and have a couple of kids. That she avoided monthly karaoke night with the sheriff's office and Laramie Fire Department because she had an irrational fear of singing in public and only did it at home. "The one person who has *been* there for me. Protecting me. Helping me. Sacrificing for me." She didn't realize she was moving toward him until she was touching him. "This thing between us hasn't been conventional, but it's real and I'd be lost without it. Without you." She took another deep breath. "Because I love you."

Nothing had ever felt so right or sounded so true. She eased further back into her bedroom.

And this time, he followed. "You shouldn't say those words lightly."

"I haven't."

He took her in his arms. "I want more than a night."

"I know." She slipped his jacket off, letting it hit the floor, and then hers.

"I want everything with you."

She unbuckled his belt, transfixed by his piercing gaze. "Then we're on the same page."

"But how? What about your job? Your family?"

Putting her hands on his cheeks, the scratchy stubble forming a beard tickling her palms, she brought his face to hers. "We're going to be together. We'll discuss the details later." After they made love.

His mouth took hers and he kissed her, a deep, sensual kiss that had her moaning and losing her balance. Digging her hands into the material of his shirt, she wanted him inside her, no long foreplay, only the fast, frantic rush of passion. She pulled the Henley over his head and started unbuttoning her shirt.

"Wait," he said, and she hoped he wasn't going to come up with another reason why they couldn't be together. "We're going to do this slow and easy. I want you to remember the first time I make love to you. For it to burn in your memory for all the days and nights to come."

The first time I make love to you. There would be other times, other ways they'd do this.

"You hide it well."

"What?"

"Being such a romantic."

He caressed her cheek and gave her a soft grin. "Do you still have any of those bath oils and candles I bought you?"

She nodded. He bought her the most luxurious gifts. She only used them on special occasions, savoring them. "The oils are in the bathroom. I'll light the candles."

Not only was he a generous lover but a romantic, too. Jasper hadn't taken it slowly or thought of her pleasure. Within minutes, it had been done, and she hadn't felt any different, even though she was no longer a virgin.

But this...making love to Rip would change everything.

He went into the bathroom and started the water. She dug out the large, scented soy candles that smelled like a lush tropical paradise and lit them. She set one on each nightstand and carried the other two to the bathroom, where she found Rip standing in all his glory, without a stitch of clothing on.

Her mouth dropped. He was beautiful. Rugged. A work of art she couldn't wait to get her hands on. "No fair, I wanted to undress you."

"Next time." He took the candles from her and set them down. They reflected a soft white light in the mirror, providing the only illumination in the room. "There is one thing," he said.

No, no, no. "This is happening, Rip."

He smiled and it was a rainbow after a storm, glorious and filled with promise. The hot look in his eyes sparked heat low in her abdomen. "I don't have protection. I didn't plan on this."

Oh, not what she was expecting him to say. "I used a condom with Jasper."

"Please refrain from mentioning other men when I'm naked and about to make love to you."

"Sorry," she said with a shake of her head. "Anyway, I had a checkup after." She pressed her hand to the heavy stubble lining his jaw, enjoying the way it scratched her palm. "I'm clean and I take the pill."

His eyes changed. The desire from before turned even darker. "It's been a while for me, but I'm clean, too."

"Then I don't want there to be anything between us."

No barriers. No past. No secrets. Just the two of them. She wanted to open her soul to him.

He stripped off her shirt and unfastened her bra. Crouching, he pressed kisses to her stomach before slipping off her shoes. He unbuttoned her jeans and pulled them down. She touched the top of his head, balancing herself as he tugged them off.

Her knees trembled. Who was she kidding? She trembled all over.

Rip planted a kiss at the apex between her thighs, his warm breath coursing through the silky material of her panties, unraveling her in thirteen different ways. Then he gripped the waistband and slid them down, allowing her to step out of them. Leaving them on the floor, he stood and looked at her.

Fixing her attention on his mouth, the shape of his full lips, the sexy crook of his smile, she shivered. Grabbing a clip from the counter, she pinned her hair on top of her head while he shut off the faucet and checked the temperature.

Rip held out a hand, helping her into the claw-footed porcelain tub filled with bubbles that smelled divine. He climbed in on the other side, the water sloshing, and eased down, careful not to get his bandaged hand wet. His legs stretched out, and she clamped her knees together, making room for him to surround her.

In the candlelight suffusing the room, he bathed her gently, tenderly, caressing every inch of skin. No one had ever taken such care of her. Been so patient with his affection. And when he finished, she bathed him. She was familiar with the top half of his body but enjoyed the new spots she hadn't yet explored. Stroking him in places that made him groan, and she understood what he meant about liking to hear her pleasure because hearing his lit her up inside.

Every kiss, every touch, every stroke heated them until their desire for each other reached a torturous simmer. She was ready to climb on top of him and have him right there in the tub. His restraint was phenomenal.

"I can't wait any longer," she admitted.

Another heartrending smile. "Me neither."

They got out and hurried, towel-drying each other off.

Rip bent over and scooped her up off the floor, lifting her in his arms.

"You'll hurt your hand," she said, worried about him. "And what about your head?"

He was already moving out of the bathroom and set her down on the bed. "I've got this."

She scooted higher on the bed and lay back. He climbed up, prowling closer.

Excitement pulsed through her and goose bumps pebbled her skin.

Island scents drifted in the air—Tahitian vanilla, white musk, night-blooming jasmine. He settled between her spread legs, caressed her cheek with the knuckle of his index finger, moved to her mouth and stroked her bottom lip with his thumb. She caught the tip between her teeth, bit down lightly, and sucked.

"God, you are amazing," he said, his voice filled with the same awe she felt looking at him. "So sexy."

He kissed her, a searing brand of possession and passion, his hand diving between them, his fingers stroking that place she ached most. He knew precisely how to caress her to make the rush of desire flood her body, to make her tremble with longing, and she became lost. So sweetly lost in him. And this time the pleasure was both theirs to share.

His thigh settled between her legs, and she opened herself, pressing the warmth of her most intimate spot against him. Desire roared through her, so intense, so urgent, she swore the world quaked.

Need took over as he entered her slowly. She cried out, not in pain but in a kind of triumph. Gripping his hips, she urged him to move faster, deeper. Sensation swamped her with a force she'd never felt before and she wanted more. Lots more.

They rocked together as one, clinging to each other, breathing hard, climbing higher. Not just having sex or hooking up or having a fling but making love. Committing to each other.

This new dimension of their relationship was sensual and nurturing and hot and better than she'd imagined. All these years she'd been searching for something she couldn't fully define, and here she'd found it in the one man who had been there for her all along.

Rip.

Chapter Eighteen

Holding Ash in his arms, in her bed, Rip felt like he'd won the lottery. If this was a dream, he never wanted to wake from it. "How do you feel?"

"Different. Revered and ravaged," she said, and he laughed. "I wish I had waited for you. Waited for this. Instead of blowing my first time on Jasper."

He patted her butt softly, playfully. "Please, do me the favor of not mentioning him again. Ever."

"Okay, okay. But I will say one more thing."

Rip groaned.

"You'll appreciate this. You gave me my first orgasm, in the motel," she said, and he did appreciate it.

"Well, I've given you plenty of those. Five so far, not that I'm counting, and more to come. Pun intended."

She elbowed him lightly in his side. "Humble. But I am looking forward to lots of other firsts with you, like our bath." She rolled on top of him and peered down into his face. "Have you ever been married?"

"Yes." Suddenly, he wished he had been the one who'd waited for her. "It was right after I became a Raider. Spec Ops. The marriage lasted less than two years. She couldn't handle me being gone all the time. Didn't like being lonely. I came back from a deployment to find her living with another guy." The memory no longer stung. It had happened a lifetime ago.

"What was she like? I mean, what's your type?"

"You're my type." He slid his arms around her waist. "Beautiful, bold, brave. Loyal." Mandy had only been pretty. He'd been in lust with her, mistaking it for love. His ego had been more hurt than his heart when the marriage ended.

"So, I won't be your first wife," she said, and the sadness in her tone and her eyes stopped him from making a joke about how he'd never promised marriage.

"No. Not the first. But the last. The only one to matter. My dad used to talk about how my mom was the great love of his life. You're mine." He kissed her. "I love you. I have for a few years."

"Did you fall in love with me before or after you started bringing me tacos?"

"I *wanted* you before the tacos, but I think I realized I'd fallen in deep when I started bringing you candles and bath oils and—"

"And the booze."

He chuckled. "Yeah."

"There was one night," she said, slipping her leg between his and snuggling against him, "where I wanted you so bad, I came close to inviting you to my bedroom."

"Why didn't you?"

"You called me deputy and it…shifted my thoughts back into alignment."

"That's why I did it. Called you deputy all the time. To keep me focused on not crossing the line between us." He put a knuckle under her chin and tipped her face up, so he could look into her eyes. "Speaking of which, what about your job?"

Sighing, she rolled off him onto her back and stared up

at the ceiling. At the lack of eye contact, he braced for what she might say.

"Don't get upset, but the sheriff suspended me because I misled him about the DEA mission, and the current status of our relationship prompted an investigation."

"What?" He leaned up on his forearm and peered down at her face. "I can talk to him. Try to clear it up."

She pressed her index finger to his lips. "I'm not worried about the internal investigation. I'll be cleared, but I still quit."

He moved her finger from his mouth. "Ash, you can't."

"I already did. The sheriff asked me to reconsider, said he didn't want to lose a good deputy and that the investigation was only procedural. I told him that a law enforcement officer has to do things by the book. But to get Todd, it required me to bend the rules. I had to work in the gray. I don't regret it and I also don't think I should wear the badge anymore. Todd was arrested and when he's found, he won't slip out of those charges. He was the only reason I became a deputy in the first place. I achieved what I set out to do. You were in the hospital, and suddenly, you were all that mattered to me. So, I quit. It's done. Tomorrow, we'll tell my parents and Ida that we have to leave. Together. Besides, I can find a new job wherever we decide to make our new home. Not law enforcement of course, but something to help people that also pays the bills."

He wrapped an arm around her waist. "You don't have to worry about paying bills. I bring in plenty of money."

Turning onto her side, facing him, she raised an eyebrow. "Clean, legit money?"

He chuckled. "Yeah, of course. I started a company. Ironside Protection Services."

"I've heard of it. That's you? How were you able to hide

being the owner from the DEA? It didn't come up in their deep dive on you."

"I was Special Forces. I know how to hide things I don't want others to know. Over the years, I've expanded a great deal into Montana, Idaho and Colorado. I employee a lot of veterans."

"Guess I could do protection work."

He trailed his fingers over her spine, loving the feel of her nestled against him. "I bring in close to a million a year. You can do what you want. Handle management. Source intel. Lead a team. Stay home with me and we can practice making babies."

She sat up and stared down at him. "A million *dollars* a year?"

"Yep."

"And you pay your taxes?"

He laughed. "On time. Every year. I swear it's all aboveboard. You can trust me, honey."

"I know I can. It's just I had no idea."

"That's the point. For no one to know."

"You're full of surprises. The good kind." She gave him a peck on the lips and hopped out of the bed. "I'm going to go to the bathroom and clean up."

"I'm starving."

"There's a strawberry rhubarb pie on the counter and shepherd's pie in the fridge."

"Both are my favorite."

"I'm aware. I've been paying attention, too, over the years and I had planned for you to stay here. The strawberry rhubarb is from the Divine Treats café and the shepherd's pie is from my mother's kitchen."

He pulled on his boxer briefs. "Want anything?"

"Glass of water." She paused, thinking. "Ooh, this is a

night to celebrate. Calls for Clase Azul. I'll meet you in the kitchen. Give me a couple of minutes." She disappeared in the bathroom, shutting the door, and he heard the faucet turn on.

His head buzzed. Not from pain. Not from swelling. From this high of being in love, of knowing that Ash loved him back, wanted to build a life together.

He padded down the hall, passing her living room, and entered the kitchen.

A draft sent a chill over him. The back door creaked. Slightly ajar. The bottom windowpane had been busted in, broken glass on the floor.

Then he sensed movement behind him before he heard it.

He grabbed the first thing within reach—a cast-iron skillet from the dish rack on the counter—and swung around.

The iron pan collided with the barrel of a twelve-gauge shotgun that Freddy was holding. A blast exploded, shattering the window over the sink.

Rip swung again, smashing the pan against Freddy's fingers and then across his head, sending him to the floor in a whirling sprawl.

Heavyset Clive had a baseball bat. Tall, burly Arlo limped forward, raising a 9mm.

Over their shoulders, Rip glimpsed Todd Burk stalking down the hallway toward the bedroom.

"Ashley!" Rip ducked, taking cover behind the kitchen island as Arlo opened fire. He grabbed the shotgun from an unconscious Freddy.

When those men, former brothers, had attacked him at his home, he'd gone easy, only dislocating a kneecap.

Now they were here, going after Ash, and he'd show no mercy.

SINGING TO HERSELF in the mirror, she wondered where they'd go, if he already had a city or town picked out. Would they even stay in Wyoming?

Boom.

"What the hell?" She shut off the water and listened.

"Ashley!"

Her heart stuttered. *Rip.*

She snatched the long purple kimono robe from the hook on the back of the door, put it on and tied the belt.

Gunfire erupted deeper in the house, from the kitchen, sending her pulse skyrocketing. She opened the bathroom door and froze. Todd Burk stood on the other side. In her bedroom. His black hair was wild, his eyes crazed. He had her in height, he had her in weight, and he was holding a hammer.

In milliseconds, she located her gun and pepper spray. Both in her purse. On top of the dresser that Todd had pushed in front of the closed bedroom door.

Panic wanted to ice her brain. It snaked through her belly, slithered up her throat, made her hands shake until she balled them into fists. Fear threatened to swallow her, but her anger, her seven years of grief, her bottled-up pain were stronger.

A vicious smirk tugged at his mouth, and he raised the hammer.

She kicked him in the crotch as hard as she could. As he doubled over, she rammed the fleshy part of her palm up into his nose. Once. Twice. Bone crunched. Then she kicked him again, this time thrusting the heel of her foot into his gut, shoving him back, putting space between them.

More gunfire came from the kitchen.

Todd stumbled and fell near the dresser, blocking her escape, but the hammer slipped from his grip and clattered to the hardwood floor.

She bolted for her nightstand on the other side of the room.

Cursing and grunting, Todd was up. He leaped onto the bed with the hammer in his hand.

She grabbed the handle of her top drawer and pulled it open, but Todd lunged, taking her down to the floor. The breath was knocked from her. Lights starred behind her eyes when her head rapped hard against the floor. She still held the handle, but the drawer had been yanked free from the nightstand, the contents spilling around her.

She felt around for what she was looking for. She'd seen it fall to her left.

Crouched on top of her, Todd raised the hammer. She swung her forearm into his head, across his face. A move Rip had taught her after she graduated from the academy to keep her from breaking her hand. Then she went for his eyes, raked furrows down his cheek.

He howled like a wounded animal. Ashley grabbed his arm holding the hammer with her hands and bit him, as hard as she could, drawing blood.

The hammer fell, but with his free hand, he punched her. The blow stunned her, but she kept moving.

His bloody hand was shaking. She only wished she'd been able to take off a finger.

Head clearing, she scrambled with him for the hammer. His hand closed over it first, but she didn't stop fighting for it.

"The boys are taking care of Rip. So you and I can play."

Todd's face was close to hers, his body pinning her in an obscene way. His wrist was slippery with his own blood.

She cursed as she lost her grip.

Smiling, in control of the hammer, he ripped open the top of her robe, exposing her breasts. "I want a taste of what Rip's been protecting all this time before I kill you."

She sagged, but reached out, searching the floor with her fingers, hoping, praying, the weapon might be nearby.

There! She found it. Her hand closed around cool aluminum. "You're not man enough to take what's his."

A lecherous smile curled his lips and something in his eyes made her stomach clench like a fist. "We'll see when I'm done with you."

With her finger, she flipped the on switch. Blue sparks snapped and sizzled, drawing his gaze down to her hand.

She shoved the stun gun into his side.

Todd let out a piercing wail, falling off her to the side, shuddering and convulsing. The hammer dropped to the floor.

One to two seconds of contact caused unbearable pain, muscle cramps and dizziness. She shocked him again. Todd and his flunkies had broken into her house, assuming she was alone and weak. They had been thinking four against one. Had planned to do unspeakable things to her and then kill her.

A geyser of pain and rage welled up in her and exploded. She hit him with her fists. In the face. In the gut. In the stomach. Screaming, she kept punching. The red haze clouding her vision darkened every time she landed a blow.

She never heard Rip calling her name. Or the battering of the door. Or him busting it down and shoving the dresser aside.

His arms were around her waist, her back pressed to his chest, and he was hauling her off Todd. She was still swinging and kicking when he carried her to the corner of the room.

"Ashley!"

She wasn't sure how many times he'd yelled her name before it registered.

"Look at me. Not him."

Chest heaving, she tore her gaze from the sight of Todd, crumpled and bleeding on her floor, to Rip. Met his eyes. Those riveting blue-gray eyes anchored her. The immediate connection calmed her. The red haze of fury dissipated, and tears fell from her eyes.

"I need to know. Right now," Rip said.

"What? Know what?" Then she realized he'd been talking to her, but she hadn't heard him.

"Todd Burk. Do you want him dead…or in prison? I need to know, right now before I call 911."

She glanced back at the man who had killed her brother, who had caused her family unfathomable suffering.

"Look at me when you decide." Rip's voice was sharp, sobering.

Finding his gaze and holding it, she took a long, ragged breath. "I want him to burn in hell for what he's done." Staying focused on this man, whom she loved, whom she was safe with, who would do anything for her, she then thought about her brother, remembered the promises she'd made her parents when she joined the sheriff's office. "But I want him to rot in jail first."

She wanted justice.

Not vengeance.

"Good choice, honey." He sat her down in a chair. Yanked a cord from the lamp on the bedside table. Tied Todd's hands behind his back. Ran from the room for a minute. Hurried back with duct tape and a phone pressed to his ear. "The four escapees the marshals are searching for broke in and attacked us. I believe the officer outside is dead."

Rip finished the call on speakerphone, giving the 911 operator Ashley's address, as he doubled the restraints on Todd's wrists with the tape and bound his ankles.

He grabbed their clothes and ushered her to the hall. Quickly, he dressed her and himself. Looking her over, he wiped blood from her face, and she winced from the tenderness in her cheek where Todd had hit her.

"Sorry I didn't get to you sooner," he said, regret heavy in his voice.

She leaned against him, needing his strength, his support, and he wrapped her in a bear hug. "He had a hammer. He was going to rape me." She shivered at the prospect of what might have happened if Rip hadn't been in the house. But he had been there dealing with the others. "I don't know what choice I would have made if you hadn't stopped me."

"I do. You would've made the right one." He tightened the embrace. "I believe that. I believe in you."

"But how can you? After the way I hit him. I didn't think I'd be able to stop."

"Todd had that coming and deserved everything you dished out. Deserves far worse. But I know because in all the years when you weren't sure what side of the law I was on, you never asked me to put him down like a dog, shoot him unaware in the back and bury him in a deep hole somewhere no one would find him. You never would have."

It had crossed her mind, but she could never bring herself to utter the words. To ask someone to commit murder. Not that Rip would have ever gone through with it. He was a good man, the best kind of man, who believed in justice. Not revenge. "What about the others?"

"Two are still breathing, but they're broken. They're going to have a tough time in prison wearing casts."

She pressed her head to his chest. "I'm glad it's over. I'm glad you're here."

"I'm the one who's glad. That you're safe and okay."

"What if you hadn't stayed? What if you had gone back to your trailer?" A shudder racked her body.

"But I'm here. Because you're stubborn and persistent. Because you had the guts to tell me how you felt about me and then had your way with me in bed to get me to stay."

Pulling back and looking up at him, she gave him a grim smile.

"That's my Ash, head held high, a warrior to the bone." He took her chin between his thumb and index finger. "I'm never leaving you again. It's you and me together from now on."

She nodded. "Together."

He lowered his mouth to hers and kissed her, long and slow and deep, and her heart melted as everything else faded away.

Ten months later

RIP STOOD BESIDE ASH, with his arm around her shoulder, in front of Ida Hindley's grave in Millstone Cemetery. Though he couldn't be with Ida during her last months, he was comforted knowing that she had lived to see her ninetieth birthday, and in the end, had been surrounded by love and hadn't been alone, thanks to Ashley's parents.

"It was a lovely service," Ashley's mother said to the small group.

Only her parents, Quill and JD had been invited. An announcement about her passing would be put in the paper along with her obituary once Rip and Ash left town again. They'd only flown in for the funeral.

"Of course, it was." Rip smiled, looking at her simple

headstone that read *Ida Hindley, Beloved Wife, Mother, Auntie and Friend*, along with the years of her birth and death. "Auntie Ida planned it herself. She claimed it was so I wouldn't have to do it and that's partly true, but she was also a perfectionist and wanted it done right."

Ashley's father laughed. "Even when it came to making the bed. If I didn't do hospital corners, it was done wrong."

Fond memories sprang to mind and his chest filled with gratitude and love. "Thanks to her, making a bed and shooting were the two things I didn't have to worry about learning how to do when I joined the Marines."

"She was a good woman," Quill said.

"With Rip and Ashley gone, Ida appreciated you two paying her visits," Mrs. Russo said to Quill and JD.

JD nodded. "She played a mean hand of pinochle and enjoyed taking our money."

"I didn't know pinochle was a gambling game," Ash said, resting her head on Rip.

Quill laughed. "It was the way Ida played it."

"Tired?" Rip asked Ash, tightening his arm around her.

"Starving." She put her hands on her belly, nearly the size of a basketball, and rubbed. Her wedding ring, a diamond eternity band, sparkled, catching the light. "I'm always hungry."

"I was the same when I was pregnant." Her mother put a hand on Ash's rounded tummy. "You said you'd tell us the sex in person. We've been waiting."

"What are you having, man?" Quill stepped closer. "Boy or girl?"

Rip looked at her. "Do you want to tell them or should I?"

Ash shrugged, a mischievous gleam in her eye. "Let's do it at the same time. One, two, three. Boy."

"Girl."

Everyone looked at them, confused.

Her father's face lit up. "Oh, my! Twins? Is my jelly bean having two beans?"

Ash nodded. "A boy and a girl."

Everyone took turns giving them hugs and offering congratulations.

Then her mom broke down in tears.

"Don't cry." Ash kissed her cheek and comforted her. "This is good news."

"The best news possible." Her mom sniffled. "It's just that your dad and I retired early. With Ida gone, we have no reason to stay here. We miss you. We want to see the baby, the babies when they're born, watch them grow up, but..."

Rip took out a handkerchief and gave it to her. "Ash and I have been talking about that. We were wondering if you wanted to come live with us. Well, not in the same house. But walking distance close."

Her mother went slack-jawed with surprise and looked at Ash as if to check whether the proposal was real.

"Yes, Mom. We want you guys with us if that's what you want."

Ash had broached the subject and he had been open to it. They had even made plans to bring Ida. He'd always wanted a big family. If he could give his kids grandparents, who wanted to be hands-on and in their lives every day, then he would. It was also a huge plus that he'd make his wife ecstatic in the process.

An easy win-win.

Her father grabbed him in a bear hug. "Thank you, Rip."

"Sir, you're more than welcome. We're happy to have you."

"We told you at the wedding. No more sir or ma'am or

Mr. and Mrs. Russo. It's Dante and Emily. Or if you'd prefer, Mom and Dad. You're not our son-in-law, but our son."

They'd gotten legally married at the Justice of the Peace in the United States, only the two of them. Then had a small ceremony in Paris with Ash's parents and Auntie Ida. At the Place du Trocadéro, overlooking the Eiffel Tower. Ash had wanted to do it in Europe, since she'd never been, and he thought she'd love it. Her parents and Ida had been impressed and her mother couldn't stop crying happy tears. For their honeymoon, they'd traveled for a month, going wherever Ash wanted.

"All right. No more formalities." Rip nodded, sticky emotions surfacing. He'd have to work his way up to calling them Mom and Dad. "Don't sell your house. Don't change your routine. Just have two bags packed and ready. One day, we'll call with instructions. Follow them to the letter. Don't say goodbye to anyone. Okay?" It was similar to how he'd handled things for the wedding. The obstetrician thought the babies might come early. He was planning for a December birth and to have her parents relocated by Thanksgiving.

"Yes, yes," Dante and Emily both said.

"Will we ever see you guys again?" JD asked.

The district attorney had plenty of evidence to put Todd, Freddy and Arlo away, including for the murder of the police officer who had been assigned to protect them. Clive hadn't left Ash's house alive. Fortunately, the case was so solid against the others it didn't require either of their testimonies in court. Their sworn affidavits would suffice. Many of the Sons of Chaos had been arrested, including Stryker, when the prostitution ring was busted. But the Sandoval cartel was still a potential problem waiting to happen.

"No, you won't." Rip shook his head. "I'm sorry."

"We understand." Quill patted him on the back. "Thanks for still kicking Ironside work to the Warriors."

"It'll help keep the club legit," JD said, proudly wearing his president patch.

"Now that's all settled, can we eat?" Ash asked.

"Let's go to the house," Emily said. "I have plenty of food prepared."

"Good. I'm hungry." Quill patted his own round belly, heading for his bike.

Once they finished lunch, they would go to the Laramie Regional Airport, where Rip had a chartered plane waiting. Staying any longer than the day wasn't wise. Not a chance he was willing to take with his family, now that the cartel knew his name and involvement in the seizure of the drug camp.

They started for the car when Ash stopped suddenly.

"The babies are kicking." She put his hand on her belly.

After a second or two he felt it. Like a powerful one-two jab from inside her. Took his breath away every time. "They're so strong."

She smiled. "Fighters like their dad."

"And their mom."

"I was thinking about names. How about Hatch Angelo and Elizabeth Ida?"

The suggestions warmed his heart, choking him up in a way he didn't expect. This beautiful woman never stopped surprising him in the best ways. He nodded. "Great choices, but only if you really love those names."

She pressed a palm to his clean-shaven cheek. "I love you. And I think those names would make us both happy."

"Thank you. For loving me. For marrying me. For giving me this family I've always wanted." Far too long he'd been looking to the motorcycle club and the Marine Corps to give him that intangible piece missing to make him feel whole. But this was it. Ashley, the babies, her parents, even Quill and JD. This was what he'd been missing.

"I wish I'd seen it sooner," she said. "How remarkable you are. Seen that I could trust you. That we were meant to be."

No, he rejected that. Immediately. He looped his arms around her and pulled her close. "Everything happened as it was supposed to. Without all that came before, we would never have been here. Sometimes things have to happen, to push us, to show us, to get us where we never thought we'd be."

Not in a million years had he thought it possible for Ash to be his wife and the mother of his children, that he would even ever be a father.

"Then I'd go through it again." She stared at him with light and love. "All seven years. Walking through fire. To get to the other side, to be here with you now."

He really had won the lottery, because Ash was the remarkable one.

The great love of his life.

* * * * *

THE PERFECT MURDER

K.D. RICHARDS

Chapter One

He'd worried for years waiting for Franklin Brooks to ex-
haust all of his appeals. And now the last appeal was over,
and he should be able to relax, confident that another man
would be paying for the crime he'd committed. But he
couldn't relax. Because Chelsea just wouldn't let it go.

He couldn't believe Chelsea Harper, a third-grade teacher,
had the skills to hack into the LAPD's computer system, but
whoever she'd gotten to do it had been good. If he hadn't
had the foresight to flag Lily Wong's case file, he would
have never known it had been accessed and downloaded re-
motely. The hacker hadn't left a trail, either. Thank goodness he'd been notified the moment the file was accessed.
Knowing about the hack while it was happening was the
only reason he'd been able to follow it back to its source.
After that it had been easy to search through the hacker's
computer and find out who'd hired him to steal Lily's file.

He hadn't meant to kill her. His precious Lily. He'd tried
to make her understand they were meant to be together.
She wouldn't listen.

Killing her had been an accident. His rage had exploded,
and before he realized it, she was dead.

Franklin getting blamed for it had been a fluke. A convenient fluke.

He hadn't had to run. He hadn't had to leave his life.

But if Chelsea Harper succeeded in her quest to clear her father's name, he might have to now.

No. No, he wouldn't let her destroy his life.

He finished his breakfast, loading his dishes into the dishwasher and straightening the kitchen before he prepared to leave for work. Years of monotonous, solitary drudgery among boxes and in dark rooms had given him a super-power. Invisibility. It would come in handy. He'd need to keep an eye on Chelsea. And, if he had to, deal with her the same way he'd dealt with Lily.

Chapter Two

Chelsea Harper paused for a moment just inside the West Security and Investigations West Coast offices. The private investigations firm was located in a single-story brick building in West Hollywood. She passed through double glass doors into a small lobby where an attractive twenty-something Latina woman typed on a computer behind the reception desk. The decor was sleek and masculine with dark leather sofas and an uninspired snapshot of the iconic Hollywood sign on the white wall.

"Hello," she said, giving the receptionist, whose name plate read Bailey Lee, a smile. "I'd like to speak with Travis Collins, please."

Bailey returned her smile with one that looked genuine. She tapped a few keys, her smile slightly dimming when her gaze returned to Chelsea's face. "Is Mr. Collins expecting you?"

"No." Chelsea bit her bottom lip. She had considered calling to make an appointment, but she'd been afraid that Travis Collins would refuse to see her, so she'd opted for an ambush instead. "But I'm hoping he can make time for me."

"And your name is?" Bailey asked, reaching for the phone receiver.

"Chelsea Harper."

Bailey spoke quietly into the receiver for a moment. "Mr. Collins will be right out. You can have a seat while you wait if you'd like." She motioned to the leather sofas with one hand and reset the phone receiver with the other.

Chelsea was too nervous to sit. She backed away from the receptionist's desk but stayed standing. She examined the photos on the wall, not really seeing them. For maybe the hundredth time, she wondered if she was doing the right thing bringing on an investigator. Especially this particular investigator. For a second, she considered turning around and leaving, but Travis Collins rounded the corner before she could make a break for it.

She'd seen him on the news and had read several online articles that mentioned him while she was investigating PIs, so she knew he was thirty-five years old and an attractive man. Real-life Travis Collins was not just attractive, he was impressively masculine. He was tall and lean and wearing a suit that fit him like he had been born in it. His short, cropped hair was shot through with the beginning of gray. He moved toward her with a stride that was both confident and noble. His dark brown eyes fell on her face, and she watched as he quickly sized her up from head to toe.

His gaze met hers as he approached, and she saw the moment he recognized her. It had been a long time since anyone recognized her like that, but she wasn't surprised that he had. Her face had been in the papers almost as much as her father's during his trial, reporters hounding her to no end. And Travis was a detective and a private investigator, trained to remember details.

"Chelsea Brooks?" His expression was a cross between surprise and shock.

"It's Chelsea Harper now."

"You got married?"

She shook her head. "I took my aunt and uncle's last name after…" The press and social media had made it impossible to keep her father's name even during the years she'd lived in San Francisco immediately after college.

He nodded. "I understand."

She doubted that he did but kept that thought to herself. "What can I do for you?"

"I'd like to hire you."

One of his eyebrows cocked upward. "Hire me?"

"Yes. I understand you have left the LAPD and are a private investigator now." She waved a hand vaguely to encompass the lobby. "I want to hire you to help me prove my father's innocence."

His brow came down now as his eyes narrowed suspiciously. "Let's go into a conference room. We can talk more freely there."

He led her down a hallway to a small glass-walled conference room. She took a seat at the large round table, and he offered her coffee and water, which she declined. She was too anxious to drink.

Travis sat across from her at the table. He looked like he wasn't sure how to start the conversation. Finally, he said, "Why don't you tell me exactly what you're hoping West Investigations can do for you?"

She cocked her head to the side. "As you know, my father was convicted of the murder of Lily Wong, his former girlfriend."

Of course he knew. He had not been involved in her father's case, but he had been on the force, and Lily's murder was big news for more than a year. Chelsea knew it might seem odd for her to seek his help in proving her father's innocence. She'd spent countless hours debating whether he was the right man for the job. But West Security and Investigations was one of the best PI firms on either coast, and in the years since her father had been convicted, Travis had proved he was willing to go up against the system in general and the LAPD in particular to do the right thing. She was going to need that kind of courage and conviction if she had any hope of winning her father's freedom.

"He's exhausted all his appeals. The only way to get him out of jail now is to prove he was wrongly convicted."

Travis's expression remained sympathetic. "These past seven years must have been hard for you," he started.

"You have no idea, Mr. Collins."

"Call me Travis, please."

"Travis. And you can call me Chelsea. Travis, my father is innocent. He did not kill Lily Wong."

She watched him stiffen in his chair. "Ms. Harper—"

She held up a hand, stopping him. "I'm sure you heard that a lot as a police detective, but you're not a cop now, so I hope you'll hear me out."

He hesitated before nodding that she should continue.

"My father has always maintained his innocence. In the years since his trial, I've gathered as much information as I could, news articles, police reports, whatever I could get my hands on, and I've pored over them." She wasn't sure how he would react to the conclusions she'd drawn from her review of the police investigation, but if there was any chance of them working together, it was best to get everything out in the open now. "Frankly, the police investigation was lacking. They homed in on my dad and never looked at anyone else."

The look he gave her was one of disbelief. "It may seem that way to you, but a jury convicted your father."

"Based on the limited evidence collected by the cops and presented by the prosecutor," she responded fiercely.

"Ms. Harper, I know we are talking about your father. I'm sure you love him, but I don't have time—"

"I'm not here to waste your time, Mr. Collins," she interjected sharply. "I'm here to hire you. I want to clear my father's name and get him out of prison. But more than that, I want Lily's real murderer to pay. Whoever killed her has gotten away with the crime for all these years. My dad wants to rectify that." She paused for a moment before adding quietly. "And my dad wasn't the only one who cared about Lily."

"Chelsea, it has been seven years. I wouldn't even know where to begin."

He may have thought that statement would deter her, but it showed he was thinking about where to begin. A good sign in her book. "There are discrepancies in the witness statements." She reached into her handbag and pulled out a crinkled letter-size envelope. "My aunt received this note last week. I think the witness who placed my dad at Lily's house, Peter Schmeichel—"

Travis gave her a look that drew a smile from her along with a shrug.

"Hey, I didn't name him. Take it up with his parents. As I was saying, I think the witness who placed my dad at Lily's house perjured himself on the witness stand."

She handed him the letter and envelope and watched as he read it once, then once more. She knew the words by heart.

Peter Schmeichel lied. He didn't see your brother at the dead girl's house that night.

Travis shook his head. She was losing him. "This isn't evidence." He turned the envelope over, looking, she was sure, for a return address or some indication where it might have come from. There was nothing but a postage stamp indicating it had been mailed from California. No help.

"I know." She nearly growled the words. "The police detective I took it to all but laughed at me and the prosecutor wouldn't even meet with me. But if it's true—"

He cut her off. "If, and that's a very big if. We don't even know who sent this." He held up the note.

She didn't need to hear the suspicion in his voice to know what he was getting at. "You think my father, or I, sent the note. To what end? If I could get anyone to believe me, they'd just go find Peter, and he'd stick to his story. What would sending the note to myself get me or my dad in the end?"

Suspicion still clouded his face, but he said, "I'm willing to concede that it makes no sense for you or your dad to send the note, but that doesn't make the note true."

"But it's worth looking into. It might be my father's only chance." She hated the pleading tone of her voice, but if pleading was what it took to get him to help her, she'd do it. She reached out and took his hand in both of hers. His brown skin was smooth, and she couldn't help noticing how perfectly her hand fit with his. "Please. Please. Just come with me to visit my father tomorrow at the prison. Listen to his story. If you still don't believe him, I'll never bother you again."

The expression on his face was inscrutable.

She took her hand back. "At the very least you'll get paid for a day's work."

"One day. That's all I can promise you."

"And you listen with an open mind," she countered.

"And I'll listen with an open mind," he agreed.

The tension she had been carrying inside of her eased. Over the first hurdle and only hundreds more to go.

"If you give me your contact information, I will have the paperwork emailed to you. You can read it and sign it tonight and give it to me tomorrow. What time are we expected at Chino?" he asked, referencing the California Institution for Men by its common nickname.

Chelsea nodded. "Yes. Visiting hours start at eleven."

"I'll pick you up at your place at ten then. Let me walk you out."

He walked her to the entrance and shook her hand before she pushed out into the Los Angeles heat. She could feel his eyes still on her as she stepped off the curb. She was in the middle of the street when the roar of an engine came from her right. She froze as a black sedan careened toward her. Seconds passed as she processed the moment. Then her brain finally sent the message to her feet to move.

She leaped for the opposite curb. A sharp pain whipped through her hip right before she hit the pavement and rolled between two parked cars.

It felt as if the pain was coming from everywhere. She struggled to take in a breath.

Then Travis Collins's face appeared, hovering over hers. "Chelsea? Are you okay?" His voice sounded as if it was coming from a distance even though he was centimeters away.

She wasn't sure how to answer that. She struggled to push herself up into a sitting position, but gentle hands held her down.

"Don't move. An ambulance is on its way." He lifted her head gently and rested it on his knees.

"I don't need an ambulance."

"You were clipped by a car. You definitely need to be checked out at the hospital."

Sirens wailed in the distance. A man in a suit jogged to Travis's side. "I tried to catch him, but he got away."

"Did you get a look at the license plate?" Travis asked the man.

The man was hunched over, hands on his knees, trying to catch his breath, but he shook his head. "Sorry, dude. The guy must have been drunk or something."

"That was no drunk driver," Travis said, looking down at Chelsea, his gaze serious. "I think someone just tried to kill you."

Chapter Three

Travis rode with Chelsea in the ambulance to the hospital and didn't leave her side while the doctor checked her over. She was lucky. She had a few bruises and a deep gash on her arm that needed a handful of stitches, but she had no broken bones or permanent damage. She sat on a gurney in the curtained area of the emergency room, clutching Travis's hand in a death grip while the doctor stitched her arm.

The day had taken a very unexpected turn. He had planned to wrap up his current case, a fraud investigation for an insurance client who suspected a business owner of faking a series of thefts from his store. Travis had caught the owner on camera taking stock that had supposedly been stolen from the store from a self-storage locker and selling it out of his home. He'd already forwarded the photos to his client, but he needed to put the finishing touches on his report. That had been the plan for the day before Chelsea Harper walked into the West offices.

Chelsea squeezed his hand, and he glanced down at her face. He could tell she was trying to hide it, but she was in pain. That thought sent a bubble of anger rising in his chest.

Over her shoulders, he saw the automatic doors to the emergency room open. Kevin Lombard, his boss and West

Security and Investigations' operations manager, strode in with Tess Stenning, head of the West Coast office.

He gave Chelsea's hand a squeeze and rose. "I'll be right back."

Chelsea clutched his hand. "Don't leave me?"

"Of course not. I'm just going to talk to my boss. Right over there." He jerked his head to where Tess and Kevin waited for him.

He could feel Chelsea's eyes following him as he crossed the emergency room.

"How is she?" Kevin asked. Like Travis, Kevin was a former cop who had signed on with West Security and Investigations when the firm opened up its West Coast office.

"Okay. She had a gash on her arm that required stitches, but otherwise she was unharmed."

"That's a relief," Tess said. "I don't know how I would have explained to Ryan and Sean if a client got seriously injured right outside our offices." Although Tess was the head of West Security and Investigations West Coast division, she reported to Sean and Ryan West, the co-owners who remained in the firm's New York headquarters.

"Were you able to get any info from witnesses about the car or driver?" Travis asked. He'd given Tess a quick description of the hit and run before leaving for the hospital with Chelsea.

Tess shook her head. "Nothing. But we're working on getting security footage from the surrounding businesses. Unfortunately, the angle wasn't good enough to get a clear shot from our own cameras."

"Someone knew Chelsea was coming to see me. This wasn't an accident."

Tess nodded. "That or they were following her, but either way I agree this doesn't look like an accident."

"Do you think it was a warning or…" Kevin let the rest of the sentence hang.

Travis shook his head, his rage barely contained. "I don't know, but you better believe I intend to find out." His jaw clenched, and a hot rage bubbled in his gut. "Let me know when you get that security footage from the nearby businesses."

There was no reason for him to feel so protective of Chelsea—he barely knew her—but he did.

"Already on it," Kevin responded.

Tess gave Travis a searching look. "Bailey said Ms. Harper came in without an appointment and asked for you specifically. Do you two know each other?"

"Yes and no. She's Franklin Brooks's daughter. I wasn't involved in the case, but he was convicted seven years ago for killing his former girlfriend."

"And why did Ms. Harper want to speak with you?" Tess pressed.

"She wants to hire West Investigations to prove her father's innocence."

"Wait." Kevin held up a hand. "You said her father has already been convicted."

Travis sighed. "He was, but he never stopped professing his innocence. He's exhausted his appeals, but Chelsea says she's found evidence that a key witness may have lied at his trial."

Both frowns deepened.

"Okay," Kevin said. "That's all fine and good, but her father has been convicted and his appeal denied. I don't see how we can help."

Travis held his hands up, hoping to ward off his bosses' arguments. "Hey, I know what it sounds like. So does Chelsea. She's asked me to meet with her father tomorrow, and

I've agreed." He held a hand up higher stopping the oncoming protest. "I've made it clear to her that's all I'm agreeing to. One meeting. I'll hear Franklin Brooks out, but I've promised nothing."

Tess and Kevin groaned.

"I know. I felt the same way. Until the hit-and-run," Travis responded pointedly.

"The two things may not be related," Tess countered.

Travis shot her a look.

She shrugged. "I said they may not be related."

"Unlikely." Travis ran a hand over his head. "Chelsea comes to me about proving her father's innocence, and she's not ten steps from the office when someone tries to run her down? Something is going on here whether Franklin Brooks is innocent or guilty."

"And she's willing to pay our fee for this investigation?" Tess, ever the businesswoman, asked. "It may be a lot of expense for nothing."

"I'm not going to lead her on. One day. Limited expense, then I'll let her down as gently as possible." He thought about Chelsea having to take her uncle's name just to get away from the press, and anger bubbled. Whatever her father had done, she didn't deserve to be punished for it.

"You know digging into this could put you at odds with your friends at the LAPD, right?" Tess stated the obvious.

Travis frowned. "I doubt very much anyone at the LAPD considers themselves my friend. At least not anymore. And if, and I know it's a very big if, Chelsea is right, I want to make it right."

"I don't know how much of her father's story is true, but the lady has definitely acquired an enemy," Kevin said, shooting a glance at the bed where Chelsea was still getting stitched up. "There is one thing we should consider." Kevin hesitated before continuing, "Chelsea could have set this up herself. Hired someone to drive that car at her."

The look on Tess's face said she'd thought of this as well.

Chelsea's fear-filled brown eyes popped into Travis's head, and he instinctively rejected the idea. "You didn't see her face when she was lying there in the street. She was stunned and terrified. She didn't do that to herself." He glanced over his shoulder to where Chelsea lay on the rolling bed alone now, the doctor having finished her stitches. He turned back to his colleagues in time to catch them sharing a look. "What?"

"Do you think you might be too close to this to be objective?" Tess asked.

"No," he answered quickly. Maybe too quickly. "Look, do I feel sorry for her? Yes. She was twenty-two years old when her father was convicted. The local media around this was not kind to her. She had to take her aunt and uncle's last name to get away from it. But every convict professes their innocence. Franklin Brooks is guilty."

"But..." Kevin cocked an eyebrow.

"But something is going on here, and my gut tells me Chelsea might have put herself in real danger."

Tess shook her head. "Not another one. I'm surrounded by knights in shining armor."

He was no knight. But he was convinced something dangerous was going on, and he was going to find out what it was.

TRAVIS DROVE CHELSEA home after taking her to have the prescription the doctor had given her filled. He had suggested she call someone to come stay with her. She'd told him she would consider it, but she really just wanted to be alone. Still, she did leave a message for her cousin Victor, telling him she'd had a minor run-in with a car but that she was okay and resting at home. She was sure she'd have to answer for that less-than-descriptive message but hoped it would wait until tomorrow.

She swallowed two of the pills the doctor had prescribed and made a large bowl of popcorn for dinner. She usually loved to cook, but she didn't have the energy tonight, nor a taste for takeout.

When the popcorn was ready, she carried it and a large glass of water (since alcohol and painkillers didn't mix) to the sofa and flipped through the movie channels. *Batman*, the one with Michael Keaton, was on, and she'd just settled in to watch when the sound of the front door clicking open drew her attention.

Only Victor and her aunt Brenda had keys to her house, so she wasn't surprised when her cousin appeared in the doorway between the kitchen and family room a moment later.

"Chelsea Antoinette Harper, are you okay?"

"I'm fine, Victor. I told you that in my message," she said, moving the blanket covering her legs to the side and starting to rise.

"Do not get up." Victor marched across the room and sat next to her on the sofa. Gently, he pulled her into his arms and gave her a sideways hug. "I can't believe you didn't call me."

"I knew you were at work."

Victor was a teacher just like her, but he had elected to teach summer school. Chelsea usually did, too, but she'd planned to devote this summer to doing everything she could to finally free her father.

"I would have dropped everything if I'd known you needed me. You know that."

"I do. But like I said, I'm fine, and I wasn't alone."

Victor's eyebrows went up.

"The private investigator I hired was with me."

"Private investigator?"

"Yes. I hired him to help me with my father's case. I've done a lot by myself, but I think I could use some professional help."

"Chelsea—"

"I know you think I should just get on with my life, but—"

"It's not that I don't believe in Uncle Franklin's innocence," Victor started. He had taken a more measured approach to her father's predicament than his mother, who wanted nothing to do with her older brother, but Chelsea knew Victor had his doubts. He'd never laid them all out for her, preferring to remain Switzerland between Chelsea and Brenda.

"I get it, Victor, I do."

"I'm just worried about you. You said you were at the hospital with your private investigator. Was he with you when you got hit?"

"I was leaving his office. He was inside, but he saw it."

"Does he think the hit-and-run is connected to your investigation?"

"I'm sure it isn't," she lied.

"Uh-huh."

"Are you going to do something pedestrian, like order me to stop investigating?"

"You know me well enough to know I would never do anything pedestrian. I am worried about you, though."

"Don't be."

"Oh, don't be. Well, poof, I'm no longer worried. You know it doesn't work that way. You're family."

"So is my dad."

"I'm not saying he's not…"

"I know, and I know you don't mean anything by it, but I can't drop this."

"Do you really think you can turn up something the police didn't? Even after seven years?"

"I don't know," she said, exasperated. "Maybe not. But I have to try everything I possibly can to get my father his life back."

Victor bumped her shoulder with his. "You're amazing, you know that?"

"Well…" Chelsea flipped her hair over one shoulder and vamped.

"And so humble, too." Victor tossed a piece of popcorn at her. "By the way, this—" he circled the popcorn bowl with his index finger "—does not qualify as dinner. I'm going to call Novita's. Do you want me to order something for you?"

Chelsea sighed inside. It looked like she wasn't going to get her quiet, restful night at home, after all.

Chapter Four

Travis suggested rescheduling their appointment to meet with Franklin Brooks, but Chelsea insisted they keep it. If they missed their prearranged visitation time, it would be at least another week, probably considerably longer, before Chelsea could get set up another time to visit her father.

Travis had taken her home after her discharge from the hospital and promised to return the next morning at ten to take her to the prison. When she opened her front door to him that morning, she only looked slightly more rested than when he dropped her off the day before. But she grabbed her purse and locked the front door to the house, ignoring his renewed suggestion of putting off the visit.

It was a forty-minute drive to Chino. They passed the time with pleasantries. Chelsea told him all about her plans for her third-grade class in the fall. It was clear she was a passionate and engaged teacher, dedicated to doing her best for each of the kids who passed through her classroom doors. He wasn't surprised, given how zealously she was championing her father's cause.

The prison was a blocky, red-brick, one-story structure. A high fence topped with razor wire wound around the perimeter. Travis drove through the main gate and to the visitors' parking lot. He parked the car, then led Chelsea into the prison.

Prisons always felt like...well, prisons. The air was thick with the smell of disinfectant and despair. It hit him the moment he walked in. He and Chelsea got in line behind another family queued up to sign in and go through the series of indignities required in order to see their incarcerated family member or friend. The guards at the desk were efficient, checking names on driver's licenses against the names on the list of visitors allowed inside, then waving each person on to the lockers.

Travis and Chelsea showed their identification and stored their personal items—his wallet and her purse—in a locker before going through a set of metal detectors. After lining up again, they were led along with the other visitors to a large cream-colored room.

Fluorescent lights flickered overhead, and a half-dozen cafeteria tables lined the walls on either side of the room. The visitors trampled down the middle aisle, claiming seats at various tables. A mechanical buzzing echoed through the room after they were all seated.

Prisoners clad in drab gray jumpsuits, with Department of Corrections and their prisoner numbers penned on the left side of their chests, shuffled into the room.

Franklin Brooks was one of the last men to enter. He had aged quite a bit in the seven years since Travis had last seen him. His dark brown dreads had gone mostly gray. He'd lost weight but gained muscle. His skin was sallow, and his eyes were hooded, undoubtedly from the horrors he'd seen behind bars. But his smile when his gaze landed on Chelsea was pure and filled with love.

"Hi, Daddy." Chelsea stepped into her father's arms.

Brooks's arms tightened around his daughter, and his

eyes closed. The hug went on long enough to draw a cough and a frown from a nearby prison guard.

The prison had strict rules about touching. Brief touches such as hugs and handshakes were allowed at the beginning and end of visitation hour.

Brooks pulled away, his gaze moving to Travis. His smile fell into something more akin to a grimace. "Mr. Collins, thanks for coming."

Travis took Brooks's outstretched hand and shook it briefly. Travis sat next to Chelsea on one side of the table, and Brooks sat across from them on the other side.

"I wasn't sure Chelsea would be able to convince you to come see me, but I should have never doubted my girl." He smiled across the table at Chelsea.

Chelsea reached for her father's hand, giving it a quick squeeze before pulling back. "Travis has agreed to hear you out before he decides whether to help me investigate."

Travis frowned. He still had no intention of taking on investigating Franklin Brooks's case. As far as he was concerned, the justice system had spoken. He was more inclined toward investigating who had attempted to hit Chelsea.

"It would be best if you went over the details of your case. Starting at the beginning."

"The beginning," Brooks said acidly. "I'm not sure where that is, but I'll try." He took a deep breath and let it out slowly. "I wasn't a good father."

"Daddy—" Chelsea reached across the table for her father's hands.

"No, sweetheart. I wasn't." Brooks gave her hands a quick squeeze before pulling back. "If it wasn't for your aunt Brenda and uncle Darren taking us in and doing the lion's share of rearing you, I don't know where we would have been." His gaze went back to Travis's face. "Brenda is my sister. She and her husband took care of Chelsea like she was their own. Making sure she did her homework. Had clean clothes. Stayed away from the wrong crowds when she was a teen. She acted as Chelsea's parent after her mother died and while I drank too much, too often. Catted around with women when I should have been home, raising my daughter. I'm ashamed to say I never really grew up. At least not until I got here." He motioned to the prison walls. "And didn't have a choice."

Travis hadn't traveled all the way to Chino to hold a therapy session with Brooks. If the man was feeling remorse over how he'd lived his life, he was sorry, but he wasn't a therapist. "I understand," he said, nodding for Brooks to go on.

Brooks smiled knowingly. "Yes, of course. I don't want you to think I'm wasting your time, Mr. Collins. I just want you to understand what our life was like back when—"

Travis tapped into his store of patience. "When Lily Wong was killed."

Brooks glanced at Chelsea who nodded her encouragement. "Yes. Like I said, I dated a lot of women back then, but Lily was different. I loved her."

"How did you meet Lily?"

Brooks smiled, his eyes going glassy as if he was remembering. "At the park. She'd gone to a yoga class, and when she got back to her car, it wouldn't start. She called the garage where I worked, and I was sent out with the tow truck to see if I could get her car started. I couldn't. I had to tow it in, and by the time we got back to the shop, I had a date for the weekend."

"So, you two hit it off right away?" Travis asked.

"Right away. She was just so beautiful and so fun. And

funny, a real quick wit. Everybody loved being around her. You remember, don't you, Chels?"

"I do." Chelsea grinned. "She always made me laugh."

Brooks laughed then, too. "Always."

"When did the relationship start to sour?" That was one thing Travis remembered clearly from the trial. As good as things may have been between Franklin and Lily at the beginning of their relationship, it definitely hadn't been good around the time of Lily's murder.

Brooks's face fell. "When my drinking picked up. I'll be the first to admit it got out of hand. I've been in AA since I got to this lovely establishment. But it took me a long time to admit I had a problem."

"What happened the day Lily was killed?" Travis asked, getting to the reason he was there. It hadn't been his case and he only remembered bits and pieces of the news reports that had come out about Lily's murder and Franklin's conviction. And it was always best to hear a story directly from the source.

Brooks let out a sigh. "I've gone over it hundreds, thousands of times in my head. I convinced Lily to meet me at Billiards, a bar we like to go to. She had broken things off with me about a month earlier, sick of my drinking. And yes, my cheating on her. I had been trying to get her back. Cleaning up my act and proving to her that I could be the man she deserved." Brooks paused, looking down at the table.

Chelsea shifted in her seat. It couldn't have been easy for her to hear her father talk about his faults, but her expression remained nonjudgmental.

"Lily and I had a couple drinks. We talked, but she wasn't buying that I had changed. She said she was through. She deserved better, and she'd moved on." Brooks's gaze rose. "She said she'd met someone new. I got angry. I yelled at her. Said horrible things. Things I didn't mean. She left the bar, and I followed her to her house."

"And then what happened?" Travis pressed. Visitation was only for an hour, and they were already nearing half an hour in. He wanted to make sure he got as much detail from Brooks as possible before he left.

"Lily wouldn't let me in her house. I can't say I blame her. I was angry. We argued some more on her front porch, and then I left. That's the last time I saw her. I swear. I went to another bar, I could never remember the name of it, just some dive, and drank myself stupid. I'm not sure when I left or how I got to the park where Lily and I met, but I know I woke up there in the parking lot the next morning with one helluva hangover. I went home, and I was sleeping it off when the cops showed up and took me in."

It was a story full of holes, which was probably why the lead detective had homed in on him in the first place. "And you have never been able to recall any specifics about what you did or where you went after leaving the bar? Not in the last seven years?" It didn't seem likely.

Brooks shook his head. "It's like the hours after I left Lily are just gone."

Travis's disbelief must have shown on his face.

Brooks's expression hardened. "Mr. Collins, I know you don't believe me."

"Your story is hard to believe."

Chelsea turned an angry gaze on Travis. "You said you would listen with an open mind."

"And I have. I just don't believe the story I'm hearing. Open mind or no."

Chelsea's cheeks mottled in anger. "What about the hit-and-run? How do you explain that, or do you think it's just a coincidence that the very day I seek your help proving my father's innocence someone tries to run me down?"

"What?" Brooks's roar had most of the heads in the room turning in their direction.

Two of the guards headed toward them. "Keep it down, Brooks, or I will cut this party short," a beefy guard with a shaved head said in a gruff smoker's voice.

Brooks never took his gaze from his daughter. "What is this business about a hit-and-run?"

Chelsea's expression slipped from one of anger to one of chagrin. She clearly hadn't intended to tell her father about the hit-and-run, but the cat was out of the bag now. "I wasn't going to say anything. I didn't want to worry you." Her gaze slid from her father's face to the guards, who were still standing close by, and back to him nervously.

"Chelsea Antoinette Brooks. What is going on?"

Travis sat silently, watching the family drama play out.

"It's nothing to worry about. I was crossing the street yesterday when a car almost hit me. You know Los Angeles traffic. It was probably just some jerk racing off to an appointment."

Brooks held Chelsea's gaze for several long beats before turning to Travis. "You were there, yes?"

"It happened outside my agency's offices. I was inside the building, but I saw the whole thing from the window."

Brooks's eyes probed Travis's face. "Do you think it was just a drunk driving too fast and not paying attention?"

Travis could almost feel Chelsea willing him to say yes. But this was a father concerned about his daughter. If the roles were reversed, he would want the truth. So, he gave it to Brooks. "No, I don't. It looked like the driver was aiming for Chelsea."

Chelsea growled angrily next to him.

"I don't want you to investigate," Brooks said determinedly.

"Daddy—"

"Mr. Collins," Brooks said, looking Travis in the eye. "Thank you for coming out here today, but your services are no longer needed."

"It's not your decision to make," Chelsea ground out.

"It's my case and my life. That makes it my decision," Brooks shot back.

"It's my money," Chelsea countered.

The guards were looking their way again, and Travis didn't like the expressions on their faces. "Okay, let's just take a minute, and both of you cool down," he said. "I may not believe you, Brooks, but I don't not believe you, either. I don't know. The prosecutor's evidence against you was strong. But your sister recently received a note saying that Peter Schmeichel lied about seeing you at Lily's house around the time of her murder."

"Of course he lied. I may not be able to tell you exactly what I did after I left the bar that night, but I know—" Brooks pressed a fist over his heart "—in here that I didn't kill Lily."

"That's not going to be enough to get you out of jail," Travis responded.

"That's why I need your help," Chelsea countered.

"No," Brooks hissed. "I will not put you in danger."

Chelsea opened her mouth, but Travis spoke first. "It may be too late to avoid that."

"Then I want to hire you to protect Chelsea," Brooks said. "I don't know how much you charge, but I'll get it."

"Daddy, I don't need protection."

"Mr. Brooks, I'm not a bodyguard."

"You're a former cop. You served and protected for a living."

Chelsea slapped her hand on the table. "Is anyone listening to me? I don't need a bodyguard."

They had pushed the guards to their limit. The bald one came up behind Brooks. "All right, Brooks. That's enough. Time to go back to your cell."

Brooks didn't move.

Travis knew the situation could very easily and very quickly escalate. "I'll keep an eye on Chelsea," he said.

Beside him, another growl rumbled in Chelsea's throat.

Brooks's shoulders relaxed a fraction of an inch. "Thank you," he said, rising.

The guard put a hand on his shoulder and started turning him away, but Brooks resisted, looking at Chelsea. "Baby girl, be careful. You mean more to me than anything. Including my own life. I love you."

Brooks turned with the guard and let them lead him away then.

Chelsea fumed silently beside Travis while they collected their things and exited the prison. She didn't speak until they got to his car.

Travis opened the driver's-side door, but Chelsea glared at him over the car's hood. "What the hell was that?" she asked.

Travis sighed. He'd been asking himself the same question for the last several minutes, but he knew the answer. "That was me taking your case."

Chapter Five

Travis stood on Chelsea's welcome mat waiting for her to answer the door and wondering if he had made the right choice, agreeing to help her. Kevin hadn't been thrilled when Travis told him they were officially on the case. But something about Franklin Brooks's desperation to protect his daughter had gotten to Travis. That and the nagging suspicion that despite the evidence against her father, Chelsea might be onto something. When he'd dropped her off after leaving the prison, they'd agreed to meet up at her place later that evening to go over the files she'd collected.

Now the door opened, and Chelsea stood in front of him clad in yoga pants and a long-sleeve T-shirt, her feet bare. She'd put her hair atop her head in a messy bun from which curly tendrils fell to frame her heart-shaped face. The overall effect was sexy as hell.

"Hi," she said.

"Hey," he replied. "Can I come in?"

"Sorry. Yes, of course." She stepped back to allow him inside.

He followed her down a short hall, trying not to stare at her figure as he did, but it was hard not to. He'd always been attracted to curvy women, and Chelsea definitely had curves in all the right places. There was a grace to her that only came from being completely comfortable in her own skin. Her dark brown skin looked as if it had never seen a blemish, but it was her eyes that really pulled him in; violet-colored orbs that made him think of seduction.

He pulled his attention away from her and noticed that they had reached a living room, which opened up to the left, and a dining room was to the right. The dining room table was covered with boxes, and two big blue binders were stacked on top of one of them.

Chelsea paused in the entrance to the dining room. "This is my war room so to speak. Everything I have been able to find on my dad's case is in here."

"It seems like you've been able to get a lot."

"In some respects, yes. In others, not nearly enough." She began walking again, leading him to the kitchen at the back of the house. There was a second hall off the kitchen, and he could see three doors that opened onto it. Two bedrooms and a bathroom, he presumed. The house was small but cozy.

He sat on one of the two stools at the island counter. "What is all this?" He eyed the pots on the stove across from where he sat.

"I'm fixing us dinner. Beef shank ragù. I hope you like beef."

The smell had his stomach growling. He hadn't eaten since breakfast, and he suddenly realized he was ravenous. "I definitely do. But that sounds fancy."

Chelsea lifted the top of one of the pots and peeked inside. Obviously satisfied with what she saw, she placed the top back on. "Just a few more minutes. And it's really not that fancy. The pressure cooker does most of the work. I'm just cooking the pasta now. I figured we could eat and then get started going through the files."

"That works for me."

She smiled. "Great. Can I offer you something to drink? Water. Soda pop. Wine. I've also got beer."

"Beer for me, please."

"Is Corona okay?"

"Fine."

Chelsea pulled two bottles of Corona from the fridge and opened them both before sliding one his way.

He was glad she seemed to have gotten over her anger at him from that morning. It would definitely be easier to work together. He took a sip before speaking again. "So, I take it you like to cook?"

"Yeah." She took a pull from her bottle. "I find it relaxing. My aunt is an amazing cook, and I learned a lot from her. When I moved out on my own after college, I didn't want to get into the habit of eating out all the time. Not that I could afford to. How about you?"

"Do you mean do I cook? No. Not really." There were a handful of things he could make, but nothing like what she was talking about. "I'm pretty good at breakfast foods. Pancakes. Waffles. Even French toast, but nothing approaching beef shank ragù. I'm not even sure what a ragù is. Assuming we aren't talking about Chef Boyardee."

She laughed, and he felt warmth spread through his chest and limbs. "No. Definitely not. A ragù is basically just a meat-based sauce. The meat is braised and cooked in the sauce slowly over several hours. It's common for it to be served over pasta."

"So fancy spaghetti and meat sauce."

"Fancy spaghetti—" She fisted her hands on her hips, but her eyes sparkled, so he knew he hadn't actually offended her. "Go sit at the table." She pointed to the round table in the kitchen. "I'll show you fancy spaghetti." She laughed again, a slow sexy turnup of her mouth that sent a jolt through him. This felt a lot like flirting, something he did not do with clients.

Not that he didn't date. He did, usually quite regularly, although he'd been in a slump for the last several months. What he didn't do was relationships. Too messy, too likely that someone would get attached.

He never wanted to feel the pain of losing someone he loved again. The car accident that had taken the lives of his parents and his older brother, and had nearly taken his own when he was only ten, had left a wound that he wasn't sure would ever heal. He didn't think he could live through losing the woman he loved, and he was going to do everything he could not to ever put himself in that situation.

Maybe it was time to call one of his friends with benefits who understood that he was not looking for anything more than a pleasant weekend between two consenting adults. He'd been working a lot lately, so maybe after he put this case to bed, he'd take some time off. Maybe take a trip to Las Vegas or even splurge and fly to Hawaii. He lived frugally, so he could afford it.

He glanced at Chelsea, wondering if she'd ever been to Hawaii. He was positive she looked fabulous in a bikini. His groin tightened, and he shook the mental image from his head. She was a client, he reminded himself.

"Do you mind if I wash up before we eat?" he said, feeling the need to put a bit of distance between himself and Chelsea.

"Oh, sure. The bathroom is just down the hall." She pointed to the hall off the kitchen, confirming his earlier guess. "Second door to the left."

The bathroom was on the dated side but clean. He washed his hands, taking more time than usual to give his body a chance to settle down. On the way back to the kitchen, he passed the open door to what looked to be Chelsea's bedroom. He surveyed the room from the hall. A queen-size bed was on the far wall, with a night table and lamps on either side of the bed. On the other side of the room was a dresser with a bunch of bottles—perfume, hair products and who knew what else—on top. There were also framed photos. Several of her, Franklin and a woman who had to be Chelsea's mother based on the resemblance. One of her father, Chelsea and a woman Travis figured must be Chelsea's aunt. The second photo was of a younger man he didn't recognize. Maybe a boyfriend?

A knot of jealousy formed in his stomach.

"Everything okay in there?" Chelsea called out.

"On my way," he called back, leaving the doorway and striding back into the kitchen. "I'm ready to try this ragù."

Chelsea had set the table while he'd washed his hands. She plated the food and brought it to the table.

He took a bite, the flavors bursting in his mouth. "Wow," he said. "This is amazing."

Chelsea's eyes sparkled. "See, I told you. Better than spaghetti and meatballs, right?"

He agreed, and they ate in silence for a few moments, enjoying the meal. A part of him felt as if he should make conversation, but then he remembered this wasn't a date. And the silence wasn't bad. It was actually quite comfortable.

After a while, Chelsea cleared her throat. "Can I ask you a question?"

"Sure," he said hesitantly.

"Going to the state's attorney about the corruption in your department. That had to be hard."

That was an understatement. Two years after Brooks's conviction, the FBI indicted several LAPD officers and detectives for bribery, money laundering and other crimes related to accepting money, gifts and other favors from local gang members to look the other way regarding their criminal activities. Not long after the initial news reports came out, Travis's name was leaked to the media as the source of the investigation that ultimately led to the charges. And then the organized campaign to ruin him kicked off. It had worked. Most of his colleagues wouldn't talk to him, refused to be partnered with him and certainly couldn't be trusted to have his back. He'd had no choice but to leave the force.

His stomach twisted. "That's not a question," he responded.

"I know. The question is why did you do it? I mean, you had to know you would be vilified even if the corrupt officers were arrested and charged."

He looked into her eyes. "I did it because it was the right thing to do."

She held his gaze for a long moment. She looked as if she was on the verge of a response, a response that he was surprisingly eager to hear, but the doorbell rang before she spoke.

"Excuse me," she said, getting up from the table and going to the door.

He waited until she disappeared from the kitchen to follow her. He heard the front door open, and then Chelsea spoke.

"Simon, what are you doing here?" she asked, irritation lacing her tone.

"One of my colleagues told me you were in the hospital last night. Why didn't you call me?"

Travis peeked around the corner, careful to stay out of sight. Chelsea's back was to him, and the man—Simon, Chelsea had called him—hadn't noticed him. He took in the man's wavy black hair, blue eyes and beige-colored skin that shone in a way that could only be achieved with regular facials. He wore pressed chinos with a crease down the front and a starched white button-down. All he needed was a sweater thrown over his shoulders and the preppy look would be complete.

"Why would I call you?" Chelsea said.

The man sighed as if the answer was obvious, but Chelsea was just too dim-witted to see it. "Just because we aren't married anymore doesn't mean we can't care about each other, does it?"

"I haven't seen or heard from you in months, Simon. And when we were married, you cared so much about me that you cheated on me. Repeatedly."

Simon sighed again. "Chelsea, I want us to get past the past. We should look toward the future."

"We don't have a future."

"Can I please just come in? I don't want to have a conversation with you on the front porch for the whole neighborhood to hear."

Travis stepped around the wall separating the foyer from the rest of the house. "Chelsea, is everything okay here?"

Simon leaned around Chelsea. His eyes narrowed, and he made a show of sizing Travis up. "Who is this?"

"None of your business," Chelsea answered.

"This is my house," Simon shot back.

"Was your house. You seem to have forgotten I got the house in the divorce. You said it was a dump and you wanted to move to a condo on the beach."

Simon's expression turned contrite. "I said some things during our rough patch that I didn't mean. That's one of the things I wanted to talk to you about."

"I don't care what you want to talk about, Simon. I want you to leave." Chelsea started to close the door.

Simon's hand shot out, preventing it from closing. "Chelsea—" He stepped forward as if he was prepared to force his way into the house.

Travis crossed the few remaining steps separating him from Chelsea. He filled the space Simon would have used to slide past her into the house. "The lady asked you to leave," he said.

Simon was an inch or two shorter than Travis, but he looked up at him now with a glower. "I think you should leave. This conversation is between me and my wife."

"Ex-wife," Chelsea corrected. "Ex being the most important part, and if you don't leave now, I will call the cops."

"If you don't leave now, you will need an ambulance, not the police," Travis amended in a voice so cold it served as a warning.

Simon must have heard it. Anger still blazed in his gaze, but his hand dropped to his side, and he took several steps away from the door. His gaze swung to Chelsea, his expression turning pleading. "We need to talk, Chels. It's important. I'll call you to find a better time," he said.

"You do that." Chelsea closed the door. She turned to face Travis. "Sorry about that. I don't know what possessed him to show up here out of the blue. He's never done that before."

Travis held up his hands. "You don't owe me an explanation." And she didn't. Her ex-husband was clearly an ass, but he had reminded Travis why he didn't do relationships. "I think we should take a look at those files now," he said, turning his back on Chelsea, but not before he saw something resembling hurt flash across her face.

Chapter Six

Chelsea cleared the kitchen table of their dinner plates and got a pot of coffee started while Travis moved into the dining room. The evening had taken on a decidedly chillier tone after Simon's unwelcome visit. She couldn't help but be annoyed at Travis's change in attitude after Simon left. She hadn't invited Simon over. But her ex-husband did have a way of rubbing people wrong. Unfortunately, she hadn't noticed that character flaw until after they'd said *I do.*

"Would you like some coffee?" Chelsea asked, heading for the kitchen ten steps away. Nothing in her small house was more than ten steps from anything else. Small was all she could afford, but she made the space feel like home.

"Yes. Black please," Travis answered.

She finished loading the dishes in the dishwasher and poured two cups of coffee. She brought the mugs to the table, setting his next to him, then carrying hers to sit across from him.

"You have done a lot of work in a short time." He flipped through the binder that held a timeline of Lily's last days.

"I've tried to reconstruct as much of the timeline as I could. It's been years, though, and there are still missing pieces." Chelsea reached across the cluttered table and pulled the second binder in front of her. She'd constructed biographies for each of the witnesses who testified in her father's case, including Lily's friends and family and the cops who had testified. She also had copies of relevant reports, news articles, internet posts and anything else that she could find relating to the case, but she could save those for later.

Her father had already told Travis about the last time he'd seen Lily. Now, she walked Travis through her father's trial and appeals, pulling documents from binders and boxes to support her statements as she went along. The recitation took hours, and by the time she was finished, she had covered the dining room table with papers.

She took a sip of the now-cold coffee, exhausted but also energized. She could see doubt about the case against her father in Travis's eyes. He'd taken copious notes and had asked a lot of questions, good questions, some of which she hadn't thought of.

He flipped through the binder to Lily's biography. "You've tried to contact Lily's friends and family?"

She nodded. "I was hoping someone might listen and at least concede that the police work wasn't as thorough as it could have been. Maybe support my dad's appeals, but none of Lily's family or friends would speak to me when I approached them about my father's possible innocence."

That wasn't completely true. A few of Lily's friends had plenty to say about what a monster her father was and how much they hoped he rotted in jail, but they wouldn't talk to her about anything that could help her prove his innocence. Even when she'd pointed out that if she was right and that her father was innocent, Lily's killer was still out there. She understood why Lily's friends and relatives didn't want to talk to the daughter of her accused murderer. She didn't blame them, but it made her investigation harder, and she couldn't help feeling some resentment toward them for it.

Travis flipped to the autopsy report. The description of Lily's wounds and the photos were gruesome. The brutal nature of the attack was one of the reasons the cops had been convinced the killer had to be someone who knew Lily and whose anger was personal.

"How did you get this?" Travis asked.

"If I told you, I'd have to kill you," she joked flatly.

The autopsy hadn't been easy to get. It had been part of the trial but wasn't included with the transcripts that were available to the public. She'd had to resort to searching the dark web for hackers and praying that she wasn't walking into a scam or a police sting. It had not been cheap, but it had worked. The hacker had gotten her the autopsy report and the police report in the case. She paid and hadn't asked any questions.

Travis's eyebrows rose.

"It's better you don't know. Let's just say with enough money, anything is attainable."

He seemed to let it go. For now. "How long have you been trying to free your father?" Travis asked.

She met his gaze straight on. "Since the day he was arrested."

Travis's brow rose. "You believe that much in his innocence?"

"Yes," she said, steel in her voice. "He is innocent." She'd never believed in anything more than that her father, for all his faults, would never kill anyone. "My father loved Lily. And she loved him. I think that's why she met him that night at the bar. She may not have wanted to be with him, but she still cared about him. He didn't do this." It didn't escape her notice that her statement echoed Simon's comments from earlier. "And I won't stop until I prove he's innocent."

"Okay," Travis said with a nod.

Her shoulders relaxed when she saw that even if Travis didn't quite believe in her father's innocence yet, he at least believed that she believed it. That was a start. At least she wasn't completely alone in this anymore. Her father now had one person on his side with the knowledge, expertise and resources that could lead to his freedom.

Travis flipped several pages in the binder. "We need to speak with Peter Schmeichel and Gina McGrath. If Peter admits that he lied and Gina confirms it, that could go a long way to getting a judge's attention."

"Gina used to live next door to Lily. She worked as a nurse. I went to the house after I got the note about Peter's confession, but Gina doesn't live there anymore. The current occupant has been living there for years and had never heard of Gina." Chelsea grabbed the photos she'd taken of Lily's old house. She'd taken them more than a decade after the murder, but the home hadn't changed much in those years. "In the statement Gina gave the police on the night of Lily's murder, she says she was taking the trash out and saw my dad and Lily arguing on the porch. That was hours before the medical examiner says Lily was killed. My dad admits to the argument, but he swears he left and Lily was alive."

"Gina didn't see him leave?" Travis's eyes darted over the testimony.

"No. She went back into her house before my dad left."

Travis gave the note accusing Peter of lying a quick once-over, then flipped through the file until he got to the section on Peter. "And what can you tell me about Peter?"

"He was Gina's boyfriend back then," Chelsea admitted. "According to Peter's testimony, he left Gina's place the night of the murder around 1:00 a.m. He says he saw my dad leaving Lily's house at the same time. That my dad was disheveled and in a rush. His statement is what put my father at Lily's house around the time the medical examiner says she was killed." She flipped to a different page in the binder. "Mr. Schmeichel has a criminal record for dealing drugs, assault and burglary. Amazingly, he's managed not to do all that much time in prison even though he's a career criminal. He was arrested a week after Lily's death and that's when he told the cops about seeing my dad at Lily's house."

"And you find that suspicious," Travis stated the obvious.

"Of course I do. Why wouldn't he have approached the cops earlier if he'd really seen my dad that night?" She turned to yet another page in her binder. "And Gina's statement says Peter was at her house all night. No mention of him leaving at 1:00 a.m."

Travis frowned. "Could be an oversight. Witness statements often don't match exactly."

"The cops didn't interview Peter right after the murder. At least, there's not a statement from him that I could find."

"We need to talk to him," Travis conceded.

"His last known address is in the binder, but he's not exactly what I'd call stable. I can't say for sure that he still lives there."

"We'll find him wherever he is," Travis said with confidence. He looked up from the notebook, the gaze he pinned on her intense. "You've done a good job with this so far. Better than some professional private investigators I've had the misfortune to run into."

She nodded her thanks for the compliment and lowered her gaze to the papers on the table. Her cheeks were on fire, and her heart was thundering. "You guys should consider hiring more teachers. There's no one more resourceful on the planet."

Travis grinned and her stomach did a flip-flop. "I'll keep that in mind," he said.

CHELSEA WAS DAMN IMPRESSIVE. When Travis thought about what life must have been like for her since her father went to prison, he felt for her. "Tell me about Lily," he said.

Chelsea moved to open the binder to Lily's page.

Travis put his hand over hers, stopping her from flipping the pages. "You knew her. Tell me about her in your own words."

He could see genuine grief on her face when she thought about Lily. "What do you want to know?"

"Tell me how she and your father met. What was their relationship like? What did you think about her?"

"I was nineteen when they met. Between work and school, I was busy and not around very much, but she was nice. I was glad my dad had someone who seemed to care about him. He and my mother had married young, and then they had me. My mother passed away when I was ten, and my father dated a lot while I was growing up, but Lily was his first serious girlfriend after my mom passed. She did my hair for me for free, and we both loved action movies, so we'd always catch opening weekend of the new ones together. She was just great. She treated me more like a little sister than her boyfriend's daughter."

It was clear Lily's father hadn't been the only one who'd loved Lily. "How did you feel about her breaking up with your dad?"

Chelsea's gaze slid away from his. "I didn't really have an opinion."

Travis waited a beat, but Chelsea didn't add any more. "If this is going to work, you have to be honest with me. About everything."

"I'm not lying." But Chelsea still wasn't meeting his gaze.

"Maybe not, but you're holding back."

Chelsea sighed. "You already know my dad was a heavy

drinker back then. He was never violent, but he could be really mean when he had too many. I suspect Lily got tired of it."

She flipped to the page with Lily's biography. Hers was one of the only profiles that had a photo with it. Lily had been quite beautiful with a slim, heart-shaped face and straight dark hair. Her dark brown eyes were ringed with gold on the outer edges, and laugh lines creased the edges of her mouth.

Chelsea rubbed her thumb over the photograph as if she could touch Lily's cheek. Her gaze shifted out the window. It was clear that she'd been transported back into her memories. Travis wanted to reach across the table and comfort her. He suspected that she needed it. With her aunt not believing in her father's innocence and her father in prison, she was isolated. Alone.

And he needed to remember that. She was vulnerable, and she'd come to him for help.

"I skimmed Lily's half sister's testimony at the trial," Travis said. "She said Lily was finished with your father. That it was over, and she made that clear to him. Lily was dating someone else. But she didn't say who that person was."

"We never found out who the other man was. If there was another man. If Lily was seeing someone new, why did she meet my dad at the bar that night? And it seems odd that Lily told no one about him."

"Your dad also said Lily told him she was seeing someone new."

Chelsea shrugged. "Maybe that was her way of letting him down easy. I don't know. But I know that Lily's family, the cops, the prosecutors, everyone decided my father had committed the murder just hours after Lily's body was found. They never looked at anyone else seriously."

They were going to have to find a way to get Lily's friends and family to talk to them if they wanted to find out if her mystery man existed. He didn't anticipate that it was going to be easy.

Chelsea looked deflated, and he didn't like it. He preferred the aggressive, take-charge, uber-organized woman on a mission to save her father. He wasn't sure he believed her father was innocent, but he admired her determination. And he wanted to give her closure. One way or the other. He had a feeling that it had been some time since she had genuinely smiled. For one fleeting moment, the urge to be the man who put that smile on her face consumed him.

"Do you know the name of the salon where Lily worked?" he asked instead.

"The salon she worked at closed a few years ago. But I know Lily's best friend and former coworker, Rachel Lamier, opened her own salon, Snips, in Venice. She wouldn't talk to me when I called her, though."

"We have to start somewhere. Maybe I'll have better luck. If you're up for it, we can pay a visit to Rachel tomorrow morning."

"I'm up for it, definitely."

"Great." Travis looked at his watch. "It's getting late so I think I should go." He rose.

She stood and walked him to the door.

"Make sure you lock this behind me." He tapped the lock.

"Don't worry about me."

But he was worried about her. He'd made a promise to her father to watch out for her, and he intended to keep that promise. "Good night, Chelsea. Sleep tight."

Chapter Seven

Chelsea spent a restless night flitting in and out of sleep. A part of her was excited. She felt like there was finally some movement behind her investigation. Another part of her was nervous. This was her father's last chance. If she didn't find some evidence to convince the authorities that they'd convicted the wrong man for Lily's murder, her father would spend the rest of his life in jail.

At 7:00 a.m., she gave up trying to sleep and went to the basement where she kept her treadmill. A forty-five-minute workout burned off some of her nervousness, but her injured hip throbbed afterward. She took a long hot shower to soothe the pain and, when she got out, found a text message from Travis telling her he was on his way over. She dressed quickly in a yellow floral dress and braided her long light brown hair into a goddess braid encircling her head. She was still debating which pair of sandals went best with the outfit when the doorbell rang.

Travis stood on her doorstep, two steaming to-go cups in hand. Despite the already warm late June morning, he wore blue jeans. He'd paired them with a white short-sleeved collared shirt that brought out the flecks of gray in his brown eyes. Not for the first time, she noted how devastatingly handsome the man was.

Travis's brow quirked up. "Can I come in?"

Chelsea's body flooded with embarrassment at how long she'd been standing in the doorway thinking about him. "Yes. Of course. Sorry."

She stepped back to allow him to pass by her into the house. He headed straight for the dining room, where she had cleared a small square of space on the table for her laptop. She'd spent some time after he left the night before scouring social media for more of Lily's prior coworkers with no luck.

"How was your night?" she asked, accepting the cup of coffee Travis handed her. "Thank you." She popped the lid off her coffee and took a sip. She was pleasantly surprised to find it was exactly how she liked it, with milk and more sugar than she probably should have had. She was touched that he had paid attention to the several cups of coffee she'd plowed through while they'd worked the day before. She closed her eyes and wrapped her hands around the warm cup, taking another sip. It was good. Almost as good as the expensive stuff she bought from the specialty coffee shop not far from her house, her one splurge.

She opened her eyes and found Travis watching her, his gaze intense. Sexual awareness flooded through her. "What?"

"Nothing." He shifted his gaze away, focusing on setting up his tablet next to her laptop. "How are you feeling? Any pain?"

Part of her wanted to push to know exactly what he was thinking when he was looking at her, but she let it go. "A little. Nothing a couple of ibuprofen can't fix. Did you have any luck finding our eyewitness Peter Schmeichel?"

"I think I have a line on him."

"Really?" She felt herself perking up at the news. "That's great."

"Don't get too excited. I don't have anything concrete like a location yet, but I'm working on it."

"Still, great." She took another sip of her coffee. "Hopefully, Rachel will give us some useful information as well. Snips opens at nine."

Travis looked at his wristwatch. "It's still early. The shop won't be open yet."

Chelsea put her coffee down and eyed her phone. "Are you sure it wouldn't be better for me to call and make an appointment when they open? Rachel might be more receptive to answering our questions if we don't ambush her."

Travis shook his hand. "I come from the school of thought where it's better to ask forgiveness than permission."

"Alrighty then. An ambush it is," Chelsea teased. "I'm just going to go finish getting dressed."

In the bathroom, she popped open the bottle of ibuprofen and took two pills, then brushed her teeth and reapplied her lip gloss before rejoining Travis.

"What are you doing now?" She looked over his shoulder at the screen of his tablet.

"Just pulling on some of the threads, one of which I hope will lead to Peter Schmeichel. He's done a good job of staying under the radar. He hasn't filed taxes in years or applied for disability or unemployment. I can't find any relatives or even an address for him."

Chelsea frowned. "I thought you said you had a line on him."

"I have other oars in the water, don't worry," he responded confidently. "I'll find him. It's just unusual for someone to disappear so completely."

"Do you think there's something to it? Like maybe he's disappeared to avoid someone or something. Like the law?"

Travis shrugged. "Maybe. I'll keep digging."

Since they had an hour to kill before they needed to leave for Snips, Travis continued his search for Peter while she tried to locate as many of Lily's former coworkers as she could. It was slow going; most salons didn't list their stylists by name, so she had to cobble together information from old websites and social media. Travis didn't seem to be having much better luck based on his grunts and sighs.

At ten minutes to 9:00 a.m., Travis closed the cover of his tablet. "Are you ready to head out to see Rachel?"

Chelsea closed her laptop. "As ready as I'll ever be."

They climbed into Travis's car, and he headed for Venice. Rachel had opened her shop, Snips, six years earlier. Based on its fashionable location, it seemed like she was doing very well as a business owner. Rachel had been interviewed by the police during their investigation, but she hadn't testified at Chelsea's father's trial. Chelsea didn't know what or if Rachel could tell them anything that might be helpful in proving her father's innocence, but she hoped the woman would be less hostile toward now that more time had passed. She was still hopeful Rachel might be able to tell them something about Lily's life around the time of her murder that they didn't already know. Maybe point them in the direction of this mysterious boyfriend, assuming he existed at all.

They parked in a garage and walked the two blocks to the salon. Chelsea noticed several women turn and shoot very feminine gazes and smiles at Travis as they made the trek to the salon. A pang of jealousy stirred inside her, but Travis didn't seem to notice the women's stares. Or maybe he was just used to them. He was a very attractive man, there was no doubt about that. Maybe if they'd met under different circumstances… But they hadn't. And she needed to focus all her attention on her father's case.

One of the women passing by them tripped on some uneven pavement she hadn't noticed because she'd been staring at Travis.

He reached out a hand, steadying her. "Are you okay?"

"Yeah…yes. Thank you." The woman's words came out breathily.

Chelsea rolled her eyes and shot a death glare at the woman. The woman's cheeks pinked, and she hurried on.

Travis turned to her, his eyes sparkling with mischief. "That wasn't very nice."

"She's a grown woman falling all over herself because you have a nice—"

He looked like he was trying not to laugh. "A nice what?"

"I'm sure you know you're a very attractive man."

"Am I now?" Travis said in a teasing tone.

"Can we just get to the salon, please?" Chelsea picked up her pace.

Now Travis did let loose with a hearty laugh. "Slow down. I want to hear more about how attractive you find me."

"I did not say I found you attractive," she shot back, heat flooding into her cheeks. "I said you know you are an attractive man."

"A very attractive man, you said."

"Is this really the time for this conversation?" she asked, nearly sweating with embarrassment.

Travis caught her arm as they arrived in front of Snips. "I think it's a great time for this conversation."

A gust of wind blew a napkin down the street, but it did nothing to cool the heat burning through her.

Travis stared at her with an odd look she couldn't place on his face. "I think you're very attractive, too."

Chelsea's heart thumped in her chest, her pulse picking up even more steam when Travis took a step closer to her. She could see that his brown eyes were rimmed in gold. She saw heat in them.

Travis reached out a hand, running two fingers down her cheek, sending her into a full-body blush. He leaned in closer, and she closed her eyes.

Someone bumped into her shoulder. Chelsea glanced at the woman and recognized her as Rachel from her social media accounts.

Rachel Lamier had shiny, bouncy, shoulder-length red hair that only a professional could have achieved. It framed her square-shaped face and deep-set blue eyes. Rachel appeared to be about the same age as Lily would have been. Chelsea couldn't help but feel a twinge of sadness at the thought that Lily hadn't had the opportunity to live the years that Rachel had.

Rachel tore her gaze from Travis, who was seemingly the cause of their minor collision, and turned to Chelsea. "Oh, sorry. I wasn't looking where I was going."

Chelsea chuckled knowingly. "That's okay. I understand. You are Rachel, aren't you?"

The slightly amused expression on Rachel's face changed to suspicion. "Yes. Do I know you?"

"I'm Chelsea Harper. I'm actually here to speak with you."

Rachel's shoulders relaxed. "Oh, well, I have a client scheduled in a few minutes but if you can come back this afternoon, I'm free after 1:00 p.m." Rachel shot another glance at Travis, no doubt wondering about his presence.

"I'm not here to have my hair done. I was hoping to speak to you about Lily Wong."

Rachel started. "Lily? Why?"

It was Chelsea's turn to shoot a glance at Travis. He picked up on her train of thought right away. "Ms. Harper is Franklin Brooks's daughter." Travis handed Rachel a business card. "She has hired me to look into her father's case."

"I don't have anything to say to you," Rachel spat.

"My father is innocent," Chelsea replied firmly.

"We'll only take a moment of your time," Travis interjected. "Please."

The seconds stretched until Chelsea was sure Rachel was going to say no and walk away. But Rachel surprised her. "Ten minutes. Then I have to prepare for my client. What do you want to know about Lily?"

RACHEL LED CHELSEA and Travis to her office at the back of the salon and closed the door. The office was no bigger than a closet and so cluttered as to be claustrophobic. Rachel cleared off the sole chair in front of her desk, and Travis gestured for Chelsea to take it. She did, and he stood next to her facing Rachel who took a seat behind the desk.

"I don't know how I can help you," Rachel said. "It's been a long time, and the cops caught Lily's murderer as far as I'm concerned." She shot a venomous look in Chelsea's direction.

Even though he understood where Rachel was coming from, Travis felt a surge of protectiveness. Chelsea didn't deserve anger from Lily's friends and family. Even if her father was a murderer, she'd done nothing wrong. And if she was right, and Franklin was innocent, she was one of the bravest women he knew.

Chelsea didn't seem to be letting Rachel get to her,

though. Her expression remained polite, almost as if she hadn't seen the nasty look Rachel shot at her, although Travis knew that she had.

"We understand why you feel that way," Travis said soothingly. "You want someone to pay for what was done to your friend."

"I do, yes."

"But what if the wrong person is in jail? What if Lily's killer is still out there? Walking free? You wouldn't want an innocent man to pay for a crime he didn't commit."

Rachel bit her bottom lip. "Of course I wouldn't want that."

"Me, either. That's why I agreed to take this case. If Lily's killer is still out there, we need to find him and have him brought to justice. Anything you can tell us, no matter how insignificant you might think it is, could help."

From the look on her face, his words had gotten through to Rachel. "I'll tell you what I can, but I warn you it probably won't be much."

"Thank you." Travis smiled, melting more of Rachel's iciness. "Can you tell me what Lily was like?"

Rachel smiled. "She was the most caring person you'd ever meet. Everyone from her coworkers to her clients loved her." It was similar to the way Franklin and Chelsea had described Lily. Of course, people tended to speak well of the dead even when they hadn't been very nice people in life, but he had a feeling that Lily had genuinely been a good person who was liked by many.

"Did you and Lily hang out a lot outside of work?" he asked.

"I wouldn't say a lot, but we did hang out a few times."

It looked like Chelsea had wisely decided to let him take

the lead on questioning Rachel, so he forged on. "Did Lily ever mention a new boyfriend?"

Rachel's face scrounged as if she was thinking back. "No, not that I remember. She broke up with Frank a few weeks before she was killed." She shot another look Chelsea's way, but this one was far less venomous. "I don't remember her talking about dating anyone new."

"Did she ever talk about Frank with you? Do you know why they broke up?"

Rachel nodded. "Yes, she talked about him all the time. She really loved him, but I got the feeling that she was fed up with his drinking near the end. I don't think she wanted to end it, but she didn't know what else to do. Or how to help him. She stopped hanging out with me as much after work once they broke up. I don't know much about the relationship after that."

Travis poked and prodded along that line of questioning for a bit more, but Rachel didn't have more to offer about Lily and Frank's relationship.

"Is there anything else you can remember about that time?"

"Well, there was one thing. Lily had been having some trouble at her house."

Chelsea sat up straighter in the chair next to him. "What kind of trouble?"

"She complained a couple of times about some strange stuff that was happening. Her car had been vandalized with someone throwing eggs on her hood. And she thought someone had been in her house, but nothing was missing. I told her it was probably just teenagers goofing, you know. It didn't seem serious."

"Did she call the police?"

"I don't think so. Like I said, we both thought it was prob-

ably just some of the rowdy teens who lived in her neighborhood. And it wasn't like there was anything missing or
permanently damaged." Rachel shrugged. "What were the
police going to do?"

Probably nothing, but he made a mental note to check
if Lily had filed a police report anyway. "Did you tell the
police about the vandalism when they interviewed you?"

"Oh." Rachel seemed surprised by the question. "I'm
not sure. Probably not. They seemed so sure that Frank had
done it when they talked to me. Most of their questions were
about him, and his and Lily's relationship."

Travis shot a look at Chelsea. She was pressing her lips
together as if she was trying not to let certain words spill
out of her mouth.

Rachel pressed a hand over her mouth. "You don't think
the stuff with her house had anything to do with her murder, do you? I mean…" She cut a look at Chelsea. "If Frank
is innocent, and I didn't say anything…"

"Right now, we are collecting information. We don't
know what is relevant and what isn't, but you've been very
helpful." Travis rose as did Chelsea next to him. "If you
think of anything else, give me a call."

He opened the door, but Rachel spoke again before he
and Chelsea stepped out of the office. "I met Frank a couple
of times. When a cop said he killed Lily, I couldn't see it.
I know people have dark sides, but he just didn't seem like
the type. He loved her. You could see that whenever they
were together. Even when they were fighting and arguing."

Chelsea gave a small smile. "Thank you for saying that."

Rachel tapped the side of Travis's business card against
the palm of her hand. "Would you let me know what happens? If it wasn't Frank who killed Lily, I'd like to know. I
want to see the person who hurt my friend in jail."

"I will." Chelsea nodded. "And like Travis said, if you can think of anything else, please let him know."

They headed out of the salon. Travis glanced at Chelsea as they walked to the car in silence, but she looked lost in her thoughts. He'd give anything to know what she was thinking, but her face gave away nothing. They were back in the car before she spoke again.

"Well, what do you think?" she asked, fastening her seat belt.

"The vandalism and possible break-in are something to explore. I take it you didn't know about that." Travis started the car and pulled out of the parking lot.

"I didn't. And if my dad did, he never said anything to me. And it didn't come up during his trial either," Chelsea added bitterly.

He could understand why she might be bitter. It certainly would have helped her father if the jury had heard that Lily had been the victim of vandalism and possible break-ins just weeks before she was murdered. Of course, it might have also hurt him if the prosecution had been able to imply that Franklin was behind the vandalism and break-in. You never knew with a jury.

"Rachel wasn't sure if Lily called the police, but I'm going to check into whether she made a police report about the events at her house," he said, laying out his next steps.

"Okay, and what should I do?"

"Did Lily have any social media presence?"

Chelsea nodded. "Yes, she had a couple social media pages. Why?"

"Take another look at them. We need to figure out if this boyfriend really existed. If he did, it's likely he's in those feeds somewhere. Don't just look for the obvious, though. Look for anything out of the ordinary for Lily. A new restaurant. Changes to her normal routine. Anything that might have changed between the time she and your father broke up until her death."

Chelsea frowned. "Rachel didn't seem to think Lily had a new man in her life."

"That's what she said, but I noticed some hesitation. Like maybe there was something she didn't want to say. Often people don't want to say anything that might make their friends look bad, especially when those friends can no longer defend themselves."

Chelsea shrugged. "Okay, I'll see what I can find."

"In the meantime, are you up for a little field trip?"

"A field trip? Where?"

"I want to get a look at Lily's old house. Get a feel for the place and the neighborhood and how someone might have gotten in and out without being seen."

The air in the car stilled. Lily's old house…which also happened to be the scene of her murder.

"I understand if you don't want to go with me. I can drop you off at your place if you want."

"No," Chelsea said quickly. "No, I'll go with you."

"Chelsea, you really don't have to—"

"It's okay. It's been a long time, and I want to be involved in every part of the investigation."

"Okay. Let's go back to the beginning." Travis said, turning the car in the direction of Lily's old San Fernando Valley neighborhood.

Chapter Eight

Chelsea gave Travis an address that she knew by heart, and he plugged it into the GPS and drove. He stopped the car across the street from Lily's old house. It looked bigger, cheerier the last time she'd seen it. Lily had been proud of her little home, keeping the square patch of front lawn neat and trimmed and the window boxes full of flowers and herbs. Now it looked as if the current owners hadn't put any effort into its upkeep.

Travis turned to her. "You can stay in the car. I just want to take a quick look around."

Her gaze didn't leave the forlorn little house, but she answered him. "No, I want to go with you."

They climbed out of the car together. Chelsea stopped at the top of the cracked walkway and looked at the house. The house itself hadn't changed, but it had lost its sheen. Gone were the colorful flowers in the flower beds. The lawn was overgrown. The windows were filthy with grime and dirt.

Chelsea pointed to the house to the right of Lily's old place. "That's where Gina McGrath lived."

The neighboring house looked only slightly better kept than Lily's. Chelsea knew from her investigation that Gina no longer lived there.

She and Travis made their way up the cracked walkway

to the front door. Travis knocked on the door, then peered through the front window. "I don't think anyone is living here at the moment."

Somehow that made her even sadder. Lily was gone, and her house was empty.

"I'm going to head around back," Travis said. "See if I can find an open door and take a look around."

Chelsea nodded. "Let's go."

Travis hesitated for a moment, searching her face. Whatever he found there clearly didn't please him, but it must have been enough to let him know she wasn't going to fall apart on him.

They walked through the tall grass around to the back of the house. Although the back door was locked, it was flimsy enough that Travis needed only to give it a good shove to get it to pop open.

"Travis," Chelsea hissed. "That's illegal."

"I'm just going to take a look. Get a feel for the crime scene. You can stay here if you want."

They both knew she wasn't going to do that despite her protests.

She hadn't been in Lily's house since before the murder and then only a handful of times. There was a generously spacious living room/kitchen/dining room setup followed by a short hall. Travis was right. There was clearly no one currently living in the house. There was no food in the fridge, and the water and electricity had been shut off. The sun was still high in the sky, but with no lights to turn on inside the house, shadows crisscrossed the space.

Travis aimed the flashlight on his phone toward the hall. Chelsea followed him past a bathroom and a small bedroom. Lily's bedroom was at the end of the hall. A king-size bed still rested against one wall, its headboard leaning precariously forward.

Chelsea's mind flashed back to the crime-scene pictures from the file her hacker had gotten for her. Lily lying on the bed. Cuts on her face, neck and hands. Her sheets were covered with blood. The report indicated she had fought. Her nails had been broken off in several places. And she had been stabbed six times. *Overkill*, Chelsea remembered reading in the detective's notes. It was one of the reasons the police believed Lily had more than likely known her attacker.

Chelsea was suddenly overwhelmed by a wave of emotion. The room was too small, and everything in it was too close to her. She'd looked at the crime-scene photos dozens of times, but somehow, she'd been able to detach in a way she couldn't while standing in Lily's old room. In the space where she'd been killed.

Almost as if he could feel her inner turmoil, Travis reached out and pulled her into his arms.

"Breathe. Just breathe slowly."

"All the violence, the anger. He stabbed her six times. Why?" Tears slid from her eyes.

Travis laid his cheek on her head, pulling her in closer. "I don't know, honey. I do know whoever did this is a coward. And we are going to figure it out."

She leaned into his warmth, letting the spicy scent of his cologne wrap around her. Despite the circumstances, in that moment, she felt safe. Protected. She stepped out of his arms, wiping the tears from her cheeks. "Can we get out of here?"

They retraced their steps through the house to the back door. They rounded the house just as a man got out of a red Mazda in the driveway next door.

He looked at them, surprise on his face. "Hello? Can I

help you?" A curly mop of brunette curls bounced on the man's head as he pulled himself the rest of the way out of his car and slammed the driver's-side door.

Travis made his way forward, his business card extended toward the man. "I'm Travis Collins, a private investigator. This is Chelsea Harper, my associate. We're looking into the death of the woman who used to live here."

"Lily," the man said.

Chelsea shared a quick look with Travis.

"Yes," Travis confirmed. "Did you know her?"

"A little," the man answered. He looked to be a few years younger than her father, mid-to late-forties.

"Would you mind if I asked your name?"

"I'm Jace Orson."

"And how long have you lived here, Mr. Orson?"

Jace darted a glance at his house as if he was thinking about making a run for it. "About eight years. A little closer to nine."

"So, you lived here when Lily lived next door," Chelsea said.

"Yes. It was so sad when she was… Well, you obviously know if you're investigating. I thought they caught the guy who did it. A boyfriend or something."

"There have been some new developments," Travis said quickly.

Jace's face registered surprise.

Chelsea frowned. She had a feeling he'd spoken up so quickly to cut off her chance to argue that the man in jail for Lily's death had been wrongly convicted.

"Do you remember seeing anything unusual around the time that Lily was killed?" Travis asked. "Maybe a stranger hanging around? Or a vehicle that seemed out of place?"

"No." Jace shook his head. "But it's been a long time. I would have told the police if I had."

"Do you remember seeing or hearing Lily argue with anyone? Ever see her upset with anyone?"

"Well, sometimes she and the boyfriend of hers got into it." He rolled his eyes. "Loudly. I don't know what she saw in him. I could tell he was a loser. I wish she had listened to me."

Chelsea stopped angry words from springing forward and instead asked, "Listened to you?"

"Yeah, I may have mentioned that she could do better than the bum she was seeing. For a while there, I actually thought she had taken my advice."

"Why?" Travis asked.

"Because a new guy started coming around for a while, but he wasn't around for long before the loser boyfriend was back."

Chelsea's heart pounded. "The new guy, do you remember his name?"

"No, sorry. I don't think I ever knew it. Like I said, I didn't know Lily that well."

Well enough to call her boyfriend a loser, Chelsea thought, still fuming.

"Can you describe the man you saw?" Travis pressed.

"Oh, man. No, I don't think so. I'm only even thinking about this stuff because you guys asked. I try not to remember what happened right next door to me."

"I understand," Travis said in a conciliatory tone. "Do you happen to remember where you were when Lily was killed?"

Jace frowned. "I don't think I like what you are suggesting."

"Trust me I'm not suggesting anything," Travis said with

a smile. "I'm just trying to draw as complete a picture as possible of the last moments of Lily's life."

Jace hesitated for a moment before answering. "Well, I do remember where I was as it happens. I was out with friends that night."

"One more question for you. Do you know where the neighbor on the other side of Lily's house moved to?"

Jace looked over Chelsea's shoulder at the house that used to be Gina's. "Sorry. She hung around for a little while after Lily died, but a lot of people got freaked out by a murder happening on their street. And, well, a lot has changed over the years."

"Thanks anyway for your help," Travis said, grabbing Chelsea's hand and backing away. "If you think of anything else, could you please give me a call at the number on the card? Anything you remember could be helpful."

"He's not going to call," Chelsea said as they got back into the car. She watched Jace watch them for a moment before he went into his house and shut the door.

"That's okay. He confirmed that another man had been visiting Lily around the time of her death. We need to find that man."

Chapter Nine

"Where to next?" Chelsea asked when they were back in the car.

"I'm headed back to my office to see if I can track down Peter and Gina. I'm taking you home so you can get some rest."

"I don't need to rest." But something about saying the word set off a yawn.

"You do need to rest. You could have been killed, and I noticed that hitch in your step back at Lily's house. Your hip is hurting you."

"I'll be fine."

"Rest. Investigations take time. A lot of the work is waiting for something to break."

Frustration swelled in her chest. "My father has been in jail for seven years now. I don't want to waste any more time."

Travis glanced across the car at her. "I get it, I do. I'll call you if I get any news. Until then, there's nothing for you to do."

She didn't like it, but she wasn't willing to argue with him about it. Not when she had an idea about who might be able to help them. But she knew Travis would want to go with her, and in this case, she was sure she needed to make this visit alone.

He turned into her driveway moments later. Travis walked her to her door and waited on the porch until he heard the lock click into place. She watched as he backed out of her driveway and waited five minutes before she grabbed her purse and keys and headed back out.

She'd made the short drive from her place to her father's best friend's house hundreds of times over the years. Bill Rowland, or Uncle Bill as she'd called him since she was a little girl, was a second father to her...

She turned the radio to her favorite nineties pop station and willed the tension in her shoulders to let up.

A short time later, she pulled to a stop at the curb in front of a suburban brick ranch in Winnetka. The flower beds lining the front of the house were filled with neatly trimmed flowers and hedges, and the grass was freshly cut. A tall maple tree stood stoically in the yard, his green leaves waving in the slight breeze cooling the day. Uncle Bill had taken up gardening in his semiretirement with the same passion he'd had for his auto mechanic business.

She walked to the front door and rang the bell. Seconds later, the door swung open, and Uncle Bill stood before her.

Uncle Bill smiled, happy to see her as always. The joy on his face sent a pang of guilt through her for not visiting more often. Uncle Bill had never married or had children. He had a brother in Arizona, but for the most part he'd always been on his own. Chelsea and her father were his family. He had been there for her as much as Aunt Brenda had, even though the two hadn't always seen eye to eye. Brenda Harper was conservative, quiet, a rule follower at heart. And Uncle Bill...was not. Gregarious, outgoing, always up for a laugh, that was Uncle Bill. He'd kept the same boisterous personality into his retirement years.

"How's life treating you, kid?" he asked, grabbing her into a bear hug. He held her there for a moment before pulling back and searching her face. "Everything good?"

Uncle Bill was one of the most empathetic people she knew. Which was why he'd always known when she was feeling down or nervous or needed someone to talk to.

Chelsea nodded and forced a smile. "Yes, everything is fine."

"Are you teaching this summer?" he asked as he led her into the small living room where a glass of lemonade and a small plate of cookies rested on the coffee table in front of his lounger.

"Not this summer. I decided to take some time off."

"Good for you. Oh, let me get you a glass of lemonade. I got chocolate chip cookies from this new bakery near the grocery store. They aren't too bad," he said, turning for the kitchen.

"No, Uncle Bill, I'm not thirsty or hungry. I just need to talk to you."

He turned back to her. "Are you sure?"

She assured him that she didn't want any refreshments, and he reclaimed his glass of already poured lemonade before settling into his battered brown easy chair.

Despite an active lifestyle, he'd begun to develop a little pouch in his tummy. At fifty-four years old, Uncle Bill was fortunate to have worked hard, built a sound business and saved enough that he only went into work a couple of days a week now. The rest of the workweek he left to his shop manager and employees, most of whom had worked for him for years, to handle. Her father had been one of those employees before he was arrested and convicted of Lily's murder.

Uncle Bill had never believed his best friend was a murderer and had even offered to pay to hire a better lawyer for her father. But Franklin's pride hadn't allowed him to accept what he considered charity. Not even from his best friend.

"So, what brings you to an old man's door today?"

"You are not an old man, and I'm sorry I don't visit more often."

Uncle Bill waved her comment away. "Ah, don't worry about it. You're young. You have a life to live. I get it. So, what brings you by today?" he repeated.

Chelsea sat on the edge of her uncle's brown leather sofa, considering how to ease into the conversation she needed to have. Deciding that there was no easy way to ask, she just plunged in. "I need to ask you something, and it might be a little upsetting."

Uncle Bill frowned. He placed his lemonade on the coffee table. "You're scaring me. Are you sick?"

"No, no, it's nothing like that."

"Is it your aunt?" Aunt Brenda and Uncle Bill didn't get along, but Chelsea knew he would do anything for her aunt because of her.

"No, she's fine, too. We're both fine." Chelsea took a deep breath. "I've hired a private investigator to help me prove Dad didn't kill Lily."

Uncle Bill looked at her, his face twisted with surprise. It took him a moment to speak. "What? Why?"

"Why? Because he's innocent. And I need your help proving it."

"Chelsea—"

"Could you just answer some of my questions, please?" she interjected before he could argue with her.

Uncle Bill sighed. "Sure, you know I'll tell you whatever you want to know."

"Well, during my investigation, I found out a couple of things that I didn't know about Dad and Lily's relationship."

"Things like what?"

"Did Dad ever tell you that Lily was seeing someone else?"

Uncle Bill looked uncomfortable. "I don't know if I should be talking to you about your father and Lily's relationship."

"Uncle Bill, I'm not a child. This could be important."

"At the end there, when your dad and Lily were finally calling it quits, he might've suspected she was seeing someone else. But I don't think he had any real proof."

"I spoke to Dad. He said Lily told him she was seeing someone else."

Uncle Bill's eyes went wide, and he pushed himself up straighter in his chair. "Yes…yes, but your father said she wouldn't tell him who the other man was."

"That's right. She didn't tell anyone his name, and the prosecution wasn't able to figure out who he was."

Her uncle slumped back down in his chair. "Honey, you know how emotional breakups can be."

That she did. Her recent confrontation with Simon flashed through her head before she shook it away. This wasn't about her and Simon. It was about her father and Lily.

The police never even considered this new guy, but if Lily had been seeing him, the man could know something about her murder. Or be her murderer. "I know you were only friends with Lily through Dad, but did you suspect she was seeing someone? Do you have any idea who this person might be?"

Uncle Bill's gaze slid away from hers. "I don't know, honey. It was all a very long time ago."

It felt as if he was holding something back, but she didn't

know how to get him to tell her what it was. Just like her father, Uncle Bill's first concern was always protecting her even when she didn't need protecting.

"Why are you digging into this now?" he asked. "I thought your father's conviction had been upheld on appeal?"

"It was. The only chance he has now is to prove his innocence. And that's what I'm going to do."

Uncle Bill sighed. "I'm sure your father wouldn't want you to spend your time like this."

"Like what?" She threw her hands up in frustration. "Getting an innocent man out of jail? I can't think of a better way to spend my time."

Uncle Bill scooted to the end of his chair and reached out to take her hands. "I'm just worried that this obsession isn't healthy for you."

"Uncle Bill, an injustice has been done." She knew she sounded like a zealot. Maybe she was, but was zealotry in the interest of justice so wrong?

Uncle Bill dropped her hands and looked away.

"What is it?" she asked.

He held his gaze on the picture window for a long moment before turning back to her. "Chelsea, your father has exhausted his appeals. Every court that has looked at his case has determined he is guilty."

"What are you saying?"

His sigh this time was heavier and laced with something she couldn't quite name. Regret, maybe. "Maybe we have to face a hard truth."

"A hard truth? You mean that my father killed Lily? It sounds like you have already faced this truth."

"I've offered to hire better attorneys for your father, several times. He's always refused."

"He's proud."

"Or he feels guilty. Maybe he feels like he deserves the punishment he's getting."

"He has always professed his innocence. And he has appealed his conviction."

Uncle Bill shook his head. "He pursued that appeal for you. Because you wanted him to."

A heavy silence fell over the room while Chelsea struggled against fury and a sense of betrayal. Uncle Bill was supposed to be her father's best friend. He stood by her father even when Aunt Brenda, his own sister, didn't believe in him. He'd known her father for longer than she'd been alive. If he didn't believe in her father's innocence, what chance did she have convincing anyone else? She couldn't remember ever feeling so alone.

"I need to go," she said, surging to her feet.

"Oh, Chelsea. Don't leave like this. I just don't want to see you get hurt."

"I've already been hurt. I have spent the last seven years without my dad. I've had to change my name in order to get the press to stop hounding me. My own aunt believes her brother is a murderer. Everyone has turned against Dad, but I won't. I know he loved Lily. He didn't kill her. And I'm going to prove it. To you. To everyone."

Chapter Ten

After dropping Chelsea at her house, Travis fought the Los Angeles traffic to the West Security and Investigations offices. He strode through the glass entrance and nearly ran into his boss.

"Just the man I was looking for," Kevin said with a smile.

"Really? You must have ESP."

"Well, I looked for you in your cubicle a moment ago. You weren't there, so I was headed out to grab a decent cup of coffee, but seeing as you're here now, it will just have to wait."

"You got something?" Travis asked, following Kevin across the polished tile floor to his office.

Kevin gave them a brief nod and kept walking. "How is Chelsea recovering from the hit-and-run?"

"Better than I'd be. She's still got some pain," Travis said, recalling the ibuprofen she'd swallowed with her coffee that morning, "but she's going to be fine. She's tough."

Kevin slid a sidelong glance at Travis, appraising him. "I have to agree. That was quite a tuck-and-roll she did to get out of the way of that car's path."

They stepped into Kevin's corner office. Light streamed in from the bay of windows. The office was decorated in a minimalist fashion that was simultaneously masculine with lots of dark wood and leather. Kevin's office was one of the largest on the floor, second only to Tess's. Dual sleek silver monitors sat on a desk. Kevin tapped on the keyboard, and the large flat screen mounted to the opposite wall glowed to life. A black-and-white image of the street a few yards from their office building appeared.

"We were able to get security footage from several of our neighbors," Kevin said. "You can take a look at all the tapes, seven in total that caught glimpses of the car that hit Chelsea. I've spliced them together to approximate the route the car took." He tapped the keyboard again, and the tape began. "There's the car. A late model sedan. It sits across the street there idling while Chelsea is inside our offices. It appears this guy followed her to her meeting with you."

The black Oldsmobile sat about twenty feet from the front of the West Investigations building. Waiting.

Travis hoped to see the outline of the driver, but he or she had the sunshade pulled down, covering the top of their face. The recording was too grainy and from too far of a distance to make out any distinguishing features on the driver.

He and Kevin watched as Chelsea walked out of the front of the building and started to cross the street. His body tensed, anticipating what was about to happen. The Oldsmobile pulled away from the curb as Chelsea stepped into the street and accelerated toward her. Travis's heart thundered, watching Chelsea turn toward the danger and freeze for a moment. Then she was in motion, running for the opposite sidewalk. The car swerved into her path. She leaped for the sidewalk as the right front side of the car clipped her hip. That leap had probably kept her from suffering far greater injuries. It may have even saved her life. Chelsea hit the pavement just short of the curb and rolled between two parked cars. The sedan sped off.

"Can you rewind the tape and slow it down? Focusing on the sedan's driver."

"I've pulled some still photos, but there hasn't been a good enough shot to get an identification," Kevin said while he rewound the video. He handed Travis the photos, but he was right. They were worthless.

They watched the video again at a slower pace, but the driver wore a baseball cap pulled low over his brow and sunglasses in addition to having used the sun visor to conceal his identity.

"Did any of the cameras get a shot of the license plates?"

Kevin shook his head. "There were none."

Travis's stomach sank. The lack of license plates along with the driver's efforts to shield his identity confirmed what he already suspected. The hit-and-run hadn't been an accident. Someone had specifically targeted Chelsea. The still unanswered question was, had the driver meant to kill her or was this just a warning to back off investigating her father's case?

Either way, it meant Chelsea was in danger. It was impossible to believe that the hit-and-run wasn't connected to Chelsea's efforts to prove her father's innocence. Had Lily's killer somehow found out about Chelsea's investigation into the murder and decided to put a stop to it? If so, how had the killer learned about the investigation? There were dozens of names in Chelsea's binder, and Chelsea had said she'd reached out to several of Lily's friends and family before coming to him for help. Any one of them might want her to drop her investigation, either because they believed Franklin Brooks was in jail where he belonged or because they wanted to protect themselves or someone else. But right now, the hit-and-run driver appeared to be a dead end.

"Have we had any luck tracking down Peter Schmeichel?"

Kevin shook his head. "Peter doesn't appear to have a fixed address. I pulled his criminal record. It's as long as my arm, mostly drug offenses. A couple of assaults and batteries." He handed Travis a sheaf of papers. He hadn't been kidding about Peter's criminal history. The guy was a career criminal.

"Humph." Travis wasn't buying it. "What about locating Gina?"

"I've had better luck with that." Kevin tapped his keyboard, and Travis's phone chimed with the incoming text. "That's her current work and home address. She moved to San Bernardino about a year after Lily's death."

"This is great, thanks." Travis noted the address was about an hour away from Los Angeles. He could have just called Gina, but interviews were always more fruitful face-to-face. Plus, he wasn't convinced Gina had told the police everything she knew about Lily's murder. But she would tell him.

"Can you also check if Lily ever filed a police report for vandalism or a burglary at her place?" He explained what Rachel had told him and Chelsea, as well as the information that Jace, the neighbor, had given them about a possible new boyfriend.

"I'll see what I can do, but it might take a bit of time to search police reports from seven-plus years ago that may or may not exist."

Travis's phone rang. He looked at the screen and saw the call was from Chelsea.

"Hello?"

"Did you call my aunt?" Chelsea asked without preamble.

"What? No, why?"

"I went to my uncle Bill's house—he's my dad's best friend—to ask him what he remembers about Lily and my dad's relationship, and my aunt called me as I was leaving. Someone called her asking a bunch of questions about me."

"You were supposed to be home resting," he said, tamping down his anger that she'd gone out alone.

"You said I should rest. I never agreed to it. Anyway, my aunt is more important."

"What kind of questions did the caller ask?" Travis said.

"I don't know," she answered, her voice rising. "Aunt Brenda said a man called saying he was a friend, and he asked questions about me and Dad. Then he said that it could be dangerous for me to continue on my quest to get Dad out of prison."

"The caller threatened you?" Travis growled.

"Not in so many words. I'm headed to my aunt's house now to check in on her."

"Send me her address," he said, already moving toward Kevin's office door.

"If you need any backup, give me a shout," Kevin said as he left.

Travis nodded to let Kevin know he heard him and kept moving. His phone dinged in his ear. He pulled it away long enough to see that Chelsea had sent him her aunt's address.

"I'm on my way. I'll meet you there in twenty minutes," he said, racing from the office.

Chapter Eleven

He ate his lunch. A turkey sandwich on wheat, light mustard, heavy on the mayonnaise with a diet Coke. He ate alone as usual. His coworkers barely acknowledged him. He bet if asked most wouldn't even know his name. Some might not even recognize him if pressed. He knew how to blend in. How to go unnoticed. How to be unseen even when people were looking directly at him. That gave him space. To remember. To think. To plan.

She hadn't backed off after the hit-and-run. Chelsea Harper was tough, a fighter. Part of him admired her for it. But the other part, the bigger part, hated it. Hated her for making him feel this way. For turning him into a ball of nerves. For making him sneak around, hiding in the shadows, jumping at every shape and sound.

This would not do.

She was going to cause trouble, he knew it. But he couldn't just get rid of her.

She was going to keep asking questions. Ask even more questions, better questions, now that she'd hired a private detective. Dammit to hell and back.

Why wouldn't she just give up investigating Lily's case? Everyone else had. The whole world was convinced that Franklin Brooks killed Lily Wong. They'd convicted him and thrown away the key. No one cared anymore. No one except Franklin Brooks's daughter.

She was bringing it all back to the forefront of everyone's mind. What if someone remembered seeing him? What if that drugged-out fool grew a conscience? Admitted he'd lied? What if Chelsea and her private investigator succeeded in getting the police and prosecutor to reopen Franklin's case?

He couldn't let that happen. Too bad just killing her wasn't an option. But that would surely attract more attention than he wanted. Franklin Brooks's daughter getting killed when she was pressing for his case to be reopened. Shouting from the rafters to anyone who would listen that her father was innocent. The cops wouldn't be able to just write it off as coincidence.

He wasn't sure what it would take to get her to back off, but he had to figure it out.

He had to stop her.

He'd made it this long without anyone suspecting him. He didn't intend to go to jail.

Chapter Twelve

Chelsea pulled into her aunt's driveway just as Travis pulled to a stop in front of the house. She didn't slow down to let him catch up with her as she headed to the front door. The door opened as she lifted her hand to knock.

"Aunt Brenda, are you okay?" Chelsea let her gaze roam over her aunt from head to toe.

Aunt Brenda was a willowy woman with dark brown hair that had gone mostly gray and keen hazel eyes. She'd had surgery on her knees two years earlier that had left her with a slight limp, but she kept in shape by swimming regularly at the local recreation center.

"Of course I'm okay. You don't think a little old phone call is going to do me in, do you?"

"Well, no," Chelsea said, "but you seemed upset."

"I was upset for you, not me." Aunt Brenda leaned to her right, looking around Chelsea. "Who's he?"

Chelsea glanced over her shoulder at Travis, who was standing several feet behind her. His eyes swept over the street before coming back to land on her and her aunt. "This is Travis Collins, the private investigator I hired to help me get Dad out of jail."

Her aunt's face twisted into a scowl. "Waste of time and money if you ask me."

She hadn't asked, and it was her money, Chelsea thought, but she bit back that retort.

"Ladies, might I suggest we take this discussion inside?" Travis nodded toward the interior of the house.

Her aunt's scowl deepened, but she stood aside and let Chelsea and Travis in. The door snapped closed behind them, and Aunt Brenda turned, crossing her arms over her chest. "Is he the friend who called me?"

"No," Chelsea said through gritted teeth. "We don't know who called you. That's what we are hoping to find out."

"Chelsea, you know I try to put your father and all that nastiness that came with his trial behind me. I don't want to dredge all that up. I would think that you'd feel the same way. Picking at this scab could ruin your life."

Chelsea took a deep breath. Her aunt looked so much like her father, especially when she was mad, it was hard to look at her and not see him. In some ways, it was comforting, like still having a piece of her father with her. In others, it made her yearn for all that she had lost. "Seeking the truth is not going to ruin my life."

Aunt Brenda threw her hands up in the air and stomped past Chelsea and Travis into the kitchen. "Well, I want no part of it. Tell your friend never to call me again."

"Aunt Brenda, you aren't listening. I didn't tell anyone to call you."

"I don't understand you." Aunt Brenda looked around the kitchen as if understanding might be hiding on top of a cabinet or behind the toaster. "Why can't you just go on with your life? Forget about your father. Find a nice guy to settle down with and have a family of your own."

"I have a family. You, Victor, Uncle Bill and Dad." Chelsea emphasized her last word.

Her aunt let out a sigh of frustration, but her eyes were

tinged with fear. "If you dredge this up again, people may realize who you are. Who your father is. What will they think of you?"

"I don't care what people think about me."

"That's obvious," her aunt shot back.

This was an argument they'd had dozens of times before, and neither was going to give in to the other. It wasn't why Chelsea had come to her aunt's house, either, so it was best to move on.

"On the phone, you said that the person who called was a man. Did he give you a name?" Chelsea asked.

Aunt Brenda shook her head, her expression contemplative. "I don't think so. He just said he was a friend of yours."

"Did the call come in on your home phone or your cell phone?" Travis asked.

Aunt Brenda nodded to the black handset and cradle on the kitchen counter. "Home. I hardly bother with that cell. Only a few people even have the number."

"Do you mind if I take a look at the incoming call log?" Travis asked.

"Knock yourself out."

"How long ago did you get the call?" Travis reached for the handset and pressed a button.

"Maybe an hour ago." Aunt Brenda glanced at the clock on the microwave. "I called Chelsea right after."

"Can you remember anything else about the call?" Chelsea asked, pulling her attention back to her. "Background noises? Did the man have an accent? Anything you remember could help us identify him."

"I don't know, Chels. It was a regular call." Her aunt grabbed a dishrag from the sink and wiped haphazardly at the counter.

Chelsea knew her aunt cleaned when she was worried.

She felt a moment's guilt for being the cause of that worry, but not enough to stop investigating.

"He said he was a friend of yours and that he knew we were investigating your father's case," Aunt Brenda continued. "He was concerned that you were in over your head. Those were his exact words, in over your head and that you could get hurt." Aunt Brenda scrubbed at a mark that had been on the counter for as long as Chelsea could remember.

She reached out and covered her aunt's hand with her own, stilling it.

Aunt Brenda's gaze met hers. "I asked what he meant by saying you could get hurt, but he just hung up."

Chelsea pulled her aunt into a hug. "I'm not going to get hurt."

"The number the call came in from was blocked," Travis said, replacing the phone on its cradle.

Chelsea pulled back from the embrace with her aunt but kept one arm around the older woman. "Now what?"

"Now you stop this madness." Her aunt shrugged out from under Chelsea's arm. "I've already lost a brother and a husband. I won't lose you, too."

"You won't lose me," Chelsea said.

"No?" her aunt spat angrily. "You think I don't know what's going on here? That call was a warning. A threat."

Another stab of guilt cut through Chelsea. She hadn't told her aunt about the hit-and-run earlier because she didn't want to worry her. But now didn't seem like a good time to tell her, either.

"I'm sorry, Aunt Brenda, but I have to do this. I'll be careful, and I have Travis to help me. He's a former cop and a private investigator. We've already turned up some good leads that the police didn't follow up on seven years ago. I'll be careful, I promise."

Her aunt shook her head, a single tear falling over the crest of her cheek. "I can't talk you out of this, but I won't be a part of it." She turned and rushed from the room. A moment later the sound of a bedroom door slamming carried into the kitchen.

Chelsea let out a heavy sigh.

"She loves you," Travis said, coming to stand next to Chelsea.

"I know."

His voice lowered. "She's not wrong about the potential danger."

Chelsea studied him. "Did you learn something at West's offices this afternoon?"

"We probably shouldn't talk about it here." Travis had a look down the hallway where her aunt had disappeared.

"Come on. I haven't eaten since breakfast, and I'm starved," Chelsea said. "You can tell me the bad news over food."

"Do you have any particular place in mind?"

Chelsea flashed a weary smile. "My favorite place isn't too far. Follow me."

Chapter Thirteen

"Eight fish tacos coming up." The teen behind the food truck window shot a toothy grin at Chelsea as she passed him the cash for the food. He made change and handed it back to her.

"This is your favorite place to eat?" Travis asked when they stepped back to wait for their food.

"One of them, yes." She held up a finger. "It's affordable. The tacos are the best on the West Coast." She held up a second finger. "And the views can't be beat." She spread out a hand to encompass the waves lapping against the sands of El Segundo Beach. Tucked under her other arm was the blanket she kept in the trunk of her car.

The views were spectacular, which was why this was one of her favorite places on earth, even with the crush of people mobbing the shoreline along the water.

"Eight fish tacos," the teen called out.

Chelsea grinned up at Travis. "And the service is quick," she added, walking back to the food truck to grab their order. She handed the bag of food and two canned iced teas to Travis.

At the edge of the beach, they shucked their shoes, and Chelsea carried them and the blanket down the beach until they found a spot that was not as crowded. She spread the blanket out over the flat sand, and they sat down.

"Do you do this often?" Travis asked. "Dine on the beach?"

Chelsea handed him two tacos. "I spent a lot of time here with my dad when I was growing up. It's not too far from Aunt Brenda's place, and it's cheap, so it fit right into our budget."

Travis unwrapped one of the tacos and ate half of it in one bite. "It must have been nice to have a beach so close to home."

"It was great. I take it you didn't grow up in Los Angeles."

Travis shook his head. "I grew up in the Midwest." He didn't give her any more information, instead stuffing the remaining portion of the taco in his mouth.

"I like to come here and think. After my dad was arrested, it was one of the only places I could go for a while where people didn't recognize me. I could blend into the crowd of beachgoers."

"It must have been hard for you after your father was arrested."

"It's like everyone—not just the cops, but my friends, my aunt—everyone believed that my dad did it. And because I didn't, I became one of the bad guys, too."

"I'm sorry."

Chelsea took a bite of taco, chewed and swallowed. "Victor was really the only person to stand by me. I mean, I know he thinks my dad is where he belongs, but he doesn't treat me any differently than he did before." She brought the iced tea to her lips.

"Victor?"

"My cousin. More like my brother. He's my aunt Brenda and uncle Darren's only child. We grew up together."

"Is he in one of the photos on your dresser?"

Chelsea made a face. "My dresser?"

"I noticed the photos that you have on top when I went to the bathroom at your place yesterday. I didn't go into your room," he added quickly. "I promise."

"Oh, yeah, that's Victor."

"Your cousin." Something passed over Travis's face.

"Yes. My cousin. Why?"

"Nothing. I just thought he might be a boyfriend."

She laughed. "You met Simon, so you know my track record with men isn't good. I haven't even had a date in, I don't remember how long."

He wiped his hands on a napkin, but not before Chelsea saw a satisfied smile on his face. Wait… He'd thought Victor was her boyfriend, and now that he knew he wasn't, was he happy she was single? Maybe he'd even been a little jealous. The idea of it made her insides do a happy dance before she reminded herself they could only have a business relationship.

Travis cleared his throat. "Listen, I wanted to tell you what the team at West has been able to turn up." Whatever he might have been thinking or feeling, it was gone, replaced by his usual professionalism.

She sighed internally, wiped her own hands on a napkin and set her iced tea to the side. "Great. Shoot."

"We got video of the hit-and-run from the businesses surrounding the office. This was no accident, Chelsea. The driver followed you to the office and waited for you to come out. He never swerved. In fact, he aimed for you."

Travis's words stole her breath. She'd suspected the hit-and-run wasn't an accident, but to have it confirmed was to face the fact that someone out there wanted to hurt her. Badly.

Travis put a hand on her arm. "Are you okay?"

Chelsea nodded slowly. "Yeah, just processing."

"We weren't able to get a good look at the driver's face or the tags on the car, but we know to watch out for a black sedan now."

"Okay," Chelsea said on a long breath.

"And this might be a good time to mention how bad an idea it was to sneak off to speak with your uncle earlier—"

Chelsea scowled. "I didn't sneak anywhere. I'm a grown woman. I can go where I please."

He held up his hands. "*Sneak* was the wrong word. But that hit-and-run was intentional. You need to be careful. At least let me know your plans so I can have your back even if I disagree with them."

She felt her ire dissipate. "Okay. I'll keep you in the loop from now on."

"Great. Now, can I ask what you and your uncle discussed?"

She filled him in on the conversation with her uncle. "Unfortunately, he didn't remember anything that could help us."

"Well, I do have some good news. We got an address for Gina. She's living in San Bernardino now."

"That's great. Are you going to give her a call or—"

"I was thinking we could take a trip up there and talk to her in person."

"Even better. Let's go," Chelsea said, starting to push to her feet.

Travis laid a hand on her arm again, keeping her on the blanket. "Slow down. I have to get some things in order first. Gina is working as a nurse at a local hospital. I don't want to have to ambush her at her job, so I need to try to get her schedule to see if we can catch her at home."

Frustration bubbled in Chelsea's chest, but she'd hired Travis for his help so she needed to take it. "Whatever you think is the best plan, I'm on board. When do you want to go?"

"I'm thinking about tomorrow afternoon."

Chelsea collected their trash and stuffed it into the taco bag. This time when she stood, Travis stood with her. Her feet sank into the sand and combined with her excitement and haste, she lost her footing.

Travis grabbed her, his hands winding around her waist, steadying her against his hard body. She angled her head to look up at him and saw desire in his eyes. The same desire that she felt.

Travis sucked in a breath that made her knees go weak again. He bought his mouth down, nearly touching hers. They stood there a moment, hovering at the edge of an invisible line.

A shriek ripped through the air a moment before a young girl came tearing down the sand.

Travis's arms dropped from her waist, and he took three large steps back. "I should get you home." He turned away, bending down to collect the blanket and their shoes.

Chelsea let out the breath she'd been holding. The young girl's parents ambled by, their arms loaded down with stuff, completely oblivious to the moment they'd interrupted.

But it was good that they'd been interrupted. She and Travis were obviously attracted to each other, but crossing the line could have repercussions neither of them needed at the moment. But now she just had to figure out a way to forget how she felt in his arms.

THAT WAS A near miss, Travis thought as he followed Chelsea to make sure she got home without incident. He'd almost kissed her. The way she'd melted against him had almost made him forget that she was a client. And that he didn't do relationships. He also knew Chelsea wasn't the kind of woman who did casual relationships. Luckily, that screaming kid had come along and brought him back to his senses. As soon as he was sure Chelsea was safe and sound inside her house, he'd head home and take a long cold shower and pretend nothing had happened.

He pulled into Chelsea's driveway behind her car and got out.

"I'm fine, Travis. You don't have to see me to my door."

He stopped next to her. "I do, actually. I promised your dad I'd watch out for you, and I mean to keep that promise."

"Fine," she huffed, turning and marching to her porch. She opened her front door and froze.

Travis immediately grabbed her and moved her behind him so he was between her and the interior of the house. It looked like a cyclone had blown through her living room. Bloodred paint splattered the soft gray walls and just about everything else in the living room. A single word—*Stop*— had been written across one wall, red paint dripping down from each letter like a horror movie.

"Stay here," he ordered before entering the house. He swept through the living room, dining room and kitchen as well as the bedrooms. They'd all been trashed, but only the living room had been splattered with paint.

He returned to the doorway to find that Chelsea had ignored his admonishment to stay outside. She reached for the wall.

"Don't touch anything," he began, but her fingertips were already covered in paint.

"He did this. The man who called my aunt and tried to run me over," she said, sounding as if she was in a daze. He recognized that she was in shock. "The man who killed Lily."

Travis strode over to her, tilting her chin until she was looking at him, really looking at him. "We're going to get this guy. I promise you." He took her into his arms, not caring if it was professional or not. Her home had been invaded and violated, and she needed comfort. Hell, he could use a little comfort himself. When he first stepped up to the door and saw all that red, he'd thought…

Of course, that was what this psycho wanted. To scare Chelsea. Scare her enough that she'd back off. Her home looked like the site of a grisly murder.

"Let's go outside, and I'll call the police." He led her back to his car and got her safely inside before bypassing 911 and punching a familiar number into his cell. Less than ten minutes later, a gold sedan screeched to a stop behind his car.

Travis stretched out his hand toward the man who approached. Detective Gabe Owens was the only person from his police days that he kept in touch with, and only sparingly. Owens had joined the LAPD a couple of years after Travis and had still been in uniform when Travis left the force. That was probably the only reason Owens hadn't shunned him like the rest of his former colleagues. He'd still been idealistic enough to believe that Travis had done the right thing.

But it had been over a year since he and Owens had last grabbed a drink together. Gabe had aged, as they all had. The flaming red hair Travis remembered was more orange now, at least the part that hadn't completely turned gray. But more than anything it was Owens's eyes that had changed. He had the eyes now of a man who had seen too much.

"Hey, thanks for getting here so quickly," Travis said.

"No problem. I wasn't far. So, you said someone vandalized your friend's home."

"My client," he responded automatically, then remembering their near kiss, he added, "and friend kind of."

Owens shot him a knowing look. "Okay, tell me about this client/friend kind of."

Travis shoved off the embarrassing description of Chelsea and gave Owens a quick rundown of the investigation, the recent threats against her life and now her coming home to a paint-splattered mess.

"You always did like the complicated ones," Owens said.

Travis wasn't sure whether Owens was referring to cases or women. He wasn't sure he wanted to know.

Owens insisted on clearing the house himself. Travis and Chelsea waited on the front step until he returned.

"It doesn't look like anything was stolen, but would you come inside and have a look?" Owens asked Chelsea.

Travis and Chelsea followed Owens back into the house. The way the place had been trashed, but it didn't seem like the perp had been looking for anything in particular. He'd just been bent on destruction. The televisions in the living room and Chelsea's bedroom had been smashed as had most of her china and several lamps. Her clothes were thrown around her bedroom, some clearly destroyed, and nearly every cabinet and drawer had been pulled out and their contents dumped. The papers Chelsea had collected in her investigation had been torn to shreds and littered the dining room floor.

"Where's your binder, Chelsea?" Travis asked.

"My binder—" Chelsea looked at him for a moment, confused, until understanding took over. "Oh, thankfully I had one in my car with me, but I think I left the second one on the dining room table."

Travis followed her around the house, an arm that he hoped was comforting around her shoulders. Finally, they returned to where Owens stood, making notes for the incident report, in the living room.

"It's hard to tell for sure," Chelsea said, "but I don't think anything is missing, just destroyed." She pointed to the dining room where the files she'd compiled on her father's case had been ripped and torn to shreds.

"Do you have any idea who could have done this? An ex-boyfriend?" Owens glanced at Travis. "A current boyfriend?"

Travis caught the look Chelsea shot at him before she answered, "Not exactly."

Owens's bushy brows rose. "What does that mean, exactly?"

"My ex-husband paid me an unexpected visit the other day, but I don't think he would do something like this."

Travis had taken an instant dislike to the man, but he had to agree with Chelsea. Whoever had done this had exhibited a lot of uncontrolled rage. Simon seemed like the type of guy who wouldn't have wanted to muss his hair. But looks could be deceiving, so he was glad Owens insisted on taking Simon's information down. Travis would also be checking into Simon more closely, something he should have thought of earlier.

"Can you think of anyone else who may be angry with you?" Owens asked Chelsea.

Chelsea shot Travis a look that seemed to say *where do I start?*

Travis stepped in, adding more detail to the brief explanation he'd given Owens outside. He explained Chelsea's theory that her father was innocent of the murder he was in jail for and that they were revisiting the case.

"And you think whoever did those things did this?" Owens summarized.

"Who else?" Chelsea responded sharply.

"I'm just trying to understand, Ms. Harper."

"I think it's the obvious answer, Owens," Travis seconded.

"And you think that person also really killed Lily Wong?" Owens asked.

"Yes," Chelsea answered definitively.

At the same time Travis said, "We don't know."

Chelsea shot him a look that would have turned him to dust if it could have.

Travis knew she thought her father's innocence was an absolute certainty, but he still had questions. Someone clearly wanted her to stop investigating, but that didn't mean that person was Lily Wong's true killer. It was just as possible that someone didn't appreciate Chelsea making waves.

Owens gave them both a long look. "Well, we don't usually dust for prints when nothing has been taken, but as a courtesy to you, Trav, I can have the boys come out. It may take them several hours to get here, though."

"Thanks," Travis responded. "I appreciate it."

"I'll write up the incident report. You need it to file a claim with your insurance company for the damages and replace your things."

"Thanks," Chelsea responded.

"Do you have a place to stay until the lock gets fixed?" Owens asked.

"She will be fine," Travis interjected before Chelsea spoke. "I'll take care of it."

Chelsea shot him a second disgruntled look.

"Here's my card." Owens handed a card to Chelsea. "I'll have the report ready for you in a couple days. You can call me directly if you have any more trouble."

"Thank you," Chelsea repeated, this time in a voice so

small it tore through Travis. She didn't deserve this. To have her home violated in this way.

Owens started for the door, and Travis followed him outside. "Owens, look, I know I'm not a favorite citizen of the LAPD—"

Owens held up a meaty hand. "Look, man, you did what you felt was right. I respect that."

Travis was surprised. It had been some time since he'd spoken to a former colleague. At best he'd been treated like a pariah after he turned several of his colleagues into internal affairs for evidence tampering. At worst, he'd fielded threats that had him sleeping with his gun by his side. No one had ever indicated they believed he'd done the right thing by turning his colleagues in. "Thanks."

He said goodbye and went back inside the house.

"You can't stay here tonight," he said as Chelsea picked up the shattered remnants of a photograph of her and her aunt.

"Where else am I going to go?"

"You can get a hotel room."

She let out a strangled laugh. "You're kidding. I live on a teacher's salary. I can barely afford my mortgage and I've had to cut back in order to pay West's fee, and I can't leave with the lock smashed in like that."

"I can fix the lock, temporarily at least. But it's too dangerous for you to be here. Whoever is doing this is currently escalating. You shouldn't go anywhere alone until we find this guy and put him behind bars." He hesitated for a moment, considering the idea he'd been tossing around in his head. "You could stay with me. I have a spare room."

Chelsea studied him. "What did you mean when you said you didn't know if the person who did this is the person who killed Lily? You can't possibly believe all this—"

she spread her arms out encompassing the destruction in the house "—isn't related to her death."

"It's definitely related, but we have no proof that the person who is doing this is Lily's killer."

"You still think my dad did it, don't you?"

"I haven't made any conclusions yet."

Chelsea stared at him for another long moment before turning and starting down the hall toward her bedroom.

"Chelsea, you might be angry with me now, but your safety—"

"I'm not stupid or foolhardy, Travis. I'll take you up on your offer of your spare bedroom."

He breathed out a sigh of relief.

"I'm going to see if I have enough undamaged clothes to pack a bag," she said, still not looking at him. "You should be able to find something to keep the door closed until I can get a locksmith here."

He watched her disappear into her bedroom, all the while something tugged at his insides. He was losing the battle to ignore his growing feelings for Chelsea. And even scarier, he was realizing that he wasn't sure it was a battle he really wanted to fight.

Chapter Fourteen

The next morning, Chelsea blinked her eyes open, her heart racing as she took in the unfamiliar room, then settled when she remembered where she was. In Travis's guestroom. In Travis's apartment. Because her home was not safe. Although the temperature in the room was a tad on the warm side, a chill went through her.

Travis had shored up her front door enough that it would hold for a night as long as the vandal didn't return to inflict more damage. She glanced at the clock on the nightstand—8:00 a.m. She'd slept later than usual.

She supposed she shouldn't be surprised. The day before had been long and trying, and she'd spent an hour after Travis got her settled in the guest room searching Lily's dormant social media pages for any hint of her mystery boyfriend, to no avail. It was enough to make her contemplate pulling the covers up over her head and hiding. One day in bed, a very comfortable one at that, was that too much to ask? But she had too much to do to hide out, no matter how much she wanted to or how enticing the mattress was.

She took a quick shower, then gathered her hair into a bun. Efficiency was going to have to trump fashion until she was back in her own place with all of her own things. She slipped on a pair of black slacks, a burgundy knit top and black ankle boots. As she stepped out of the guest room, she smelled coffee and sautéed onions.

She found Travis in front of the stove making omelets. His back was to her. He wore a pair of gray sweatpants that clung to well-shaped buttocks. A black T-shirt stretched over the muscles of his arms and back. She allowed herself a moment to take him in completely before reminding herself that romance wasn't in the cards for them, no matter how delectable the man whose house she was now sharing. She gave herself a shake and entered the kitchen.

"Good morning," she said as she walked over to the coffee pot.

"Good morning," Travis responded without turning. "The omelets are almost done."

Chelsea poured herself a cup, adding cream and sugar, which Travis had already placed next to the carafe. She turned to find him staring at her. "Is everything okay?"

Travis blinked and turned back to the omelets. "Yeah, these are done. Have a seat."

Chelsea sat at the kitchen table, contemplating the look she'd seen on Travis's face. It was almost as if the sight of her had stunned him speechless. But that couldn't be, could it? He had been the one to pull away from her the day before at the beach. She was sure he'd been about to kiss her, and she would have let him. Heck, she wanted him to kiss her. As much as she'd tried to keep things professional between them, there was undeniably an attraction there.

Travis slid an omelet onto the plate in front of her.

"This looks great," she said as he slid a second omelet onto the plate across from hers.

He put the pan back on the stove and took his seat. "Thanks," he said. "I'm not much for cooking, but as I said, I can handle breakfast and a few simple meals."

She took a bite. "This *is* great. You can be in charge of breakfast every morning as far as I'm concerned." Heat rose in her cheeks as she realized what she'd implied. That they would be having breakfast together every morning. Hopefully, she'd be able to get a locksmith to her house today, and this would be the only time they had breakfast together. The thought made her sad.

They ate in silence for a few minutes. Finally, Travis spoke up. "I got Gina's schedule at the hospital. She works the 9:00 p.m. to 9:00 a.m. shift. I thought we could drive out to speak with her after we get your door fixed."

"That's great, but I haven't even contacted a locksmith yet."

"I hope you don't mind," he said. "I contacted the locksmith that West Investigations keeps on retainer. He'll meet us at your place whenever you're ready."

"That's great. Thank you. Could you arrange for him to come by this morning? Detective Owens left me a voicemail while I was in the shower to say he'd finished dusting my house for fingerprints, so I can get out of your hair today."

"You're welcome. And you're not in my hair. Actually, I wanted to talk to you about staying here for a few more days."

"Staying here?"

"We could stay at your place, but I do think you'd be safer here. For one thing, I have a security system, and you don't."

"Wait. Slow down. Why would I need to stay here or you stay with me if I change the locks?"

"Even with your locks changed, you'll still be in danger. I don't think it's safe for you to be at your place. Or alone generally."

"I can't hide."

"I know. And I'm not asking you to. Staying with me or

me staying with you at your place would be a deterrent to whoever has been targeting you. They know someone has your back."

"You?"

"Me."

Warmth spread through her. "It still feels like hiding. I don't like the idea of being run out of my own home."

"I can understand that, but think of it more as taking precautions. Not running or hiding."

She raised her coffee mug to her lips, thinking. There was some validity to what Travis said. If someone broke into her home again, having Travis there would certainly be better than being alone. And she had to admit, as much as she wanted to go home, she was still a little afraid. A couple more days in Travis's bed wouldn't be a hardship. *In Travis's guest bed*, she mentally amended. Alone. Her cheeks heated again, and she fought the urge to fan herself.

"Okay. Um, I'll stay here."

He smiled. "Great."

"Great." She brought the coffee mug to her lips again.

"I'd like to take you out to dinner tonight."

Chelsea spat coffee onto what was left of her omelet. Travis rounded the table but paused when she held out her hand to stop him. She was embarrassed enough. She didn't need him patting her back like a father trying to burp an infant. She caught her breath enough to sputter, "Dinner?"

"Yes. I would like to take you to dinner." He handed her a napkin.

She wiped at the coffee dripping down her chin. "Why?"

"Because you've made dinner and showed me where I can get the best fish tacos on the West Coast. I'd like to do something nice for you. And you mentioned it had been a while since you went out for a nice meal."

Oh, so that was it. He felt sorry for her. "You don't have to do that."

One of his shoulders rose in a shrug. "I know I don't have to. I want to." He picked up his plate and carried it to the sink before turning back to her. "It's just dinner. We have to eat, and it's not fair for you to do all the heavy lifting. I can't cook dinner, but I'm a champ at paying for it," he joked.

That got a smile from her. Why not? He was right. It was just dinner. Dinner with a colleague, kind of. They were working together, after all. *And living together for the moment*, a little voice chimed in. She ignored it. "Okay. Yes. I'd like to go to dinner with you."

Travis's shoulders relaxed. "Tonight then. Meet you in the living room at 8:00 p.m."

A tingling sensation ignited her body. It had been a long time since she'd been on a date. Even if it was just a friendly dinner date. After she cleared her father and got him out of prison, she would get a life. Aunt Brenda was right about how Chelsea should find someone to settle down with and start a family. Someone better for her than Simon ever was.

Her gaze went to Travis, who was still looking at her in a way that made her pulse pound. Places inside her that had long been dormant awakened.

Whoa, girl. She didn't need to ask to know he wasn't the settling-down type, but her body didn't seem to have gotten that message. Luckily, her brain was still in control. She wanted a real connection with someone, not just a roll in the sack. Not that rolling around with Travis wouldn't be fun. She was pretty sure he would be extraordinary in bed. But the moment would be fleeting. She didn't need the additional emotional drama that playing with a man like him was sure to cause.

No. Friends were all she and Travis could ever be. And she'd keep saying that for as long as it took her to believe it.

Chapter Fifteen

Travis helped her straighten up her house as much as they could while the locksmith fixed her door. Dealing with the paint-splattered walls would take more effort and lots of primer, but she was glad Travis had offered to help. Even though she'd agreed to stay with him for a few days, she felt an urgency to erase the vandal's presence from her home.

The locksmith was not only good at his job, he was also fast. It took him less than an hour to change the locks and add a dead bolt at Travis's request. She had to admit the dead bolt did make her feel safer. She hoped the hesitance she felt being in her own home would pass quickly.

After she paid the locksmith, they headed to Gina's address.

Gina worked the nine-to-nine overnight shift, and when they pulled into her street a little after eleven o'clock, they saw a woman in blue scrubs matching her general description just getting out of a car parked in the driveway.

Chelsea and Travis headed up the concrete walkway to the front porch.

Gina turned toward them, a mask of distrust on her face.

"Gina McGrath," Chelsea said when they reached her, giving her a smile.

Gina's gaze cut to Travis, then back to Chelsea. "Who's asking?"

"My name is Chelsea Harper. This is Travis Collins. We are investigators."

"Investigators? What do you want with me?" Gina was dressed in scrubs, but even with their loose fit, Chelsea could see the woman was painfully thin. Gina's eyes were sunken, and her muddy brown hair was short and straight. Her lips were covered in bright red lipstick. She looked older than her forty-something years.

"We're looking into Lily Wong's murder. We understand you used to be her neighbor."

The frown on Gina's face hardened. "That was a long time ago. I told the police everything I know. I don't have anything more to say."

"We aren't with the police," Travis said. "We're conducting a separate investigation."

"Evidence has come to light suggesting Franklin Brooks may not have committed the murder," Chelsea added.

The comment clearly surprised Gina. She let the bag of groceries slide through her hands. Two apples rolled in opposite directions across the porch floor.

Travis went after them and handed the apples back to Gina.

"Thank you," she said, placing them in the bag again.

"If we can just speak to you for a moment," Travis said, trying again. "Please, it could help free an innocent man."

Gina hesitated for a long moment. "Come on in." She stepped back, allowing Chelsea and Travis to walk into the house, then closed the door and headed to the kitchen. She set the groceries on the counter and took a carton of milk from the bag. She put it in the fridge, then turned to face them, wariness in her eyes. "What kind of questions do you want to ask me?"

"We want to know about the night Lily died."

She reached into the grocery bag and pulled out a loaf of bread, not looking at either Travis or Chelsea. "Like I said, I already told the police everything I knew."

"We understand that, but sometimes things come back to us later. Details that we don't remember right away," Travis said.

Gina sighed. "I don't think I'll ever forget anything about that night. You don't forget the details of the day your neighbor was murdered."

"Can you tell us about it?" Travis asked.

Gina sighed a second time. "I got home from work late. Peter was there. I'd stupidly given him a key, which he took as an invitation to essentially move in. The house was a mess. I remember garbage day was the next day, and Peter hadn't taken the trash out. We argued about it, and I eventually ended up taking it out. That's when I saw Lily and Frank. They were on her front stoop talking."

"On the front stoop. Not in the house?" Chelsea said.

"On the stoop. They weren't arguing or anything, at least not that I could hear, but it kind of looked like Lily didn't want to let him in the house." She shrugged. "That's the vibe I got anyway."

"Why did you get this vibe?" Travis asked.

"I don't know. It was the way she was standing. Like right in front of it like she was blocking it so he couldn't come inside. Like with her arms crossed."

Gina looked at Chelsea for understanding. She got it. Arms crossed, defenses up, the universal signal among women that they weren't interested in whatever the man in front of them was saying at the moment.

"Like I said, it was just a feeling I got."

"So, you definitely didn't see Frank go into the house," Chelsea pressed.

Gina shook her head. "I can't say for sure they didn't go inside, but I didn't see them go inside."

"And Peter didn't go outside with you? You're sure about that."

"I'm sure."

Chelsea cut a glance at Travis. That confirmed the contradiction of Peter's statement at trial and at least suggested that the writer of the note was telling the truth. "In his testimony at trial, Peter said he took out the trash that night. That's when he supposedly saw Frank and Lily arguing and Frank follow Lily into the house," Travis said.

Gina reached into the grocery bag, avoiding their gazes again. She turned her back on them, putting canned peaches into an overhead cabinet.

"Gina, was Peter in the house or not?" Travis asked softly.

"He never left the sofa that night. I'm not a liar." Her back stayed to them.

"But Peter is?"

Gina turned and looked at them. "Peter had problems back then."

"He was arrested for possession about a week after Lily's murder. Carrying enough drugs to have been charged with a felony," Travis said. "It would have been his third strike, which meant he was in danger of serving serious time behind bars."

Gina didn't respond.

"So maybe Peter saw an opportunity," Chelsea picked up the narrative. "Tell the cops what they want to hear about

Frank and Lily, and they'd look the other way regarding his charges."

"I don't know anything about that," Gina said, still avoiding looking directly at them.

"But you suspect," Travis pressed her.

Gina flattened her lips into a thin line but stayed quiet.

Chelsea moved across the kitchen and stood directly in front of the woman. "Gina, I'm not just doing this to right a wrong. Franklin Brooks is my father. He has spent the last seven years of his life in jail separated from his family who loves him because of a lie."

Gina sighed and finally looked Chelsea in the eye. "I don't know anything for a fact, but I told the cops the truth. I didn't know about what Peter told them until later. They believed him over me, and the cop seemed pretty sure that Franklin killed Lily so—"

"So, you just left it," Chelsea said, unable to curtail the hint of anger in her tone.

"What was I supposed to do?" Gina challenged. "The cops had their killer."

"Let's stay focused on the night Lily died, okay?" Travis interjected. "Did you see Franklin leave Lily's house that night?" he asked Gina.

"No," she responded.

"Did you notice anything or hear anything at all unusual after you saw Lily and Franklin?"

Gina scrunched her face as if she was thinking. After a beat, she responded, "Unusual, no. I put the trash out by the curb, waved at Lily and she waved back."

"Wait a minute." Travis said. "Did you see Jace Orson? He said he was out with friends the night Lily was killed."

Gina laughed. "Jace? Out? With friends? No way. If he

wasn't at work, he was at home, and I'm pretty sure he didn't have any friends."

"That's what he told us," Travis said.

"Well, then he lied. He was definitely home and I saw him."

There was no mention of Gina having seen Jace in her statement.

"Did you tell the cops about seeing Jace that night?" Travis asked.

"I don't know. I don't think so. They were mostly focused on the argument I had seen between Lily and Franklin."

"Do you have any idea where we can find Peter now?" Chelsea asked.

"Last I heard he'd moved to Monterey, but that was eons ago. I haven't seen or heard from him in years. And good riddance."

They thanked Gina and headed back to the car.

"We need to find Peter and talk to Jace Orson again," Chelsea said as they fastened their seat belts.

Travis flashed her a grim smile. "You read my mind."

Chapter Sixteen

Chelsea Harper just would not back down. He'd watched her house. Seen the locksmith come to fix the door. Watched through the windows as she and the private investigator cleaned up inside. He had a clear view into the house now since he'd slashed the curtains and pulled them from the wall.

It looked like they were pretty cozy with each other. Downright domestic. Maybe the obvious attraction between the two would distract Chelsea from her investigation.

He didn't hold out much hope for that, but women were fickle. Lily had proven that, hadn't she? She'd left Franklin, and then—just when he'd been about to make his move, to show her the right man for her was right in front of her— she took up with that other guy. The memory of seeing her with the new guy sat like a stone in his gut. It still made him want to scream at times.

The memories of Lily both comforted and tormented him. He hadn't meant to kill her. He'd wanted her. He'd loved her. He still did. His stomach churned. Things had just gotten out of control. *He'd* gotten out of control. He had only been trying to make her understand. Understand that they were meant to be together. But it had all gone so wrong.

He'd hoped that Chelsea could be easily scared off her

investigation. But when he'd seen her dining room, her research, everything she'd collected on her father's case, he'd known that would never happen. And then they'd gone and tracked down Gina.

This had the potential to be bad. Really bad. Chelsea would keep digging until she found the truth. Until she found him.

He knew what it would take to get her to stop now. But it was dangerous, too dangerous. He shouldn't even be thinking about it, but he was. He had always hoped it wouldn't come to this, but he'd also known that if it did, he'd do what needed to be done.

It seemed like the time had come.

His rage boiled, stoked by once again being forced to do something he didn't want to do. Forced to lose control.

He needed to get out of here before he did something stupid. He'd do what he had to do, but he needed to think. To plan. Whatever he did, it couldn't come back on him. He didn't want the authorities to even think of his name in relation to Chelsea Harper's.

He started the engine and pressed the accelerator. He needed to think. He had to figure out how to stop Chelsea and the private investigator before they ruined everything.

Chapter Seventeen

Jace Orson didn't answer the door at his house when Chelsea and Travis dropped by. Travis had used West's resources to dig up a phone number for him, but Jace hadn't answered his call, either. That, and Gina's surety that Jace had been home the night of Lily's murder, was enough to make Chelsea want to track him down and force the truth out of him immediately.

But Travis pointed out that they had no power to force anything out of anyone. They weren't the police. And Jace not being at home didn't really mean anything anyway. Travis had confronted this kind of thing many times when he'd been on the police force: a witness or neighbor just hadn't wanted to get involved with a police investigation, so they claimed not to have been home or seen anything. It wasn't uncommon, unfortunately.

Travis left a message for Jace, asking him to call, and then suggested to Chelsea that their best course of action would be to give Jace a little time to get back to them. Keeping things cordial went a long way toward getting people to help when you were a private investigator, he explained.

He could tell Chelsea didn't like it, but there was nothing more they could do about Jace right then.

Hoping to get some good news, he suggested they stop

by the police station and see if Owens had made any progress finding out who had vandalized Chelsea's house. Travis didn't relish walking into the station, so he called Owens on his cell and arranged to meet the detective in a small park near the station's parking lot.

When they arrived, Travis parked in one of the visitor spaces. It had been almost four years since he'd left the force; been forced to leave, really, since he could no longer trust that his colleagues would have his back when bad stuff happened. Still, he felt a little tug in his chest looking up at the building that had been his professional home at one point.

They got out and made their way to the lone picnic table on the small patch of land next to the parking lot.

"Where is he? I don't see him," Chelsea said, shading her eyes from the glaring sun and scanning the short expanse between the station and where they stood.

Travis checked his phone to make sure he hadn't missed a message from Owens. He hadn't. "He probably just got caught up in something. He'll be here."

"Well, well. I thought I smelled something foul."

Travis stiffened, instantly on alert. He turned and found Detective Robert Ward. Ward had a wrapped sandwich in one hand and a to-go cup in the other. They were from the deli two blocks over that was a frequent cop stop for lunch. Travis missed their pastrami on rye, but he hadn't dared patronize the place since he had resigned from the force.

Ward swaggered toward them, a glower on his face. He cut a glance at Chelsea, dismissing her quickly, for which Travis gave small thanks. Ward hadn't worked on Franklin Brooks's case, so he likely didn't recognize Chelsea.

Ward could have been out of Central Casting playing the stereotypical not-so-bright middle-aged cop. His shirt strained against his belly, and his sport coat was several years out of fashion.

Travis folded his arms over his chest and angled himself so he was slightly in front of Chelsea. "Ward," he greeted the man without a hint of warmth in his tone.

"What are you doing here, Collins? I hope not looking to get your job back," Ward sneered.

"I've got a job."

Ward snapped his fingers theatrically, as though he'd forgotten. The sound was like the crack of a whip in the otherwise quiet park. "That's right. You're a PI now," he said. "That's a club that doesn't mind a Judas is in their midst."

"Who is this jerk?" Chelsea said from behind Travis. Her voice was low enough that he didn't think Ward heard. Or maybe Ward was just so focused on his hatred for him that he couldn't be bothered to respond to Chelsea's slight.

Either way, Travis gave his head a slight shake and nudged Chelsea a little farther behind him. He didn't think Ward would lash out physically, but the man's disdain for Travis was clear. Who knew how worked up he would get himself?

"Every one of the cops I turned into internal affairs was either fired or forced to resign from the force," Travis responded.

"Internal affairs pigs covering their behinds," Ward spat. "That doesn't mean anything. I knew those men. They were good cops."

"They were supposed to uphold the law, not break it." Travis knew he was talking to a brick wall. Ward was not the kind of cop who would ever see it his way.

"Don't give me that crap. We do what we have to do to get the bad guys off the street."

"Not when it means becoming the bad guy."

"Who decides who's a good guy and who's a bad guy? You?" Ward scoffed.

"Well, it sure as hell shouldn't be you," Travis shot back.

Ward's face reddened. But before he could mount a comeback, Owens jogged over.

"Ward, the lieutenant is looking for you."

Ward cut a glance at Owens, but Owens kept his expression impassive. Ward shot one last venomous look at Travis before stomping away.

"I'm sorry if you're going to catch flak for meeting with me," Travis said to Owens when Ward was out of earshot.

Owens waived his apology away. "Don't worry about it. The vandalism at Chelsea's house is my case. Officially, I'm meeting with her. If she wants to bring you along…" He shrugged. "Who am I to argue?"

Owens was a good man and a good cop.

"So do you have anything for us?" Chelsea asked, getting the meeting on track.

"I wish I had better news," Owens answered. "Your ex-husband has an alibi for the vandalism. He was in surgery all day. Confirmed by multiple people. The fingerprints turned up nothing. They were all yours, Travis's or too smudged to be of any value. Whoever broke in probably wore gloves. I've turned up no witnesses. Not surprising since most of your neighbors were at work. I'm sorry, Ms. Harper."

"Please, call me Chelsea."

Nothing but dead ends, Travis thought, frustrated.

"I have to get back inside, but listen…" Owens stole a glance over his shoulder at the station before turning back to Travis and Chelsea. "I have a bad feeling about whatever you two have gotten yourself into."

"Are we still talking about the vandalism or Chelsea investigating her father's case?" Travis asked.

"Both. As you well know, they are probably one and the same. That's part of why I have a bad feeling. All I'm trying to say is be careful."

All three of them looked at the police station now. Ward had disappeared inside, and Travis had no doubt several of his former colleagues were at that very moment discovering he was currently nearby.

"There are a lot of people who would like to see you go down," Owens said in all seriousness. "By any means necessary."

Chapter Eighteen

Chelsea and Travis stopped by the hardware store and picked up cleaning supplies and paint and primer to cover the mess the vandal had left on her living room walls. When they got back to her house, Chelsea started cleaning and getting the house back in order while Travis broke out the primer and got to work on the walls.

It was slow going, both painting and cleaning. Chelsea made note of items that weren't salvageable and would have to be replaced. Included in that list was pretty much every piece of paper she hadn't had in her binder. Thankfully, the most important stuff she'd scanned and saved to her computer. But printing everything out again would be another big job she'd need to tackle at some point.

She worked on her bedroom first, cleaning until she felt like she'd rubbed out the destructive presence of the stranger who had invaded her private space. She saved the clothing she could; the vandal had cut up several shirts and skirts and several of her bras and panties. The thought of a stranger handling her things made her stomach turn. She gathered the rest of her clothing into her laundry basket to be washed. Then she turned her attention to the other rooms in the house.

The carpet in the living room had been splattered with

paint along with the walls and would need to be taken up and replaced, but the kitchen and dining room floors got a thorough mopping. She cleaned until her hip protested, then headed into the living room to see how Travis was faring.

Red paint wasn't easy to cover, and the vandal had splattered all four of her living room walls. Travis had finally gotten enough primer on the walls to cover them, but there was no time to move on to painting.

Chelsea packed a few more clothes, including her favorite little black dress and the strappy heels she'd bought months earlier even though she'd had nowhere to wear them then. She had somewhere to wear them now. Contrary to her frequent reminders that this wasn't a date. They were working together to clear her father, and that was what she had to keep her focus on. But it definitely felt like a date when Travis picked her up in his living room at 8:00 p.m. sharp as they'd agreed. Wearing black dress pants and a button-down blue shirt that hugged his chest under a dark sport coat, he looked...delicious.

She was glad she'd opted for her little black dress when they stepped into the Fireside Grill, one of Los Angeles' nicest steak houses.

"This is a nice place," Chelsea said.

Travis's brow quirked up. "You didn't think I was going to take you to a nice place?"

"I... I didn't mean to imply—"

"I was joking. You made me a gourmet meal. I'm returning the favor." He turned to the hostess and gave his name for the reservation.

Chelsea wasn't sure if her ragù would qualify as gourmet, but she wasn't going to turn down dinner at the Fireside Grill, either.

The hostess led them to a table in an intimate corner of

the restaurant. She handed them each a menu and left them with a promise that their server would be with them soon. Chelsea's stomach flip-flopped. *Not a date*, she reminded herself.

The restaurant was fairly busy. This was probably just one of the only tables available. Still, she couldn't help but feel a little nervous energy. She could tell herself it wasn't a date all she wanted, but she hadn't been out with a man in longer than she was willing to admit, and her body seemed anxious to make up for lost time.

The flickering candle at the center of the table cast a shadow on Travis's face that made him appear even more ruggedly handsome than he already was. Leagues sexier actually. For a brief moment, she wondered what he would do if she rounded the table, sat on his lap and kissed him silly.

"Chelsea?" His voice pulled her from her fantasy.

She shook herself out of her racing thoughts and focused on the present. "Sorry, yes?"

A small, knowing smile crossed Travis's face. "Where did you go?"

"I was just thinking about the menu," she said, heat crawling up her neck. There was no doubt he knew she was lying. The menu was still closed in her hand. She opened it and hid behind it. She spent the next several minutes choosing her appetizer and entrée and reining in her libido.

The waitress stopped by their table and they put in their drink order. They continued to make small talk until the drinks arrived and then ordered their appetizers and entrées.

"So, um, do you have any siblings?" Chelsea asked, taking a swig from her glass of wine.

Travis's lips quirked up. "Do I have any siblings?"

"Give me a break," Chelsea laughed. "This is awkward. I'm trying to make conversation."

Travis chuckled, the low rumble sending a tingle down her back. "Okay. I'll lay off." His smile dimmed. "I had an older brother. He died when I was ten. He was thirteen." Travis lifted his wineglass to his lips.

"Oh, I'm sorry," she said, kicking herself. "I didn't know."

"Of course you didn't. It's fine." He laid his index finger over the rim of his glass. "I don't mind talking about him. Charles, his name was Charles. He was a cool kid. At least I thought so. As far as I was concerned, he hung the moon." He smiled again.

Chelsea laid her hand over his on the table. "How did he die, if you don't mind my asking?"

"It was a car accident. He, my parents and I were in the car when we were hit by a drunk driver. Charles and my mom and dad didn't make it."

Her heart broke for him. "God, Travis. I'm so sorry."

He pressed his lips tightly together. "Thanks. I spent the next eight years in foster care. Twelve homes in eight years to be exact. I think it's why I went into the marines. I craved structure after such an unstable childhood."

"And how long did you serve?"

He turned her hand over and traced the lines on her palm, sending a charge up and down her spine. "Eight years," he said with another chuckle. "A psychologist would probably have a field day with that coincidence."

"Was it just a coincidence?"

"Yes. Maybe. I don't know. After a while, I just felt like my time in the corps was up."

"And that's why you joined the LAPD?"

"Yeah." Now his laugh turned mirthless. "Not my best decision."

"I think it was a great decision." She took another sip of wine. She needed to be careful. She wasn't a big drinker.

Not much of one at all really. She didn't want to make a fool of herself tonight. "You brought corruption to light."

"Yeah, well, my former colleagues aren't as appreciative as you are."

"They should be. Dirty cops make the good ones look bad. They should want to out the bad ones, and if they don't, they should get into a different line of work. Preferably one that keeps them away from the public," she added passionately.

He grinned. "You sound like a real-life avenger. Or a member of the Justice League or something. A real-life superhero."

She dipped her head. "I'm no superhero. I just hate seeing injustice go uncorrected."

"I bet you're a superhero to your dad."

Before she could think of what to say to that, their food arrived. She had opted for the lamb while Travis had more traditional fare for a steak house and ordered steak. They both had veggies on the side, and the waitress refilled their wineglasses before leaving again.

Chelsea took a bite of her food and moaned slightly as the spicy flavors mingled with the lamb hit her tongue. "This is amazing," she said around the food.

"I'm glad you like it," Travis said, his eyes sparkling. He cut into his steak. "A buddy of mine is the executive chef here. That's how I was able to get a reservation at the last moment. I was hoping to introduce you, but he's out of town."

"Well, your buddy sure knows what he's doing. You should get him to teach you."

"I think I'll stick to omelets and pancakes." Travis popped a piece of steak into his mouth, and they spent the next few minutes eating in companionable silence.

"I told you something about me," he said at last. "It's your turn to tell me something about you."

Chelsea leaned back a bit, surprised by his question. He hadn't shown much interest at all in her life outside of looking into her father's case. But she had asked him questions about his personal life. It was only fair that she answered his questions about hers. "You already know more about me than most people."

"I know about your father's case," he said pointedly. "I want to know about you, Chelsea."

She took another sip of wine, shifting in her seat. "What do you want to know?"

"Anything. Did you always want to be a teacher?"

She put her glass down and picked up her fork again but didn't bring it to her mouth. "No. I wanted to be an attorney, if you can believe it."

Travis pointed at her. "Now that I can believe. Why didn't you go to law school?"

She shrugged. "Money. After my dad was convicted, I needed to get a job quickly if I wanted to help pay for the appeals. I found a position with a small private school in San Francisco and got my master's degree at night. Then I switched to the public school system and moved back here to be closer to Aunt Brenda and Victor. And my dad. Don't get me wrong, I love my kids—"

"But you still think about law?"

"Sometimes. I mean, it's hard not to consider it. I almost feel like I don't need law school now. I have practically lived the law for the past several years."

"It couldn't have been easy."

"It wasn't. When I got word that Dad lost his last appeal…" She let the thought hang, mostly because she couldn't adequately put into words the desolation she had felt. She guessed this was how he felt talking about his family. Time to get this dinner conversation back on track. "What do you like to do for fun?" she asked, spearing another piece of lamb.

"Fun?"

"Yes," she said with a laugh. "You know, enjoyment. To bring pleasure to your life."

He leaned forward, the candlelight sparkling in his eyes along with a hint of something sensual. "Believe me, I enjoy pleasure, and I know many ways to have fun." His gaze raked over her face.

A part of her wanted to look away, but a bigger part wanted to lean into the suggestion he was making. She felt ready to burst into flames under his gaze.

"How are you two doing over here? Can I get you anything else?" the waitress singsonged, oblivious to the moment she had interrupted.

"We're great, thanks." Travis leaned back in his chair, but his gaze didn't move from Chelsea's face. "We'd like to see the dessert menu, please."

"Certainly," the waitress said, sailing off to get the menus.

"I probably shouldn't."

"Come on now, weren't you the one who just mentioned fun? Where's the fun in skipping dessert?"

Were her eyes deceiving her or had he licked his lips after the word *dessert*? She was really on the edge of bursting into flames. Any minute now.

The waitress brought over dessert menus, and Chelsea scanned hers, thinking about the unexpected turn the night had taken. When Travis suggested dinner, she figured it was a pity thing. *Poor Chelsea who hasn't been out on a date in forever.* But she was not only enjoying spending time with him and getting to know him a little better, she enjoyed his flirting. *Wait.* Was that a pity thing, too? Was he throwing her a bone?

She glanced at him over the top of the menu. Even if he was, so what? This non-date couldn't mean anything anyway. It was nice getting to know him, and the flirting was a much-needed ego boost. She felt that she understood him a little better and trusted him a little more, but that was all this could lead to.

When the waitress returned, Chelsea ordered the chocolate mousse and he got the seven-layer cake. They both ordered coffee. They chatted more about their lives until the dessert arrived.

This time it was Travis who moaned when he tasted the cake. She was glad she was sitting when he did. Her knees wouldn't have held her up.

Travis placed a bite of cake onto his fork and leaned across the table with it outstretched toward her. "Try it."

Hunger for a very different kind of dessert seared through her.

"You like it?" he asked.

Her first attempt at answering failed. She leaned back in her seat and cleared her throat before trying again. "It's good," she said. "Great, really."

They finished their desserts quickly, and Travis paid the check. They picked up their coats from the coat check and stepped out into the night.

"Thank you for a wonderful evening," Chelsea said.

"You're welcome." Travis shot her a heated gaze.

The valet rushed toward them, and Travis handed over his ticket.

The brisk wind sent a shiver through Chelsea. Travis put his arm around her, pulling her into his side. "Is this all right? Better?"

The spicy scent of his cologne snaked under her nose. "It's fine. Thanks." She looked up at him and found his face only centimeters away from hers.

Travis sucked in a breath and leaned closer. His lips slowly lowered until they were covering hers. She sighed, opening farther and letting him pull her in closer. The kiss was gentle but hot in a way she'd never experienced before. His hips pressed against her, and she felt the length of him. How much he wanted her. As much as she wanted him.

The kiss went on and on but not long enough. A boisterous group turned the corner, laughing loudly and heading to the restaurant.

Chelsea pulled away, her entire body still ignited from Travis's kiss. A kiss that had been everything she'd imagined and more, but the doubts and second thoughts were already creeping in. She needed him to get her father out of prison. That was the most important thing to her. Even if being in his arms made her forget about all the obstacles she was facing. But she could not mess that up. No matter how strong her feelings for Travis were growing.

She took one step back and then another, putting distance between them. She watched disappointment flit across Travis's face. Disappointment she knew was mirrored in her own expression. But this was for the best.

The valet pulled Travis's car to a stop at the curb in front of them and got out.

Travis turned to the young man.

A loud bang split the air, and Chelsea dropped to the pavement.

Chapter Nineteen

Chelsea jerked to one side, then fell to the sidewalk. In two steps, Travis was by her side, shielding her with his body. Tires squealed, and people were yelling around him, but all he could see was Chelsea's teary eyes staring up at him, her face contorted with pain. Blood poured from her arm, her sleeveless dress giving him a good view of the wound.

"I've got you. I've got you, Chelsea." He stripped off his jacket and button-down shirt and used the latter to press on the wound. She moaned.

"It's okay," he said. "You are going to be okay."

"Oh, man. Oh, my God. He shot her," the valet said in a high-pitched voice filled with panic.

"Call 911. Tell them we need an ambulance and that we have a gunshot wound. And tell the dispatcher that the victim is Chelsea Harper. Ask them to notify Owens," Travis barked out orders.

"Yes, sir. Got it." The valet dashed away.

"It hurts," Chelsea moaned.

"I know, baby. Hang in there. Help is on the way."

How had things gone bad so fast? He'd let down his guard. Been distracted. He'd let his attraction to Chelsea cloud his judgment, and she'd paid the price. If she died… He shook the thought away. She wasn't going to die. He pressed harder on the wound in an attempt to slow the bleeding.

The sound of sirens cut through the air, letting him know that the EMTs were close. Moments later they arrived, a man and a woman in blue. They pushed him to the side so they could kneel next to Chelsea. He stayed close, though, not wanting to let her out of his sight.

She must have felt the same way. Her eyes didn't leave his face even as the EMTs worked on her.

"Sir?"

Travis snapped his head to the right. A uniformed police officer stood next to him.

"Could you step over here and give me your statement of what happened?" the officer said.

"I'm not leaving her," Travis snarled.

The officer frowned. "Sir, I need to get your statement."

Travis gave the officer a succinct version of the moments leading up to Chelsea getting shot without moving away from her side.

"Let's get loaded up," the male EMT said. He and his partner lifted Chelsea onto a gurney and began pushing her toward the ambulance. Travis moved to follow.

"Hey!" The officer he'd been talking to put a hand on his forearm to stop him. "You need to stay here and finish giving me your statement."

Travis shook off the officer's hand. "I am not leaving her," he repeated.

"It's okay, Officer."

Travis and the officer turned as Owens stopped next to them. "I can get his formal statement at the hospital."

The officer scowled at Owen's badge but stepped back.

Travis jogged to catch up with the gurney, and Owens hustled to keep up.

"What happened?" Owens asked.

"Drive-by. I didn't see the driver. Black sedan. I can't tell you anything about the plates. They were covered. Just like with the hit-and-run video, although this was a different car." Travis pulled himself into the back of the ambulance.

"I'll meet you at the hospital," Owens said.

Travis turned and shot Owens a look that had made lesser men tremble with fear. "Owens, when we find this guy, I want to be the one to take him down. Understand?"

TRAVIS WATCHED THE doctor examine Chelsea from the corner of the room where he'd been since the EMTs had rolled her into the hospital on a gurney. Watching over her like he should have been doing before she was shot. He was still kicking himself for letting his growing feelings for her sway his professionalism. Chelsea's injury might not be lethal, but it was painful. He could see that from the semi-glazed look in her eyes.

"Travis? Are you still there?" Kevin's voice cut through Travis's thoughts.

"Yeah, I'm still here," he said into the phone.

"Are you sure you're okay? I can come down to the hospital."

"No, I'm fine. Chelsea's going to be okay, too." The bullet had only grazed her arm, thankfully.

"Good. Then you should know that I was able to get an address for Peter Schmeichel. He does still live in Monterey. I found his name and a photograph in a church bulletin. Looks like he volunteers a lot of his time."

"Send me everything you got." Travis glanced at Chelsea again. "I'm not sure when I'll be able to make a trip to Monterey." The picturesque town was nearly a six-hour drive away. "But I have a buddy who owns a condo there.

I'll give him a call. See if I can crash there for a night or two in the coming days."

"If you need me or Tess to head up there for you..."

Travis looked at Chelsea again. He didn't want to leave her side, but he knew this investigation better than Tess or Kevin, and he wanted to see how Peter would respond to his questions. "No. I'll go." He ended the call with Kevin.

Seconds later, his phone pinged with a text containing Peter's address and the church bulletin Kevin mentioned. Travis shot off a quick text to his friend asking if his Monterey condo was available for the next several days and whether he could crash there, then walked over to the bed where Chelsea lay.

"You are very lucky," the doctor said as she finished the last of Chelsea's stitches. Dr. Lacey's curly brown hair was bound on top of her head with a hair tie, and wrinkles creased her forehead. Intelligent eyes indicated that she knew what she was doing. She pulled off her gloves and tossed them onto a metal table next to Chelsea. "I'll prescribe a painkiller, but you'll be able to sleep in your own bed tonight."

Chelsea cut a look at Travis. "Not exactly, but thanks, Doctor."

Dr. Lacey made notes on a tablet. "It may take me a little while to get your discharge papers together. Just hang tight. We're a bit understaffed tonight."

"As long as I don't have to stay overnight, I'll be fine," Chelsea responded.

"You shouldn't be so eager to leave," Travis said after the doctor left the room. "At least we know you're safe in the hospital."

Chelsea tilted her head and looked at him. "I'm safe at your place, too."

"I'm not so sure about that anymore," he muttered, running a hand over his head.

Chelsea studied him. "What does that mean?"

"It means I'm the reason you got shot."

Chelsea frowned. "Did you hit your head?"

"Chels, I'm serious."

"So am I. Did you hit your head when you threw your body over me? Because admittedly things happened fast, but I don't recall you shooting at me."

"I was distracted. I should have been paying attention. I should have seen the sedan and the gun before the shooter got off a shot. If I had been doing my job—"

"Wait a minute." She held up a hand. "I hired you to help me prove my father's innocence, not throw yourself in front of bullets for me."

"I know, but of the two of us, I'm the professional."

Chelsea pushed herself up straighter in the hospital bed. "Oh, get over yourself. You are no more responsible for me getting shot then I am. You're not a superhero. If you had seen the guy and thrown yourself in front of me, you would have been shot. Would you be saying the same things to me right now if our roles were reversed?"

"I'd tell you that you weren't to blame," he reluctantly admitted.

"Okay, then, I don't want to hear any more of this macho 'I should have protected you' baloney."

Despite everything, he smiled.

A moment later, that smile fell as Chelsea's aunt Brenda barreled through the door.

"There you are. Oh, my God, Chelsea." Her aunt threw herself on top of Chelsea, her sobs filling the room.

Chelsea flinched with pain from her aunt's jostling.

Travis took a step toward them, intending to prod the

older woman away before she inadvertently hurt her niece any further. But the man from the photo on Chelsea's dresser, her cousin Victor, strode in after Brenda.

Victor sized Travis up quickly. "You must be the private investigator my mom told me was helping Chels."

Travis nodded, bracing himself for the same anger Chelsea's aunt had thrown his way at her house.

Victor thrust his hand out. "Victor Harper, Chelsea's cousin. More like a brother. Thanks for looking out for my cuz."

Travis shook Victor's hand, surprised by the friendly greeting.

"Chelsea told us how you used your own body to shield her and that you tried to stop the bleeding," Victor explained.

Chelsea had called her family herself after the doctor determined her wound wouldn't require surgery and they'd been waiting for her to get stitched up. She'd wanted privacy for the call, so Travis had stepped into the hall while she was on the phone. Apparently, she had embellished his role.

"I really didn't do that much," he countered to Victor.

"Yes, he did," Chelsea called from the bed.

Chelsea's aunt lifted herself from Chelsea's body and made a half turn. "You," she said, stalking across the room to Travis.

Victor moved quickly, getting out of the path of his mother.

Before Travis knew what she was about to do, Aunt Brenda had her arms wrapped around him. She buried her face in his chest, still crying.

"Thank you," she said, her voice thick with emotion. "You saved my Chelsea."

Travis rubbed her shoulder awkwardly. "You're welcome, but really I—"

Aunt Brenda reared back, fire mingling with the tears in her eyes. "Don't say it was nothing. It was everything to me. To Victor. Chelsea is family. She told me you ruined a beautiful shirt, and you stayed with her when she was scared. That's not nothing."

"She would have done the same for me," he said, still unsure what to do with the older woman's praise.

"That is true," Aunt Brenda said. "My Chelsea has a big heart." She patted one of Travis's cheeks. "So do you. I can tell."

"Thank you," Travis said, touched by her words.

"I was rude to you the other day when you came to my house. Let me make it up to you? You have to come to dinner. Do you like mashed potatoes and gravy? I make them with real potatoes. None of that powdered junk. Milk and real butter, that's the secret to getting them nice and fluffy." She patted his cheek again.

Victor edged up to his mother. "Okay, Ma. I think now is not a good time to try to feed the man." He wrapped an arm around his mother, but she shrugged him off.

"It's always a good time to feed a man." Brenda turned back to look at her niece. "You hear that, Chelsea?" She winked at her.

"Aunt Brenda," Chelsea groaned.

"Ma," Victor lamented.

Travis held back a chuckle, but he was struck by a sense of longing. He never let himself think about what might have been if his family had lived, but occasionally a memory would creep up on him. They had been a happy family. Content to be in each other's company. His brother had teased him sometimes, and it had annoyed him then, but Travis would give anything to have his brother tease him again. Or fight with him. Having people in his life who cared enough to fight with him and for him... It had been a long time since he had that. Maybe too long.

He told himself he didn't need it, but watching Chelsea with her aunt and her cousin, who had raced to the hospital the minute they learned she was hurt, made him realize he'd been lying to himself. He wanted people in his life, that sense of belonging to a family. Maybe even this family.

He watched Chelsea's aunt and cousin fuss over her while foggy images of what his future could look like played through his head. What if he let Chelsea in?

The door to the room swung open, and Dr. Lacey strode back in. "Well, it looks like the gang's all here. I'm going to have to ask you to step into the hall while I talk to Miss Harper about caring for her wound. When we're done, she will be all set to go home."

Victor ushered his mother out into the hall.

Travis started to follow but stopped at the sound of Chelsea's voice.

"Hey, are you okay?" she asked him.

Was he? He wasn't sure. He felt like a raw nerve at the moment. But he wasn't going to trouble Chelsea with his kaleidoscope of emotions. Especially not when he wasn't sure what to make of them himself.

Instead, he smiled. "I'm fine. Great, now that we know you're going to be okay."

"Okay," she said, a note of skepticism in her voice.

"I'll be waiting for you when you're ready to go home."

Chapter Twenty

Travis helped Chelsea into his guest room, then left her to change into her pajamas. It had been a long and arduous night, and she was exhausted. And despite knowing she was safe now, a thread of fear still lingered. She could hear Travis walking around the house, checking all the locks on the doors and windows, she suspected.

She'd changed and was crossing from the attached bathroom to the bed when he appeared at the bedroom door again.

"Here. Let me help you." He put an arm around her shoulders, walked her to the head of the bed and turned down the bedspread with one hand.

"You know, I'm not an invalid. I can walk."

He eased her down onto the bed. "I know you aren't, but you should take it easy for a while. And speaking of taking it easy, Kevin found an address for Peter Schmeichel. It's in Monterey, so I was thinking I could have Kevin or Tess stay with you while I go speak to him."

Chelsea swung her legs up onto the bed and under the bedspread. "Without me? No way." She shook her head. "I'm going with you."

He sighed. "I had a feeling you'd say that. We'll go in a few days then. Once you've had some time to rest."

"I don't need rest, and I don't want to put off talking to Peter. We can go tomorrow."

Travis pulled the covers up to her waist. "You were just shot."

She tamped down the fear that threatened to rise. "It was a graze."

He rolled his eyes. "Semantics."

Chelsea grabbed his hand. "Travis, please. We're close. I can feel it. I don't want to wait. I need to do this."

He sighed again. "Okay. As long as you're feeling up for it tomorrow, we can go. But if you don't feel like it when you wake up tomorrow, you have to promise you'll tell me." He looked into her eyes, and she saw how serious he was. "I won't compromise your health."

Warmth spread through her chest. She squeezed his hand. "I appreciate you looking out for me." She threw good sense to the wind and leaned forward and kissed his mouth quickly, softly.

He stroked her cheek with the pad of his thumb. "Get some sleep." He stood and headed for the door.

"Travis?" Her heart pounded in her chest. She felt a little foolish, but fear pushed her forward.

Travis turned.

"Would you mind staying with me tonight? Just sleeping. I'm embarrassed to admit it, but I'm still a little shaky after, well, everything."

"You have nothing to be embarrassed about," he said, heading back to the bed.

She scooted over to make room for him. He toed off his shoes and slid in beside her still in his clothes. She relaxed against him. He wrapped an arm around her waist and gathered her close. The faint smell of his cologne still lingered even after the night they'd had.

"I feel safe when I'm with you."

"I'm glad I make you feel safe."

His breath tickled the skin on her neck, causing her pulse to pick up. She'd meant it when she asked him to only sleep next to her, but her body didn't seem to want to cooperate. Lying next to him was sweet torture but still torture. "You do," she said.

"You know, when I woke up in the hospital and the doctor told me that my parents and brother had been killed, that was the most scared I thought I could ever be. Until today. I've never been more scared than I was when I saw you lying on the pavement with a gunshot wound."

"I'm sorry I scared you like that."

He shifted so he could look at her. "You don't have anything to be sorry about. I'm just so glad you're safe." He held her more tightly against his side.

She snaked a hand up around the back of his neck and leaned forward. As soon as their lips met, his control seemed to snap. He ravished her mouth, sending a groan through them both. Blood pounded in her ears. She deepened the kiss, letting her hand move down from his neck to his chest before venturing farther south. He stopped her before she reached below his waist.

"Wait. Chelsea. I…" He panted. "I think we should slow down. This… We… I'm not a relationship guy," he blurted.

She stiffened.

"I mean… I didn't mean. I just wanted to be upfront about—"

"I get it." She slid away from him.

"I'm not trying to hurt you. Obviously, I'm attracted to you, but you deserve a man who is going to be all in, and I'm not that guy."

"I said I get it, Travis," she said, her tone more caustic

than she'd intended. She couldn't be mad with him for saying out loud exactly what she'd been telling herself for days now. She let out a breath. "You're right." She laid her head on his shoulder. "You'll stay until I fall asleep?"

"Of course. Whatever you want."

When she woke the next morning, the side of the bed where he'd been was cold.

TRAVIS WAS UP at six the next morning. He normally went to the gym, but he wasn't about to leave Chelsea's side, so he settled for a pared-down workout in his bedroom. The drive to Monterey took about five hours, and he wanted to arrive by early afternoon, but he was loath to wake Chelsea. She needed rest to heal. Part of him hoped she would sleep late so he'd have a reason to put off the trip for another day and give her more time to rest, but he should have known it wouldn't be that easy. He heard her moving around the guest room shortly after 7:30.

He still had a knot in his throat thinking about their conversation the night before.

You did the right thing.

He knew he had. Chelsea deserved the truth from him. He wasn't the type of man who did relationships, no matter how brilliant, sexy and fearless the woman. And Chelsea was all of those things. She deserved someone who could commit to her. That wasn't him.

He'd just finished cooking the first batch of waffles when Chelsea entered the kitchen. She looked much better than she had the night before. The color was back in her cheeks, and she appeared rested. But her body language was closed off. She gave him a weak, polite smile as she headed for the coffee maker. "Good morning."

"Good morning. I hope you like waffles," he said.

"I do."

"How many?"

"Two, please."

He handed her a plate with a couple waffles he'd just taken off the iron.

She took it without meeting his gaze. "Thanks."

He had never done the awkward morning-after dance before. He rarely stayed the night. He blew out a silent breath and put two more waffles on the griddle for himself. When they were ready, he sat across from Chelsea. They ate in uncomfortable silence for several minutes.

"Are you still up for the trip to Monterey?"

"Absolutely." Chelsea dabbed her mouth with a napkin and rose. "I just need to pack a few more things. When do you want to leave?"

The clock on the stove read 8:15 a.m. "Does nine o'clock work for you? We should get there around three if we don't make a lot of stops and don't hit traffic. Peter works the three-to-eleven shift at a plumbing supply distributor, so that will give us a little time to settle in at the condo before going to see him."

"That's fine. I'll go get ready." She all but ran from the kitchen.

He sighed. There wasn't anything he could do about the awkwardness except hope it passed. He cleaned up the kitchen before gathering his own overnight bag. Chelsea met him at the car at nine o'clock sharp, and they headed out.

He headed north on US 101 toward Santa Barbara. It would be marginally faster to take the I-5 north, but the 101 ran along the coast and provided a much better view. They kept the conversation light and mostly talked about the case. As he hoped, some of the awkwardness from the night before ebbed the farther they got from his house.

Chelsea fell asleep somewhere around Pismo Beach. He shut off the radio to let her sleep, content to make the drive in silence. He couldn't help but note how he seemed to be content to do just about anything when he was with her.

She woke as he exited the freeway and drove into what was known as Old Monterey just before 3:00 p.m. They drove past a gallery, specialty markets, several restaurants, pubs and coffee shops. Everything about the area screamed small-town America.

"Do you like seafood?" he asked her, turning the car away from the downtown area.

"Yeah. I love it," she said, stretching.

"Great. I need to make a stop before we get to the condo."

Travis drove a few miles before he pulled into a parking lot twenty-five yards from the wharf.

"Where are we?"

"This is my favorite place to buy seafood." He opened his door.

Chelsea pushed open her door and followed Travis into what looked like an aluminum shack. Inside there were several rows of tables with seafood displayed on ice. Running along the far wall was a counter with more fish behind glass.

The muscular young man behind the counter greeted them. "What can I get you folks?"

"Two lobsters, a pound of shrimp and a half pound of crab."

While the clerk pulled his order together, Travis walked around the shop collecting the other items he'd need to prepare lunch, as well as a six pack of beer.

"This seems like a lot," Chelsea said, following him.

"Trust me," he said.

They went back to the counter and gathered their order. "Anything else I can get you?" the man asked.

"That should do it," Travis said.

The clerk put everything into bags and rang them up. Travis paid, and they got back into the car and headed a little farther up the coast until they reached a strip of beachfront condos. He pulled the car into a short, shared driveway. The ocean was visible just beyond the side of the house, the water a brilliant calm blue past a smooth expanse of sand.

Travis had spent many weekends decompressing here. His friend actually owned a couple condos as investment properties, but it looked like the left side of the house was empty at the moment. Inside, the condo was renovated and well maintained. Two good-size bedrooms opened up off the large living/dining/kitchen area. A wide balcony jutted off the back of the condo, looking out into the ocean.

"Take whichever room you'd like," Travis said, placing the grocery bag on the counter. He grabbed the lobsters and put them in the fridge.

Chelsea carried her bag into the room on the left. It was slightly bigger and had a better view in his opinion. It was the room he usually slept in, but he was happy to give it up to her.

He opened one of the beers and put the others in the fridge. Then he grabbed a large pot from a lower cabinet and filled it with water, setting it on a burner to boil. Next, he got started preparing the easy crab dip recipe he always used, then arranged some crackers on a plate and scooped cocktail sauce into a small bowl. When the water came to a boil, he pulled the lobsters from the fridge. The cool air had done its job putting the crustaceans to sleep. Cooking them this way seemed less cruel than throwing them into boiling water while they were still active.

He was spreading the shrimp out on a platter next to the cocktail sauce when Chelsea stepped out of her bedroom.

"This is a gorgeous place. And these photos," she said, stopping next to a nighttime photo of the ocean just beyond her bedroom door.

Travis poured her a glass of wine. "My buddy who owns the condo is a photographer."

"He's really good." Chelsea crossed to the kitchen and took the glass of wine from him.

He smiled. "He's Myles Messina."

Chelsea's hand froze with her glass halfway to her lips. "Myles Messina, the famous photographer?"

Travis nodded.

"Wow. How do you two know each other?"

"Myles was in foster care with me for a year. We managed to keep in touch after we aged out of the system."

"I didn't know he was in foster care." Chelsea sat on one of the kitchen counter stools.

"Yeah, he's a real success story."

"Both of you are." Chelsea brought the wineglass to her lips.

Heat traveled through him at the compliment. He lifted the plates with the shrimp and crab dip and carried them to the balcony door. "Can you open this for me?"

Chelsea grabbed the door handle and turned it. They stepped out onto the deck. A glass-top table with four wrought iron chairs stood center stage.

"Don't sit yet." Travis set the food on the table, then went back into the house. He returned moments later with two towels and his beer.

They both sat. Travis took a deep breath of ocean air, feeling it calm him. There was something special about the beach air here. Cleaner. He took another sip of beer and watched Chelsea reach for a shrimp and dip it into the sauce.

"Oh," she moaned, sending a spirit of need to his lower region. "This is amazing."

"Yeah, the crab house makes the best cocktail sauce. Homemade by the owner," he said, trying not to think about how his body had reacted to her moan.

Her brows rose. "I thought you said you couldn't cook."

"You'll notice there's nothing that had to be seasoned or braised or anything much more difficult than dropping things into a pot of boiling water or mixing crab dip."

Chelsea laughed. "How often do you come here?"

"Recently, not as much as I'd like to. Work has been busy."

"Well, I can see why you like it." She leaned her head back against the chair and closed her eyes.

God, she was gorgeous.

They said in silence for a while until Chelsea said, "The lobster should be ready by now, shouldn't it?"

Travis got up. "You're right." Chelsea started to follow. "No. You stay. Enjoy the view. I've got this."

He transferred the lobsters from the water onto a large platter and carried it outside with a dish of clarified garlic butter. He went back inside for the wine bottle and dinner plates.

"You know, I can get used to being served like this," Chelsea teased, grabbing a lobster and putting it on the plate he slid in front of her.

And I could get used to serving you. The thought popped into his head unbidden.

No. This was nice, but that's all it was. A nice moment. That's all it could be.

But even as he thought, he couldn't quite convince himself that was all this was.

"Do YOU NEED anything else?" Travis asked her, still standing next to the table.

"I don't think so. Sit. Relax," Chelsea said.

He sat down next to her. They ate in companionable silence until her phone rang. She pulled it from her pocket. Simon. She made a face and declined the call. The phone rang again a moment later.

"If you need to take that, you can," Travis said.

"No, it's just Simon." She declined the call again.

Travis's mouth twisted into a frown.

For some reason she felt she had to explain. "He's been calling me since I, we, threw him out of my house."

"Why?" Travis groaned.

"I don't know. I haven't taken his call."

Travis seemed relieved to hear her say that. She got the feeling he didn't want her taking Simon's call any more than she wanted to talk to her ex-husband.

Chelsea dipped a piece of lobster in butter. "This is the best butter I've ever tasted." She popped the lobster in her mouth. A little bit of butter dripped down her chin.

Travis reached out and swiped it away with his thumb.

The waves crashed against the sand, and electricity crackled between them.

Travis ran the pad of his thumb over her lips.

She knew she would probably kick herself later. He'd made it quite clear he was not available for anything serious, and she didn't do casual hookups. But she didn't care about any of that at the moment. She had to kiss him, the desire more than she had the will to fight off.

She leaned forward, closing the distance between them. Kissing him felt like a strong wave had crashed into her, dragging her underwater. His hands roamed over her shoulders, then down her back. He seemed to feel just as much urgency as she did.

Travis pulled back first. "We shouldn't do this." He slid his chair away from her.

"You're right," she said, turning away from him, her pride smarting. She was a glutton for punishment.

Travis rose. "I'm going to get us a couple of bottles of water." He went inside.

Water. He probably thought she'd had too much to drink. Maybe she had. He was right, she shouldn't have kissed him. No matter how good it felt. It was stupid.

Travis returned with the bottled waters, and she took the one he offered.

"How about a walk on the beach?" she suggested, mostly to get away from the scene of the kissing crime, as it were.

He agreed, and they set off along the beach, keeping a respectable distance between them. Travis told her a little bit more about his older brother, recounting several childhood stories. She reciprocated, telling him about growing up with Victor.

They'd made it about a mile down the beach when her phone began ringing again.

"Are you sure you don't want to take that?" Travis asked.

She silenced the ringer this time. "Absolutely sure."

"You know, I can't see the two of you together. How did you two meet?"

"Aunt Brenda took a fall four years ago. Simon was her orthopedist. I should have known better, but Dad's first appeal had just been denied, and I was in a tough place. We got married too quickly. Only five months after we met."

"That is fast."

"Too fast. We didn't really know each other at all. I think we were both infatuated with how different we were. Or maybe that was just me. I've learned that Simon always has ulterior motives."

"And what was his ulterior motive for marrying you?"

"I think he thought it would upset his father. Bringing a poor, Black girlfriend home. And to be truthful, I think his father was concerned at first."

"At first?"

"Funny enough, my former father-in-law and I had more in common than Simon and I did. Gerald passed away about six months ago."

"I'm sorry for your loss."

"Thanks. Gerald was a doctor like Simon, but he came from nothing. A poor boy from southern Texas. Worked his way through college and med school. He was brilliant and came up with a revolutionary procedure for conducting intestinal surgery. That made him a legend in the medical field and a millionaire many, many times over. I think Simon's issues stem from feeling like he can't live up to his father. I think Gerald thought that I might be good for Simon."

"But you weren't?"

Chelsea laughed. "Our marriage was a disaster. Before the first year was out, I realized I'd made a mistake. Simon was already stepping out with one of his coworkers. Our marriage didn't last much longer. I kept in touch with Gerald, though. He was a good man."

"He didn't have a problem with who your father was?"

She pushed a lock of hair from her face. Gerald had never bought up her father, at least not with her, but she was sure he'd cautioned Simon. "I'm sure he didn't love that his daughter-in-law had a convict for a father, but he was never anything but supportive."

"That's cool. He sounds like a good guy."

"He was. Can I ask you something?"

"Sure."

"You told me you don't do relationships." Her heart thudded uncontrollably. "Have you ever considered it? You know, doing a relationship."

Travis stopped walking and turned to look out at the ocean. He didn't answer her.

"I'm sorry. I shouldn't have asked." Chelsea said as her phone vibrated, indicating another incoming call.

"You should take that," Travis said, turning back to the condo. "I'm going to clean up. Peter should be getting a break soon."

She ignored her phone and watched him walk away.

Chapter Twenty-One

His nerves were on edge. Shooting at Chelsea had been a
rash decision. Stupid. Especially since he hadn't killed her.
The cops would have no choice but to investigate a shooting. They weren't the brightest bulbs in the pack, but even
a dim bulb gave off some light. What if some upstart detective believed Chelsea's rants about her father's innocence?

He'd done it again. Let his emotions, his anger, take over.
It was Chelsea's fault, just like it had been Lily's. They confused him. Forced him to take action when he just wanted
to be left in peace. Lily had paid the price for angering him.

Blood roared in his ears. He could feel his life veering out
of control again. Like it had when Lily was alive. He wasn't
sure how to regain control, but he knew he had to. Chelsea
Harper had to be dealt with. Once and for all.

Chapter Twenty-Two

Salinger's Wholesale Plumbing and Fixtures was located in an industrial park in Salinas about twenty miles from Monterey. Travis had called ahead and, using the bogus excuse of having talked to Peter earlier about some plumbing part, found out that Peter was scheduled to work that day from three to eleven that evening and that he usually took his dinner break around 7:00 p.m.

The manager of the warehouse pointed Peter out to Chelsea and Travis. Peter was pulling several large boxes on a dolly cart from one end of the warehouse to the other where the truck bays were. He wore a blue-gray jumpsuit unzipped enough for Travis to see the white T-shirt underneath. His name was stenciled on the jumpsuit's left side, and worn work boots covered his feet. He slowed and stopped as Travis and Chelsea approached.

"Peter," Travis said with a polite smile that he hoped would put the man at ease. "My name is Travis Collins. This is my associate Chelsea Harper. Can we speak with you for a moment?"

"About what?"

"Lily Wong," Chelsea answered.

Peter's body stiffened, going on full alert. "I don't have anything to say about that."

"I think you do, Peter," Travis said firmly. "Chelsea's aunt received an anonymous note saying you'd lied at trial. I think you sent it."

It was a shot in the dark, but from the way Peter paled, Travis knew he'd hit his mark. If Peter had sent the note, it meant he felt remorse for what he'd done. That was good for them.

"We have spoken to Gina." Travis paused for several beats, letting that statement percolate in Peter's head, leaving him wondering just what his ex-girlfriend had said about the night Lily was murdered. "We'll buy you dinner. Your manager said your break starts soon. Anywhere you want to go. Just give us ten minutes." Travis could see the man's resolve cracking. "Ten minutes, and you get a free dinner. How about it?"

"Ten minutes," Peter agreed. "There's a Thai place two blocks down. I'll meet you there in fifteen minutes."

"Thank you," Chelsea said before she and Travis turned and left the warehouse.

"You think he'll show?" she asked as they got into Travis's car and headed for the restaurant.

"I think so. If he doesn't, we'll track him down again and ask a lot less nicely."

Thankfully, they didn't have to. Peter arrived at the restaurant fifteen minutes later as promised. Their waiter had already left three waters and three menus on the table. Travis wasn't hungry, and apparently neither was Chelsea. They both had coffee. Peter went all in, getting stir-fry with soft-shell crab, the most expensive item on the menu. Travis only hoped the coming conversation would be worth what this dinner would cost.

When the waiter left to put their order in with the kitchen, Peter asked, "What do you want from me?"

"I don't know if you know, but Franklin Brooks is my father," Chelsea said.

Peter squinted at her from across the table. "I didn't recognize you. Yeah, yeah, I remember you now from the trial."

"My father has exhausted all his appeals. Barring the truth coming out, he's going to spend the rest of his life in jail."

Peter's gaze slid from Chelsea's. "I'm sorry to hear that."

"Are you?" Chelsea leaned forward. "Because I think you know my dad is innocent."

Peter wouldn't look at either of them. "I don't know anything."

"Mr. Schmeichel." Travis jumped back into the conversation. "We are trying to get an innocent man free from prison. We need your help."

Peter remained silent.

"My father's life is at stake. If you don't tell the truth now, he'll die in prison," Chelsea added.

Peter reached for his glass of water and took a long pull on the straw.

Chelsea and Travis waited.

Finally, Peter spoke. "The court said he's guilty."

"In part based on your testimony. But we all know that what you said on the witness stand wasn't true," Chelsea countered.

"Are you calling me a liar?"

"I think you may have seen a way out of a jam, and you took it," Travis said, avoiding the question.

"Oh, yeah? And you got all this figured out based on what?"

"Based on the fact that Franklin was somewhere else at the time you say he was at Lily's house. On the fact that Franklin has always professed his innocence. And on the fact that your recollection of seeing Franklin at Lily's house at the time of her murder is undermined by Gina's statement."

"Gina," Peter scoffed. "The cops didn't believe her."

"No, they didn't," Travis agreed. "But then they had an incentive not to believe her. A woman killed in her own home. The community was scared and demanding someone be arrested. The recent ex-boyfriend is an easy answer. They just needed enough evidence to slap the cuffs on him. But they had enough evidence to slap the cuffs on you."

Peter's angry gaze slipped away but not before Travis got a hint of the guilt there, too. He kept going. "You were arrested about a week after Lily's murder. Your third strike." Travis softened his tone. "No one could blame you for wanting to avoid prison. Did one of the detectives hint that they would be willing to make a deal if you had seen something helpful regarding Lily's murder?"

Travis half expected Peter to erupt with anger and denials, but neither came. Peter looked down at the table and sighed.

"You know how we found you?" Chelsea asked.

Peter looked up and shook his head.

"The church bulletin. Your name popped up as a parishioner of the month. You do a lot of good work at your church."

"I do," Peter confirmed.

The waiter returned with their food then. It took several moments to get settled, but when the waiter left again, Travis decided to push Peter a little harder. "You know, Chelsea and I don't think you were involved with Lily's murder. But I work with a team, and we bounce things off each other. It's been pointed out to me that you could have made up the story regarding Franklin not to get out of the drug charge, or at least not just to get out of the drug charge. That maybe you had another reason for wanting to throw suspicion on Franklin." Travis let the implication hang over the table.

"What are you suggesting?" Peter glared, ignoring his lunch.

"Well, and I'm just spitballing, but Lily was an attractive, professional, intelligent woman. A catch. And she was back on the market. We know she was dating again. And Gina mentioned you two were having trouble. Arguing a lot. Maybe you made a play for Lily. She said no, things got out of hand."

"No," Peter spat.

"Then what really happened?" Chelsea asked. "I know it wasn't what you testified to at my father's trial."

"You don't know anything."

"Oh, but we do." Travis said. "We know you lied. The cops may have dismissed Gina seven years ago, but we wouldn't let them get away with that now. And someone has been targeting Chelsea. Attempting to run her down, vandalizing her home, even shooting at her. That makes me very angry, Peter. It makes me think someone has something to hide. Maybe someone who has already lied under oath. Where were you yesterday between 8:00 and 11:00 p.m.?" Travis asked, giving the time period when Chelsea had been shot.

Peter pushed his chair back and started to stand. "I don't have to listen to this."

"Sit. Down."

Peter hesitated, half standing, half sitting for a fraction of a second before reclaiming his seat.

"Peter, my father has been in prison for seven years," Chelsea said in a soft voice. "You seem to have changed your life, turned over a new leaf. You're helping people now. Help my father. Right this wrong."

There was a long silence where no one at the table so much as moved beyond breathing.

Peter spoke first. "I have to admit I lied."

"You have to tell the truth," Chelsea responded.

"You sign an affidavit under oath saying that your testimony at Franklin Brooks's trial was inaccurate."

Peter laughed bitterly. "Inaccurate is just fancy talk for lied."

It was, so Travis stayed quiet.

"Everyone will know I'm a liar and I could get in real trouble."

"Everyone will know you're correcting a wrong," Chelsea countered. "Making amends for a mistake that you made. There's nothing shameful about that."

Peter's chin dropped to his chest. "I lied." His voice was so soft Travis wasn't sure he heard it. "I lied," Peter said, louder this time, and Travis nearly cheered.

Peter looked at Chelsea. "You said I've turned over a new leaf. Well, I've tried. I kicked the drugs. I started going to church. I got a decent job, but I've always felt guilty about what I did to your father. I don't know if he's innocent or not. The cop said he did it, and I didn't see any reason for both of us to go to jail back then, so I lied. But it was eating me alive that an innocent man might be sitting in prison in part because of me, so I sent the note to your aunt. I… I was too scared to go to the prosecutor myself, but I hoped that someone would look into it. Make sure a mistake hadn't been made."

Chelsea let out an audible breath.

Even Peter looked lighter. Like a weight had been lifted from his shoulders. He looked Chelsea in the eyes. "I'll sign your affidavit. I don't know how much it will help your father, but it's time I told the truth."

Chapter Twenty-Three

"I can't believe he admitted he lied," Chelsea said not for the first time since she and Travis had left Peter. They'd just walked into the condo, and she was euphoric. "I'm going to get my dad out of jail, Travis." She'd always believed that she'd do it someday, but someday finally felt like it was coming soon.

"Slow down," Travis said, probably attempting to temper her enthusiasm. But even he was grinning. "We still have a lot of work to do before we can go to the prosecutor."

But they were closer, and she had him to thank. Without thinking, she threw herself into his arms. "Thank you," she said, wrapping her arms around him and hugging him tightly. "You don't know what this means to me. What it means to me that you've helped."

His muscles flexed under her hands. "I will always be there for you, Chelsea. Whenever you need me."

The air between them was charged. She knew if she looked into his eyes now she'd see in them exactly what she was feeling. Want. Desire. Need. She leaned back, and there it was. She knew that there were a lot of good reasons they shouldn't do this, but she didn't care about any of them. She wanted Travis Collins, and from the look and feel of him, he wanted her, too.

She feathered a light kiss over his lips.

He sucked in a ragged breath. "What are you doing?"

She didn't answer right away. Instead, she kissed each corner of his mouth before dotting light kisses along his jawline. "What do you think I'm doing?"

"Chelsea—"

"Travis, I don't want to hear about all the reasons we shouldn't do this. I already know the reasons not to. I'm telling you that I want you. Do you want me?"

"You know I do, but—"

She pressed a finger to his lips. "No buts. No doubts. Just us, right now."

He growled, placing his palms on either side of her face and pulling her to him. His lips met hers in a kiss that was ruthlessly efficient. He lifted her. She wrapped her legs around his waist and let him carry her into his bedroom.

His chest rose and fell. She felt the beat of his heart and gazed up into his face. A heady desire coursed between them. Then his mouth met hers, kissing, nibbling, suckling. Somewhere in the heat of passion they both shed their clothes. Her lips were swollen with his skill. They were both breathless by the time he slid down her body, kissing her neck and shoulders before lavishing her breasts with attention.

He grabbed her wrists, pulling them both over her head, and rolled her flat onto her back. Then he came down over her, straddling her. He worked his way down her body, leaving a trail of kisses across her belly before making his way lower. She responded by opening herself to him, body and heart. His fingers explored her, and she sighed, giving in to the intimate caress and riding the wave of release when it came. The aftermath of her orgasm was still rippling through her when he came up over her again, having sheathed himself with a condom. Gently he coaxed her thighs open, his large hands clamping around her hips as he eased himself into her, filling her body, heart and soul.

The realization that she had never wanted a man the way she wanted Travis tore through her, frightening and exhilarating at the same time. Then he took up a rhythm, and all she could feel was him. Her release this time was an explosion that sent shock waves through her body, made all the more potent by the fact that Travis found his release right along with her. Within minutes, they fell asleep, wrapped around each other.

They awoke sometime before dawn and made love a second time. She fell back into a satiated slumber, pressed into Travis's side, knowing that her life would never be the same again.

THE EVENTS OF the night came rushing back as Chelsea awoke still in Travis's bed. Her gaze shot to the space where he'd slept, but the other side of the bed was empty. No sound came from anywhere else in the condo, either.

They had driven to Monterey together, and she knew Travis wouldn't abandon her. It wasn't a surprise to find a note from him next to a fresh pot of coffee saying he'd gone for a run on the beach. He was giving her time to wake up and go back to her own room, she knew.

She would never forget the night of passion they'd shared. He had driven her to heights she hadn't known existed. She didn't, couldn't, regret making love with him, but it didn't change anything. A part of her, a big part of her, was disappointed about that, but Travis had been honest with her from the beginning. This thing between them could go no further than the physical.

She poured her coffee and took it with her back into her bedroom.

Travis returned to the condo while she was in the shower. She heard him in his bedroom while she was getting dressed and packing to head home. She took her time getting ready, brushing her hair and applying her makeup and trying to tamp down her nervousness about seeing Travis after their night together.

When she walked into the living room, he was perched at the kitchen counter with his phone to his ear. His expression was serious, and when he waved her over and put the phone on speaker, she forgot all about her nerves. "Kevin, Chelsea is with me now."

"Good morning, Chelsea," Kevin's voice called through the phone.

"Morning." Chelsea shot Travis a questioning look.

"I was just telling Kevin about Peter admitting that he lied on the stand and agreeing to sign a statement saying so."

"It will take some work to iron out the logistics, but we'll get a lawyer started on it today," Kevin said.

"That's great. Thank you," Chelsea responded.

Travis cleared his throat. "Kevin and I were also discussing something else."

Chelsea had a feeling that *something else* was something she wasn't going to like.

"Even with Peter's statement, it's going to be an uphill climb getting the prosecutor to reopen the investigation," Kevin said gingerly.

She knew what Kevin said was true, but it didn't make it any less frustrating. "I sense you have an idea that may help."

"We have been talking," Travis jumped in, "and we both

think it will go a long way if we can get Lily's sister, Claire, to support reopening the case."

"I agree, but she has refused to speak to me."

"I know," Travis said, "but maybe with Peter retracting his statement, and knowing now there was another man in Lily's life, she will reconsider."

"Hey, I'm all for trying," Chelsea agreed.

"Good. Lily's sister lives in Santa Clarita. It would just be a little detour on the drive back to Los Angeles to stop in and see if she'll talk to us."

"I'm up for it," Chelsea said.

She was still high on having gotten Peter to admit to his falsehoods and relaxed from a night of incredible lovemaking. It felt like the tide might finally be turning in her and her dad's favor.

Chapter Twenty-Four

"This is it," Chelsea said, pointing to a mailbox with the address that they had for Claire Wong, Lily's half sister on their father's side. Claire had been twenty-two years old at the time of Lily's murder. She'd been in court every day of Chelsea's father's trial. Chelsea was sure the woman wouldn't be happy to see her, but she hoped Claire would be willing to listen. After all, if she was right, the wrong man was in jail for her sister's death. Claire had just as much incentive to get to the truth as Chelsea did.

Travis brought the car to a stop in front of a slightly run-down home surrounded by a good-size yard with mature trees and bushes. He and Chelsea sat in the car for a moment after he shut off the engine.

"Claire lived in LA at the time of Lily's death," Chelsea said. "She moved out here sometime after she inherited this place from her grandparents."

"It looks like it could use some TLC," Travis said.

"Claire was a community college student seven years ago. I don't know what she does now. Maybe she can't afford it."

"The background check I pulled on her had her employed at a small boutique in town." They sat in silence for another several seconds before Travis said, "Shall we?"

As they got out of the car, Chelsea noticed the curtains

in the front window flutter. "Someone is inside, and they know we're here."

They walked up the front steps carefully since they appeared ready to crumble at any moment. The door opened before they had a chance to knock.

"What do you want?"

Claire Wong looked like a much older version of the young woman Chelsea had seen each day at her father's trial. The Claire standing in front of Chelsea now had aged two decades in the past seven years. Her pallor seemed to have a grayish tinge as if she didn't get enough sun. Her brown eyes and hair were dull and lackluster. She wore a sweater that was several sizes too big and jeans that did nothing to flatter.

Travis smiled at her. "Hi, we're sorry to bother you. We're looking for Claire Wong."

The woman's eyes flicked to Travis, then back to Chelsea. "Why? Who are you?"

"My name is Travis Collins."

"And my name is Chelsea Harper, although it used to be Chelsea Brooks."

Claire looked as if she had been slapped. "You're Franklin Brooks's daughter. I remember you now." She started to shut the door.

Chelsea slipped her hand around the door, stopping it from closing in their faces. "Please, we just want to talk," she said quickly.

"I don't care. I want you both to leave now."

"New information has come to light that exonerates my father. Don't you want to know the truth? Who really killed Lily?"

"Your father was convicted," Claire spat.

"What if the police, the prosecutor, everyone got it

wrong? What if they just took the easy way out, and Lily's real killer has been walking free all this time? Since I started looking into my father's case, I've almost been run down, had my home broken into, and I've been shot."

Claire jolted, her eyes widening. "Oh, my God."

At least now she was listening. "That tells me someone doesn't want me looking into Lily's murder too hard, and I have to ask myself why that is."

Claire eyed Chelsea for a long moment. She prayed Claire was really thinking about what she had said.

Finally, Claire jerked her head at Travis. "Is he a cop?"

"I'm not a cop," he answered. "I'm a private investigator helping Chelsea get to the truth. We need your help in order to do that. Please."

After a moment, Claire opened the door and let them in. She led them to a kitchen table but didn't offer them anything to eat or drink. They sat.

"What do you want to know?" Claire asked hotly.

"Tell us about Lily," Travis said soothingly, taking the lead.

Claire visibly relaxed, a smile turning her mouth up and bringing some light into her eyes. "She was a great big sister. We had the same father, but he was never around for either of us. My mother died when I was nineteen, and Lily, she just jumped right in as a surrogate mother. Well, she'd always been somewhat of a surrogate mother. She was fifteen years older than me. I looked up to her like she was some sort of goddess." Claire laughed shortly. Then her smile fell, and her eyes hardened. "She was all I had, and your father took her from me."

"No," Chelsea said firmly. "I never believed that, and now I'm this close to proving it."

"How?" Claire crossed her arms over her chest, but a

flicker of doubt flashed in her eyes. "What is this information you claim to have?"

Chelsea looked at Travis who nodded.

"We've learned that the eyewitness who said he saw my father leave Lily's house around the time of her murder lied."

Claire blinked, surprise widening her eyes. "Really."

"Yes," Chelsea answered. "He's agreed to sign a statement to that effect, too. He feels guilty for his part in putting my father in jail."

"That...that doesn't mean anything. It doesn't mean your father didn't kill Lily."

Travis interjected quickly, "We've also discovered that Lily likely had a new boyfriend whom no one ever questioned."

Claire's gaze moved away from Chelsea's face. Something about it struck Chelsea. "But you knew that already, right?" she asked.

Tears spilled down Claire's cheeks. "It doesn't matter. Your father killed Lily."

Chelsea fought the urge to reach across the table and slap the woman. She fisted her hands under the table.

Travis must have picked up on her anger. "Claire, do you know who Lily's new boyfriend was?" he asked softly.

Claire was quiet for so long Chelsea began to think she wouldn't answer. "No," she finally responded in a small voice. "She didn't tell me his name, and I never met him. Lily only said she had to be careful."

"Careful?" Travis pressed gently. "Why did Lily have to be careful?"

Claire shrugged. "I don't know. I didn't ask her."

"Did you tell the police this after Lily was killed?" Chelsea asked, the anger in her voice too potent to conceal completely.

Claire noticed. "No," she said bitterly. "The cops said Franklin did it. I know he drank a lot, and he wanted to get back together with my sister, and she didn't want to. I didn't think it would help to throw some innocent guy to the cops."

"An innocent guy who didn't step forward after Lily, the woman he'd been dating, was murdered," Chelsea shot back. "Doesn't sound all that innocent to me."

"Telling the cops would have just muddied the waters," Claire said angrily. "They would have written Lily off as some promiscuous woman who got what she deserved. They had her killer, and I wasn't going to let him get away with it."

"The killer has gotten away with it," Chelsea said, acid in her voice. "For seven years while my dad sat in a jail cell because you didn't tell the truth."

Claire's eyes hardened. "How dare you? I loved my sister."

"Okay," Travis said. "Let's just everyone take a step back here. Breathe. We all want the same thing. To see Lily's killer pay for his crime."

Charged silence crackled between Chelsea and Claire. Lily's sister was just as bad as the cops and the prosecutor in her father's case. They'd all jumped to conclusions, and her father had paid the price.

"Lily may not have told you the name of the man she was seeing before she was killed, but is there anyone else she would have told?" Travis asked.

Claire pulled her gaze from Chelsea, but her scowl remained. "Maybe her best friend, Gina. But like I said, Lily said she had to be careful, so I'm not sure if she told her, either."

"Do you still have any of Lily's belongings?" Travis asked. "Any old diaries or address books or anything where she might have mentioned this man?"

Claire hesitated. "I found an old diary of Lily's and some other things out at our father's place after he died."

"At your father's place? Why would she keep them there?" Travis asked.

Claire shrugged. "She lived with him for a while before she moved into her own place. Maybe she just forgot them."

"Would you mind if I took a look?"

Claire hesitated again. "I don't see how it could help." But she rose and disappeared into another part of the house.

"Are you okay?" Travis asked softly.

Chelsea shook her head but didn't give him any other response. She definitely wasn't okay. She didn't know what she was exactly. Livid at the authorities. Appalled at Claire's callousness with her father's life. She couldn't put her current state of mind into words. She wasn't sure there were any words to explain it.

Claire reappeared with a small box in her hands. "You can take it with you."

It was an obvious dismissal, but Chelsea didn't much care. She wanted to get out of this house and as far away from Claire as she could as soon as she could.

"But I'd like to have it back," Claire amended.

"I'll make sure you get it back as soon as possible," Travis assured her.

"I CAN'T BELIEVE HER." Chelsea said when Travis had driven away from Claire's house.

"I know that was hard to hear, but at least Claire confirmed for us that Lily did have a new man in her life. That was good. Hopefully something in this box will point to who he was."

"I can't wait until we get back to LA to look."

"Okay, how about I find us somewhere to eat, and we can see what's inside?"

They stopped at a diner about a mile from Claire's house. They ordered food, then Travis leaned over to look as Chelsea opened the box.

"A high school yearbook." Chelsea pulled it out. A bear was on the cover with his arms spread wide. A school year was embossed in gold between them. She flipped a few pages. She found Lily's graduation photo and stared for several long seconds before passing the yearbook to Travis.

"We should look at this more carefully later." He set the yearbook aside.

Chelsea reached back into the box and pulled out a small book. This one said *Diary* across the front. Chelsea opened the cover. The first entry was from January of the same year. She sighed dejectedly. "It's probably just her high school diary. It's not going to help us."

Travis took the diary from Chelsea's hands. "I don't know," he said, carefully flipping through pages. "I can understand why Lily may have left her high school yearbook at her father's place, but her diary? It seems like she would have taken it with her to make sure that her innermost thoughts stayed private."

Chelsea shrugged. "She was eighteen when she wrote it. Maybe she just forgot about it."

Travis turned another page. "She didn't forget." He slid the book over so Chelsea could see the date on the page he had open two thirds of the way into the diary. It was dated two months before Lily was killed.

The handwriting was more refined than in the earlier entries, but it was still clearly Lily's.

"It looks like she started writing in her diary again before she died. Maybe she left it at her father's because she was being careful, as her sister mentioned." Travis said.

Chelsea grabbed the book. She flipped through several pages. All of the ones toward the end were dated from that fall. She looked up at him, confused. "Why would Lily have felt she needed to be so careful?"

"My guess is if we read these entries, we'll find out."

She flipped to the end of the diary. "Usually I avoid spoilers, but I'll make an exception in this case. If Lily was having trouble with the new man in her life, and he killed her, her last entries will probably be the most telling."

Travis couldn't argue with her logic although he wanted to read the old diary carefully as soon as possible.

Chelsea scanned over the pages, reading quickly. "She was dating someone, but she didn't say his name. She only gives his initials. WR. She sounds worried." Travis watched as she swallowed hard. "She's worried about telling my dad about the new guy. How he will react," she said, her eyes not leaving the page.

"Does she say why?" Travis asked softly. If Lily was afraid of telling Franklin she was moving on, that gave support to the people who believed Franklin had killed her out of jealousy and possessiveness.

Chelsea didn't answer right away, but the book slid from her hands and onto the table. She turned to look at him, her eyes glazed over as if she'd been stunned.

"Chelsea, what is it?" He reached for the diary, which had fallen closed when she dropped it.

"Lily. She wrote that she was worried about how my father would take it when he found out she was seeing his best friend. Bill Rowland," Chelsea murmured. "Travis, Lily's new boyfriend was my uncle Bill."

Chapter Twenty-Five

Uncle Bill opened the door and smiled when his gaze landed on Chelsea. It was a smile she couldn't return. She still couldn't bring herself to believe that her father's best friend had been sneaking around with Lily behind his back. There had to be another explanation. Something that didn't involve Uncle Bill betraying her father.

"Well, hello there. Isn't this a pleasant surprise?" Uncle Bill said.

"Uncle Bill, this is Travis Collins, the private investigator I hired to look into Dad's case."

"Nice to meet you, sir." Travis extended his hand.

Uncle Bill started for a moment, possibly surprised by Travis's formality. "Well, it's nice to meet you, too."

"I'm sorry for dropping by without calling first," Chelsea said, both anxious to get answers and terrified of them at the same time. "Do you have a minute to speak with us?"

"I always have time for you, sweetie. Come on in." Uncle Bill led them into the sunroom. "I'm taking advantage of every nice sunny day we have left."

His battered old recliner faced the glass wall of windows. Across from it was a matching love seat, slightly less worn. To his left was an end table with a pitcher of water and a coffee mug on top. The day's paper lay open on the seat of the recliner, clearly having been discarded there when he rose to answer the doorbell. Uncle Bill folded the paper along its creases and tossed it onto the floor before sitting.

She and Travis claimed the love seat.

"Sorry, I don't have any refreshments prepared right now. The market is on my list of things to do today. I can get you water if you'd like?" Uncle Bill made to get up, but Chelsea lifted a hand to stop him.

"That's okay. We're good."

"Okay," he said, sitting back into his recliner. "What can I do for you then?"

"You know I've been looking into Lily's murder," Chelsea said.

Uncle Bill nodded slowly. She could tell this was a subject he didn't want to talk about.

"Lily's sister finally agreed to talk to us. Lily wanted to keep it a secret because her new boyfriend was a friend of Dad's. She found Lily's diary after Dad's trial, and in it Lily mentions seeing a man whose initials were WR."

Uncle Bill's leg jiggled, and he wouldn't look at Chelsea. "I don't know what you're talking about."

"Sir, we could go back through your phone and computer records, if necessary, but it would be better for everyone, for Chelsea, if you told us the truth now," Travis said.

Chelsea suspected he was exaggerating. They didn't have any authority to obtain, much less search, Uncle Bill's computer, and nothing they'd uncovered to date was enough to compel the police to reopen her father's case.

But Uncle Bill didn't know that, and even if he did, tapping into his feelings for her seemed to do the trick. He looked at her with eyes shining with tears. "Does your father know?"

Chelsea felt tears well in her own eyes. "No, and I'm

not sure I'm going to tell him. It depends on what you tell me now."

"Nothing I can say will change anything."

"It will bring us one step closer to finding the truth, sir," Travis said.

Uncle Bill stared out the window for a long moment before answering. "Okay. What do you want to know?"

"How did your relationship with Lily begin?" Travis asked.

Chelsea was happy to let him take the lead questioning her uncle. She had too many emotions swirling through her to focus on asking the questions they needed answers to at the moment.

"We met when she and Franklin started dating. She was an amazing woman. Too good for Franklin. Too good for me as well."

"And when did the two of you begin your separate relationship?"

"Nothing happened until after Frank and Lily ended things."

"Did Lily end things with my dad because of you?" Chelsea chimed in, bitterness lacing each syllable.

"No. Lily wasn't that kind of woman. She was faithful to your dad even when he wasn't faithful to her," Uncle Bill spat. His gaze flashed with anger that Chelsea met with anger of her own.

"Okay," Travis said in a quelling tone. "How long was it after Lily and Franklin broke up that you two got together?"

"I don't know," Uncle Bill said, shifting his gaze to Travis. "You have to understand Franklin was very volatile during those days. He was drinking and stepping out on Lily a lot. We were both concerned about him. He'd always been a heavy drinker, but it had gotten so much worse, and neither of us knew what to do about it. We tried talking to him, but he would just get angry. We spent a lot of time commiserating, and one thing led to another." Uncle Bill's eyes shifted back to Chelsea. "But like I said, nothing happened until it was over between Lily and Franklin."

He seemed sincere, but Chelsea wasn't sure she could believe him. After all, he'd been lying to her for the past seven years.

"You visited Lily at her home, correct?" Travis said, pulling Uncle Bill's attention back to him.

"Sometimes, yes."

"What about the night she was killed? Were you two still together then?" Chelsea asked. All the fire seemed to have gone out of Uncle Bill. He stared down at the tiled sunroom floor. "We were."

"Did you tell the police about your relationship after Lily was killed?" Chelsea asked.

Uncle Bill looked up. "No," he answered, his voice small.

"So, you just let Dad take the fall?" Disgust at the man sitting in front of her swept through her body. She hadn't known him at all.

Uncle Bill looked at her, his eyes imploring. "I didn't kill Lily. I may be a coward for not telling the cops about my relationship with her, but I did not kill her."

"Where were you the night Lily was murdered?" Travis asked.

"I'll never forget it. I was out with my employees. Celebrating the opening of my second shop. I would have loved to have Lily there with me, but we were still taking things slow. Keeping our relationship to ourselves so we didn't hurt Franklin." Uncle Bill stared out of the windows again, but this time it was clear he was looking into the past. "He was supposed to be there, too, but he never showed up."

Probably because he was meeting with Lily. It was the perfect time, since Lily would have known that Bill wouldn't show up to interrupt them.

"So, you think Franklin might have killed Lily?" Travis returned to his questioning.

Uncle Bill shrugged. "I don't know. He was a mean drunk, but I had never seen him be violent toward anyone. But who else could it have been?"

"Maybe Lily had a third boyfriend?" Chelsea said bitterly.

Uncle Bill's expression turned to surprise as if he'd never even considered the possibility. But if Lily had been playing around with her father and Uncle Bill, it was more than possible she had other companions. It seemed she wasn't as nice as she led everyone to believe she was.

"Did you know if Lily was having difficulties with anyone specific?" Travis asked.

Uncle Bill's forehead crinkled. "What do you mean?"

"We were told she had a vandalism incident and a possible break-in at her place."

"Oh, yeah. I think she mentioned something like that. But nothing came of it. Probably just kids messing around."

"Did she ever find out who did it?"

"If she did, I don't remember. You might try asking her neighbor. Kind of a busybody." Uncle Bill rolled his eyes. "Knew everything that happened in the neighborhood."

"Gina McGrath?" Travis asked.

"Gina? No." Uncle Bill shook his head. "I was talking about the guy. John. Justin. Something starting with a *J*. He was always in Lily's business."

"Jace," Chelsea supplied the name.

"Maybe," Uncle Bill said, sounding unsure. "It's been too long for me to be certain."

Chelsea shot a glance at Travis, but his gaze was locked on Bill's face.

"Lily thought he was a nice, if somewhat lonely, guy," Uncle Bill continued, "but he gave me the creeps."

"He did? Why?" Travis pressed.

"Well, he was always finding reasons to come over to Lily's place. And more than once, I caught him looking at her from the windows of his house."

A spidery feeling crawled down Chelsea's back.

Uncle Bill snapped his fingers. "If you ask me the cops should have taken a much harder look at that guy."

Chapter Twenty-Six

Travis spoke to Kevin on speaker as he drove away from Bill Rowland's house.

"So, Franklin's best friend was seeing Lily at the time of her death. Man, that is some friend," Kevin summarized the information Travis had just conveyed.

Travis cut a look at Chelsea who still seemed to be in a state of shock. "Chelsea's in the car with me."

"Oh, sorry, Chelsea," Kevin apologized.

"No, you're right. I'm struggling to wrap my mind around how Uncle Bill could have done this to my dad."

"We will need to check on Bill's alibi for the night of the murder," Travis said.

Kevin groaned. "Confirming a seven-year-old alibi. Give me something hard, why don't you?"

"Sorry." Travis stopped at a corner to let a jogger cross the street before making a right-hand turn. "Bill Rowland swears he had nothing to do with Lily's death but—"

"But he's been lying for nearly a decade, so we can't trust anything he has said," Chelsea interrupted.

Travis stole a glance at her. She was focused on the scenery outside the passenger window, avoiding his gaze.

"Bill gave us the names of the employees he remembers being at the party the night of the murder. Some of them no longer work for him, so they don't have a strong incentive to lie for him if they were ever inclined to do so." Travis ordered the virtual assistant on his phone to send the list of names to Kevin. Seconds later, he heard a faint ping come from the other side of the line.

"Got it," Kevin said. "I'll get started on running down this alibi. What are you going to do?"

"I think the most important thing right now is to focus on the information Bill gave us," Travis said, slowing to a stop at a red light. "If Jace Orson was at home the night Lily died, and he lied about it, we need to know why."

"Agreed," Kevin said.

"I'm going to drop Chelsea off at her house, and then I'll come into the office," Travis replied.

"Wait, what?" Chelsea finally tore her attention away from the window to look at him. "Drop me off? No way."

"Guys, I'm going to hang up," Kevin said before quickly ending the call.

"Chelsea, Jace Orson might not be involved at all." But Travis's gut was telling him that wasn't the case. "But if he is, he's probably the person who tried to run you down and vandalized your home and shot at you. He's dangerous."

"He's dangerous to you, too, then."

"But I'm trained to deal with dangerous people, and you aren't. You hired me for a reason. Let me do my job."

She looked like she wanted to argue with him. Instead, she pressed her lips together tightly.

"Listen." He tried a different approach. "I'll reach out to Jace again. When we spoke to him, we weren't thinking about him as a suspect in Lily's murder. I'll see how he responds to the suggestion that he lied about where he was the night of the murder. Maybe there is some innocent explanation."

"You don't believe that, or you would take me with you to talk to him." She was too astute for her own good.

"There is a lot West can do, but ultimately we have to turn this case over to the cops and the prosecutor if you want to get your dad out of prison. Let me do my job. I'll let you know what's happening as soon as I can."

Chelsea stayed silent, the tension building in the car to the point he couldn't stand it anymore.

"I can't take the chance that you'll get hurt again if something goes wrong," he said softly. "You've already been shot. I can't—I don't think I could survive it."

Chelsea hesitated for a beat longer. "Okay. I'll sit home twiddling my thumbs."

He let out a sigh of relief and a bark of laughter at the same time. "I doubt that. Actually, I was thinking you could call your cousin, Victor, and have him stay with you."

"Stay with me?"

"I don't want you to be alone. Maybe Victor could help you finish painting."

Now Chelsea laughed. "You don't know Victor. Painting would be the last thing he'd want to do, but I will call him."

She made the call while he drove. Victor was waiting for them in front of Chelsea's house when they pulled up a little while later.

Travis put the car in Park but didn't shut off the engine.

Instead of getting out of the car, Chelsea grabbed his forearm. "This feels like one of those moments in the movies when the hero goes off to face the bad guy and doesn't come back."

He lifted a hand and caressed her cheek. "This is not a movie, and I'm no hero."

"I beg to differ with that last part." She leaned forward

and placed a fast, hard kiss on his lips. "Promise me you'll be careful and come back to me safe."

He knew it was a fool's promise. Nothing was ever certain in life. But if it alleviated even a moment of her worry, he also knew he'd make that promise a million times over. "I promise."

It was a promise he had every intention of keeping.

Chapter Twenty-Seven

Damn. Damn. Damn. He had been reduced to sneaking into his own house through the back door. It had been all he could do to control his temper and not slam the door as he went in. The last thing he needed was to draw more attention to himself. His neighbors kept to themselves for the most part, but he had no idea who else Chelsea and her private investigator had spoken to. Whether they'd spread their suspicions about him to his neighbors. But he knew they were looking for him. He knew that they knew, or at least suspected, he killed Lily.

He shuddered. Thinking about how it would feel to have everyone know that he killed Lily. They'd look at him the way they looked at Franklin Brooks. Worse than the way they looked at him. The rage was threatening to take over again, but this time he didn't try to stop it. He didn't want to control it anymore.

He headed into his bedroom and went straight for the closet. Pushing aside the clothes folded neatly on the overhead shelf, he exposed two boxes. One held his mementos. The other his gun. Chelsea had left him no choice. His life as he knew it was over. But that didn't mean he couldn't exact some revenge before it all exploded for good.

He took the gun from its case, holding it for a moment,

feeling the steel in his hand, its weight and balance. Then he slid in a loaded magazine.

He'd given Chelsea Harper the chance to walk away before.

He wouldn't give her that chance this time.

Chapter Twenty-Eight

Chelsea took a step back and eyed the newly painted living room walls. It had taken her and Victor the better part of the evening to paint over the walls with the light blue shade that she'd selected, but she liked the results.

Chelsea set her roller down on a piece of newspaper. "Ready to start doing the trim?"

Victor groaned. "We don't have to do it all in one day."

"I want to get my house back together. And I don't want to have to prep the room a second time just to do the trim."

Victor groaned again, shooting a glance at the sand and eggshell paint cans. "Well, can we at least take a break? The pizza will be here soon, and I'm starving."

"Okay, but after we eat, we knock this trim out. I want to get my home back."

The sound of gunfire burst from the television speakers, drawing their attention. Their pending project would have taken considerably less time if Victor hadn't brought along the *Dark Knight* trilogy on DVD. She and her cousin shared a love of action and superhero films, and even though they'd seen the Christian Bale movies nearly half a dozen times each, Chelsea loved watching them again with her cousin.

Victor's attention was glued to the television, but Chelsea's eye landed on a white envelope she hadn't noticed on the television stand earlier.

"Hey, what is this?" she asked, crossing the room and picking up the envelope.

Victor glanced over at her, then back to the television. "Oh, it was wedged between your screen door and your front door when I got here. It must have been delivered while you were staying with Travis."

"Yeah, I guess." She turned the envelope over. The return address was for a law firm in San Diego.

Victor cleared his throat.

Chelsea pulled her gaze from the envelope to look at her cousin. "What?"

"About Travis."

"What about Travis?"

"I know you're a grown woman, but I worry about you. You're my cousin, and you're like a sister to me. I don't want to see you hurt again."

"Travis is nothing like Simon."

Victor held his hands out. "I'm not saying he is. Just that it seems like the two of you have grown close. This investigation is a lot. You're close to maybe finally proving your father's innocence, and that could leave you emotionally vulnerable."

"Emotionally vulnerable?" Chelsea teased.

"Ugh, I mean the last thing I want to do is talk to you about your romantic life. Just know that if that man hurts you, he will have to answer to me."

Chelsea smiled and threw her arms around her cousin. "You know how much I love you, don't you?"

Victor squeezed her in a tight bear hug. "I do. And I love you, too."

The doorbell rang, signaling the arrival of their pizza. "I'll get it." Victor stepped out of the embrace.

"I'll grab some paper plates for us," Chelsea said, heading for the kitchen while opening the envelope she still held in her hand. She stopped just inside the kitchen, shocked at the information in the letter.

Her father-in-law had made her a beneficiary in his will. The letter was brief and didn't get into details about exactly what she'd inherited, but it invited her to reach out to the lawyers to discuss the issue more fully as soon as possible.

So, this was why Simon had been so desperate to talk to her. She wondered if he knew what she had inherited. She was debating whether to call the lawyers right then when Victor screamed, "Chelsea! Run!"

There was a loud crack, a groan and then a thump.

Someone was in her house.

Despite Victor's order to run, her feet felt as if they were glued to the ground. Her brain finally sent the message to move, but she knew she couldn't just leave Victor. "Victor?" She started for the front door.

He was lying face down on the floor in front of the door. The man standing over him looked up.

Jace Orson.

Jace smiled at her, and her stomach twisted into knots. "Chelsea. Good to see you again."

She turned and ran back into the kitchen. Jace's footsteps pounded on the hardwood floors behind her. She grabbed at a counter drawer, reached inside and pulled out a knife.

"Ah, ah, ah. I wouldn't do that if I were you."

She turned to find Jace pointing a gun at her.

"Put down the knife, Chelsea."

She didn't have any choice. A knife couldn't beat a bullet. Her shoulder throbbed at the memory of having been shot. Jace was even closer now. If he pulled the trigger, he wouldn't just graze her this time. It would be a direct hit.

The knife clattered as she let it drop to the countertop.

"Good girl. Now come here."

She didn't move.

Jace crossed the kitchen in three long strides. "I said come here!" He grabbed her arm, wrenching it behind her back in a painful twist, and pulled her tightly against his chest. "From here on out, you do exactly what I tell you. Do you understand?"

Her eyes filled with tears of terror. She nodded.

"Say it!" Jace yelled.

"Ye-yes," she stammered.

"Good. Now move."

"My cousin… He needs help."

"The guy at the door? He'll be fine. At least he will be as long as you do what you're told."

"You didn't… Is he?" A different kind of fear flooded through her.

"He's not dead. I told you he's fine for now. I just needed him out of the way to get to you." Jace pulled on her injured arm drawing a wince forcing her forward. "We need to go."

"I'm not going anywhere with you." She struggled against him.

"No?" Jace yanked her into the hallway where Victor still lay on the floor not moving. "Maybe I'll have to show you how serious I am." He pointed the gun at Victor's head.

"No! No, I'll go with you." If going with Jace kept Victor safe, kept him alive, she'd go. She would trade Victor's life for hers.

She let Jace push her forward, stepping over Victor's

prone form and out the front door. Travis would come for her. She just had to do everything she could to stay alive until he did.

THE WEST SECURITY AND INVESTIGATIONS offices were busy with activity when Travis arrived. He'd gone to Jace's house before heading to the office, but no one answered. It looked like he hadn't been there for a couple of days, which didn't necessarily mean anything, but Travis's instincts were buzzing. They were onto something.

The first thing he did when he got back to the office was request a rush background check on Jace Orson. The company they worked with was good and promised to have something to him within two hours. He also tried calling Jace at his accounting firm, but his boss said he hadn't heard from Jace in days.

Travis spent the next couple hours calling Bill Rowland's alibi witnesses for the night of Lily's murder. He'd just gotten off the phone with one of them when his computer dinged with an incoming email. Jace Orson's background report. He read it quickly, then printed out a copy before hurrying into Kevin's office.

"I think I got something." Travis handed the report to him.

"What is it?" Kevin flipped through the pages, scanning.

"Jace Orson has a red Mazda registered in his name." He reached across the desk and helped Kevin flip to the relevant page. "Chelsea and I saw him get out of that vehicle the day we met him. But he also has a black Oldsmobile in his name."

Kevin made the connection instantly. He looked up from the pages in his hand with a sparkle in his eye that said they'd just hit on something significant. "Just like the car that tried to run down Chelsea."

"Exactly," Travis responded excitedly.

"Okay, it adds to the questions we want to ask Mr. Orson, but it doesn't exactly help us find him."

That, unfortunately, was true.

"Did you find a second residence? Maybe a family member's place where he might be staying?" Kevin handed the papers back to Travis.

"No," Travis said, his frustration doubling. "Both of Orson's parents are deceased. He's an only child. The Oldsmobile was his mother's. It looks like he inherited it when she died three years ago, but the registration is still active, so it's likely he has it stored somewhere."

"Could be in a paid parking spot or in a self-storage unit. If he used it in a hit-and-run, he wouldn't want to park it in his driveway where everyone could see it. That could also be where he's hiding out. Assuming he is hiding out," Kevin added pointedly. "He could just as easily be at a conference or on vacation."

Travis shook his head. "I checked with the IT firm where he works on my way back to the office from his house. He hasn't been in for the last three days. He didn't call in sick or arrange for time off. He probably won't have a job when, if, he shows up."

"So, he's nuking his life." Kevin frowned. The concern in his tone was unmistakable, and Travis shared it.

"Yes." If Jace was at the point where he no longer cared about showing up for work or at his house, he might feel like he had nothing left to lose. That could mean he was desperate, and desperate people were very dangerous. "But it gets worse. The IT firm is a state contractor. I recognized the company's name from my time with the LAPD. They provide the IT guys for the police department's help desk. Orson's boss told me that Orson was assigned to the Hollywood police station until early this year."

"So, Orson had access to all the LAPD's police files."

Travis nodded. "It's possible. I'd even go so far as to say, given what we now know, that he knew Chelsea was looking into her father's case."

Kevin stroked his chin. "It wouldn't be hard for a computer technician to tag a file, so he's notified when it was accessed."

"No, it wouldn't be hard at all," Travis agreed.

"Okay, well, all we can do is keep searching for him," Kevin said, turning back to his computer. "In the meantime, we've got an attorney working on the affidavit for Peter Schmeichel. He's hopeful that it will be done by the end of the week or early next at the latest."

Travis frowned. That gave Peter plenty of time to change his mind. He hoped that didn't happen. Peter seemed remorseful about his lies.

"I reached out to three of the nearly dozen names Rowling gave me," Kevin said. "They all remembered the party and confirmed that, to the best of their recollection, Bill was at the party the whole night. One person was even able to send me photos of Bill with a dozen other people. The metadata from those photos confirms the dates and times Bill gave us."

"That's a pretty airtight alibi."

"Yeah, I'm not feeling Rowland for a murderer," Travis responded.

"But you are feeling Jace Orson?"

The knot in Travis's chest twisted tighter. "I am. Now we just have to prove it."

His phone rang, and he plucked it out of his pocket.

"Hello?" The voice on the other end spoke so fast that it took him a moment to realize it was Victor, Chelsea's cousin. "Victor, slow down. I can't understand what you're saying."

"It's Chelsea. She's been... I think she's been kidnapped."

JACE PUSHED CHELSEA toward his car, the barrel of the gun pressed into her back. He opened the passenger door and shoved her over the middle console and into the driver's seat before climbing into the passenger seat himself. He handed her the keys and ordered, "Drive."

She started the engine without protest and pulled from the driveway, praying some nosy neighbor was watching her be kidnapped and was on the phone at that very moment calling out the cavalry. She gripped the steering wheel with white knuckles, her entire body on alert as she assessed her situation.

It was dire. Jace held the gun below the view of the window but pointed it at her with his finger on the trigger. His eyes were on the road.

"Where are we going?"

"Just drive," he responded.

So, she did. When they neared the interchange for an older, underused stretch of road, he directed her to it. "Make this right."

She did as she was told, still trying to formulate a plan. It was late, and the old highway had seen a drop in traffic since the nearby freeway had been built. She hoped someone had seen her kidnapping and called the cops, but she couldn't count on it. If she wanted to get out of this situation alive, she'd have to do it on her own.

She took a deep breath, trying to remain calm and focus on finding a solution. Her first order of business was making sure Jace didn't just decide to kill her and be done with her. He had, she was sure now, killed Lily, but she still had no real idea why. Maybe if she could get him talking, she could get an answer and distract him enough so that she could get away.

She swallowed the ball of terror in her throat and spoke. "You killed Lily."

Jace's body stiffened, but he didn't respond.

Chelsea continued, "You killed her, and you let my father take the blame for her murder. Why?"

"He deserved it. He never treated my Lily like she should have been treated. Like the treasure she was. I tried to tell her she deserved better."

"You tried to tell her?" She remembered he'd said something similar the day she and Travis met him.

"I thought she understood. She broke up with him, but then she started dating that other guy."

Uncle Bill. "Is that why you killed her? Because she wouldn't date you?"

"She was mine."

"She was her own person. She belonged to herself, and she didn't deserve what you did to her," Chelsea growled, forgetting her fear for a moment. She glanced away from the road to take a look at Jace.

He showed no remorse at all. His eyes were cold and emotionless. Empty. "She was mine, and now she is mine forever." He stared out the front windshield, his voice eerily calm.

That was probably as close to a confession as she was likely to get from him. His calmness was the most terrifying part of her current ordeal. Jace didn't seem to be bothered in the least at having killed Lily. Just like he wouldn't be bothered at all by killing Chelsea.

Her pulse raced as an almost uncontrollable urge to get

out of the car and as far away from the monster beside her racked her body with tremors. But she needed to keep calm and clearheaded if she had any hope of surviving this. Jace had eluded justice for seven years. He might be a sick monster, but he wasn't stupid. She had to keep him talking until she had a plan.

"So, what now? You can't hope to get away. The private investigator I've been working with knows you killed Lily. The cops probably know I'm missing by now and are looking for me." She hoped that part was true. "They'll realize that you kidnapped me sooner rather than later."

Jace finally showed some sign of emotion, his face twisting into a mask of rage. "Just keep driving and shut up!" His fury blew through the car.

Chelsea stopped talking. She'd blown it, and now he was going to have to drive to some remote area and kill her. Well, she wouldn't go down without a fight.

Several minutes passed in silence. They crested a hill, and Chelsea saw headlights shining a dozen yards in front of them. A hasty, dangerous plan formed in her head. There was no time to think it through.

As the truck passed by them, she slammed on the brakes, her seat belt yanking her back sharply. Jace jerked forward, too, the gun flying from his hands and landing on the floor well in front of him. His head banged against the dashboard.

She wasted no time throwing the car door open and running toward the truck. It had already passed by them, but their sudden stop had the truck slowing. She ran.

She heard the passenger door to the car open behind her and a gunshot ring out.

Chapter Twenty-Nine

Travis's heart raced. He was more afraid than he had ever been in his life. Victor had calmed down enough on the phone to explain that he'd opened Chelsea's door to a man pointing a gun toward him. After he'd yelled out a warning to Chelsea, he'd been knocked out. When he'd come to, Chelsea and the man were gone. Victor had gotten a quick look at the car the man drove, and although he didn't get the license plate, the description matched Jace's red Mazda.

A patrol car was already at Chelsea's house, but Kevin drove Travis to the police station. Travis burst into the police conference room and barked, "What do you know?"

Detective Owens rose from his seat as did the other man at the conference table.

"You can't just come bursting in here, Collins!" Lieutenant Zach Grady blustered. Grady had been in charge of the precinct while Travis was a cop. They hadn't gotten along even before Travis went to Internal Affairs about his dirty colleagues.

"Slow down, Travis," Owens said, stepping between him and Grady. "We are already doing everything that can be done. The BOLO is out. Squad cars all over the city are on alert. I notified the state police myself, and they're combing the interstate. They're also standing by to offer any other support we might need." He put a hand on either of Travis's shoulders. "We'll find her."

That was all fine and good, but Owens hadn't answered Travis's question. How had Jace gotten to Chelsea in the first place?

"How did this happen?" Travis bit out again.

Owens looked at the lieutenant and got a nod from his boss before answering. "It looks like Jace got the jump on Chelsea's cousin."

Travis vibrated with anger.

"When Victor Harper came to, he called it in. We got there quickly and set up a perimeter, but we think Jace had a ten-to fifteen-minute head start on us."

Ten to fifteen minutes. It didn't sound like much, but a car could turn that into significant distance. Especially since they didn't have a clue where Jace was heading.

"Mr. Harper is in the hospital. He probably has a concussion, but he'll be okay." Owens darted a look at the lieutenant.

"What?" Kevin asked, looking between the two police officers.

"Mr. Harper was pistol-whipped," Owens answered.

Pistol-whipped. Jace had a gun. So, Chelsea might already be—

Travis wouldn't let himself think about it. Except he couldn't stop. Chelsea had been kidnapped by an obsessed killer. A man who had already killed once and who probably knew the authorities knew it. He had nothing to lose by exacting revenge and killing Chelsea.

Don't hurt her. Please don't hurt her.

But Jace would. That was his plan. To kill Chelsea.

Travis had to find them first.

"Like Owens said, we're doing everything humanly possible to find Ms. Harper," Grady chimed in.

"You have someone at Jace's house?" Travis asked.

Grady nodded. "We're executing a search warrant now."

Travis turned for the door, stopping only when Owens grabbed his arm. "Where do you think you're going?"

"To Orson's house to help with the search."

Owens shook his head. "You know you can't be there."

"Chelsea and I have been looking into Lily Wong's case. I have more insight into this guy now than either of you do. I may see something that clues us in to where he's taking her that your guys won't."

Owens looked at Grady again, an entire conversation taking place between the longtime colleagues without a word spoken.

Finally, Grady nodded again. "You can't touch anything," he said to Travis before turning to Owens. "Go with him."

Orson's house was swarming with officers when Travis and Owens arrived. Travis was out of the car before Owens shut off the engine. They stepped inside the house together.

Travis forced himself to take several deep breaths and think. People were creatures of habit. There had to be something in the house that hinted at Jace's plan. He had to find it. He walked through the house with Owens, touching nothing just as Grady had directed. He didn't need to touch anything. Not yet anyway. He needed to get a feel for how Jace lived first. How he used the space. That was likely to tell him where Jace would hide anything of value.

As he did, he thought about Chelsea. She was a fighter. She had proven that by fighting for her dad when everyone, including him, thought it was a lost cause.

Owens spoke quietly to one of the officers in the hall.

When he returned, Travis knew the news wasn't good. "So far they haven't found anything, but we aren't done looking."

Ignoring Lieutenant Grady's admonishment to look and not touch, Travis went to Orson's bedroom.

The officer searching the room spun around as he entered. "Hey, you can't be here!"

Owens stepped into the room behind Travis with his badge out. "It's okay, Officer Johnson," Owens read the name on the officer's chest. "He's with me. Why don't you go help in the basement?"

Officer Johnson trotted out of the bedroom.

Travis marched to the nightstand and yanked the door open.

Owens didn't say a word about Travis ignoring the lieutenant's instructions. Instead, he went to the closet and picked up searching where Officer Johnson had left off. After a few minutes, he called, "Hey, I think I've got something."

Owens pulled a metal box from the closet and set it on the bed as Travis walked over to join him. The box had a flimsy lock. Owens borrowed a flashlight from one of the officers in another room, and with two solid hits, the lock gave way.

Inside were photographs. Hundreds of them of Lily from years ago and dozens that had been taken more recently. Of Chelsea. There were even a few photographs of Travis. Orson had clearly been watching them. Of course he had.

"This is creepy," Owens said. "Jace was stalking Lily Wong."

"And Chelsea," Travis added.

The detective's cell phone rang. "Owens." He was silent for a moment, then said, "Lieutenant, I'm going to put you on speaker so Travis can hear." Owens hit a button on the screen. "Okay, Lieutenant. Go ahead."

"We just got a call from a driver out on Old Route 1. They said they passed a red Mazda, and a woman jumped out. Followed by a man with a gun. The passerby reported shots fired."

Travis went numb. "Chelsea. Is she—"

"The driver who called it in said a man shot at his truck. The bullet didn't hit him or his vehicle, but it scared him. He drove off but called it in as soon as he was sure the shooter wasn't following him."

"So, we don't know if Chelsea—" Travis started.

Lieutenant Grady cut him off. "I've got units rolling in the direction that the man said the car was headed. And the state police are putting a chopper in the air."

Travis looked at Owens.

Owens pulled his keys from his coat pocket. "I'll drive."

CHELSEA THREW HERSELF onto the paved highway. Tires screeched, and she lifted her head in time to see the truck tear off down the highway. Tears rolled down her cheeks as she watched the brakes fade into darkness.

Then Jace was there beside her.

"Get up," he ordered.

She looked up into the barrel of the gun. She stood.

He grabbed her arm and turned her around roughly, so her back was to him. The cold metal of the gun pressed against her temple. His breath touched her cheek, his voice pure rage. "I should shoot you right now but I'm not going to make the same mistake I made with Lily. When I'm finished with you nobody will ever find your body."

She didn't want to die. Not when she was so close to freeing her dad. Not at the hands of the man who had destroyed both of their lives. And not when she had finally found someone, she could see having a future with.

"Pl-please, no," she stammered.

"Don't worry. I have plans to make you pay for ruining my life. You don't deserve a quick death. Now, get back in the car. Move!"

Shaking uncontrollably, she walked with him to the car. Again, he directed her to the passenger side and pushed her over behind the wheel.

"Drive!" he yelled, pressing the gun into her side hard enough to make her yelp.

She got the car moving again.

"Faster! You just made a huge mistake. And I'm going to make sure you pay for it."

"You don't have to do this."

"I'm not going to jail."

"You didn't have any problem letting my father go to jail," Chelsea said, fury rising in her.

"Just shut up and drive!" Jace screamed.

The hysteria in his tone was enough to temper her fury and ignite another wave of fear. She knew she shouldn't antagonize him any further. Her attempt to escape hadn't gone the way she hoped, but the driver of the truck had gotten away. Surely, he had called the police. She just had to hang in there for a little longer.

They'd driven another several miles when she noticed the flashing lights in her rearview mirror. Jace noticed them at the same time.

"Faster." He slammed his hand down on her right thigh in an attempt to push the accelerator to the floor. The car sped up, but the next time she checked the rearview mirror, the flashing blue lights were closer and had doubled.

A voice came over the police cruiser's speaker. "Pull over."

"Don't," Jace said through gritted teeth.

She didn't stop the car, but she slowed. She wasn't sure what the cops knew. Did they know Jace was holding her against her will? Or had they only been told about a man who had shot at another driver? Would they open fire at the car with her in it?

She eased up on the accelerator even more.

"Don't stop." Jace reached across the car again, this time grabbing the wheel. The car veered across the center line in the road.

Chelsea yanked the wheel in the other direction, but she overcompensated. They went off the road completely this time, hitting the ditch beyond the shoulder.

Jace screamed next to her.

All four wheels left the ground for a brief moment, and then they were rolling. Once. Twice. The windshield cracked, and the driver window shattered into hundreds of pieces, scattering glass over the front seats.

Chelsea was completely disoriented, unsure which way was up as the car finally came to a stop.

Jace moaned.

She turned her head slowly, but pain still exploded in her skull. The car was upside down, balanced on its top, but their seat belts held both of them strapped to their seats. Yet somehow Jace had managed to hold on to the gun.

Chelsea's eyes widened, her pain forgotten as he raised the gun and pointed it in her direction.

OWENS AND TRAVIS rounded a curve in the highway, and Travis quickly took in the scene. The Mazda was fishtailing, swerving from one side of the road to the other before it dropped into the ditch at the side of the road. The sickening crash of metal nearly stopped his heart.

Travis watched in terror as the car rolled several times

before coming to a stop. "Chelsea!" he screamed, open-ing his car door before Owens came to a complete stop, and raced toward the accident. The police cruiser that had been following along with them pulled over on the opposite shoulder of the road. Travis drew his gun as he raced past it, pushing aside the nearly paralyzing thought that Chel-sea might be dead.

She wasn't dead. She couldn't be dead.

But she could be badly injured. The crash was bad. The Mazda was upside down.

He got to the driver's side of the car and knelt. Chelsea was in there, but the passenger seat was empty. "Chelsea? Baby, answer me, please?"

Chelsea turned her head slowly toward him. "Jace. He got out. Ran away."

"Don't worry about him. We'll get him."

A shot rang out, shattering the back window that had somehow remained intact after the crash.

Chelsea screamed.

Travis ducked down behind the rear of the car. "Jace! Give it up! You're surrounded."

But Orson clearly had no intention of giving up. Travis could hear him moving through the trees and shrubbery on the other side of the ditch. If he got enough distance between himself and the road, he stood a good chance of getting away.

Travis went back to the driver's-side window. "Chelsea, I'll be back. Hang in there for me, baby," he said, and then he took off after Orson.

Orson was fast, but Travis was motivated. He wasn't going to let him get away.

Orson pushed through the branches with Travis right be-hind, closing the distance. Travis put on a burst of speed and threw himself at Jace's back, slamming the man onto the pine-needle-covered ground. Jace's gun flew out to the side.

Anger flooded through Travis's body. He flipped Orson onto his stomach and drove his fist into the killer's face. He had never been so enraged or scared. This man was a killer. He had kidnapped Chelsea, and he probably planned to kill her.

Orson struggled, but Travis used his weight to hold him down while he pounded his fist into the monster's face. He wasn't sure how many times he hit him before he felt someone pulling him away.

"Travis, stop. Enough."

Owens dragged him off Orson. A second officer grabbed Jace's arms and slapped cuffs on his wrists.

"Go back to Chelsea," Owens ordered. "The EMTs got her out of the car, and they're about to transfer her to the ER."

Travis didn't have to be told twice. He backtracked through the woods at a run. "Chelsea!" he called as he cleared the trees. He spotted the gurney being lifted into the ambulance and raced forward. "Chelsea!" He ignored the EMT's protest as he hauled himself into the back of the ambulance.

"Sir, you can't be in here," the EMT said with a glower.

"It's okay. I want him here," Chelsea said.

The EMT shrugged and closed the back door and called to the driver to get them moving.

Travis sat on the bench across from the gurney and stroked Chelsea's cheek while the paramedic started an intravenous line in her arm.

"Hey, you're going to be okay, Chels." Travis leaned down and kissed her on the lips. "I have never been more afraid in my life. When I saw your car flipped over—"

She took his hand and squeezed. "I'm okay. Did you get him?"

Travis squeezed back. "We got him. He won't hurt anyone else ever again."

She sighed. "Then it's over. My father—"

"It will take a little more time, but your father is coming home." Travis stroked her cheek. "You did it, Chels. You got the truth and freed your father."

THE LAST SIX hours had taken Travis on a roller coaster of emotion, but the doctors had checked out both Victor and Chelsea and declared no permanent damage had been done to either. The cousins would be spending the night in the hospital, though. It had taken Victor, Chelsea and a doctor to get Brenda Harper to go home and get some rest, but she'd finally relented. Now it was time for Travis to do what he knew had to be done and say goodbye to Chelsea.

"They aren't going to let me out until tomorrow," Chelsea said, sounding displeased when he entered her hospital room.

"Well, I'm sure the doctors know what's best."

Chelsea pushed herself up straighter in the bed. "I was thinking that I could make dinner for us tomorrow when I get home. It would be nice to get back in my own kitchen."

She reached a hand out to him, but he didn't move closer to the bed to take it.

"You should probably rest when you get home," he said in a flat voice that sounded nothing like his own.

Chelsea let her hand fall to the mattress. "What's wrong?"

"Listen, Chelsea. We got the evidence you need to prove your father's innocence. Orson is in jail. West Investigations will work with you to get whatever evidence you need to the prosecutor."

"Oh." The hurt look that crossed her face nearly crushed him.

Silence fell.

"I told you I don't do the relationship thing," he said quietly.

"Yes, you did. If that's what you want, I guess that's it."

His heart felt like it was being squeezed in a vise. He wished he could be different, but it wouldn't be fair to either one of them.

"Thank you for everything," she said quietly.

"If you ever need anything, just call, okay? Anytime, day or night. I'll be there."

"Goodbye, Travis."

"Goodbye, Chelsea." He forced himself to turn away from the bed before she could see the tears welling in his eyes and walked out of the room.

You did the right thing, he repeated as he walked to his car and drove home.

Then why did it hurt so much?

Chapter Thirty

A week had passed since Chelsea had been released from the hospital. There was still a lot to do before her father was released from prison, but the prosecutor's office had filed the necessary paperwork with the court. There was little reason to wait once Jace Orson confessed, which he'd done once the police presented all the evidence they had on him. He was behind the call to her aunt, the hit-and-run and the shooting in front of the restaurant. Most important, he'd admitted to killing Lily.

Chelsea couldn't help wondering how different her life and her father's life would have been if the cops hadn't had tunnel vision seven years earlier. Or if they hadn't accepted Peter's lies. When she thought about it, the anger threatened to consume her, so she tried not to. It worked most of the time.

She tried to stay busy and keep her mind off Travis, too, but that didn't really work, either. She felt as if a part of her was missing. She hadn't realized how deeply she'd fallen for him until he walked away. She wanted to be angry at him, but he'd been honest with her. He told her from the start that he didn't want anything permanent. She was the one who had hoped for more.

But it wasn't to be. She needed to get herself together and

get over him. She repeated that mantra a hundred times a day, but it didn't seem to be working. She still ended every day crying herself to sleep.

Aunt Brenda had demanded that she and Victor appear for family dinner at her house that evening. Her aunt had struggled with the news that she'd been wrong about her brother for so many years. It had taken a few days, but she had finally got up the nerve to call Franklin two days earlier. Chelsea had only been able to hear her aunt's end of the call, and there had been a lot of crying, but it seemed like the siblings wanted to work on building a new relationship.

Aunt Brenda set a big bowl of mashed potatoes on the table and took her seat. She had also cooked a ham, cabbage, homemade biscuits and apple pie for dessert.

"You made a feast, Mom." Victor leaned over and planted a kiss on his mother's cheek.

"Yes, well, we are celebrating." Aunt Brenda beamed. "Franklin is coming home to his family, and it's all Chelsea's doing." Her aunt reached for her hand. "You have grown into an amazing woman, and I could not be prouder of you, sweetie."

"Thank you, Aunt Brenda. And I have an announcement to make, too. We have something else to celebrate. I've decided to go to law school."

Working on her dad's case had shown her just how much she loved helping people and the law. There were too many innocent people in jail. One was too many. And she could do something about it. She'd done her research, and there was still time for her to apply for a spring semester at several area law schools. She could even take a course or two at night as a nonmatriculated student during the fall term and have them count toward her degree when she enrolled as a student.

"Wow, Chels. Congrats," Victor said.

"There are so many people out there who need someone who knows the law to fight for them. I think I can do that for others."

"I know you can," Aunt Brenda said.

"I also spoke to Gerald's estate lawyer," Chelsea went on.

Victor scoffed. "Yeah? I bet Simon was none too pleased to hear they'd reached out to you."

"He was not. It was his job to inform me of the bequest as his father's executor." Chelsea piled mashed potatoes on her plate. "He wanted to get on my good side first."

"Ho ho! That means Gerald must have left you something good."

"Half the estate," Chelsea said.

Her aunt's fork dropped onto her plate with a clang.

Victor's mouth hung open. "Half his estate?"

"Apparently, Gerald wrote the will when Simon and I were married, specifically noting that Simon would take half and I would inherit the other half. He never changed his will. It was why Simon suddenly showed up again and has been calling me."

Victor whooped and raised his water glass with a grin. "Here's to Chelsea becoming an heiress."

"No. I spoke to Simon. I told him that I'd sign over my bequest to him as long as I could keep enough to pay for law school. He was more than happy to accept my proposal."

"Chelsea," Victor groaned.

"It's the right thing to do, Victor. I don't know if Gerald just never got around to changing his will or what, but he meant more to me than money. And I think he'd be happy that I'm going to graduate from law school debt-free. I know I am."

Victor groaned again. "You are too good, cuz."

Aunt Brenda tapped Victor's hand. "There is no such thing as 'too good,' Chelsea has made her decision, and that's that. Now let's eat."

They ate dinner and dessert, and when they were finished, Aunt Brenda insisted on cleaning up everything herself. Victor and Chelsea retired to the living room where Victor pulled up *Iron Man*, her all-time favorite Marvel movie, on Aunt Brenda's television.

"So have you heard from Travis?" Victor asked while the opening credits played.

"No," Chelsea said without looking away from the television. "And I don't expect to." She could feel Victor staring. "I don't. I hired him to do a job, he did it adequately, and now it's over."

"He did it adequately?" Victor's tone was incredulous. He reached for the remote and paused the movie. "It was clear that there was something going on between you two. Now it's just over?" He shook his head. "I don't believe that. You don't do casual relationships."

Chelsea tried forcing back the tears that threatened, but one got away from her.

Victor looked mortified. "Oh, I'm sorry. Don't cry. I shouldn't have brought it up." He wrapped her in a hug.

But it was too late. The floodgates had opened. Chelsea leaned into her cousin's arms. "He didn't want me, Victor. He didn't want me."

TRAVIS SAT AT his desk at the West Security and Investigations office. Phones rang. A meeting was being held in a conference room. Kevin had been holed up in his office all day. It seemed like everyone was busy except Travis.

He hadn't been able to get motivated since he walked out of Chelsea's hospital room and out of her life a week earlier. He needed to shake off his malaise, but all he'd thought about in the last week was Chelsea.

This had never happened to him before. Usually when he ended a relationship, he was able to move on quickly. *Because you never really cared about those women. You never loved them.*

It felt like with each day that passed without Chelsea he hurt even more. Missed her more. He needed to get his head on straight, like Kevin had said.

He glanced over the top of his cubicle wall and saw that his boss's office door was finally open. Thirty seconds later, he knocked on Kevin's door.

Kevin looked away from whatever he'd been reading on his computer monitor.

"Got a minute?" Travis asked.

"Absolutely. What's up?"

Travis crossed to one of the chairs in front of the desk and sat. "I wanted to know if you had anything for me. I'm a little light right now, and you know I like to keep busy."

Kevin's head tilted to the side. "To be honest, I'm surprised you aren't with Chelsea. We can manage around here without you for a few days. You should take some vacation time, you have certainly earned it."

"I don't think that would be a great idea. Chelsea has a lot on her plate right now. Recovering and getting her father out of prison." His gaze slid away from Kevin's face. "Her job is over, so I think it's best we both get on with our lives."

Kevin leaned back in his chair and frowned. "That's what you think is best?"

The pain that had been lingering in Travis's chest for days now became more acute, but he continued to ignore it.

Kevin shook his head, a pitying look on his face. "I thought you were smarter than this."

"Smarter than what?" Travis snapped. "You told me to get my head on straight. It's on straight now."

Kevin looked at him directly. "You think this is what I meant when I told you to get your head on straight? Because right now it looks like you have your head up your—"

Travis growled, cutting him off. "What did you mean then?"

"Man, I can't answer that question for you. Only you can. If you really think letting Chelsea go is the answer, then maybe it is." Kevin shrugged. "Maybe you don't deserve her." he turned back to his monitor. A dismissal.

Travis rose. He made it to the office door. "You really think I could make it work with Chelsea?" he asked, his hand on the doorknob but his back still to Kevin.

"I think when two people want a relationship to work, they make it work. The question is do you want to make it work?"

That was the question.

Chapter Thirty-One

It had been two days since his talk with Kevin, and Travis was no closer to figuring out how to live without Chelsea. He had made a little progress on the professional front, though. Kevin had assigned him to a case that was little more than busywork, collecting files from the Parks and Rec Department. He was heading up the steps of the municipal building when he caught sight of Chelsea's cousin, Victor. He considered turning away to avoid having to make small talk with the man, but Victor's gaze fell on him before he could make his getaway.

The anger marring Victor's face had Travis reconsidering turning and walking away.

Victor increased his pace, coming to a stop in front of Travis. "What the hell did you do to my cousin?"

Travis's heart rate increased. "What are you talking about? Did something happen to Chelsea?" She hadn't called. He'd told her to call if she ever needed anything.

"Yes, something happened to her. You. You happened to her."

Travis's chest tightened even more, but this time from confusion. "I don't understand. Is Chelsea okay?"

"No. She's not okay. She's heartbroken."

He felt himself relax a little, but his chest still felt as if an anvil sat on it. Heartbroken?

"She cried," Victor said, a note of mortification mingling with the anger in his voice. "She cried and said you told her you didn't want her."

"I never said that!"

Victor crossed his arms over his chest. "What did you say then?"

"I—" He hadn't said he didn't want her. He couldn't say that because it wasn't true. But he hadn't told her how much he wanted her, either. He hadn't told her that he loved her. And he did.

He groaned. Kevin was right. His head was up his—

"I told my cousin that if you ever hurt her, you'd be answering to me, and I meant it," Victor said, pulling Travis's attention back to him.

"You're right," Travis responded quickly.

Victor looked at him, confused. "I am? About what?"

"Everything. I'm an idiot. I love your cousin, and I stupidly pushed her away because—"

"Because you're an idiot." Victor grinned.

Travis smiled back. "Yes."

"Good. At least we agree on one thing."

"Look, I need your help."

"Is it helping you make a grand romantic gesture for Chelsea?"

"Let's not get carried away."

Victor tsked. "You are an idiot. If you want to make up with my cousin, you very much need to get carried away. It sounds like you definitely need my help."

CHELSEA PARKED HER car in front of Aunt Brenda's house and got out. The interior of the house was dark, but Victor had called her an hour ago and insisted she meet him there. Since she hadn't been doing much, just rewatching the *Black Panther* movies for the umpteenth time, she'd agreed to. Three more weeks of summer, and then she'd be back at work. The new school year, new students and law classes had to take her mind off Travis, right? She sure hoped so.

She turned her key in the lock on her aunt's door, walked inside and gasped.

A carpet of red rose petals lined the hallway leading to the kitchen.

Was her aunt seeing someone? She would be mortified if Victor called her here to break up his mother's date night.

"Aunt Brenda? It's me, Chelsea."

The voice that called back wasn't her aunt's.

"Chelsea." Travis stepped out of the kitchen, and everything inside her melted. He wore a dark suit and held a dozen red roses in his hand.

"Travis. What are you doing here?"

"I needed to talk to you."

Her heart ached, but she wasn't ready to open it up again and possibly have it shattered further. "About what?"

"About us."

She looked away from him. "There is no us. You made that clear. You don't want me. You have your own life, and I'm not a part of it."

His lips flattened. "You think I don't want you? That's the furthest thing from the truth."

Her eyes met his. "Of course I think that. You left. You walked out on me."

"I was wrong," he said. "I swore to myself I wouldn't let myself love anyone so that I never had to hurt the way I hurt when I lost my parents and brother. But I hurt her anyway.

When I lost you. Worse even because I lost you because I was an idiot."

Chelsea couldn't help it. Hope swelled in her chest. "And you're not an idiot anymore?"

"No. I'm not afraid of being hurt. I'm afraid of living another second without you in my life. I want you, Chelsea. I've never wanted anything more than I have wanted you. And I hope you still want me, too."

Something released inside of her, letting her heartbeat again. She ran into Travis's arms. He held her tightly. Tight enough that she could feel the beating of his heart.

"I love you. Don't you ever leave me again."

"Never again. That's a promise."

Epilogue

Chelsea waited in a private room in the prison family area with her aunt Brenda, Victor and Travis at her side. She'd waited years for this moment, when her father would walk out of prison a free man, but the last two weeks waiting for his release had been some of the longest of her life.

Travis took her shaking hands in his and brought them to his lips.

"I've dreamed about this day for years, and now that it's here I'm so nervous," she said, giving him a small smile.

"That's understandable." He pulled her close and wrapped his arms around her. "You're an amazing woman. I don't know anyone else who would have fought so hard for someone they loved. Your father is lucky to have you." He leaned in close and said in a voice that sent a shiver through her, "I'm lucky to have you." He pressed a kiss to her lips.

They broke apart just as the doors opened.

A pair of guards led her father into the room. He'd changed out of his prison uniform and into the new slacks and cotton pullover that Brenda had bought for her brother.

Chelsea couldn't help the cry that tore from her throat when she saw her father for the first time as a free man. "Dad." She crossed the small room quickly and threw herself into her father's arms.

She felt his tears falling on her shoulder as he squeezed her tightly. It had been so long since they'd had more than a brief touch. She didn't know if she could bring herself to ever let him go.

But after several minutes, her father stepped back and opened his arms to his sister. Aunt Brenda stepped into her older brother's arms, fat tears sliding down her cheeks.

When she turned, Chelsea noted that Victor was also crying. Even Travis's eyes were red. She stepped back to his side, and his arm slid around her waist.

"Okay, enough with the tears," her father said with the widest smile Chelsea had ever seen on his face. "I've been waiting years to say this. I'm going home!" He kept one arm around his sister and threw the other one around his nephew before heading for the door, laughing.

Chelsea watched her family step out of the room, then looked up into Travis's eyes. "I'm so glad you were here to share this moment with me."

He gazed at her with so much love in his eyes, her breath caught. "I'll always be by your side. There's nowhere else I'd rather be."

* * * * *

COMING SOON!

We really hope you enjoyed reading this book.
If you're looking for more romance
be sure to head to the shops when
new books are available on

Thursday 19th December

To see which titles are coming soon, please visit

millsandboon.co.uk/nextmonth

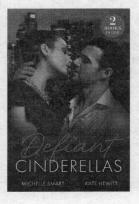

LET'S TALK

Romance

For exclusive extracts, competitions and special offers, find us online:

- 🅕 MillsandBoon
- 𝕏 @MillsandBoon
- 📷 @MillsandBoonUK
- ♪ @MillsandBoonUK

Get in touch on 01413 063 232